JANUS

JOHN PARK

CZP

ChiZine Publications

FIRST EDITION

Distributed in Canada by
HarperCollins Canada Ltd.
1995 Markham Road
Scarborough, ON M1B 5M8
Toll Free: 1-800-387-0117
e-mail: hcorder@harpercollins.com

Distributed in the U.S. by
Diamond Book Distributors
1966 Greenspring Drive
Timonium, MD 21093
Phone: 1-410-560-7100 x826
e-mail: books@diamondbookdistributors.com

Library and Archives Canada Cataloguing in Publication

Park, John Melvyn, 1948-
    Janus / John Park.

Issued also in an electronic format.
ISBN 978-1-927469-10-1

    I. Title.

PS8631.A74797J36 2012   C813'.6   C2012-904097-5

Issued also in electronic formats.

ISBN 978-1-927469-10-1

CHIZINE PUBLICATIONS
Toronto, Canada
www.chizinepub.com
info@chizinepub.com

Edited by Sandra Kasturi
Copyedited and proofread by Brett Savory

 Canada Council   Conseil des Arts
for the Arts   du Canada

We acknowledge the support of the Canada Council for the Arts which last year invested $20.1 million in writing and publishing throughout Canada.

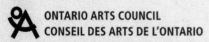 ONTARIO ARTS COUNCIL
CONSEIL DES ARTS DE L'ONTARIO

Published with the generous assistance of the Ontario Arts Council.

Printed in Canada

JANUS

PROLOGUE

Had the stars changed?

He opened his eyes. A small room, unlighted, and a square window of stars beside his head.

Had they changed?

Why had he thought that? Why was it important?

Memory started to leak back.

A blue-white segment of planet, Earth, his home. Then what? The shuttle—the transfer. The Knot. And the stars changing?

What else?

He couldn't remember—

And his arms, his ankles, his chest—strapped down, the electrodes—

A timeless interval of noise and terror.

Voices.

"He's coming out if it *now*."

"Get these fucking things off me! Who do you think I am?"

Then a glare of light, and two white-coated men watching.

He was back in his body. They had been talking to him. His throat hurt, and his arm. His eyes ached. But he was free of the straps. Perhaps later he would remember how it had happened.

The taller man said. "Better? How much do you remember now?"

Darkness.

The stars—was that what he had seen, the stars swirling together?

He gasped as if he had fallen into an icy lake. His jaw locked. *Cold and dark and empty. The lights clotting and draining away . . .*

He heard himself moan.

"Your name," said the man. "Do you remember your name?"

He groped desperately, close to drowning, then breathed. "Grebbel," he whispered. "Jon Grebbel."

"Good. It'll be all right now. I'll tell you again. This is the planet Janus. You decided to emigrate and the shuttle brought you through the Knot. The jump's just from Earth orbit, but it takes some people this way—amnesia. We're in a dirigible, a blimp, on the way from the landing field to the main settlement. They'll help you when you get there. Just keep taking deep breaths now. It won't be much longer."

Inside his head: the lights all draining away . . .

The next time he looked, the sky was blue-black about two brilliant moons, one high, one very low. Below was the silver thread of a river, and in the distance a cluster of lights. A little later the dirigible turned, hiding the moons and showing a sky faintly washed with light above a serrated horizon. He watched the ghostly aurora play over the sky of his new home.

ONE

For Elinda Michaels, each waking was a journey between worlds—a passage that shrank half-remembered nightmares into morning shadows and left them lying harmless on the rush mat beside the bed.

But her clock showed her this wasn't morning. And it wouldn't be daylight for another twenty-odd hours on this godforsaken world. A bar of moonlight reached from the foot of the far wall to the edge of the pillow beside her face. Outside, the distant construction machinery was still silent. There were the permanent bass whisper of the river, a rustling from the woods, perhaps the wind, perhaps a night browser, and a deeper, persistent humming. As she recognised the sound, the moonlight vanished and then came back. A delivery, she thought sleepily, one of the dirigibles working graveyard again.

In the official morning, under the lights on the landing field, the gasbag would be floating like a long, dull silver bubble, and its red-eyed crew would be besieged in the cafeteria by the night shift wanting gossip from back there.

But that wasn't what had woken her. As she reached across the bed, to where her lover had curled up in sleep, she realised why she had been listening to the quiet. She rolled onto her side. The bed beside her was cold.

"Barbara," she whispered, then sat up. She spoke the name aloud, and the stillness swallowed her voice. She pulled the blankets around her shoulders and gnawed at a fingernail. "Barbara, if you've gone off to sleep in the living room, you'll freeze." Beside her, the moonlight was edging onto her pillow.

"Answer me, will you."

Elinda wrapped a blanket around herself and got out of bed. She shivered. In the living room, the couch with its neat pile of unfinished embroidery was undisturbed. "God damn it. I don't want to start playing hide and seek at five o'clock in the morning again. We could talk about it, you know." Only the moonlight shifted, minutely. "We could have tried talking about it. Shit, didn't you even bother to leave a note?"

Most of Barbara's clothes were still in the closet, but her flashlight, parka and boots were gone from inside the front door. Elinda got dressed, made a cup of herb tea. Outside, the sky was paling where the second moon was about to rise, and silver edged the ice fields across the valley. "Another midnight hike, is that it? Brisk morning exercise, and back before I'm awake? No need to explain what I don't know about? That it? You'd better hurry, dear; I'm off to work when I've finished this." She wondered when she had started talking to herself.

She finished her tea and dropped the ceramic cup into the sink. Then she sat down again, opened the slatted blind over the kitchen window and stared along the shadowed valley, with its rampart southern wall, thinking how the water would cover so much of it when the dam was complete—sandstone and black earth, woods and undergrowth and everything that crawled and burrowed and flapped there, hidden under a weight of black water.

Her hands were rapping out a fast nervous rhythm on the wooden table. She watched them with a remote fascination as if they were unconnected to her. All the fingers were bitten around the nails. How long had she been doing that? How many other habits and memories were hidden behind that blank wall in her mind?

She pushed herself up from the table. "That's it, lover. I'm gone just as soon as I can get my coat on."

Beside the coat stand she and Barbara had built, she paused and looked back at the bedroom and the corner of the rumpled bed visible through the open door. She shook her head impatiently and shut the door behind her.

The row of homes stretching beside hers was dark and quiet. She resisted the temptation to slam the door, shoved it closed and set off.

JANUS

The cold air was invigorating. She walked briskly down the slope, keeping to the gravel path beside the woods. Photolures glimmered among the trunks like fallen stars. The second moon was just clearing the rim of the mountains. Visibility was good: to the south, across the river the white peaks known as the Angel's Hand gleamed like a set of talons from fifteen kilometres away. Almost overhead a pink blossom of aurora opened, bright enough to compete with the moons.

No one else was out. By the time she passed the next cluster of squat timber bungalows on her right, the lower slopes of the valley wall behind her shimmered darkly in the light of both moons. Higher, a white tracery of brooks and waterfalls reached down the unwooded upper slopes, then converged into a couple of streams that vanished into the woods. Ahead of her, mist eddied over the river and the coffer dam.

When the path curved she could see below her last night's dirigible moored at the landing field.

On her left she passed a track leading back up into the woods. Patches of snow still lay across it, between hollows of half-frozen mud. In the first patch there were footprints. They left the snow, went through the worst of the mud and were lost in the moonshadows as the track curved behind the trees. Elinda stopped. The prints were fresh—clear bootprints. She knew where the track led—to a stream you could cross on stepping stones, and up and along the valley wall. She had walked it several times with Barbara. Who had always been fastidious about keeping her boots clean.

The woods gave a long muted roar in the morning breeze, and the fronds swayed above her. A handful of dead leaves, like tiny brown gloves, released from last winter's snow came pattering towards her. She shivered. "Screw it," she whispered. "If that's you, just don't track mud all over the carpet when you do decide to come back, that's all."

▲

She was too late to catch the crew of the dirigible in the cafeteria. Only a few tables were occupied, mostly by rock-cutters and a couple of security men. She didn't want to talk to any of them this morning, and carried her cornflakes and soya-yoghurt towards an empty table; but then she saw someone else, a slim muscular man with black curling hair. On impulse she went to join him.

"Good god, Carlo," she said, sitting opposite him. "Your latest kick you out of bed?"

He rolled his eyes theatrically. "If you'd seen how I fought—how I had to tear myself away—you'd have wept. And I thought it was merely duty that compelled me, not knowing that fate had decreed our paths would entwine this morning."

"Yeah, fate can be nasty that way." She found she wasn't in the mood for banter. Hearing the stiffness in her voice, she grinned to compensate.

"Oh, so cruel, to a poor bachelor. Why are the prettiest ones always the coldest?" Carlo peered quickly at her and changed moods. "But fate will tear us apart soon enough. A new man came in on the gasbag last night. One, count him, one, from what was supposed to be a cargo shuttle. He was delayed somewhere up the pipe by medical complications." He sipped at his steaming coffee. "Don't ask me what, I only work here. And now he's lined up for a session with the memory machine as soon as he's through orientation. So of course Dr. Henry decides this is the occasion to try out his new algorithm, and guess who has to overhaul the machine and refresh our dear ruler's overtaxed mind with what we do in his clinic. Are you going to tell me your excuse, or shall I start believing in fate again?"

She preferred to deflect his question. "Dr. Henry is going to watch a memory session?"

"He may well try to participate if we're not careful," Carlo said. "Just as soon as he comes in from his morning constitutional. He's forgotten how long it's been since he did any practical work."

"Phillip Henry with mud on his boots. Have I slept a couple of years longer than I thought, or were you telling lies about him all this time?"

"We don't evaluate the data, ma'am, just pass it along."

She tried to chew a mouthful of cereal and finally swallowed it in a lump. "You still believe that machine of yours works, Carlo?"

He sipped again, then wiped his finger through the wet circle the mug had left on the table. "With patience, and a little luck," he said, "yes, it works." He hesitated. "At least, most people seem more comfortable with themselves after they've recovered some of their past."

"So which didn't I have?" she asked, and heard the note of strain return to her voice. "The patience or the luck?"

He peered at her again. "Both, perhaps. I did feel we were making progress when you gave it up. I'm not used to failing with a young woman. Are you going to give me another chance?"

"I don't know," she muttered. "My memory isn't coming back on its own, that's for damned sure. It wasn't very complicated—I just wanted to find out why I came here, what I wanted to be, or do."

He nodded. "And how's Barbara?"

"Okay." She bent her head as she scraped the last of the cereal from the bowl. But there was no reason not to talk about their relationship with him, was there? "She's started going for midnight walks again."

Carlo leaned back and watched her. "I think," he said, sounding professionally cautious, "anything that reduces tensions might help you both. You're both afloat in strange waters, not sure what you dare cling to. Perhaps you make too many demands on each other, because there are too many uncertainties in your lives. It might be good if you both decided to try again."

Elinda shook her head. "I don't know. She's sure she's happy enough as she is." Except, she admitted to herself, that Barbara kept writing down her dreams and trying to analyse them: she felt it was now that mattered, not the past. If there was anything to be done, she had to do it on her own. "We haven't been talking much lately, again," Elinda muttered.

"All the more reason for you both to try something like that. Keep it in mind, at least." Carlo looked at his watch. "And now I'd better tear myself away and start putting Dr. Henry's toy through its paces. Take care."

▲

The hut where she had her desk was still locked. Probably neither Larsen, her boss, nor Christopher, their assistant, would be in for half an hour yet. Rather than sit and be tempted to brood, she decided to make her morning inspection of the Greenhouse. She put her key back in her pocket and headed past the hut.

The Greenhouse lay across the road from landing field and occupied almost as much land—terraced into the slopes and enclosed under shells of automated glass panels. As she entered, banks of strip lights under the transparent ceiling were starting to glow in a simulated dawn.

The crops grew in trays of coarse sand. Each tray was fed its own nutrient mix from a set of troughs mounted on brackets above it. Nitrate, phosphate, trace elements . . . She walked the aisles, checking levels in the tanks, assuring herself that the sensors were in place, that none of the diseases they had fought were reappearing.

At the far end, up the fourth flight of steps, were the vats where waste vegetable matter was processed into something like milk, and the cloned animal protein was grown. It worked both ways, Larsen had told her when she had started working with him: terrestrial life couldn't eat the local food—plant or animal—without getting sick, but the crops they grew were safe from local pests for the same reason. If they could just get crops to grow in the natural soil, the colony would be one step nearer independence. Larsen himself spent long hours in the microbiology lab in the clinic working towards that end.

She made a mental note of a couple of problems and headed back to the office. On the way she caught sight of Carlo walking from the landing field towards the clinic. Beside him was a stocky, blond man who moved slowly, peering about him in a manner that could have meant either uncertainty or intense concentration. He must be the new arrival. He looked in her direction, but didn't seem to notice her. Something made her think of snow, and warmth shared in a shelter from biting winds. She wondered when Barbara would return. Two steps to the man's left, the taller, angular figure was Dr. Phillip Henry, the administrator, smiling animatedly and apparently talking non-stop while he pointed out things the others paid no attention to. Under the entrance light at the clinic she saw there did indeed seem to be mud on his boots.

She shook her head and went inside.

Someone had been in long enough to switch on the lights and turn on the heat, but she had the office to herself. She hung her coat behind the door and went to her desk. It faced south the window with a view of the river and the mountains. On a bright afternoon she had to squint to read her computer screen. As usual, the desk was littered with spare memory sticks, a couple of hardcopy botany texts and several piles of paper. The sheets had all been erased and recycled several times for reminders, lists, flow-diagrams, arithmetic, bits of computer code. Every unused space had been filled with her doodlings—curling, involuted shapes, chains of circles, blacked-in or empty. She could almost believe she was looking at an alien language, and wondered what Barbara, with her armchair dream analysis, would make of it all.

She felt a pang of irritation, and switched on the terminal to confirm that what she had seen of the Greenhouse fitted the facts as the machine saw them. She began working through the energy and mineral budgets, and was fully engrossed when the door opened.

"Early, this morning," said Niels Larsen, carefully unbuttoning his coat. Something in his voice made her turn to look at him. He was wearing his usual black sweater; his clipped grey goatee and the lines that ran down from his nose around his mouth emphasised the doleful length of his face. "Did you take breakfast in the cafeteria before you arrived?"

She glanced at the time flashing in the corner of her terminal screen. "About an hour ago. I couldn't sleep this morning."

He pulled a carefully folded sheet of paper from his coat pocket. "You didn't see any of these?"

The paper was a notepaper-sized leaflet printed in standard typeface capitals, and apparently photocopied. She read:

WAKE UP!

THIS PLACE IS A FRAUD!
IT IS A TOXIC DUMP FOR CRIMINALS
THEY HAVE PUT MURDERERS, RAPISTS AND
PSYCHOPATHS AMONG US
AND THEY NEVER TOLD US

EVERYONE!

GO TO THE COUNCIL
MAKE THEM TELL YOU WHAT IS GOING ON!

"It appeared on the datanet this morning," Larsen said, "and someone printed it out. Of course the file has been erased by now, but there were copies of this on most of the tables when I went in for coffee."

She shook her head. "There was the usual stack of stuff waiting for distribution when I was in. I didn't bother to read them."

"Whoever is responsible must have put them out in the last hour, then."

"Someone's either crazy or very sure of themselves," Elinda said. "I wish I had a paper budget like that." She shook her head. "I'd say it's just a practical joke, but it's too expensive for that. Someone probably believes this. I almost wonder why anyone would be so melodramatic."

"It's not a good omen for our new world, whether they're crazy, malicious or overconfident," Larsen said. "Secret criminals or secret lunatics. It seems the worm is in the apple."

"I'd take the lunatic myself," Elinda said "—as long as they stop at handing out leaflets." She looked at him. "Or do you think there's more to it?"

Larsen frowned. "We are still tied to the purse strings of our beloved home world's consortium, and I can't believe the administration there is more virtuous than others of its kind. There must be some bodies that would welcome an excuse to cut our funding." He paused and sat down. "To be honest, what really troubles me about this piece of amateur journalism is the effect it may have on our community, whether it contains any truth or not. This is a very small society in which to sow distrust. I certainly would not want to see a witch hunt here, when the nearest sanctuary may lie in another universe."

"You think it might not be a lunatic then? A—saboteur?"

He paused, frowning. "I feel if that were the main intention, some more direct action would have been taken. I believe—and hope—that it was merely misguided, and it turns out to be isolated and unfounded."

"We should just ignore it then? But if there is something in it . . ."

"If there is—then what?" he said. "You should understand, as well as anyone, how meaningless it is to judge a person by their past—here, particularly here. No: remember it, but leave it alone. Or are you looking for a new career as an investigative reporter?"

"No thanks," she said coolly. "I'm quite comfortable here."

"Good." He met her eyes briefly. "I'm glad."

She tried to hide how much that crumb of praise meant to her.

About five minutes later, Christopher Huson, the other third of their team, came in. Brown-haired and gangling, he always reminded Elinda of an overgrown, over-studious schoolboy, despite the fact that he seemed to have an inside track on what recreational drug market there was in the settlement. "Checked your in-box lately?" he asked. "I think there's a circular to all departments. Something to do with us putting on a sort of celebration, though I haven't seen it."

"Clearly," Larsen muttered, and turned to his computer. "Your extrasensory perception is as good as ever, Christopher. It seems our masters back home want something more immediate than possible pharmaceuticals for their money—publicity in this case. Next spring there is to be a celebration of the anniversary of the landing here and the completion of the hydroelectric plant, and as a build-up, we are to provide regular progress reports for the public networks. Which means they expect us to have our facilities looking their best."

"Does that mean I've gotta go tying plastic roses on all the pot plants in the Greenhouse again?" Christopher asked.

Larsen eyed him. "One day, you will say something of the kind that I will take seriously, and you'll spend the rest of your days on top of a firewatch tower. You can read the details later. Now," he continued, "perhaps we should get on with more current business. I'd like to think about some more experiments on germinating seed in the local soil."

They discussed possible experimental protocols until noon and then broke for lunch. Elinda had not brought anything to eat and picked up her coat to walk to the cafeteria. Then she stopped and asked Chris if he had seen the leaflets on the breakfast table that morning.

He looked up from unwrapping sandwiches. "Didn't drop in there today." He looked at the leaflet she handed him. "But you know the talk—we're the suicide squad sent here to test for hostile aliens, or we're an experiment in adapting to hydroponic food, or in mind control—that sort of thing."

"And you just laugh this off the same way?"

"What else? Am I supposed to sit here waiting for one of you to creep up and smash a video monitor over my skull?"

Elinda nodded at Larsen, who was listening with interest. "You're saying just what he said."

Chris shrugged expansively. "Had to happen sooner or later."

Outside, the air was colder. She walked briskly towards the cafeteria. The woods on the lower slopes shimmered with the ghost lights of predator and prey. Below her, two trucks were transferring gravel to the end of the growing dam. Nearer, a couple in a coracle were out on the fish farm with a flare and a scoop net—someone would be getting live protein on the menu this evening. Another couple, with three children in faded red and green parkas, were at the far edge of the landing field, under the lights, trying to get a box kite into the air. Everyone else seemed to be at lunch.

Barbara had probably come back from her adventure and was only concerned with catching up on her work in the lab. Judging from previous occasions, questions would not be welcome, but sooner or later they'd have to have it out. That meant breaking through the silence, and another fight. Or maybe the whole thing was over for good. Maybe it had been for weeks. Elinda thought about that, and found she could not decide what she felt.

Nothing was certain here, nothing had clear meaning. It was like the crops in the Greenhouse, flourishing but artificially rooted in a few centimetres of sand. She wondered again about going for more memory treatments. With Carlo. Yeah, sure—who knew what they might learn together if she wasn't careful? But, in fact, hadn't she given up too easily? She thought back to those sessions in her first weeks there, and how depressed she had been after them, so that Barbara had talked her out of continuing. Well, she was better adjusted now, wasn't she? Was that why half the time she still referred to Barbara as her roommate?

In the cafeteria neither Carlo nor Barbara was to be seen.

A group of space jockeys in the silvery coveralls with the comic-book shoulder patches were sitting at one of the tables against the far wall. She spotted the dirigible flight-crew two tables over; they were reading something and passing it from one to another, and she guessed it was one of the leaflets. A short man in olive green went over to the table and said something quiet and emphatic to the aircrew, then came away with the sheet of paper, folding it and slipping it into an inside pocket.

"Excuse me."

Someone was edging past her in the queue, heading for the door. She stepped to one side, then saw who it was. "Jessamyn." Barbara's ex. There had been a strained cordiality between them since Elinda and Barbara had moved in together. Elinda swallowed a temptation to ask her if she knew where Barbara might be. But Jessamyn looked back at the man who had taken the leaflet, then at her, and whispered, "What did she tell you?"

Confused, Elinda shook her head.

"Nothing? You don't know what she found? Shit." She was gone before Elinda could start to frame a question.

▲

Elinda found a table near the window. Sitting there were a group of hydroelectric engineers she knew slightly. They were turning to talk to the dirigible crew at the next table, but when she sat down, one of them asked her if she had seen the leaflets everyone was talking about.

She said she had.

"They *were* passed around, then," the other woman said. "Someone whisked them away so fast, you'd think they wanted to create paranoia. It's probably some crank's idea of a joke of course, but it's not funny. Some of us brought kids here to get away from that sort of thing. If you lived in Chicago during the last fifteen years—" She broke off as her neighbour elbowed her, not very subtly.

"It's all right," Elinda said. "There's always the chance something'll strike a chord."

"That wasn't—" the woman began, and stopped short. "Anyway, it's probably too much to hope we'll find out who did it, but if anything like this happens again, some of us are going to want a full investigation."

"You're assuming there's nothing to the story?" Elinda asked.

"Well—naturally. You have to, don't you? We're all in this together here. The danger is that someone'll set us against each other. I've seen it happen."

Elinda sensed that the other was wanting to bite her tongue again. "So tell me about living in Chicago," she said. "Really."

Listening while she ate, Elinda as usual found it difficult to imagine a place like the one being described. The words were familiar—bus, freeway, high-rise, elevator, rush hour, museum, phone—and she knew what images they represented, but they were no more tangible to her than the concepts labelled *angel*, *dragon*, *destiny* or *salvation*.

At the end of the meal, she caught sight of the new arrival

again, lining up for the last of the lunch menu. He wore a dark grey sweater, tight around the shoulders, and looked tense, probably aware that half the cafeteria would be looking him over. He'd missed the regular delivery, that was the trouble, or he'd be one of a group, getting proper orientation. Hard eyes, she decided. He might have a temper.

She returned to work, and the afternoon passed. She managed to accomplish most of the things she was supposed to do.

▲

On her way home, two hours later than usual, she passed the path where she had noticed the footprints in the mud that morning, but she didn't have the energy to follow them. If Barbara wanted to run around with her old flames, it wasn't up to her to snoop, was it? Was it?

And besides, when she got in, Barbara would be there, with the vegetables peeled for supper.

The bungalow was dark inside, and empty. As she stood in the hallway, with the door shut at her back and the living room in shadow, the stillness was so intense she imagined she could hear the stream in the woods nearby. She punched the kitchen lights on, slumped into one of the hard chairs beside the window and pulled pita bread from the bin. It tasted like cardboard to her now, but she filled her mouth and chewed and swallowed, and bit more off, until some of the emptiness inside her was filled.

Her eyes ached. In her ears was a memory of lapping water. But now, more definite memories were crowding in on her, of long frozen silences in these rooms, and screaming rages. Carefully she unlocked her fingers from each other and exhaled in a long ragged sigh. "God damn it," she whispered, "you're not going to make me miserable. When I find you you'd better have something to say for yourself."

TWO

Under a haze of arc lighting, the river swirled and foamed, muttered and roared. The man whose name was Jon Grebbel stared down at it from the road along the bank and tried to make sense of what he was being told. To his right, fifty metres downstream, a truck loaded with gravel inched out along a causeway that cut into the river and joined onto a metal bridge that spanned the rest of the distance to the far bank.

"One-point-five gigawatts of hydroelectric power, Mr. Grebbel," the tall grey man was saying, "that's our goal when the dam is fully operational. Enough to fuel the next generation of space probes exploring this system. Oxygen and hydrogen—until we strike oil, they're still the simplest and the cheapest fuels this side of the Knot. At the moment, of course, with the dam still under construction, we produce just about enough power for our own needs and a few launches a year."

Grebbel nodded and said nothing, turned his back to the arc lamps as the taller man moved along the path. In front of him at the top of a short slope stretched the landing field, with its control tower and mooring pylon. Black-furred slopes loomed above the field; a few greenish lights drifted and blinked. Downstream, beyond the dam, was a cluster of low buildings and above them, level with the landing field, was a huge low structure of transparent panes.

Higher up, slabs of white mountainside reared up into the moonlight and ended in fangs that cut into the sky. And above them, a great whorl of cloud, silver-edged where the moonlight shot through it, opened out, as though to suck the black sky down upon them. He could feel the funnel turning, pulling, although when he stared at any part of it, he could see no motion. Below its southern rim, spaced above the peaks on the far side of the river, two ivory moons swam in a copper-tinged haze, one gibbous, one almost full, like the stare of two unmatched eyes.

He shivered, and his mind slipped back to the cabin in the dirigible—coming out of a coma alone in a darkened room, finding himself strapped to a bed.

Get these fucking things off me! Who do you think I am? Then quiet voices: *How much do you remember? Can you remember your name?* Electric light. Hands freeing his wrists. Trying to sit up, staring at the pale walls, the careful, expressionless faces.

And the scars on his arm . . .

He turned back towards the river, trying to concentrate on the words he was hearing.

Henry, that was the man's name, Something Henry. He would have to make a point of memorising names. He wondered if he'd always had trouble with that, or if this was another part of the effect of coming through the Knot. The other man walking close beside him, looking unobtrusively guardian-like, he was Carlo somebody. Grebbel didn't think he'd heard the second name.

"You can see the coffer dam," Henry said. "We use it to hold back the water while we work on the main structure. Part of the flow is diverted through the sluiceways in the far wall of the valley; in there it drives the turbines. You can see a smaller set on this side too. The rest of the water finds its way under the bridge there." The metal-frame bridge strung with arc lights linked the far end of the main dam to an opening in the wall at the far side of the river. "When the new dam is ready, we'll be increasing the flow through the sluiceways, of course, and using a bigger set of turbines—they're being installed at the moment. By then, a lot of what you see will be under water."

From the way Henry was throwing around the word "we," Grebbel guessed he was a senior bureaucrat who never got any closer to the actual construction site than he was now.

But when had this mystery called Jon Grebbel learned to think such thoughts? He looked around, tried to connect what he could see with what he had been told. A long, narrow valley, steep as a knife cut on its southern side, the river close to its estuary here. Looking upstream, he would be facing east, most of the settlement on the slopes to his left. The hidden source of the river would be high in the mountains there; and beyond them, the salt flats where the shuttle must have landed.

You took the shuttle to Earth orbit, one of the voices had told him; *then the transfer out to the Knot. Is anything coming back now?*

Several hundred metres away, floodlights on the landing field still lit the dirigible that had brought him. It had been winched to the ground, and two men were working on one of the motors. The cabin was an elongated grey box slung underneath. Enough room for a couple of dozen men maybe, or—what?—five or ten tonnes of cargo?

"Well," said Henry. "As you seem to be one of the unfortunate thirty percent, let's get along to the clinic so we can get started on your memory."

From . . . Winnipeg. Manitoba, he'd said. *I was—a technician. Yes. I learned blood-typing in college, and circuit theory and some calculus and— My father had brown eyes and a moustache—*

Grebbel shivered in the morning chill. He'd have to learn to call this darkness morning, to accept whatever they decided was morning. Ninety-eight-point-something hours rotation period, they'd told him: at this season that meant nearly three days of unbroken darkness, while the temperature dropped and the winds howled overhead across the bowl of the mountains.

Janus—the god of doorways and auspicious beginnings, someone had explained.

Pink scars ran from the knuckles halfway to the elbow. He turned his wrist back and forth in the strap. Twice he opened his mouth to speak, and said nothing. He let his arm fall limp

"I guess I'm a celebrity now," Grebbel said. "I suppose you don't get that many new recruits, if you can afford to give me a red carpet treatment like this."

There's nothing else. I can't remember anything else.

"To be honest," Henry said. "I'm indulging myself a little. Since you arrived between the normal immigration flights, it was easy to make some special arrangements. And it so happened I had a new treatment algorithm worked out to help restore your memories. . . ."

"Dr. Henry was one of the originators of the therapy programme," Carlo interjected. "They were reluctant to let him come to Janus."

"Well, some of them were. Unfortunately, nowadays I spend

two-thirds of my time being an administrator; it was the only way they let me come here. So any excuse I get to do more clinical work is welcome, and the opportunity to supervise my new algorithm was too good to miss. And then it's always good to get to know one's patients before starting therapy; so I decided to take on the job of tour guide and see what it felt like."

Grebbel was beginning to wonder what was in store as therapy—and why was that making him apprehensive?—but Henry was reluctant to discuss that in advance.

"Someone else will show you where you'll be living, after this session," he continued. "You'll probably find it a little spartan at first. A lot of our accommodation isn't on the main power or water grids yet, but we have enough in the way of point sources—solar power, wood furnaces, and wells and streams and so on—to make things acceptable. Actually we're a technological ragbag of absolute essentials, worn out leftovers and cut-price deals; we'll probably strike you as a throwback to the dark ages—we still haven't got a workable microwave link for a phone system. Something to do with auroral discharges in the upper atmosphere, they tell me. And you'll find we're going back to the paper age. Man in Hut Seven has got the techniques worked out pretty well. But the first thing is to see how many of your memories we can salvage before they fade any further. This is the clinic here."

They had reached the entrance to a long, single-storey building faced with wide split logs. There was hardly anybody else around. Just a woman in a light blue parka watching them as she walked towards one of the larger buildings. The entrance lights above them seemed to bring down the dark like a black ceiling.

"The treatment wing's to the left," Carlo said. "The other way are the biology and pathology labs, for when we get time to do some research. You can scrape the mud off your boots here."

The floor was concrete; the walls and ceiling were painted in high-gloss white. Carlo led the way, past the lobby with a reception desk, and down a short corridor. His footsteps reverberated in the enclosed space. At the end was a small room containing three wooden chairs and several racks of electronic equipment. Beside a shuttered window, shelves on the far wall carried rows of bottles and steel instruments. Grebbel hesitated, rubbing the scars on his wrist.

"You can hang your coat behind the door," Carlo said. He tossed his own parka over a chair and sat beside a keyboard mounted in one of the racks. Dr. Henry folded his trench coat over the back of another chair, but remained standing where he could watch over Carlo's shoulder as Carlo began turning switches on the electronics.

The dirigible was turning. He could hear the wind and the motors thrumming. He strode to the window of the cabin and reached towards the pane.

And was met by his own face and his scarred hand outthrust.

"You want to tell me what these machines do?" Grebbel said.

"I'm afraid a detailed explanation would take more time than we have," Dr. Henry said. "But, briefly, we use a combination of electrical, chemical and sensory stimulation to restore activity in some of the brain's networks that have suffered from the passage through the Knot. The state of mind you'll experience is like a deep hypnotic trance, but we believe we've eliminated most of the suggestibility that made such states difficult to work with."

He picked up a bowl apparently made of silver basketwork. "We'll use the helmet to measure some of your brain waves, and also apply low-frequency oscillations to enhance responses in certain of the networks. The process relies heavily on feedback; so we have to calibrate your responses to certain stimuli before we start."

Carlo asked Grebbel to sit in the third chair, a complex structure covered in black vinyl, with clamps and multicoloured wires emerging from the headrest and arms. Carlo taped electrodes to Grebbel's wrist and neck, and then began adjusting the metal framework helmet to fit Grebbel's head.

"Try to relax, Mr. Grebbel. You're very tense. Open your hands and breathe deeply. There'll be no pain—at most some slight discomfort. Let your jaw relax, stop clenching your teeth. Take slow, deep breaths. That's better."

Working behind him, Carlo made some more adjustments on the helmet. Grebbel's scalp tingled as cold metal touched it, then seemed to go numb as his skin adjusted to the sensation. He saw that the scars on his wrist were bright pink. He tried to moisten his lips.

Now Carlo was in front of him again. "I'm going to give you a shot in a couple of minutes, a mild relaxant, and then we'll be ready. First, though, I'm going to calibrate your responses." He went and dimmed the ceiling light. "In a moment I'll put a pattern on the oscilloscope screen there, and I want you to concentrate on it while I ask you some preliminary questions. Okay?"

Grebbel nodded.

Blue lines tangled and leapt on the screen. Carlo fitted earphones into Grebbel's ears and spoke into a microphone. "I'll use this to get better control over your sense inputs. Can you hear me all right?"

Grebbel nodded again.

"Right then. I'm going to ask you a series of questions, and I'd like you to answer them as quickly as you can, without stopping to think about what you're going to say. Ready?"

Grebbel nodded.

"What are two and two?"

"Four."

"What is your name?"

"Grebbel . . . Jon Grebbel."

"A little faster if you can. Seven times four?"

"Twenty-eight."

"What colour is grass?"

"Green."

"How old are you?"

"Thirty-six. Thirty-six."

"Your name?"

"Grebbel. Jon Grebbel. That's all. Jon Grebbel."

"What was your occupation? . . . Mr. Grebbel, can you hear me?"

"Technician. I was a laboratory technician."

Carlo paused. "Mr. Grebbel, are you aware of anything causing you particular stress at the moment?"

Grebbel moistened his lips. "I don't know."

Carlo checked the electrodes on Grebbel's wrists. Grebbel's skin was white and sweating. The scars on his right arm were crimson.

Dr. Henry stepped forward and caught Carlo's eye. The two of them muttered by the door for a minute. Then Carlo nodded and came back. "Sorry about that. I think we'll go straight to the next stage now. I'll give you the shot, and we'll see how far we can get establishing a reference matrix for your memories."

Grebbel's sleeve was rolled up; a hypo-gun was pressed against his arm, and the flickering on the screen swelled to fill his mind.

◣

"Here, you'll be groggy for a few minutes," Carlo said, "but then you'll feel better."

Grebbel took the brownish drink Carlo handed him and sipped: something fruit-based, warm and sweet.

Seeing Grebbel look around, Carlo grinned. "The Boss doctor? Back to work for him. We're lucky, if that's the word I want, to see him twice a month."

Grebbel finished the drink and handed the glass to Carlo. As he did so, he caught sight of his wrist.

"What?" said Carlo. "I didn't catch that."

"Can I ask . . . ? You understand medicine, right? I mean . . . more than just this?"

"I've had some general background, yes."

"These scars. On my arm. How old, would you say . . . ?"

Carlo frowned. "Depends. For someone your age, with hormone treatment, even deep cuts could heal to that stage in a couple of weeks. Otherwise . . . they could be, oh, anything up to six months old. Why? Have you remembered something?"

"Months."

"Of that general order. Are you finding some associations? Don't push it yet, you're still coming round. If there is anything to be recovered at this stage, it'll probably float into your mind on its own in the next hour or so. How's your head now?"

"Bit better."

"Okay, try standing up. Exercise usually helps; so as soon as you're ready, I'll show you the town and take you to where you'll be living."

Outside the clinic, they turned onto a gravel path that led up the valley side. They passed a cluster of large wooden buildings, built low to the ground and solid. "There's a windstorm around sunrise and sunset almost every day," Carlo said. "The atmosphere's deep and a bit denser than you're used to, though you probably won't notice that unless you're a singer. But when that cloud funnel breaks up, and the winds pour though the valley, it can get interesting here. Some people are concerned about tectonics as well; we're probably clear of the worst faults, and the nearest active volcanoes are either inland or south of here, but the planning committee weren't convinced that three-storey buildings were a good thing."

Carlo pointed out the main street with the tavern at one end and, at the other, the auditorium, which doubled as council chamber and law court. Grebbel realised that what he had taken for an odd-looking greenish tower slightly north of the main street was actually one of the local trees, left standing to dominate the buildings around it.

"I'll explain a bit more about what we do here, while you get your thoughts back together," Carlo went on. "Then we'll run an informal check on how your memories are coming. You won't feel most of the benefit of each session for a day or two; so we'll be doing some more formal checks when you come back in. Anyway: as you probably know, when they stumbled on the Knot back there, practically in Earth's back yard, they didn't know what it was at first or what to do with it. Then they found it led here, and they still didn't know.

"So they sent the probes and did some exploring, and found they had a whole new solar system, at the very least, to play with, right next door—and all that implied." Carlo paused for emphasis, evidently enjoying the chance to lecture. Grebbel felt he was expected to cue Carlo with another question. He said nothing.

Carlo hesitated but then continued brightly. "What did it imply?" he asked. "That was a hard one, too. Lots of fun for people interested in theories of planetary dynamics, or comparative geology, climatology, biology. . . . Maybe the results could save some of Earth's ecology, maybe there would be some new pharmaceuticals from the research, but it would have to be a long-term venture. Eventually, with enough energy available here, it might become economical to ship produce, even fuel, back through the Knot. And that meant a decade or two spent on a resources survey of the system, to find fusion fuels. All things considered, a self-supporting colony seemed the goal to aim at. So here we are. All seven hundred of us."

"At the dam," Grebbel said finally.

"Right. Dr. Henry told you the plans. The explorers can use solar power for low-acceleration missions, but blast-off and major orbit changes still need high thrust, which still means oxy-hydrogen. At the same time, we provide a staging post for the survey of this particular world, and incidentally some normal-gravity R and R for our space-weary explorers. You'll generally find at least one shift in the tavern."

Grebbel walked on in silence, then asked, "Why are we so far from the shuttle base?"

"Geography, I'm afraid. Maybe history as well. The salt flats were one of the first areas explored, because they were a natural landing field for the shuttles, and the first supply dumps and parts depots were put there. This, on the other hand, is a lousy place to land a spaceship, but one of the best spots on this side of the continent to build a hydro plant, if you don't want it falling into a crack between tectonic plates or buried in a lava flow. Besides which, if we ever figure out how to grow anything edible in this soil, this looks like the best place to do it climatically and geochemically. And, really, we're not all that far from the landing field. It's just the other side of the mountain range."

Grebbel stared at the jagged moonlit skyline. "Too far for an afternoon walk."

"That's true. You can go for a walk in the wood, though. There are animals—you can see the imagery—but they tend to avoid us; we probably smell weird to them. Just try and stay on the main paths. But you've only just got here. You can't be wanting to get on a shuttle already."

"No—I just remembered. I was a plane spotter when I was a kid."

"Then I'm afraid you'll just have to make do with the blimps here. Fortunately, the atmosphere's deep enough for them to get above the peaks and the turbulence. They're over every day or so when the winds allow, and there are three different models. What else have you remembered?"

"I think I had a pet when I was a kid. Dog, maybe." Grebbel paused. "I've got a picture of shaggy hair and something rolling on the ground. Maybe something happened to it. Something whining and puking all the time. I don't know. If it was our dog, maybe it got hit by a car or something, and we got rid of it."

"Anything else? Can you remember where you were when you had the dog?"

Grebbel thought. "Red bricks, maybe. Concrete steps. A front lawn with a curved path—a gate and a low hedge."

"What was the number?" Carlo asked quietly. "Or the name of the street?"

"I'm trying to remember. The front door . . . all wood, painted green, but I can't see the number. And the street name was at the corner—it was out of sight because the road curved."

"That's quite good," Carlo said. "It looks promising. I'd say we've brought up an individual memory, of one particular occasion, but without enough detail yet to tell what the occasion was. Often it's nothing special—just whatever happened to be triggered by the therapy this time round and was easily recovered. The fact that it seems to have no strong emotional associations for you probably means the memory is just whatever we managed to catch in the net. Your visual memories are strongest at the moment, which is why you had to look for things like the number of your house. Later, that may turn up on its own."

"Don't you have that sort of information on my file?"

"We have some, of course, but nowhere near enough detail to replace what you've lost. And we prefer not to tell you things like that, because then you'd start relying on our files, instead of unearthing the truth by yourself."

Carlo stopped and faced Grebbel. "What you find for yourself is yours," he said, "and you'll know you can trust it. But what happens if you've been relying on our files and someone's confused you with Juan Grable, the taxi driver in Buenos Aires?" They walked on. "Let's try a bit more. Can you see the inside of your house? Is there anyone there—your family, neighbours, some friends?"

"It's too hazy," Grebbel said. "It keeps slipping away. But there's a white room somewhere. Brick walls whitewashed. And it's quite dim. Just one light bulb up in the ceiling, and I can't see a window. There's a stain on the wall."

"Well, that's quite detailed, but it's hard to see how it fits with the other memory. Maybe we should let things take their course for a bit longer." Carlo looked at his watch. "I'd better show you where you'll be staying, and then I'll have to let you explore by yourself for a while. We're short-staffed at the clinic today; one of our technicians hasn't come in. We turn left here."

They came to another long single-storey building of the usual log-and-frame construction. The roof was angled to the south. "Too much like a motel, I'm afraid, despite the photocells on the roof," Carlo said, heading for the entrance to one of the units. "If you remember such things. But you're stuck with it for the moment." He unlocked the door, fumbled with a light switch.

"Good, they remembered to bring your belongings over. I'll leave you to unpack in a minute, but I'd better give you a quick rundown first. Two main rooms. The whole block's insulated— the local timber's quite good in itself too—so you shouldn't need much power. There's a set of storage cells for the whole building under the roof. You can use the lights and so on while you're in here, but turn them off when you go out, and if you start getting a brown-out, switch everything off, or you'll be running the battery below the recommended level, and no one'll thank you if it has to be replaced. Hot water's partly solar, partly from a wood furnace. Here's the key. I think everything else is fairly obvious. You can find your way to the cafeteria, or the clinic if you need to?"

Grebbel nodded.

"First thing this afternoon, you should report to the Administration building, behind the cafeteria—there's a map on the desk there—to sort out your work detail. They'll be expecting you, and they're on part-time from other duties, so don't upset their schedule by forgetting. I think that's about it for now. When you're through there, your time's your own for the rest of the day. So make yourself comfortable, and we'll see you at the clinic tomorrow at nine."

Grebbel watched him walk away, then shut the door and leaned back against it. Closing his eyes, he drew in a long breath. He straightened his fingers one by one, eased his head from side to side, worked his shoulders loose, and slowly exhaled.

The room was sparsely furnished: white ceiling, three wooden shelves mounted on the far wall, an unvarnished wooden table under the window. A flashlight was plugged into a recharger beside the door. Two wooden-frame armchairs with foam cushions; cream-coloured plasterboard walls, and a plank floor. In the closet was another anorak and set of heavy thermal work pants like the ones he had been given in the blimp. There was a door to the bedroom, another to the bathroom, and an alcove with a sink and microwave oven. A scuffed blue suitcase and a large duffel bag had been left just inside the front door. Grebbel heaved the bag over his shoulder and carried it into the bedroom.

Then he put the suitcase on the table in the living room, fumbled a key from his pockets, and snapped the lid up.

He pulled out two folded shirts and a pair of slacks, put them on the table, and picked up a thick plastic folder that had been underneath. He weighed it in his hands, then sat down. Unopened, it lay on the table, his hands flat on either side of it. He swallowed, and carefully lifted the cover.

A lot of e-mail printouts, a few letters on white airmail paper, on lined, three-hole loose-leaf sheets; spidery in blue ink, or black squarish italics. A graduation certificate from technical college, an old driving licence, with an earnest, youthful face he could just bring himself to recognise. A passport with a holo-portrait that looked barely more familiar.

A small e-photo album.

He moistened his lips before pulling it towards him and stepping down its menu.

Bright faces, party crowds, portraits of two or three under trees, in thick-carpeted living rooms with mahogany furniture, on the steps of a beige stone building. Faces. Grinning, polite, severe, friendly, laughter-distorted, anonymous faces.

His jaw clenched. When he tilted the album towards him, he caught sight of the scars on his wrist, and stopped. He closed his eyes and did not breathe.

His hand went up to sweep the table clear.

He shuddered and brought it down slowly. His breath came out in a ragged sigh.

With fingers that shook, he squared the album parallel to the corner of the table, stacked the letters and other papers back in the folder beside it, and pushed himself to his feet.

Methodically he took his clothing out of the bags, one item at a time, carried each with his head lowered, and placed it in the cupboard. When he had finished, he stood motionless in the same hunched position, and his breathing grew harsh. He straightened up then and fastened his coat and went out, quietly pulling the door shut behind him.

Hands jammed in pockets, he walked slowly in the midday darkness, listening to the gravel under his boots, concentrating on the sights and sounds that reached him, the half-familiar tang of the alien forests—trying not to think. Something whistled in the trees.

At one point a man and woman passed him from the opposite direction, talking quietly together. Grebbel thought he heard the man say, "Who knows what he was like back then?" and laugh. And he found he had swung round, his breath surging, his hands ready to seize and twist.

He checked himself and watched as the couple walked on, oblivious, the cold air pressing against his face like a steel mask.

Then his ears were filled with the sounds of his own body, breathing again, walking.

He stopped when another sound grew to dominate them, and found he was overlooking the site of the dam again. White water thundered before him under the lights. The earth seemed to shiver under his feet. He stared at the water that piled up, that churned and lathered and forced its way through the narrow sluiceways. Its frustrated urgency made his muscles tighten and quiver.

On the far bank a dump truck emerged from a lighted tunnel entrance with a load of rubble. That would be where they were preparing to install the new turbines. Upstream was the tangle of steel pipes and tanks that was the cryoplant. He turned away from the river and looked up the valley wall. Among partly cleared timber above the little estate where his building was, there was a cluster of lights that meant more housing. And upstream of that, a white thread of moonlit water came down from the upper slopes. It vanished into the woods, glittered here and there among the trees, and evidently joined the river somewhere beyond the landing field.

He found himself wondering what the little stream would look like from above, from beyond the upper row of buildings. He tried to picture the fall of the valley from that perspective, the dark forest on the slopes below, down to the sharp division made by one of the larger roads. . . .

A siren sounded on the worksite. The icy wind was forcing itself through his coat. He fumbled to close the top button and caught another glimpse of his scarred wrist as the siren sounded again and fell quiet.

Something jarred in his mind.

Up there—or on a slope like that—he seemed to see a large isolated building, and lights spilling across the snow. In this valley, it would be up near the source of the stream. If he were there, looking down that slope, standing where that imagined building had been, the—memory—might return.

He would have to climb the slope as far as he could.

But not yet. Later, when this darkness felt more like evening.

Obscurely satisfied, he started to turn away. And the rage he had carried from his room sprang up again. He seized a rock the size of his skull, swung it over his head in both hands and heaved it out into the river. Before it splashed he had snatched up cobbles and begun hurling them—throwing furiously with either hand, stone after stone, until his arms ached and his breath sobbed in his ears. And then, as suddenly as the fury had come, he was calm again. He breathed heavily and stared at the water.

⚓

In the cafeteria he ate something that was called a cheese sandwich, paid for with a plastic card he found in his shirt pocket, then remembered his appointment at the Administration building. That turned out to be a low prefabricated structure, like a half-cylinder on its side. He wondered if it was part of a shuttle fuel tank. He followed a handwritten sign to the labour coordination office. The door was ajar and inside were a man and a woman working at small computer keyboards. Grebbel rapped on the open door and introduced himself.

"Good afternoon," said the woman, brushing back a lock of brown hair with one hand and feeling for a pencil among the pile of papers with the other. "Come on in. Mr. Grebbel, you said?" She copied something from the computer screen onto the corner of a yellow sheet of paper that had seemed to have no useable space left on it. "Just give me another moment and I'll be right with you." Her hands were rough and reddened, with grime under the nails. We've only got another hour and a half, Mike and I"— she nodded towards the balding moonfaced man, bent over his computer as though mesmerised by it—"then we've got to help with the potato harvest. Things do get a bit hectic at times."

"I'm sure."

"I've got your work detail here," she said, still concentrating on the screen, "somewhere. Fourteen," she muttered, "in Zone Three, and they wanted . . ." She groped with her left hand among a stack of folders, pulled one out and handed it to him, without apparently turning her eyes from the computer. "You can save time by looking over that profile and filling in where it asks for information. We've been short one body for three weeks now, and no replacement in sight. Not even you, though I bet you'd love to work here, wouldn't you?" She paused briefly. "They'll have to take eleven and like it."

Grebbel found a pen on the corner of her desk and worked on the form. He was finishing when she finally turned from the keyboard and faced him.

"Let's have a look," she said, and ran her gaze over the page. "Ah, that's close enough. If there's anything wrong, they can always go and ask you, can't they? Okay, here's what we've got for you. In their wisdom, they've decided that the biggest priority is to get the dam finished for the celebrations. So any cases with doubtful qualifications—that's you—are assigned to construction work. Ever remember driving a truck? They tell me it's not hard to learn. Just shifting gravel from one point to another, nothing too complicated. Here's a map. Here's who you report to. Hmm, starting tomorrow. Not much time to find your way around, but I suppose we can't all have cozy desk jobs. That okay? Any problems, drop in and see us again. The hours are on the board in the entrance."

She was back at the keyboard before Grebbel reached the door.

▲

So he had travelled from one universe to another to learn to be a truck driver.

Grebbel's hands had clenched into fists, so hard they hurt; with an effort he made them open.

He found it took an hour to walk round the perimeter of the settlement. Hours, they'd said, were unchanged at least.

A pair of winged creatures was moving in slow circles over the lights on the landing field. Suddenly their wings furled and they plummeted towards the dark woods beyond the perimeter. He imagined the scream as their talons struck flesh.

Waiting to catch sight of them again, he considered what he knew about his existence.

One. He *was*. Whatever he doubted, some fundamental core of him had existed continuously from birth until now, bridging universes.

Two. That hidden self might know more than he knew. It

might be circling in some vaulted space, awaiting the moment to plunge and strike. Why else did he find himself in the grip of sudden angers and pains he could not explain?

Three. His hands . . .

His hands that clenched into knots of pain, and hurled rocks, and bore scars . . .

The thought slipped away before he could complete it. He shook his head, then flexed his shoulders and headed on to the cafeteria.

In the lineup, he heard talk about a leaflet that had been passed around recently. He tried to get details, but none of the people he asked knew or were willing to say much more. One of them, a grizzled man in the silver astronaut costume, with his legs encased in a black composite exoskeleton, shook his head at Grebbel. "New here, aren't you? Safer if you get the official line on things here, before you go making guesses. Open council meeting at seven—why don't you drop in and see what you think of the ones who run this place before you get fed too many rumours?"

Grebbel ate quickly, still preoccupied, and then walked out onto the main street. A painted wooden sign lit from below identified it as Unter Den Linden. It was surfaced with asphalt, presumably for the trucks, although at the moment only pedestrians were using it. Along the edge of the road, mercury lights on wooden posts lit piles of grimy snow. He went past a general store and a barter shop specialising in homemade ceramic and wooden craftware. The lights ended and the street curved around a wide pond in which the reflected moons rippled. He leaned on the fence, watching as wisps of vapour curled above the surface, and below the moons, carp idled among dark weed.

He followed a group of people towards what must be the Council Hall.

A group of children ran out from between two buildings ahead of him. They passed Grebbel, shouting and chasing each other along the rim of the pond. They were all behind him when the shouts suddenly changed and there was a heavy splash. He started to turn, but the woman ahead of him had stopped and swung round so sharply he almost walked into her. Her face, for an instant, was so stricken that he stared at her.

"All right?"

She was looking past him. "Yes, I think so," she said after a moment. "Yes, it's just a soaking, it's not even knee-deep there."

The boy was pulling himself over the rim, dripping water, but evidently unhurt.

Grebbel turned back to the woman. She was blonde, with a few strands of hair straggling from the hood of her blue parka. Short nose, wide mouth, light brown eyes. He had seen her that morning on the way from the landing field. "I meant . . . Never mind."

"They're hard as diamonds at that age—or so they tell me." Her face changed. "I don't suppose you've seen . . . ?" She looked at him. "No, of course, you wouldn't have, you just arrived today, didn't you? I mean, strangers tend to be conspicuous around here, in any case, but I think I saw you on the way to the clinic this morning." She gestured along the street. "Have you had chance to look around?"

"A bit. I wanted to climb higher up the hillside, but there wasn't time."

"Up there?" She pointed. "That's where all the best people live, except when we're down here slumming. You look as though you're heading for the Council meeting. I suppose it's something you should see once. I might even go myself, but I'm meeting someone." She shifted from foot to foot, her gaze flickering from the street to his face and back again. "I'd better let you go. You can't get lost in town—just look for the Tree in the Square. Oh—keep your distance from the vegetation if you go hiking in the dark. Most of the animals seem to have learned they can't eat us—while I've been here, more people have got lost than have had trouble with animals in the woods—but the trees haven't caught on yet—spikes and thorns."

Grebbel stood and watched her walk off and then found his way into the hall. Seated at a long table on the stage were a dozen men and women. Dr. Henry sat in the centre. Grebbel had evidently arrived in the middle of a discussion. He caught references to preparations for some forthcoming celebrations, and questions about budgeting priorities and the assignment of labour from basic research to the hydroelectric project.

He waited to hear some discussion on the rumours he had heard of at dinner. When someone did stand up and ask about them, Dr. Henry, who had been quiet and efficient in directing questions to other members, took the microphone himself. He dismissed the matter as a practical joke in poor taste, warned of the danger from suspicion and paranoia in a small society, and went on to the next item.

Grebbel slipped out of his seat and left the hall. The great whorl of cloud covered most of the sky. One of the moons had vanished behind its wall. The glow of the other was making jagged white cutouts of the mountain peaks. He headed to the path up the mountain. On either side were low bulbous trees, with vague frond-like foliage.

The cold gripped his flesh. He wished he had thought to bring gloves and the flashlight. He could hear the wind now. Through a gap in the trees he saw a pale glittering bridge stretching out from one of the white peaks, and realised it was the wind tearing snow away and flinging it out into an arch. A faint orange glow pulsed in the sky beyond the snow bridge.

Ahead and to his left were lights and buildings, and instinctively he shunned them. Whatever intuition had brought him here inclined him to the woods at his right. He considered turning from the path and cutting through the undergrowth, when a track appeared leading in the direction he wanted to go. He turned onto it, stepping round a pool of mud. The track was shaded by the lacy fronds of trees shaped like beer bottles. The pale green spheres he had glimpsed from beside the river now bobbed among the fronds like tethered balloons, pulsing with light. Pink stars glowed among the undergrowth.

From ahead came the muffled rush of a stream—perhaps the one he had seen from near the dam. He could see the moon through the upper fronds. Stretches of the track still had patches of grimy snow. Footprints crossed one patch.

The trees thinned out and the path curved. Splashes of moonlight lay across it, on boulders that pushed through the soil, and then on the glitter of running water.

Something pale and winged, the size of his two hands, fluttered over his head, zigzagged towards a tree. It glimmered for a moment in the light of one of the spheres. There was a hiss and a harsh rustle, and the fluttering stopped. Grebbel listened, thought he could hear a slow dripping. He stepped away from the tree and moved on.

Tumbling over a hidden ledge, the stream rushed down to his right. He moved towards it, to see its course, thinking of winter constellations and wooded hill slopes. In the water, five, flat white rocks broke the current and formed a series of stepping stones to the far bank. He wondered how far down the slope he would be able to see from the middle stones, and then someone moved from the shadows on the far bank, and stepped carefully onto the first stone. It was a woman, and as she stepped into the moonlight, Grebbel recognised her from outside the Council Hall that evening. She moved to the centre stone and peered at the water glittering past her feet.

Grebbel coughed and stepped into the light. "Have you lost something?"

She looked up quickly. "Who is it? Where did you come from?" She laughed shortly. "Our new arrival. Is this the best they can do for you, letting you wander around in the dark?"

Grebbel shrugged and introduced himself.

"Elinda Michaels," said the woman.

"I got restless," he said. "I needed to get outside and look around. *Were* you looking for something just now?"

She gave another short laugh. "The meaning of life, would you believe? Actually I'd started out following footprints, but it got too dark. . . . Why? Did you want to help me?"

Something in him started to unwind. "I must admit," he said, "I'd never have thought of looking for the meaning of life there in a stream. Have you had any luck?"

"In a *moonlit* stream. I've never tried here before. I was looking for—something else, and I'd just decided to give up. But you'd be surprised what you can see, sometimes, in running water with the moons reflected in it." Her voice trailed away as she looked down at the water again, and quietly she added, "What you remember."

He stiffened, and she looked up at him again. "Or maybe you wouldn't be surprised."

Something held him from speaking. He felt the earth quiver with the rush of water. When she spoke again, her voice seemed to come from the stream. "Beta's clear again— the other moon. Come and see. Step carefully; the rocks are getting icy."

He joined her in the middle of the stream. Their forked shadows interlinked and undulated on the water. Grebbel looked down where the stream had carved a way through the woods down to the scale-backed snake of the river. He moistened his lips. "What is it you find here?"

"I'm not sure. There's often something—something about the reflected moons, whenever I see them. But here, now, it's something else. The valley slope and the stream running down it . . . I'm looking down, and I know it's winter, but I'm not cold, because—because I'm inside, looking out of a high window."

The moons bounced and shattered about their feet. Silver corded the stones. Slowly Grebbel said, "A wooded hill. Snow and dark trees. The sky's clear. The room I'm in must be dark, because I can see Orion in the sky quite easily. The slope falls away like this one, with the gully cut by the stream, but at the bottom, where the river is—"

"—a road and a fence with lights."

They looked at each other and did not speak. Tree shadows shifted across the path. The water hissed and splashed and leapt.

"Maybe it's not real," Grebbel said finally. "Maybe we fed each other bits of daydreams and we imagined the rest."

"You don't believe it's a real memory?"

He said nothing.

"Actually," she said, "if it is real, it's wonderful news. I gave up the therapy months ago, and this is the first sign that I haven't lost all my past. And you've recovered something on your first day here. It is wonderful. We should both be overjoyed."

"Right."

"So why are we scared?"

Grebbel knelt and plunged his right fist into the water. Shards of light flashed from it. When he stood up, his hand opened and closed spasmodically, the fingers dripping diamonds. She reached for it.

"What did you do to your arm? Those scars?"

He looked at her and at his wrist, and then at her face again. "I don't know," he said. "I don't know." The shadows shifted and the wind moaned faintly in the fronds.

⋏

"We've both remembered something," Elinda said with determination. "That's good. We have to hold on to that fact."

"Something feels—wrong."

They were walking back along the path. The rising wind roared in the woods around them.

"I don't even know why I came to this world," Grebbel said. "An enormous decision—was I running away, trying to find something—what? I can't even guess. Do you know why you came?"

"Not really. Sometimes—when I have spare pieces of paper—I draw. Just charcoal sketches—letting my fingers take over and see what they tell me. Sometimes it seems about to make sense, and I think I'm about to remember. Then my fingers won't work anymore. It's like a wall, or a mirror in my head, and I can't get at what's on the other side."

The wind roared again. They passed from moonlight to shade and back.

"Is it colder now, or am I imagining it? If it's the dawn gales starting already, we're in for a bad few hours."

"It's a bit colder," he said, and reached to put his arm around her.

She stiffened away from him. "No. Not now. I need to hold on now. I've got to hold myself together , or I'll spatter."

"Later, then—can we meet again, later?"

Around them, the trees creaked and rustled as they began to close up their fronds.

She looked at him in the moonlight, the wind starting to cut her to the bone. "Yes," she said. "Yes, we'll meet."

THREE

Elinda woke with the dawn wind roaring about the house, and a sense that she had wakened often during the night, and had dreamed continuously when she slept. The floor quivered under her feet when she went to the bathroom. The window rattled, walls creaked, and the sounds grated on her nerves because she was alone with them. Last night's notion of parading her own absence in front of Barbara had turned sour in the face of the empty place in bed beside her.

She washed and dressed hurriedly and grabbed her flashlight. Without looking at the clock, she knew she was later than she should be, and she wanted to check at the clinic before she started work.

The wind seized her at the door and shoved her onto the path. Lightning forked, flashing off a vast chaos of cloud. The thunder came as a deep hollow grating, and the dry air crackled over her skin as the beam from her lamp wavered before her. The wind tore the breath from her mouth as though she were drowning in a rushing river of air. She bent her knees, lowered her head and plunged into it.

After the first minute the storm seemed less overpowering, and then the woods gave some shelter. She lifted her head and walked more easily.

She did not turn her light onto the track leading to the stream. This morning she did not want to think about wooded slopes ending in fences, or the scars on Jon Grebbel's wrist as the moonlight shivered about them, or the footprints she had not been able to follow in the dark. She remembered four others who gone exploring alone and later been discovered dead of exposure, apparently having made no effort to find shelter.

In the woods, the darkness roared about her. Furled trees bent over, shaking. A windsower, jewelled with golden seed darts, sailed over her head and was snared by a branchnet.

When she came to the bottom of the path, in the east, over the mountains, a sullen crimson glow was the first sign of the rising sun.

Two people were working in the back room of the clinic that doubled as the stores and histology lab. Rena Schneider, the exobiologist, was there with Raul Osmon, a technician whom Elinda vaguely remembered seeing in one of the maintenance huts. Schneider looked up and said, "Good morning. I was just thinking of trying to call you at the Greenhouse. Can you tell me how long Barbara will be off? We're having to take people from the emergency room to keep up with the sample analyses and classification. If she's not too sick, we'd appreciate any help she could give us—an hour or two a day would make a difference."

Elinda bit her lip. "No, I'm afraid I don't know how long she'll be away. I was going to ask you . . . I haven't seen her since the night before last."

"Isn't that rather strange? She borrowed one of our pocket recorders three days ago, too. We're not really supposed to let them out of the building. So . . ."

"I should have checked here yesterday, or called in last night. I just thought she'd—decided to go off for a while, again. If you haven't seen her, I'm going to talk to Security."

⏶

Under a purple-black sky, the low orange sunlight gleamed on the curved roof of the Security station. It was a squat prefabricated structure that had originally been used for fuel storage. Now it housed the on-duty constabulary, a couple of offices converted to cells, and a lot of unused space. The duty officer was sitting at a desk behind a trestle table smoking a tobacco pipe while he pecked at the inevitable computer keyboard. He put the pipe down carefully away from the computer while he listened to Elinda, and the wind moaned outside.

"You know," he said, when she had finished, "the whole trouble with this here township—no one's got any healthy fear of their fellow humankind anymore. If this was a real city, like we were meant to live in, not you nor your friend would even be thinking of wandering around by yourselves at night. She's done this before?"

"Yes, twice. But only for a night."

"Well, it's not the safest way of handling problems. Remember Billy Wu, last year, fell over a cliff in the dark. And we've got one missing right now. These woods are too big to search unless you know where to start. Tell you what we'll do, though. I'll type in what you told me, and we'll make up a bulletin, with a description from the files, and put it out for people to read."

He began stabbing at the keyboard. "Now, about going searching for her . . ." He frowned and jabbed more keys. "We're a bit short of staff right now. I'll have to see when I've got people available. Why don't you come back when we've got the bulletin made up, say around lunch hour?"

"And what then?"

"Then she'll turn up. Always do, pretty well. What we need is for them biologists to discover a really *nasty* wild beast out in the woods. Keep everyone off the streets at night and safe indoors where they belong." He was still frowning and pecking at the keyboard.

"What if she doesn't turn up? You were just saying how dangerous it was—"

"You a gambling kind of person, by any chance?"

"Not really. Why?"

"Pity," he said to the screen. "If you were a gambling kind of person, I'd be staking a month's pay that your friend turns up safe and sound around lunch time."

"I hope you're right."

"Usually am." Now he looked up and met her gaze. "Look, you and your friend are RAMwipes, right?"

"What makes you say that?"

"It's part of my job—being right. We see it every few weeks: you're both barrelling around in the dark, don't know where you've come from, where you're heading, and one of you flips out for a while. Happens all the time. Maybe you don't like to hear that you're just like everyone else—"

"You're not going to do anything?" she asked bitterly.

"I can't right now. Honestly. Come back at lunch hour. But she'll have turned up by then, and you'll be glad you're not a gambling person."

⏶

Elinda walked out of the Security office. In the past, Barbara had gone off for a night when things were tense between them, had come back the next day talking of starlight and frost, and they had reconciled over the next day or so. This was looking different, and the officer's lack of enthusiasm made her feel she should have become worried sooner.

She walked past work crews clearing branches and pod husks from the streets in the half-dark. At the edge of the landing field, Jessamyn and her class of six ten-year-olds were starting to fly kites, the children in pairs, assembling a hawk and two dragons, and running with shouts and laughter into the wind, then chasing the successful flights with flashlight beams. Turned to the dawn, Jessamyn's face was as flushed and eager as any of the children's. She hurried from group to group, until suddenly all three kites were airborne, and she was not needed for the moment. Then Elinda saw the strain in her body and guessed she was thinking of Barbara.

In the office, Larsen and Chris were examining computer projections for some experiments Larsen was planning to have run in the lab next to the clinic. Elinda told them their plans would probably be delayed, because the lab was short a technician.

Larsen caught the edge in her voice and asked her to explain.

Afterward, Larsen asked, "Is there anything you feel you should do?"

She shrugged. "Try and get someone to look for Barbara—otherwise, try and follow those tracks myself."

"No. Don't go up there alone. That would be an unnecessary risk. But if you think you can induce someone in authority to organise a search, you should do it; we mustn't lose track of our basic values. If unqualified personnel are needed, we can help you ourselves."

Chris looked surprised at being volunteered, but he nodded.

"Okay," she said, and refastened her coat. "I'll let you know what happens. Thanks."

She found she wasn't ready to go and demand a search party. She compromised by going to the cafeteria for breakfast, as preparation for either a clash with authority or a hike into the woods. Without hope, she scanned the few latecomers still eating and the other stragglers like herself. Barbara was not there.

Elinda took her food to an empty table, to eat quickly and be gone. Just after she sat down, Jon Grebbel came in.

He was pale and tense, staring about him without seeming aware of what he saw. He must have come from a therapy session. She remembered the little arrowhead of wrinkles at the corner of his eye as he stared at his moonlight-dripping hand. Now he caught sight of her, and his face changed, his inward-directed tension seemed to ease. He brought his tray to her table.

"Good morning." He grimaced as he sat down. "I feel wrung out. Is the therapy always this tough?"

"You do look as though you've had some kind of workout. I don't remember it being that harrowing." She looked at his hands, gripping the edge of the table. "Do you think last night had anything to do with it?"

"I've no idea, it's only my second time." He shrugged with an apparent effort and began to eat. "I had some dreams last night, and when I woke up, I couldn't remember what they'd been about. But I seemed to be getting near them sometimes in the clinic today." He paused and when she waited, watching him, went on. "It's like climbing a cliff. You get almost to the top, and then, just as you lift yourself up to look, the earth slips away from under you and you have to start again from the bottom." He shook his head. "They finished with me half an hour ago. I needed this long to get myself back together."

His gaze had become focussed on her as he spoke. She had the slightly uncomfortable sensation of being memorised or evaluated. She wondered what his finding would be.

"Something's worrying you," he said.

She hesitated. "I'm looking for someone. If she hasn't turned up by the time I've finished eating, I'm going higher up the ladder in Security to get a search started."

"A friend."

"We're—we were very close. But recently . . ." She stopped in confusion, realising what she had said, and been about to say, and what she had not said. *I'm looking for my lover. . . .* She had dreamt of him last night, she realised suddenly. Lying alone in the bed with Barbara missing, she had dreamt of herself and Jon Grebbel cocooned in warmth, while the moonlight eddied around them like snow. She pushed her plate away. "I'd better get going."

"Wait—I've got my first shift with the trucks coming up, or I'd help you search—"

"No, that's all right—"

"—but I thought we were getting somewhere last night, remembering. You said it worked better than their therapy. I'd like to try again."

"I don't know. . . ." She pushed her chair back from the table.

"I'd like to very much," he said. "I'm sure it's important. I feel it."

She realised she was still sitting, meeting his eyes.

"After dinner, by the stream. But it won't be dark."

Had he said that, or had she spoken the words in her head?

". . . if you find your friend first, of course," he said, and smiled.

"We'll see. I don't know—"

She got to her feet and hurried out.

▲

"You're early," said the man at the desk. "Back home, we'd make you wait outside till we'd all decided lunch time was over, just to teach you humility, and by then it would be getting dark. But I guess your friend hasn't got hungry enough to come back, and you're a mite worried. Well, we're getting the bulletins copied and there's a notice on the datanet. . . ."

Elinda said, "If you don't start getting a search party organised now, I'm going up there to find her myself."

"Well, now." He glanced at his computer screen. "I've got my orders, my priorities. . . . But, hell, it wouldn't do a lot of harm if someone took a look round where you thought she'd gone. I can't leave this desk right now, so I guess we'll see if Charley feels like taking an extended coffee break. If you and she don't find anything, we'll see what we can do about the priorities."

Through heavy clouds, the low sun lit green fans, bluish leaf blades, webs of silver that swayed overhead and flailed in slow motion as they opened to the air. Elinda and Charley, the security officer, reached the turnoff towards the stream and paused, buffeted by the winds. "I'm pretty sure she went that way," Elinda said. "There were fresh tracks yesterday morning, and it was too early for anyone else who'd be likely to take that path."

"You didn't look?"

"Not all the way. It didn't seem urgent at first, and then the tracks were fading. I went as far as the stream last night, but I couldn't find anything."

"The tracks will be worse now," Charley said. "The sooner we start looking, the better."

Between patches of glistening, grimy snow, the mud was still thick. Dead leaves from the previous autumn had begun to spume away from drifts under the trees. Walking from shade to red sunlight and back, Elinda had to squint into the shadows and the wiry scrub on either side of the path.

A scaly grey burrower shuffled from the undergrowth, with the bright blue of a rider cresting its head like an orchid on a rock. The rider's head twitched upward towards Elinda and Charley, and it sent its mount scuttling back out of sight.

"Too much traffic and wind scouring," said Charley. "I can't make sense of these prints."

"Maybe it'll be easier on the other side of the stream."

"Hope so, if we're not on a wild goose chase. Be nice if we are, though. This game used to be fun." She walked on, talking into the wind, without turning to Elinda. "I haven't had much time for it here, but back home, we used to go out in the bush every chance we got, Rick and I . . ."

The stream glittered in front of them, frothing around the stepping stones. A silver-blue bird-like creature on the far bank squawked and fluttered into a tree. . . .

Elinda realised she had hardly listened to what the woman had just said. She stopped and looked at her. "You had a son? I mean—I didn't realise. What happened?"

"The sort of thing that happens to a cop's kid sometimes." They walked a few paces in silence. "Then I reckoned I'd learned enough about that world, and maybe it was time to try somewhere else."

Elinda was standing on the first stone, with the rush of the stream filling her ears. "I'm sorry," she said, too loudly. "I shouldn't have asked you that." The glare from the water stabbed at her eyes.

Charley shrugged. "It's as much a part of what I am as any of the good times." Her voice was almost drowned by the sound of the stream. "It doesn't do to pretend things never happened."

"Let's go on," Elinda said. "It's colder near the water, isn't it?"

They crossed to the far bank. Here the ground was steeper; it sloped up ahead and to the left. Snow lay in the shaded side of every hollow. None was marked by footprints. Outcrops of grey limestone pushed through the soil, with dead leaves silted up against them. An insect whirred, another avian drifted from branch to branch across the path. Something scurried in the undergrowth.

Charley pointed. "Looks like someone came this far, anyway."

"I wouldn't have spotted those. Can you follow them?"

"Sure. They're really quite clear, but they're closely spaced. Whoever made them was still following the path, but going slowly. Maybe it was too dark to see, or maybe she was looking for something."

She, Elinda, thought; they had both accepted that the tracks were Barbara's. *Maybe she was looking for something.* And—what? Got lost? Twisted an ankle? Found what she was looking for?

"The ground's drier here," Charley said. "The traces are getting hard to follow. I'm not a professional at this, you understand."

"What's that? It looks like something broke through the scrub down there."

"Right."

The path was fading among bare brown undergrowth and rocky scree. To their left an outcropping of grey rock rose almost sheer; to the right the ground fell away at almost forty-five degrees. Ten metres below them, a couple of leafless birdcatcher bushes had been broken down. If there was any more indication of what had happened, it was hidden by trees and another outcrop of rock.

They edged diagonally down the slope, the scree threatening to slide under their boots. Elinda found herself icily calm. She let Charley go first and examine the broken bushes.

"Just broken," Charley said. "No thorns, no leaves, so I might not expect to see much in the way of traces. But no shreds of clothing I can see—or anything else."

No blood.

Charley was looking around for more signs. She pointed ahead, to something beyond a large boulder, and strode towards it. As Elinda started to follow, Charley reached the boulder, looked beyond it, stopped.

Come over here," she muttered over her shoulder. "Be careful. It's steep."

The wind caught Elinda as she stumbled down and she lurched against the rock. She peered over Charley's shoulder.

A couple of metres below them was a figure in mud-stained jeans and an anorak, sprawled facedown. Brown, shoulder-length hair was matted with dirt and twigs. A few strands of the hair twitched in the breeze. It was the only motion Elinda could see. At her side, Charley whispered, "Is it . . . ?"

"There's so much dirt, and I can't see her face. How can I be sure? Yes, it's Barbara. She's—not breathing, is she?"

Charley pulled out a chunky transceiver and spent a minute fighting the bad reception to report what they had found. Then, leaning on the boulder, she picked her way down. She bent and examined Barbara. "There's still a pulse. No apparent bleeding. Her skin colour's still good. No sign of major bruising or contusions where I can see. I can't rule out a head or spinal injury yet, so I don't want to move her, but otherwise I can't see anything organically wrong. It doesn't look like anything attacked her."

"Could she have eaten something here? Alkaloid poisoning?"

"I'm not an expert on the symptoms, but it's as good an explanation as any. Let me take her pulse." She lifted Barbara's wrist.

The arm jerked out of her grasp, the legs kicked, and then Barbara's body was still again. Charley stood up quickly and stepped back. Then she turned to Elinda.

"That probably answers the questions of spinal injuries. Help me turn her over."

Barbara was as rigid as a statue. When they turned her onto her back, her arms were crossed on her chest, her face pulled down towards them. Her eyes were closed and in shadow.

Cautiously Charley bent to lift her eyelid, and Barbara came to life again. She knocked Charley away and hunched forward. Her teeth flashed and snapped. The whites of her eyes were livid against the mud on her cheeks. They jerked back and forth, and short harsh cries burst from her throat, "Ah—Ah—Ah—" Then she flopped face down at the base of the rock and ceased to move.

Elinda had fallen back against the stone. Her hands were pressed against its rough surface and air rasped through her throat.

Charley picked herself up and looked down at Barbara, breathing heavily. "We've got to get help. She broke my radio."

"You go then," Elinda mouthed. "I'll stay with her."

"Are you going to be okay?"

She nodded. "Go on."

Charley's footsteps grated on the scree. Then Elinda was alone with Barbara. She pushed herself away from the rock. Her fingers were scratched. She sat beside Barbara. She remembered walking with her in these woods, and Barbara squirming up a tree to pluck garlands of glossy purple-and-gold leaves for their hair. Slowly Elinda put out her hand and let it rest on Barbara's shoulder. After a few moments Barbara shifted uncomfortably. Elinda realised there was something hard in the breast pocket of Barbara's parka. She reached and eased it out of the way.

▲

The wind was still slapping waves against the causeway and the valley was filled with smoky red sunlight like the aftermath of an inferno.

Jon Grebbel turned the dump truck into the service bay and edged it toward the plugin. Beside him in the cab, Menzies, the foreman, looked down from his open window. "You can come another metre easy, and over to the right a bit. Better. That's it. Now I'll show you how to plug in the charger. Switch off first."

Grebbel swung himself to the ground and watched as Menzies unhooked the battery cable and plugged it into the power socket. He tried to stifle his impatience.

"Check the voltage on the meter before you leave it," Menzies was saying. "Some of these batteries get cranky after a while, and if the voltage isn't regulating, you can come back and find bits of the truck all over the scenery."

"How long do you expect me to be needed here?" Grebbel asked.

"You think you'd be happier doing something else?"

"This isn't coming naturally to me, at any rate."

"You'll get the hang of it. We'd like to keep you as long as we can, unless you totally screw up. We're short-staffed. Shit—everyone's short-staffed, to hear them talk. But if this dam isn't working by next spring's floods, it'll be another year before they can fuel their survey fleet, and the news'll be all over the networks into the bargain. You've not done this sort of job before?"

"Doesn't look like it," Grebbel said, "the way I handled that truck, does it?" He was thinking of the effects of a battery explosion, shards of metal and ceramic piercing flesh, hot alkali spraying into faces. If you were careless with a wrench when the terminals were exposed . . .

"But you can't be sure, because you're one of the unlucky thirty percent. You arrived without all your chips programmed, and they've only just started on you in the clinic, is that it? How much do you reckon you've lost?"

"Hard to say. I can remember how to do algebra, but I can't remember when I took it, or where." *I've kept what I did, and I've lost what I am.*

"That can be rough." Menzies drew his fingers through wiry, greying hair. "I've seen some . . . Well, never mind that. You work at settling in here, and what you don't get back you won't miss."

"That's what they say in the clinic, too."

Menzies considered for a moment. "If it's important enough, it'll find a way to return to you. I've seen that happen, too."

"Be nice to think so. In the meantime, what do I do? Go on autopilot?"

"That's about it. Shit, it's a shame, though. People come out here for all sorts of reasons. What it comes down to in every case, though, is that they were after some kind of a fresh start. And then a third of them find they've lost their past. They don't know what they were running from, or even if they were running. How're you going to make a fresh start if you can't look back and see where you went wrong? How in hell you ever going to do that?"

Grebbel rubbed his chin, then put on his gloves. "I heard something about a leaflet being passed around yesterday," he said, "saying some hopeless mental cases had been shipped out here. Maybe they'd be happier without their memories."

"Ah, you don't want to believe shit like that. If someone thinks that sort of thing's going on here, let then come out and point to it, so we can all make up our minds. Then I'll listen. Look, I'll tell you a case I know about. There was a man back there, not a bad sort, he'd watch the game Saturdays with the guys, go for a drink after work, Fridays. Maybe he chased the skirts on the lower end of Main Street the odd time when he'd told his wife he was making deliveries across town, but not a bad guy. Only, he started making those deliveries about every other week, and then twice a week, and then he got into the heavier stuff. Found he couldn't stop—even when one of the girls had to be taken away in an ambulance. He'd made the call himself.

"She didn't turn him in," he went on. "Maybe she couldn't describe him, maybe they weren't interested. But he was shit scared for a month. And still he couldn't stop. Knew he'd kill one of them sooner or later. And if they didn't get him before, they would then, and he'd be inside for a long time. And even that wouldn't have made him stop. But when it reached the point where he found he was looking at his own kids . . .

"Then, finally, he started looking for ways out. In the end, he turned himself in for treatment. They stirred his brains about, and made him do community work at a crisis centre, and finally let him loose in the world. But how could he go back to his old job and his friends after that? Finally, he decided there was only one place to go—out. So he applied for here.

"Of course, when he got here, all that had gone. He thought he'd just been one of those who got sick of the wages and the stinking air at rush hour and the cops clearing everyone off the streets at midnight every Friday in summer. The treatment at the clinic wasn't much help. After a couple of months he gave up on it and quit going. But he lucked out. The memories came back. And he decided, this time he'd do it right, all the way. And that's what he's done. Not one slip as long as he's been here, not even been tempted, as far as I know."

"That's interesting," Grebbel said carefully. "I'd like to think about what you said. Maybe we can talk about it some more."

Menzies nodded. "That's why I told you. There's no need to shout this right across the valley, by the way."

Grebbel wondered whether to challenge the man and ask him if he had been talking about himself or using a piece of fiction as some kind of bait. Then he decided he really did need to think about Menzies' story.

He spent the afternoon moving gravel from the river bank to

the growing dam. After half an hour he began to feel comfortable with the vehicle.

Thinking of what Menzies had said, he remembered the woman, Elinda, in the cafeteria late that morning. He was drawn by an intensity in her look, and a vulnerability. And their potentially shared hidden pasts. She was interested too, also in spite of herself, he could tell. He was reluctant to admit that his emotions were so labile, but he would not hide from himself.

Grebbel watched the smoky spears of sunlight edge along the far valley wall as he worked. He tried to picture Menzies as the actor in the story he had told, a man with two lives, the conventional family role, and the secret appetites. The mask and the true face beneath. He had been forced to choose. But what convulsions came, when he chose the mask and denied the flesh?

At the end of the shift, he ate quickly in the cafeteria without getting into any long conversations, then walked beside the river.

When he judged it was the equivalent of early evening, he turned towards the path up the valley side, to see if Elinda would keep their appointment.

▲

She was late. Grebbel had been pacing back and forth long enough to see the first moon appear like a pale dead leaf above the mountains. He watched a large membranous creature drift towards the west like a squarish kite. The local equivalent of a vulture, he thought, until it vanished above a mountain of cumulus.

He remembered the icy water glittering around their feet, as though the stones they stood on were flowing uphill. Perhaps he had misread her, and she wouldn't come. Perhaps something had happened with the friend she was looking for. . . . How close a friend?

Perhaps all his judgements were empty guesswork, and their basis in experience had been stripped away when he came through the Knot.

When Elinda appeared, she walked slowly, as though she were having to think about each step. Grebbel went to meet her, and she halted abruptly, her face half-turned from him, her eyes in shadow.

"You see," she said, in a thin remote voice, "I remembered. We both remembered to come and remember. What do you think we should remember this time? How about something really important, like the number of the bus you took to school, or what we were doing the day they liberated the mental wards in Chile. It's the fault of the moons, you see. They both pull up tides in our brains, and our thoughts keep getting pulled apart. I shouldn't be here otherwise. You can feel the tides if you want. You turn to the moons and you feel the tides in your eyes."

She lifted her face until the red sunlight spilled across it, and he saw that she was crying quietly, and must have been crying all the time she talked.

"What's happened?"

"They tried to give me a sedative, but I wouldn't. I can feel the tides now, and I have to keep my head above water or I'll go down in the mud. Face in the mud. Mud in Barbara's hair, and dead leaves—her teeth snapped and she screamed, but then she was like stone again. They say she'll be all right, and they know, don't they? But they didn't want to upset me any more, that's why they took me away from her and tried to give me a sedative. So perhaps they're not telling the truth. We took her to the clinic this afternoon, but she must have been out there all along. Ever since I woke up yesterday."

"Your—roommate? What's wrong with her?"

She shook her head and replied with more animation in her voice. "I don't know. I don't know. They've put her in the ward, sedated, but they won't tell me what's wrong. She didn't know me. I'd left her lying out there in the mud and the wind. I could have found her that morning if I'd bothered to look, but now she doesn't know me."

Grebbel's breath caught. He had a sudden impression of something filthy and hoarse-voiced that writhed and mewled—something that drooled and vomited and clawed at its own flesh, and stared about with flickering eyes that still seemed haunted by the memory of being human.

"I stayed at the clinic all afternoon," Elinda said. "Then I came here."

"Yes."

"What's the matter? Did the moons upset you too?"

"I don't know," Grebbel muttered. "A surprise just now, maybe.

Something I remembered? I don't know. She wasn't physically hurt, your friend?"

"No broken bones, stab wounds, no signs of poisoning, no marks or bruises she couldn't have got by falling over a rock."

"What could have happened, then?"

"No one wants to guess. But now I'm wondering about the leaflet I saw yesterday—about whether some people here had come out of mental wards. I've no reason to think that about her, have I? But I can't help asking myself—I mean they'd have a thirty percent chance of losing their pasts too, wouldn't they?"

"So you think—Barbara—could have been unbalanced, and you didn't know it?"

"She couldn't remember what she had been, any more than I could. But she didn't care, she always said. She wanted to know what she was now. She was always looking for hidden meanings in what you said, writing down her dreams, and things like that. It was a game to her, fun. She didn't tell me what she found, if it was anything. Of course I never thought she was insane. It wouldn't make any sense, would it, letting her live with me without warning me? Well, I'd have spat in your face if you'd tried to tell me that, yesterday. But I didn't know this could happen." She hesitated, whispered. "I didn't know I'd start suspecting her."

He looked at her as she shook her head and shivered.

"This isn't doing any good," he said. "And we're getting cold. Let's go back."

"You came here for nothing."

"Not for nothing. Just not what we hoped."

They began to walk back.

"Listen to the wind," she said. "It's almost died, but it sounds just like the falls by the dam. When I listen to them now, it always seems there are voices just underneath, trying to reach me. She worked with things like that, and I wouldn't then, I never used to listen. . . ."

"It's not a good time to be alone," he said, and put his arm around her. She was shivering minutely and constantly.

She seemed to relax, then stiffened away from him. "No, don't. I keep thinking of Barbara there in the clinic. I don't know what I'm feeling any more."

"You've had a bad shock, that's all. Are you going back to the clinic now?"

They passed from sunlight to shade and back before she answered. "No. They were going to keep her sedated overnight while they treated her for exposure. There wouldn't be any point in going back now. Tomorrow, I'll get her things from her desk in the clinic, but right now I'd better go home. There are things I have to face."

"You feel you should have found her earlier and you want to torture yourself with guilt."

"I have to think it out for myself. Lots of things. Tomorrow, perhaps I'll be sane, and we can play at remembering again."

⧨

Elinda closed the front door behind her and stood in the curtained living room while the shadows closed around her like dark water. She shivered, but it would be worse in daylight, the emptiness. She made her way to the kitchen. The wooden chair scraped in the silence. She winced and sat down with her elbows on the table.

It was there where she had left it, next to the pepper grinder, the silvery box she had found in Barbara's pocket. An audio recorder. She wasn't sure why she had taken it and said nothing to Charley, but it had felt urgent at the time to have something of Barbara's that no one else could handle or take away.

And like too much else it had turned out to be a cheat. The thing worked: it would produce a window of quivering black bars showing how much noise was in each of six frequency bands; it would display a set of numbers identifying the very second when each burst of sound had been recorded. But of Barbara herself . . .

In the clinic she had seemed calmer; though she muttered to herself, she seemed unaware of Elinda or anything around her. The sounds she made, if they really were words, were almost meaningless: "Do. What remember. Do. Do."

Elinda thumbed the replay button again. And again came the empty hissing, and the few muttered syllables, hardly even recognisable as her voice, "Testing, testing . . ." Was that to be the last coherent thought to come from her lips?

Elinda's eyes closed. She let her head sink onto her forearms. Just for a moment, rest.

Darkness flowed past her, through her. She twisted in the current and was standing on stone at the edge of the water. Her shadows forked behind her, and the moon in the water drew her eyes. It blurred and warped and began to grow. The moon rose towards her, to meet her at the boundary of air and water. It changed. Its mouth gaped and its empty eyes stared.

She was bolt upright, pushing down on the table top as though she had to hold it in its place. She choked. "Christ. Jesus fucking Christ. What was that?" She lurched to the window and clawed back the blind.

The light beat at her. She made herself stare at the mountains and the lurid sky until the ache in her eyes had driven some of the nightmare away. She smiled grimly. "Yeah. Gonna be a long night.

"Shit. Oh, shit. Barb, what's happened to you? Are you taking me with you, wherever you've gone?"

She went into the living room, then into all the rooms, snapping on lights. At Barbara's study she stopped and looked in, her hands on either side of the doorframe. It was unusual to find the door ajar. Barbara had been—was, *was*—meticulous about things like that. Elinda pushed the door fully open and went in.

There was a small, stiff-backed brown notebook on the table. It was closed, and she did not feel ready to violate its secrecy. She could find no signs of whatever Barbara had been going through. The room was meticulously tidy.

Except for the waste bin, an empty paint can covered in local tree bark. It was full to overflowing with sheets of paper, more than Elinda could remember seeing in one place. She plucked at an exposed corner. A wad of paper shifted and a couple of sheets fell to the floor. They were data sheets from the lab where Barbara worked, crumpled so that Elinda could see Barbara's quaint, backward-slanted copperplate in green ink covering their backs. Some of the phrases seemed familiar. She picked up one of the sheets and, smoothing it on the table, sat down to read it.

After a few moments she picked another sheet off the floor and compared it with the first. Then she examined the others. There were lists of names, and comments she could not understand on some of the sheets, but three were clear enough. They were a rough draft of the leaflet that had appeared two mornings earlier.

FOUR

Grebbel left the treatment room and closed the door behind him. In the lobby, he checked the room number he had written down and followed a short corridor to a room smelling of solvents. He knocked on the open door and went in. A lab and storeroom. He found he recognised fume hoods and petri dishes, a centrifuge, a microbalance, among other glassware and instruments. Near the door was a desk that looked to have been recently tidied, and a dark computer screen.

"Can we help you?" A middle-aged woman in a white lab coat approached him. She wore transparent gloves. In a far corner, a short, heavily built man was rewiring a grey-shelled instrument.

Grebbel introduced himself to the woman. He explained who he was and that he believed he had been trained as a technician and retained most of his skills. "I understand you're short of help now."

"We have been from the start," the woman said. "Now we're two short. I'm Rena Schneider, our chief excuse for an exobiologist, and that's Raul Osmon in the corner there. He comes in a couple of days a week and does our general maintenance. So they put you in the driving pool, did they? That's odd, they're usually more sensible than that. So I take it you're looking for a different work assignment, rather than just a tour of our little empire."

"That's right. I'd be willing to work here in my spare time. I thought, it might help me remember my life back there."

"What am I supposed to say, 'No'?" She pursed her lips. "But first let's see how much you really do remember."

She went back to the bench she had been working at and pipetted solutions from a set of phials into labelled centrifuge tubes. As she worked, she asked him the names and uses of pieces of equipment, and asked him to describe some standard laboratory techniques. Terminology floated into his mind; his hands knew the feel of forceps and polycarbonate glassware. At the end, she loaded the centrifuge and switched it on, and peeled off her gloves.

"You've obviously been in a lab before," she said, "though I wouldn't have guessed it was in the last five years. But I think we can give you a try-out. If you don't look like destroying the place, we'll see if we can make it official."

They arranged that he would come in for about an hour after dinner that day, and he left, feeling he had taken one real step towards recovering his identity.

⋏

The dump-truck motor whined and then howled as Grebbel took the slope too quickly. He eased off and pulled to the edge of the ramp under the loading chute. Gravel thudded into the truck, then came in a steady stream that set the cab shaking. On the windscreen, splashes of mud shivered across the unfurled fronds of the trees that clung to the far wall of the valley; a wave of slate colour and shadow with tiny highlights slithered across it as a sudden burst of sunlight struck low along its wind-tossed surface. His knuckles on the steering wheel briefly gleamed back at him from the windshield.

He thought of Elinda's friend lying out in the woods alone, with that wind tearing at her. He would have to ask Elinda what they had learned since then.

He wondered how deeply Elinda was getting under his skin. How easily had he formed attachments in his old life?

He turned onto the causeway.

The rest of the morning passed. The sun rose a few more degrees. The wind calmed. The heavy, ragged clouds began to thin; between them the sky turned smoke-blue. He parked the truck and plugged in the charger, and headed for the cafeteria.

At the entrance, a man called out behind him, "Hey, get the door for me, will you, mate?"

Grebbel turned. "Sorry, I didn't see you. I was looking for someone."

The other was the man in the silver astronaut uniform and the black exoskeleton enclosing his legs whom Grebbel had met earlier. He swayed forward, his arms out for balance. Grebbel heard the whine of motors.

"Hold it open for me, will you? Servo control's fucked up on the legs. All I can do to stay aloft today." The man was black-haired and gaunt, his face tanned and deeply lined so that his eyes peered darkly from under his brows. "Can't always predict when it'll give trouble, but I'd be fixed and back up there if this port had its priorities sorted out. Standard feedback nets, these things take; but they don't have them here, and it'll take a month to tool up to make them."

He nodded to Grebbel. "Still finding your way around here, are you? If you don't see your friend, you want to join us? There's a few of us getting tired of our own company. Bill Partridge, that's me. And over there, that's Lucinda and Olaf." The two nodded in Partridge's direction from a table by the far wall.

"Jon Grebbel." He scanned the room, briefly wondered whether to wait. "Thanks, I'd like to join you."

Partridge grimaced as he lurched and paused collecting a tray. "Too much microgee—to save you asking—" he said crisply, "and a slight disagreement with a shuttle about who had the right of way into the dock."

"So what's going to happen to you? Will they ship you back?"

Partridge concentrated on loading his tray before he replied. "Shipping back—that's a bitch of a job. The delta-vee's not as bad as it should be, but it's nothing to giggle about, and there's all the little warps and tricks the transfer does to your clocks and your hormone levels and your brain. It's worse going that way, and it's worse the second time through. No, I'm stuck this side for a week or ten yet, and not too heartbroken about it. Almost like the good old days at times. *Challenger, Columbia*—saw that one, I did—Need Another Seven Astronauts . . . But I'd give up what's left of these dry-stick legs if it would get me back on the circuit up there."

"You like your job," Grebbel commented. They had made their way to a table with the other astronauts.

"Sure as hell I like it. But they *need* us up there too. They want fuel if they're going to survey this system. Reaction mass, and no one's found an oilfield. We could put up solar arrays in orbit: need a couple of shuttles for maybe five years, or you could even ship the mirrors through in bits from the other side. Five years, ten max, and you'll get all the power you can use. If you can wait ten years, reaction mass isn't such a problem: if you're that patient, there's nothing wrong with sails or ion drives. But they want it faster—they say. That means oxy-hydrogen for the foreseeable future. So they build hydro plants down mudside here. Then you need electrolysers, compressors, cryogenics to store the stuff, and you've got to wait till all that's checked out and working before you can start lifting fuel into orbit. Sure, it's still a bit faster, and you get a chance for a look at the real estate here while you're working. But you don't gain that much."

Partridge broke off and started forking down the casserole on his plate. He gestured with his free hand, while he swallowed. "If they really wanted to do it right, they'd send a couple of ships—no crew, no life support, just smart robots—out to the gas giants. Get hold of a comet or two, or a hefty piece of ring. Eighty percent ice—all the fuel, all the reaction mass you need, and it's in orbit, right where you need it."

"So why don't they listen to you?"

"Politics. They want their colony. Something to show the voters for the money. Not much gets shipped back yet, but there's a feed into the news net damn near every ten minutes, and you'd better believe it's given some kind of priority." He made another attack on his meal.

"Perhaps there's no urgency about fuelling up for a full-scale survey, then," Grebbel said, "if we haven't found a good way of shipping things back yet."

"Sure, that's a part of it, too. But even that's to do with fuel—delta-vee, energy transfer."

"In the meantime, you're stuck down here spectating?"

"Oh, I do the odd bit of bookkeeping, check manifests on the gasbags, a bit of maintenance. I'd like to get back to the Flats—at least I'd be able to work on the shuttles there, be more a part of things. Still, being a spectator with some time on your hands has its advantages now and then. You see things everyone's forgotten about. You see how some old folk behave, and how things go on that others haven't had time to notice."

"Such as?"

"Such as—well, such as that redhead in the brown shirt off to your left. Listening to her headset, closing her eyes and rapping her fingers. Damn near every day she's here like that. Except, you get close to her—get her to open the door for you, say, and you've got good ears—there's nothing going through those phones."

"You think she's lost a few chips from her motherboard?"

Partridge leaned back, narrowing his eyes. "That's the best part of being a spectator," he said. "You get to watch and listen, but you don't have to think. Anybody asks you what it means, it's just another inexplicable quirk of human behaviour."

"Do you have any idea where we are?" Grebbel asked. If Partridge really wanted to hint at something, let him come back to it himself. "I mean if they can transmit radio signals through the Knot both ways, doesn't that mean we can't be too far from the transmitter on the other side?"

"Man, I'm a plumber, and you want the city surveyor. Or a Zen Buddhist, maybe. All I know, when they have to clean up the signals they receive at this end, it's like they'd been stretched and then not quite sprung back into shape. Like a rubber ball that'd been forced through a hosepipe, maybe. You're asking how long the hose might be, or which end has the tap on it, or maybe where the gardener is. One thing for sure: the last I knew, they hadn't got a fix on anything they could recognise here—pulsar frequencies don't match, none of the galaxies in the local group, quasar shifts—nothing fits. And needless to say, none of the local stars match anything in their catalogues. It's the same sort of place as ours, but it's not ours. Or if it's ours, it's not ours when we left it."

"You think we might be back in time? Or ahead?"

"Makes nearly as much sense as any of the other choices, which isn't a lot. But I just sit here and watch and listen. Thinking's a job for those that like it."

Grebbel frowned. "Unless it becomes a habit."

"Ah, then—it depends on what you're thinking about—it can get you in serious problems. Even here."

Grebbel raised his eyebrows and said nothing.

"Thinking, it puts all sorts of stress on the body, running those voltage pulses up and down the circuits, burning up calories, increasing the need for food, developing ulcers, overheating the skull. Stands to reason, something's gonna wear out faster when you use it like that."

"Sounds fair enough," said Grebbel. "But why here especially? And thinking about what?"

Partridge leaned back again, squinting so that Grebbel could not tell whether the man was looking at him or the ceiling. "Depends who you are," he said finally. "If you were the wrong sort of person, you might get yourself quite sick wondering about our red-headed friend—who's just leaving through the main doors now, incidentally—asking yourself if she really was two spots short on her dice. Or, if you were a slightly different type of person, you might have a morbid curiosity about what she thinks about, sitting in the middle of all those conversations with her player that doesn't make any sound playing all the time. But of course, you're not a bit like those sorts yourself."

"You've got it. I'm just curious about who I was and why I came here."

"Well there you are then. No problem at all. Nothing like the other two topics at all. Absolutely no connection whatsofuckingever."

"I was beginning to think that myself."

"There's that word again," said Partridge. "You've got to keep away from it."

"Right."

"Ah, you'll be all right. Just got to learn when to keep your head down, and you'll pick that up easy enough."

"Well, thanks." Grebbel looked around the dining area. He hadn't seen Elinda come past, and he couldn't find her at any of the tables. "It's been an interesting conversation. Though I'm afraid I can't recall a thing we talked about."

"Neither can I. Funny, isn't it?"

◢

Elinda made her way to the clinic. She had been awake most of the official night, watching an almost motionless sliver of sunlight angle through the blind, and now the daylight was harsh enough to hurt.

"Who would you like to see?" the nurse at the desk asked.

When she explained and identified herself, he began rattling keys on a terminal in front of him.

"When did you start that?" she asked. "Isn't there enough to do without keeping track of everyone who visits a patient? Are you going to start logging bedpan changes too?"

The man shrugged. "Orders. Something about trying to make the best use of our resources. A two-week test period. Okay. They'll let you see her, but only with supervision. Someone'll be along in a minute."

"Half an hour, more like," she muttered, but almost immediately Carlo appeared and nodded to her to follow him.

"I'd tell you how glad I was to see you," he said quietly. "But I'm not sure you were wise to come. Seeing her now isn't likely to set your mind at rest."

"Neither is not seeing her."

"Well, maybe. But don't be expecting too much. She still may not know you."

He unlocked a door and went ahead of her into a small white room. In a narrow, metal-frame bed, Barbara lay on her back, her face turned to the wall. Loops of grey tape fastened her ankles and wrists to the bedframe.

"Jesus Christ," Elinda whispered, "what are you doing to her?"

Carlo caught her arm. "Careful," he said, in a strained, apologetic tone. "She bites."

Elinda stared at him, then pulled herself free and went to the bed. Barbara's eyes were closed; she was breathing quickly and shallowly. Then her head rolled to the side and she muttered something.

Elinda looked at Carlo. "She's awake?"

He shrugged. "We haven't sedated her today, yet."

"Barbara," she said as steadily as she could. "Barbara, can you hear me? Do you know what happened? Tell me what I can do to help."

Barbara's eyes opened. They turned from side to side, as though they found nothing in the room to focus on. Her mouth worked. After a moment, Elinda was able to understand the words. ". . . since breakfast. Coffee then. It's curfew, half an hour, subway's not running. . . ." She thrashed against her bonds, twisting her neck to try and snap at her hands, then suddenly was still again. She began to mumble, and saliva dribbled from the corner of her mouth. Carlo came forward with a swab, but Elinda stopped him.

"Let me."

"Careful," he began, but she was already reaching over.

She wiped Barbara's chin, gently, though her fingers felt like tongs. When she had finished, Barbara seemed to be sleeping.

Carlo tilted his head towards the corridor, and after a moment she shrugged and nodded. He followed her out and locked the door.

"Well?" she said.

He spread his hands. "She's calmer than she has been, but there's no way to predict what she'll be like an hour from now."

"I meant, what the fuck's wrong with her? What are you treating her for?"

"We don't know," he said uncomfortably. "That's why we're using sedation as little as possible. We can't be certain what side effects there might be from anything we do."

"Jesus Christ. So what do you plan to do next? Garlic and silver crucifixes? Rain dances?"

"You're taking this badly. I think you're blaming yourself—"

"That's my right, isn't it? And it looks as useful as anything else being done around here." She winced and shook her head. "Sorry. I didn't mean that."

"You're taking it badly," Carlo went on, "because you've been under more strain than you need to be. I think worrying about your past has been preying on your mind these last weeks, when you've had personal problems to cope with. I've seen what can happen. . . . Anyway, I strongly recommend that you come back for therapy sessions as soon as possible."

"I'll think about it."

"Look, we're doing our best for her, all of us. But she's not the only one of you who needs help. You're going to wear yourself down to the bone if you keep on like this."

"Let me think about it, Carlo. I can't decide now."

"Okay then. You can see her again tomorrow. If there's any change before then, I'll get word to you."

She went down to the lab and collected Barbara's pair of coffee mugs, her holo of a crimson rose, a gold-nibbed pen, and half a dozen pages of notes that Dr. Schneider agreed were too cryptic to be of use to anyone else. Elinda intended to try and decipher them for clues as to what had led Barbara to prepare the leaflet.

Outside the clinic, she looked at the clouds blowing above the valley. It could still snow again that year, she thought. She remembered floundering around the landing field on skis with Barbara, neither of them sure how to negotiate any but the gentlest slopes, and both of them getting more and more frustrated until they stuck their skis in a snow bank and threw snowballs at each other for half an hour. They had laughed a lot in those days—had been able to laugh at almost anything.

She left the things she had taken from Barbara's desk in the office and then went on to the Greenhouse. She spent an hour doing an inventory of the crops ready for harvest and checking the water deionisers, and started walking back to the office. The air was cool, the wind coming in gusts with the approach of another night, and she felt a strange warmth at the idea of being cocooned in snow. Then she realised that Jon Grebbel had been in her thoughts all morning. Even while she had been wiping Barbara's face, part of her mind had been elsewhere, intent. . . .

When she reached the office, she almost walked in before she heard the raised voices.

"It has practically nothing to do with the hippocampus," Larsen's voice said in its most pedantic tone. "The whole point of those procedures—"

"I don't care about that," another man's voice broke in. "If you'd helped her the way you helped me, she wouldn't have—she wouldn't be . . ."

Larsen said something she did not hear, then added, "I'm not sure that I have helped you."

As she hesitated, the door opened and a tall, red-faced man came out. She had seen him occasionally in the Admin building: Robert Strickland—he played sweeper for their soccer team. He flinched when he caught sight of her, as though guessing she had overheard, and he was hurrying past when he seemed to recognise her.

"You're—I've seen you with Barbara Evans, haven't I?" he said. "I wonder—I'm looking for someone. Do you know Erika Frank? About your height, and blonde too, but darker colouring. She worked at the landing field in the radio room. She always wore those wooden bracelets, half a dozen of them, it seemed like, silly, clumsy things—I mean, she wears them, she works there, she—" He swallowed and fell silent, his eyes desperate.

"I'm sorry," Elinda whispered. "I don't know her. I'm sorry."

"No. Of course not. Excuse me." He turned to go.

"Just a moment. How long has she been missing?"

"That's just it—it might be two weeks. She was supposed to go back to the Flats for a training course, only I found out she never got there, maybe she never left. Somebody knows, though, somebody knows what happened to her, somebody here. Ask your friends." He peered at her sharply then turned and hurried away.

Larsen looked up quickly when she went in. "I had assumed you wouldn't be back today," he said. "But as long as you're here, you can help me check the monthly budget."

She had no appetite and worked through lunch. Chris came in, his hands grimy from helping work on a truck suspension, and reminded them about the open party at his home the following evening. Larsen, unusually irritable, twice snapped at her for not paying attention.

She worked late, and when she locked up, the sun had slid behind the Five of Diamonds, although the sky was still brilliant. She walked home through the long dusk and the cutting wind, unable to remember a thing she had done.

The bungalow was full of Barbara's presence. It seemed to her now that most of the decoration had been Barbara's ideas. Certainly the surrealist landscape painting by Jessamyn in the living room had been one of hers. She wondered what Grebbel would think of it, whether she should return it and hang one of the throw rugs instead. She wondered how important Grebbel was becoming to her, why she kept putting off Carlo's invitations to return to therapy, and why these thoughts should be filling her mind.

Barbara would have laughed at her once and taken her for a walk; more recently she would have been impatient. Brooding, she would call it. It's today that matters, and tomorrow. That's why we're here now. Let the past look after itself.

There would have been the aggrieved, defensive tone edging into her voice. And now . . . *Careful, she bites.*

Outside, shadows were sliding up the northern walls of the valley, and the swirling clouds becoming crimson-edged in the low sunlight. She ate a quick meal of leftovers, then picked up her coat from the couch and went out.

She had intended visiting Paulina and Louise next door, but met them on their front path, going out. "It's the newsfeed at the Hall tonight," Paulina reminded her. "Come along for a change."

Her tone suggested they had heard about Barbara.

She had wanted to talk, but she agreed to go, and decided it was probably the best thing to do. Their implied sympathy made her uncomfortable, and she was reminded how much she envied them their relationship.

Ahead of them, one of the bluish lights along the main street flickered and glowed, and then the others shivered into life like a string of diamonds. "They haven't got the settings right yet," Louise commented. "Lights should have been on an hour ago this time of year." She ducked her head against a cold gust.

"Yeah," said Paulina as they wandered across the road, "with all the traffic we get through here, it's a wonder there hasn't been a massacre."

"Is that why you go to these things so often," Elinda asked, "because you miss all that—freeways and traffic jams and the rest of it?"

"Sure we miss it," Louise said. "You've no idea how glamorous such memories are from this distance. It's the best reason for coming here, to make that mess look captivating."

At the Hall, the doors were open and some of the seats were already occupied. There was no reason Grebbel should have been easy to see in the dimly lit rows, but she recognised him almost immediately in the middle of a row near the back. She brought the others with her and introduced them as she sat beside him. The two of them regarded Grebbel with curiosity. Elinda wasn't sure if it contained disapproval.

The lights started to go down. "If they're starting already," Paulina said for Grebbel's benefit, "there must be a good ten minutes' worth of noticeboard to sit through. Most of it's a waste of time, but if we come any later, it's hard to get a seat. No, thank god, a false alarm." The lights had stopped fading, but the Hall was still not fully dark. Abruptly a picture flashed onto the screen. It blurred, then came into focus as a young woman's face. Beside it, a block of text appeared in plain capitals and began to roll up the screen. ERIKA FRANK HAS BEEN MISSING FOR TWO WEEKS. The portrait was replaced by a full-length shot of her with the coffer dam in the background. SOMEONE KNOWS WHAT HAPPENED TO HER. Another picture of her, beside the dirigible mooring pylon. IF SHE IS NOT FOUND BY TOMORROW NOON, THIS COMMUNITY WILL ANSWER FOR

IT. The first portrait flashed up again for a moment, and then the screen went dark.

Grebbel looked questioningly at her, and she shrugged, unready to put her doubts and suspicions into words.

"Well," said Paulina, "first those leaflets, now this. You'd think they could keep tighter control over the lunatic fringe. But then I bet only forty-five percent of the population's in the pay of security."

"Erika Frank," someone said,"—isn't that Bob Strickland's girlfriend?"

"Strickland thought so, anyway."

"What do you think it meant—'will answer for it'?" Grebbel asked.

"Probably a bluff," Paulina said, "if it isn't just a practical joke."

Before the muttering from the audience drowned everything else, Elinda thought she heard voices raised behind the stage, where the projectors must be.

Then the house lights faded completely and the screen lit again. Elinda missed most of the few noticeboard items that appeared, wondering about the threatening tone of the first item, and whether it fitted the man she had seen with Larsen. The main feature began, and she made an effort to concentrate.

There was a soundtrack with music and a commentary, but it had no meaning for her. The pictures filled her mind. Wide plains divided into olive and brown cultivated squares. A city, sprawling under low, yellowish skies. There were tight knots of freeway interchanges, thick with traffic. Weather-stained freighters moored at a dock. The water, violet-dark and greasy, licked at their hulls. Gulls fought over debris churned up by the propellers of the tugs.

I know this place, she thought. *I don't recognise any of it, but I know it. Is that why I'm shaking?*

Trucks thundered over concrete arches, where grimy rows of houses huddled on narrow streets. Words on the soundtrack she could not follow, the music beating at her.

He'd understand what I feel. He wouldn't laugh at me.

◣

And Grebbel, watching the images unfolding before him, felt his mind being squeezed into a smaller and smaller space, as though the sight of his old world was drawing his memories toward it, but they could get no further than whatever had happened in the Knot.

A map appeared on the screen. South America, his mind said, as if this was another psych test. Other pictures followed, and his mind laboured to keep up. Mountains, it said . . . Andes? Snow. Cold. With part of his mind that hid from the verbal testing game, he felt her presence next to him. Highway. Airport runway.

Blue-helmeted troops poured from transport aircraft, were shown driving through streets lined with blackened ruins, then setting up road blocks, searching buildings, directing traffic around a crater at an intersection.

Peacekeeping, his mind said. Martial law. Revolution.

Chaos.

Name? Jon Grebbel.

Nationality?

Residence?

She brushed against him in the dark, her skin chill and damp.

Name? Jon Grebbel.

Occupation?

Occupation?

Dark. All dark.

One hand to clutch in the dark.

▲

Afterwards, in the knot of people fastening coats and filing out of the Hall, they found time to talk.

"Did it strike you the same way?"

"Having trouble understanding what was happening? Yes, like—"

"—like a garbled stream of memories."

"Like trying to listen to a talk, I was going to say, when everyone's whispering around you."

"Only the whispers were inside your head."

"Maybe there's a block against understanding what we were then, maybe we'll never be able to get it back."

The crowd was dispersing. Paulina and Louise had slipped away.

"It was uncomfortable in there. I was—scared, I think."

"We both were."

"Are you sorry you came, then?"

"A bit. No."

"Neither am I."

They walked slowly down the empty street.

"I may have found a new job," he said, "substituting for your friend." He described his visit to the lab that morning. "And this evening, I spent an hour practising on some of the equipment. Do they know what happened to her?"

"They don't know a damned thing. Those leaflets, the other morning, and that missing woman at the start of the show tonight . . . We were lovers, Barbara and I."

"I thought so," he said, and abruptly risked asking: "'Were' or 'are'?"

"I . . . don't know. There's so much going on, and I don't even know what's inside my own head. I feel I've let her down. I always feel that. I have to find out what happened to her. She had something to do with the leaflets, I found evidence at home. I haven't told anyone yet. If you can look at her computer files, can you see if there's anything among them that looks like a clue."

"Yes, I'll try," he said. "What about Security?"

"I don't know. They were reluctant to go and search for her yesterday. Their priorities didn't allow it. And if she was involved in something they'd call subversive . . ."

"So you'd be on your own. I'll see what I can do to help."

"Yes. Thanks."

They followed a path, staying close together, not saying much. Behind them, the street lights went out, all together. Above them, the sky was still flushed pink and mauve.

"It's late," she said. "They use the lights to remind us it's officially midnight. We'd better get back." They turned. "I almost forgot. One of our staff is having a get-together tomorrow night. You should come—give you a chance to meet people. I'll give you the address. Have you got something to write with?"

"No. But tell me anyway. Trust my memory."

She laughed, and gave him Chris's address.

"We've got to stop meeting like this," he said.

"Maybe we will at that." She found herself giving him a genuine, uncomplicated smile. "See you tomorrow."

FIVE

Everyone called it the Factory, though it was actually a cluster of low buildings ringing a structure like a circular barn. It was where everything that had not been shipped to Janus for reasons of cost, convenience, forgetfulness or security was reinvented, imitated or faked. And it was where everything—whether crated in shockfoam, chromed and slick with grease, or put together from spare computer chips and parts of an arc welder—went for repair and maintenance.

Freya ran the Factory. She was a small, round-faced woman, with wide, innocent-looking eyes in the face of a fading seraph. When Elinda went to the service counter, Freya herself was examining a circuit diagram with a man, and apparently counting on her fingers. "Give it another afternoon," she said to him. "If you can't come up with anything by then, I'll tell them we don't do voodoo without a blood price."

She turned to Elinda. "Sorry to keep you. I've got to get back in the shop in a minute, but maybe I can help you while Peter thinks about his homework."

"Actually, I've got a question rather than a technical problem," Elinda said. She introduced herself and pulled out the leaflet Larsen had found on the cafeteria table. "I'm trying to trace where this came from."

Without giving too many details, she explained about Barbara and said she was looking for any clue as to what had happened to her.

"Medium, or message?" Freya asked. "We deal in hardware and technical information, mostly by request in triplicate, with signatures in precious bodily fluids. I like to think what messages we give out are more reliable than what you've got there."

"I was thinking of the medium. The ink or the paper—is there a chance you could identify either of them?"

Freya examined the leaflet. "One copier is much like another, and we don't have a monopoly on them here. In principle, we could set up a little forensic investigation. But to get us to do it for an unofficial request, you'd have to have something we wanted pretty goddamned badly in return, and you don't look as though you do. Five or ten lab days' worth? No, I didn't think so. Let's see. The paper might be a better bet than the ink. We don't turn out that much white paper, and it sounds as though there was a fair number of sheets in this run. Try Raul Osmon, down in Hut Seven. He runs the paper mill. He might remember something."

▲

Hut Seven gave out the smell of strong chemicals and the sound of orchestral music. The first Elinda assumed were needed for bleaching. The music stirred something within her, uncomfortably, but eluded her memory. Even after the darkness outside, the interior of the hut was dim, leaving her with an impression of grey, galvanised tanks like large bath tubs and bulky machinery with hoppers and pumps. Working on a machine part was a squat man with brown hair straggling over his eyes.

He straightened up as she came in, and she recognised him as the part-time technician who worked in Barbara's lab.

"Why, yes, hello," he said. "Aren't you the friend of Ms. Evans? I've seen you there, haven't I, often enough to remember your face. And how can we help you now?" His eyes were pale and deep set, under almost invisible eyebrows. He looked to be in his late thirties. "Raul Osmon, that's me. Always glad to assist."

Elinda brought out the leaflet and repeated her request. He took the sheet to a desk in the far corner. When he sat and switched on an angle lamp, he saw that she had remained by the entrance. He beckoned. "Come. Come. Sit here. You like Rachmaninov?"

She picked her way between the machines and the arrays of

tools in meticulous rows where repairs were evidently continuous. She realised she had been beating time to the music. "Is that who wrote it?" she said. "I didn't recognise it."

"The third piano concerto: Kusinov and the Montreal symphony under Feinstein. Just before the assassinations. But I can see you don't remember. Does that mean you've lost music along with everything else? Dreadful, dreadful."

"Perhaps I'd never heard it before."

"No, no, not you. You're a musical person. I could tell as soon as I saw you. A young woman like you—let me see your hand. There, very fine, very strong. But not large—a real woman's hand. You'd be a string player—a violinist for sure. Not a violist, scraping away buried in the depths of the orchestra. And never a bassist, heaving that black coffin about like a vampire. You might have played the cello, I think: I can see you have dark soulful stream of song within you. But I think the violin is yours. You were meant to soar above the herd, to point us toward the light. Or maybe you were a soprano."

"I don't sing," she said brusquely. "I don't like singing." In a different mood, she might have found this line amusing, but now she was getting impatient. Before she could stop him, he was off again.

"My own hands," he said "Unfortunately, the spirit is willing, but the flesh is strong. Not weak. Never think that the flesh is weak. It has its own intentions and it can enforce them. Look at these hands. Good for nothing but the bass drum. I might as well hope to play the violin with a pair of shovels. But strong. Yes, strong. I'll look up my recording of the violin works for when you come back. Tchaikovsky and Mendelssohn. Perhaps the Brahms, the Beethoven. Yes. String music for your next visit."

"In the meantime," she said heavily, "can you help me find where this paper came from?"

He rubbed the sheet between finger and thumb. His hands were large, his fingers thick and blunt, the nails surprisingly clean and well-trimmed. Holding the paper against the light, he peered at it, then sniffed it delicately. "I don't keep samples from earlier runs, you understand," he said. "There just isn't the need for that sort of record-keeping. Otherwise I'd probably be able to match this up straight away."

"It's from here, though?"

"Oh, yes, yes. Can't you smell the resin? That's not terrestrial pine, that's local. And I believe we have the manufacturing monopoly right here." He chuckled once at his joke and glanced at her. "And the texture—didn't you notice the surface? That's since we started the new sedimentation bath, three, no, four weeks ago. And I'd smell the sulphite if it was the first batch we did then: we had dreadful trouble with the bleach that week. So that narrows it down to two runs."

"And who were they for?"

"One for Dr. Henry's office. One to the histology lab. I delivered it myself."

"Thank you. That's very interesting."

"Perhaps you'd like to see how our little plant works?"

"I'm afraid I'm short of time. You've been very helpful," she told him, as convincingly as she could manage. She wanted to curse aloud : *Of course* Barbara could have taken the paper from her lab. Elinda tried to persuade herself it had been worth checking, a long shot that might still produce a clue.

"Next time—violins," he said, following her back to the entrance. Then he went to a hand-operated press, and took the handle in his blunt fingers. His forearms bulged, and water spurted from the press like rain.

⏶

Elinda's boots clattered on the wooden floor in the school entrance hall. A group of ten-year-olds dressed in anoraks came running out of one of the doors and burst past her into the floodlit Square. They ran around the tree in the north-west corner, staying clear of its overhanging fronds and even of its artificial shadows. Their shouting made her want to scream at them to be quiet, but she swallowed the urge and followed the sign pointing to the craft room.

Along the far wall was a partly coloured Mercator projection of Janus. Two large areas of their continent were painted orange and labelled *Cinnabar Sea* and *Firestone Cordillera*. In the corner beside the map, beyond two trestle tables covered with pots of paint, brushes, and small clay figures, Jessamyn was standing beside an easel with a brush and palette in her hands. Her hair was tied back and she was leaning a little towards her canvas; if she saw Elinda from the corner of her eye, she gave no sign. Nor did she turn when Elinda let the door close firmly behind her.

Elinda went round one of the tables and approached her, to see what she was working on.

"Don't stare, please. When this is ready for viewing, I'll put it on show. If you've something to say, why don't you go where I can see you?"

Elinda frowned, then walked back around the room until she was facing Jessamyn across one of the tables and could not see the canvas.

"I thought you'd be at the hospital," Jessamyn said.

"I was, yesterday."

"She's going to need someone now. Someone who understands." Jessamyn's voice shook a little.

"I'm not going to be pushed into a tug-of-war over her." Elinda could hear the edge in her own voice. "But I want to help her, I want to find out what happened."

Jessamyn looked her in the eye for the first time. "You want to find out how much of her life you were shut out of."

"I think I can help her, if I find out what she was trying to do. You work in Henry's office some of the time, don't you?"

"Some of the time, yes."

"I'm trying to track down those leaflets that appeared a couple of days ago, claiming we were a dumping ground for mental cases. I think Barbara may have had something to do with them, and the paper they were printed on might have come from Henry's office."

"Oh, aren't you the clever little girl. You're trying hard, but you don't get two chances. She's beyond your help."

"Did you put out those leaflets for her?"

"I still know more about her than you do, even if you were with her for nearly two years. You failed her and now you want to make up for everything you didn't do for her."

"That's not an answer," Elinda said stiffly. "You think hiding the truth is going to help her now?"

Jessamyn eyed her coldly, then glared at the canvas. She drew a breath and held it for a few seconds. "Yes she asked me to put the leaflets out. If she hadn't contacted me by breakfast, I was to add them to the pile to be put out on the tables."

"If she hadn't contacted you? Where was she going, then?"

"She was onto something big. But she wasn't ready to tell me. Maybe she thought it would be disloyal to you. So that's all the help you can get from me."

"God damn it, what was she doing with those leaflets? Were you helping her with that? Did you get her into that racket? Because if you did, you're the one—"

"You think she could be pushed where she didn't want to go? Jesus, she was probably trying to protect you. Protect the pure and simple-minded. And they weren't going to let me *see* her . . . ?" Jessamyn's voice had risen; now she choked and went on in a whisper. "Girl, she was digging up something—someone—big. If you go snuffling your pert little nose around that burrow, you're going to need more help than you can imagine."

"So you do know what she found, but you're just going to let it go."

"I didn't say that. You weren't listening. I've got to finish this painting. It's for the celebrations. I'd like some peace and quiet to work on it, if you don't mind."

Outside, above the streetlights, one of the moons sailed through icy streamers of cloud. The kids had vanished and the tree seemed a cowled figure that silently brooded over the curious creatures that had come to scurry in its shadows.

Elinda took several deep breaths, then squared her shoulders and went over to the clinic, where she was allowed to see Barbara.

"We have to keep her in restraints," the nurse told her. "She's always moving, squirming, trying to crawl or get up, as though there's somewhere she has to go. She mutters to herself, too—has to get in, further in. Sometimes she seems to be talking about a cave."

But when Elinda saw her, Barbara seemed almost asleep, muttering occasionally, unaware of her presence. After a couple of minutes, Elinda gave up and left the room.

Grebbel was not in Schneider's lab. At the dam then, or perhaps in therapy again. Elinda suddenly remembered the previous night. "Tell me," he had said. "Trust my memory."

He had made her laugh.

Other thoughts occurred to her then, and she found a guilty enjoyment in contemplating sensations she could not recall experiencing. Barbara was the only lover she could remember. A further thought struck her, and on impulse she went to the desk in the clinic entrance.

"Birth control?" said the technician. "I could give you an appointment almost any time with a week's notice."

"That's fine. I was just curious, there's no real . . . No. Could I make an appointment for next week?"

"Of course. Your name and chart number, please."

But when her appointment was entered into the computer, the technician looked up at her. "Didn't you know? You're down here as having chosen . . ."

"What? Tell me. No I don't want a private whisper in the back. What did I choose?"

The technician turned the screen around and pointed to a code, and its definition. Tubal Ligation.

Elinda felt her cheeks burning. She stammered something and left.

▲

In the clinic, Grebbel sat in the familiar, complicated chair, and the blue light strobed away his surroundings.

He came back slowly, aware of a dull pounding in his head. When he opened his eyes, Carlo's face interposed itself between him and the white ceiling.

"Sit and rest for five minutes," Carlo said. "We took you pretty deep that time. Wait until you feel completely comfortable before you try to get up. I'll be back in a moment."

The face went away, and Grebbel closed his eyes again. There were vague impressions of warmth, dappled shade, the scents of varnish and wood smoke. After a while, there were voices too, and at first he did not realise they were outside his mind, in the corridor beside the treatment room.

". . . no real change since they brought her in," Carlo's voice said.

"She doesn't remember anything—what happened just before she was found?" Grebbel thought he should recognise the other man's voice, but he could not pin it down.

"We don't think so," Carlo said. "But it's impossible to be certain. Most of the time, she isn't aware of us or what's around her. If anything, she's slipping. She may never regain any more normal brain function than she has now."

The two voices moved out of earshot. They had been talking about Elinda's friend, he was sure. Grebbel pushed himself to his feet and went to the door. The corridor was empty. Opening onto it were three other doors. He tried to recall how close the voices had sounded, to guess which room she was in.

He crossed to the door opposite and tried the handle. It would not turn. As he hesitated, something moved in the room. There was the rustle of bedding, and then a thick, slobbering, inarticulate whisper.

He did not move. He had a sudden clear vision of what he would see if he entered the room—the shell of something that had been human. For a moment, the corridor seemed dark and huge, the door towering, so that he would have to reach up with both hands to turn its handle. He backed away. His shoulder brushed the wall behind him, and the moment of disorientation passed. But something had tightened in his guts. His breathing was fast and urgent and he wanted to retch.

Voices sounded at the entrance to the corridor. He returned to the treatment room and sat down. Outside, the talkers stopped and began discussing something in lowered tones. Grebbel crouched forward with his fists on his knees. A memory. That glimpse in the corridor had to be a childhood memory. He tried to place it among the lawn and driveway he had seen earlier, the gold hatchback and two-storey house with its low hedge that he had come to understand as his home. It did not belong, he felt sure; that glimpse of childhood terror came from another world.

◢

Outside, Grebbel looked along the valley, where the night was coming from, and waited for his head to clear. Clouds like columns of smoke shimmered in the light of a single moon. The air was cold and clean.

As he walked to the worksite, the elongated bubble of a dirigible lifted from the landing field and moved over the river; its landing lights briefly flashed on the metal bridge that linked the coffer dam to the far bank. Then it moved upstream and hovered by the steel cylinders of the cryoplant. By the time Grebbel reached his truck, the dirigible was lifting off again, with a tank of liquid hydrogen slung beneath it, its surface already grey with frost. As it rose over the valley, still in the halo of light from the settlement, what seemed to be a pair of insects darted around it. Suddenly Grebbel recognised the two leather-winged raptors he had seen the day before. They dived at the gasbag, circled and swooped again, and then again, each time swerving away at the last moment before impact. Grebbel could imagine the furious beaks and claws, the screams of fury at the invader.

Menzies appeared by his side as Grebbel swung himself into the cab. "Watching the eagles? They've got the right idea from their point of view. We're flooding half their land."

Nodding, Grebbel said, "I was wondering if they'd know what to do with the blimp if they caught it."

"They may be just too smart for that. There were two pairs here originally. When the first blimp annoyed them, one pair started playing for keeps—managed to hole the bag a couple of times, then they got pulled into the airscrews."

"At least there wasn't a fire."

"Not so much danger of that actually. Hydrogen's not as bad as it's painted. It flies off into the sky before it can catch fire, given half a chance. Take precautions and don't cover your blimp with flammable paints, and it's manageable. But the ship was on the ground for two weeks that time—we couldn't get spares in a hurry then. Not much consolation for the two birds that got sliced, either. . . . I hear you're trying to get work at the clinic."

Grebbel looked at him, surprised.

"Word travels here," Menzies said. "It sounds as though it might be best for you, if it's something you're good with, but we've got deadlines on this job, so I'd like all the time you can give us."

"I'm wondering about splitting my time here between the two."

"Fair enough. One way and another, split lives are pretty common around here." Menzies was watching him intently.

Grebbel remembered their last conversation. "But, in the end," he said, "you have to make a choice."

"Yes," said Menzies, "if we're given the opportunity." He reached up into the cab to slap Grebbel's shoulder and turned away.

⚐

When Grebbel drove off, Menzies picked up his lunch from his own truck and walked from the parking area. He headed along the river, then turned onto a track into the woods, leading back towards the Greenhouse. After a few minutes, Niels Larsen appeared from the other direction. They unwrapped sandwiches and walked together in the wind-shaken moonlight.

"He's interested," Menzies said. "I've seen the signs. He doesn't know it yet, but he's building as much pressure as a tank of LOX."

"It's too dangerous now. We've already gone too far."

"What about getting a look at his file? He might not turn sour."

"I can't risk it since they've tightened up," Larsen said. "I think Carlo may suspect something. And in any case, I don't think we should trust their files after the last couple of times."

"What then? Do we just let them keep getting away with it?"

Larsen paced quietly, chewing, swallowing with difficulty. "I'd have to see him if we were going to do anything. . . . No, it's too risky. We should have stopped as soon as we saw what we might bring back."

"After Osmon, you mean? He hasn't actually done anything, and I'd still bet he won't as long he knows we're watching."

"I've never shared your certainty about him. And now Strickland looks like making trouble."

"You think Osmon had something to do with Strickland's girlfriend going missing?"

"No, I think you're right there. But then there must be someone we don't know about. An unpleasant thought but hardly surprising."

"Yeah. Well, we can't be responsible for everything. I just thought you should know about this new one."

"You think he's going to suffer," Larsen muttered, almost to himself. "If we acquiesce in evil again, our guilt may make us lose our nerve. I'm speaking for myself of course. But still I need something greater than myself, or—or there's nothing but ashes. You know some of this, but can you understand it?"

"I think you once learned to judge yourself harshly and you've never learned to stop."

"Well, perhaps. But there are limits to the ways we can change ourselves. That's the whole point, after all. . . . Perhaps you should keep an eye on him."

▲

Larsen watched Menzies walk back towards the dam. He remained, trying to finish his lunch, but his appetite had gone. A tenseness in his gut had been returning more frequently of late. Probably he would give himself ulcers if he took up this business again. And he could hardly go to the clinic for stress counselling.

As he walked back to the Greenhouse, he let himself remember his hard-won past—the gabled church where he had found mystery among candle flames enshrined by shadow and dark wood, and then the squalid cold huts under the blazing winter sky, where he had lost his faith, and begun the search for something to replace it.

His greatest fear was that he would succumb to his own weakness, let himself forget, content to let others take the risks, to leave things as they were, and be happy.

▲

Alpha, the first moon, was rising as Elinda descended the path to the lower-level residences and Chris's party. She had worked late, then gone home and eaten quickly, washed and changed, and then come straight out again, but the air was sharp with frost and her cheeks felt like leather.

A door opened, spilling light on four other arrivals. She hurried to join them, and they trooped into the darkened house, filled with the sound of slow dance music and a thick aroma of liquor and incense.

"Boots and coats in there, please," said Chris. "Ah—ghoul, Frankenstein and mirth, the gifts of the wise guys," as Elinda handed over the pastries she had brought. "How clever of you."

"Wrong time of year, Chris. And Barbara made them," she added with a momentary pang.

She made her way into the living room, trying not to be obviously looking for anyone. The place was already crowded. Ornate candles and a pair of battery-powered lanterns provided a dusky, golden light. At the far end, the furniture had been cleared back, and three couples were stuporously dancing. Beyond was the kitchen and another crowd. She worked her way towards it. A man in a green-and-white check shirt tried to look down the front of her blouse as he sipped from a paper cup. In an alcove at the edge of the dance floor a man in an astronaut uniform was showing an electronic folder of what looked like satellite photos to a woman hidden behind him.

". . . perpetual cyclones," he said. "Worse than here. Even the radar's patchy. You'd have to go down there and explore, and no one's going to send a dirigible into weather like that. If you know anyone in the shipbuilding business, they've got a career ahead of them."

Closing down the folder, he bent to put it in a briefcase standing against the wall. The woman thanked him and turned and saw Elinda.

"You're not at the clinic," said Jessamyn; "so you must be here investigating, right?" She carried an old coil-backed notebook, opened to pencil sketches.

"Maybe." Elinda wanted to talk to Robert Strickland if he turned up. The astronaut eyed them both and slipped away. "You've got time for your class project, too."

"I'm just passing through. Shall I give Barbara your love? She's going to need someone—"

"You said that before."

"Yes I did, didn't I?" Jessamyn hesitated, wringing the notebook in her hands until her knuckles whitened. They were blotched with paint. "You mean well, don't you? I used to think I was a charitable person, once. . . . Enjoy the party. I'd better go before I repeat myself any more."

Elinda struggled through to the kitchen and found a bottle with a hand-drawn label reading *Extra-Galactic Scotch Whisky*. Probably from Chris's own moonshine factory. She poured herself three fingers of yellowish liquid and swallowed a mouthful. As the drink seared its way down her throat, she looked around her. A lot of familiar faces, but few with names she could put to them. She realised that living with Barbara had enabled her to isolate herself from life here. One of the faces she didn't recognise belonged to another uniformed astronaut with a piratical-looking black beard. He was approaching the drinks table with a couple of empty glasses in each hand.

"Hi," he said. "Just get here? I've been here just long enough to spot a new face. I'm Martin Aguerro. They gave the shuttle crew some ground-time, but only a few of us had the good sense to come along here."

"Hello," she muttered, then introduced herself. "I'm one of the farm labourers around here. You can tell from my blunt typing fingers. Are you new in this part of the cosmos, then?"

"Just here a month now. We've been setting up the new communications satellite net. So you people won't get lost when you finally get time to explore down here properly."

"Then you didn't have to go through a lot of retraining? You didn't lose it when you came through the Knot?"

"Oh, no—we were lucky. Or maybe someone's starting to figure out how to get people through safely. The whole crew came across intact. I've heard it's the personal details that get lost most."

"Yes, it was that way with me."

"Oh," he said, "you had some bad luck, did you? Why don't you come into the other room; a group of us are talking about that sort of thing, and they're waiting for these refills."

"You remember everything, and you're happy out here? Or do you expect to go back?" she asked as she followed him through the crowd. No sign of Strickland. Nor of Jon Grebbel.

"No. I like the challenges. And the company"—with a quick smile over his shoulder—"and yes, the chances of regular two-way travel are looking better. If they can work out a good fix for the amnesia thing, you might find yourself going back and visiting in a few years."

"Maybe, but I'm still wondering what brought me here. Maybe I had some huge ambition that could only be fulfilled here—ruler of a galactic empire or something—or I'd run away with the secret to making turkey goulash. If I knew why I'd come, perhaps I'd be making plans, starting an army or a cooking school."

She followed him to a corner of the living room where a large terracotta mushroom was mounted on the wall. It didn't look like the usual work of Karl and Hannah over in Building Materials. Maybe Chris or one of his group had made it. A couple of other astronauts—an oriental woman and a short, red-haired man— were part of a group talking to Carlo. He blinked when he saw her and made introductions, then turned to listen to the woman.

"In the lab I'm keeping a rider and its host apart," she said, "and if I present the host with a stuffed oviphagus, the host goes into normal protective behavioural mode and attacks. Quite savagely. Now this rider has been conditioned from hatching to identify with the oviphage; it's almost a case of classical imprinting. In my experiment, I let it go to the host and present the oviphage again. Then the host treats the eggstealer as one of the family. I believe with a bit more work we could get it to try to copulate with the ovirattus. It's fascinating because only the local fauna show anything like this intensity of mental symbiosis."

"Does the, the host behave any differently to the rat thing after the rider has been so friendly towards it?" Elinda asked. "Does it remember what it did when the rider had control of it?"

"The trouble is, no one really understands memory," Carlo said, after the woman smiled and shrugged. "We probably know less about how it works now than we thought we did twenty years ago. They used to talk about it in terms of holograms—each individual item stored as a pattern in the whole brain. Now that seems to be too simple. The way you can lose particular chunks of information on the way here, it seems that different types of information are stored in different areas—or maybe stored in special ways. . . ."

"If you're so much in doubt," a voice said diffidently, "how do you go about treating people after we get here?" Elinda half turned and found Grebbel at her shoulder. He gave her a thin smile. She had the impression he had been listening for some time, hidden on the fringe of the group. His face was pale and she could see vertical bands of muscle in his cheeks.

Carlo shrugged and smiled. "It's the boss's area. He's a genius at what he does, but I don't think even he *really* knows why most of it works. Still, the technique does get results."

"Well, that's all that matters, isn't it?" said the woman astronaut, with just enough suggestion of sarcasm to make Carlo and Grebbel both look at her. Martin, who had been eyeing Grebbel intently, gave her a hard look and emptied his glass.

"What have you lost, after all?" said one of the others.

"That's just the point, isn't it," Grebbel said. "Who knows? And then why should we care?" He spread his arms theatrically, slopping his drink. The scars on his wrist were livid pink. "All the baggage of our past lives—cast off, abandoned, sent to another airport. Has that ever happened to you? Or you? Are you sure?

You don't remember! Congratulations! Give the lady another drink."

He leaned forward conspiratorially. "Don't breathe a word, but neither do I—isn't it wonderful? Freedom! All of that burden gone, sloughed off like an old skin, an outgrown chrysalis. And you—how do you manage to go through the days, with that much history bending your shoulders? I bet you can even recall things like your tenth birthday party, or what it felt like to be given a puppy, or the first time you put on a condom. Shit, I bet you can even remember what you *called* the things then. How can you stand it? And when you pick your nose like that, you can remember your mother scolding you. My god—maybe you even have some idea what makes you do it. With all those memories, I'll bet you can actually work out some of what makes you the way you are. Intolerable! Thank god I'm free of all that pressure—I don't even know what makes me talk like this, what makes me so happy about it all. . . ."

There was some uncomfortable laughter as Grebbel's audience tried to decide how much of his performance was foolery.

He lifted his glass to his lips, and Elinda saw how the liquid shook in it.

"A joke," he said to the group at large. "Or is it?"

"Whatever it was," said Martin, "that's enough of it."

Grebbel turned and stared at him. "You don't like the show? Strikes a bit close to the bone, somehow? Now, how could that be?"

Martin shook his head, started to turn away. Grebbel raised his voice, and the man stopped.

"Tell me, will you. Why are you offended? Because you're having to crawl in the mud with the rest of us? Because you're not up there above it all? Please tell us, tell us all."

Martin drew a breath, then shook his head and headed for the kitchen.

"Ah," said Grebbel loudly, "the burden of knowledge."

Elinda caught his eye. "Take it easy," she whispered. "And hello again."

There was sweat in the roots of his hair. He looked at her, then swallowed his drink and moved to face her, with his back to the others. Closing his eyes, he gestured vaguely. "I don't know why I did that, any of it." His voice was low now, and strained. Abruptly he swung away from her and vanished into the crowd.

She sipped at her drink, found it was empty. Someone was talking to her, telling her about his plans for the next spring. She was captivated by the whiteness of her fingers on the empty glass. The tendons in her wrist stood out, quivering. The man said something about another drink, and prised the glass out of her hand. She remembered Barbara saying *It's all right, whatever you've left behind there, it's another life, another person, let it stay forgotten*, and the secret warmth the words brought. A guilty warmth, like swallowing booze to drown a bad conscience. Guilt? She shivered and pushed her way out of the room.

Grebbel was not in the kitchen, but she saw a group outside in the back. She got her coat and boots and went out. They were huddled around what looked like a length of thirty-centimetre-diameter pipe angled towards the sky. One of the men was crouched over, apparently examining the surface of the pipe, which she belatedly realised was a telescope. Someone else was pointing out some of the brighter stars, visible though a large gap in the clouds. ". . . those three are the methylene group, and then there's the hydroxy—there, and there. It's the constellation Booze, just waiting to be named."

The man at the telescope straightened up from the eyepiece. "Anyone else?"

"What are you looking at?" she asked.

"Chronos, the gas giant. The moons are too bright to see much else. One of his satellites just came out of eclipse, I think, but it's hard to be sure."

"What about the Knot? Could you see that?"

"Not with any instrument here. Remember, it went undetected for centuries back on Earth. Have a look at Chronos here, anyway."

In the eyepiece, a silvery yellow ball bounced and shivered against a deep blue background. After a few moments, her eyes adjusted enough to pick out two lighter arcs across the disc and a dusky band between them. When she asked about them, the man explained that there were fairly regular cloud patterns on the surface, but the darker band was the planet's rings and their shadow on its surface, which were overlapping in their line of sight.

She relinquished the eyepiece to another watcher, confirmed that Grebbel was not among the crowd here and went back inside.

She finally found him crouched in the dark at the foot of the basement steps. Lengths of firewood as thick as her wrist lay snapped at his feet, their splintered ends like needles. He had another piece in his hands and was straining at it, his teeth bared, his forearms quivering with the pressure. The wood snapped with a sound like a gunshot and the breath came out of him in a snarl.

He saw her then, and let the wood clatter onto the concrete floor, and put his face in his hands.

"Why does it matter that much," she asked, "what you've lost?"

"A dark, empty box," he whispered through his hands. "It's like that—like an empty cellar. Like a nightmare . . . caves, tunnels, things snuffling . . . I haven't got the words." He fell silent for a few moments, then lifted his head and looked at her. "And how are you enjoying the party?"

"Oh," she said, and took a step forward. "I haven't been here long. I was working. I've been getting behind at work; I didn't get in at all this morning."

He nodded. "The clinic. Any news?"

"Yeah. They still don't have a goddamned clue what's wrong." She shook her head. "I was there for ten minutes, maybe. There wasn't any point in staying. She didn't know where she was, she didn't even know I was there."

"I'm sorry," he said, "if that helps at all. What about the other thing, the investigation?"

"A few hints, not much more. I'll try something else tomorrow. We can talk about it later. You must have bruised your hands. Those sticks are strong."

Grebbel shrugged. "They'll mend. I don't know where all that came from. And that's the point. I don't know—so much . . . Christ, why did I come down here?"

"It doesn't seem to be doing you any good, does it? Let's get some air."

▲

The party sounds faded behind them. Under the light of the twin moons the clouds boiled and the mountaintops gleamed like icebergs in a frozen raging sea.

"And when she told me my tubes had been tied," Elinda said, "I just panicked. I couldn't imagine that I'd do that—have done that. It was like having a stranger in my own body. . . . Perhaps I do know some of what you were going through tonight. Do you want to walk a bit further up the hill? I'm not looking forward to going into an empty home again, after seeing her like that. I haven't been doing much housekeeping lately, but I can probably find us something to drink."

At the front door, Grebbel watched her fumble a key from her pocket. Her shoulders were stiff and the tendons in the nape of her neck were caught by the moonlight as she bent towards the lock. An insect strummed, making a sound like over-taut wires in a wind; and the wind itself sounded among the trees—a long breath deeply indrawn, held, then lingeringly exhaled.

The door opened onto darkness. Stepping into it, she turned, her face a blur of moon-shadow, and gestured without speaking. He followed, and they brushed together as they pulled off boots and coats—arms and shoulders, awkward elbows.

He was in the living room, with something softer than wood under his feet. He could make out a table by the window, a dark painting on the wall, a couple of armchairs, a couch—and she was moving quietly to one wall, bending over something. A match sputtered and flared, flung her shadow against the ceiling, and left him with a vision of scalloped gold from ear, cheek and hair. Then there was a steady, paler glow. She straightened, holding an oil lamp, and put it on the corner of the table. "Emergency lighting," she said softly. "We don't open the blinds at night and I don't have candles. And I think this is an emergency, don't you?"

The light caught her cheek and hair, picked out two creases between her eyes. Her lower lip was held between her teeth, giving her a pensive look. Since they had met this evening, something had changed, but he could not have said how or when. She lifted her head a fraction and swallowed, "I can get you a drink now," she whispered. Her eyes were large and very dark. "If you want."

He shook his head, and found he could not speak.

As he reached for her, she was already moving towards him.

They held each other, and at first the warmth was enough, the weight and pressure against arms and chest. Then, almost without volition, came the need to touch, to explore. Through layers of clothing, fingers traced the curves of spines, the bulky shapes of shoulder, ribcage, scapula—moved to the skin of nape and ears, and the cushioned roundness of the skull. Lips brushed forehead, felt the softness of a cheek, worked against other lips that opened for the tongue, then moved to the throat, where teeth nipped at the skin beside the hurrying pulse, and came to rest in the smooth hollow at its base.

There was a pause, filled with the sound of breathing, as they stood on the edge of familiar, unknown realms. Leaning together, they hardly seemed to move. Then their fingers began to work on buttons and clasps, slowly, teasingly at first, then more hurriedly, getting in each other's way, until the urgency became too great, and they had to break apart and pull off what still separated them.

Again, a pause, while they looked at each other in the lamplight, a time for anticipation, for thoughts of vulnerability and delight. Slowly they moved back together. Now the explorations began again, seeking, for him, the secret touch and slide that would bring sensation, would reveal the key to her joy; for her, the ache of needs once known and fulfilled and then forgotten. Palms stroked, fingers teased and probed, and were followed by the liquid flicker of a tongue.

They had found their way to the couch, and lay face to face, one above the other. But their faces were transformed. Expressions of remote concentration intensified as their bodies worked— became gapes of astonishment protracted almost to pain. For each of them, time had ceased to flow. Space and awareness contracted to the sensation of the other and the rising tension. The world shrank to the darkened room and their two bodies. Time had stopped and yet stretched to eternity. And then it burst. One of them moaned, and then the other. As they shuddered against each other, a wave of unbeing swept them away.

▲

The light was grey. Without moving, Grebbel let it filter through his eyelids, while awareness crept back. Whatever had passed between them was spent for now, and he tried to understand it. The sense that something had taken control of him—of his actions, of even his wishes and desires—was disturbing. He felt that the direction of his life had been changed, perhaps taken out of his hands. And yet . . . he let his eyes open enough to look at the woman whose vulnerability to pleasure had given her into his power. He saw only the turn of a shoulder, the lobe of an ear emerging from a dim tangle of hair, but knew he was at the mercy of her weakness.

"You're awake, aren't you?" she said. "I've been listening to you breathe."

When he looked, she was watching him steadily.

"I dreamt of snow," he said. "I dreamt I was holding you and the snow was blowing outside, piling up, and I thought we might be able to hide under it for as long as we liked. Then there was a sound. . . ."

"I remember your arm," said Elinda. "I could feel the scars. And when you were asleep, you woke me up. You were holding your wrist and trying to say something. I thought you were crying at first, but it was something else."

"So we're still scared," he muttered. "Whatever's changed now, we haven't solved that, so where does this leave us?"

"Right here," she whispered. "Together."

SIX

Her fingers were tracing the length of his body, drawing lines as sharp and piercing as the scars on his arm. . . .

An arc light blazed through the side window and Grebbel wrenched himself back into the present and parked the truck. He took his lunch and swung down from the cab.

Menzies walked over to him, hooded against the wind. "Want to bring your lunch and come over into the galleries?" he called. "They're installing the new generators today, and one of the winches needs repairing. Another pair of hands and eyes would be welcome."

Guessing that Menzies might want to talk about memory loss again, Grebbel agreed. Icy spray stung his face as they walked over the metal mesh bridge from the coffer dam. The gallery entrance was carved into the rock. They walked into a cellar-like space lit by a row of bluish ceiling lights. Grebbel's skin prickled.

"Keep hold of the handrail," Menzies said. "Down here."

Grebbel hesitated. *Stairs*, his mind told him. A dull roaring grew to fill his ears. He shook his head and went forward. Down. Step. Down.

"We're alongside the sluiceway here," Menzies called over his shoulder. "When everything's finished, this will be part of the bypass around the turbines." He slapped the rock wall. "Security's not as tight down here as it might be. That's one reason I like to walk around here as often as I can." He looked at his watch. "They should almost be finished running tests now. In five minutes we can go and work on the winch without getting in their way. It's in the next chamber—actually in the hillside."

The gallery continued, with alcoves cut into its side every ten metres or so. One or two of these had been fitted with doors. Menzies peered into each one, flashing the beam of his light over stacks of tools or spare helmets. "Been here for weeks," he muttered at one point. "Look at the dust on them. This job needs twenty percent more personnel."

A couple of workers came past, and Menzies moved away to talk to them. Grebbel heard a name repeated with some urgency— Strickland, he thought, and tried to recall where he had heard the name—but could not hear any more. Heads were shaken; then Menzies came back. Grebbel wondered what Menzies was not telling him. He said: "You were asking about someone in particular just then. You wanted to know if he'd been seen here."

Menzies did not reply before they reached the end of the gallery. "I'm just making a routine check," he said. "It's time to get back to the turbine room."

They retraced their steps, Menzies still peering into crannies. "Looks clean enough," he said finally. "Let's see if we can get at that winch."

The air blazed in front of Grebbel's eyes. The ground heaved up and slapped him.

He was alone, sprawled on his back, peering into a fog and wondering at the quiet. After a while, he tried to sit up.

The silence ruptured. The air was full of shouts and screams. It smelled of smoke and something worse. He lurched to his feet and staggered into the chamber he had been about to enter.

Purple sparks crackled through the haze, throwing up silhouettes of jagged black machinery. The sound of voices rose like a tide, an animal noise, barely controlled. Light flickered. At the foot of the wall lay a man, his thigh impossibly bent, a gleam of white at the angle.

Awareness came and went for Grebbel. A hunched, monstrous shape fumbled towards him, then became Menzies with a man across his shoulders. "Use the truck—fetch help from the hospital."

He was in the icy dark again, pulling the truck off the causeway, and trying to remember what was so urgent. Lightning forked across a void of cloud high above him. Then he was back at the hospital, unsure of what he had told them, ears and mind buffeted by the clamour of a siren. And back in the chaos: the smell more obvious now, emergency lighting showing red pulp where hands and limbs had been. His mind had stopped working. He found he had taken one end of a stretcher and was heading back to the truck. The siren still screamed in his skull.

This time, when he reached the hospital, his head was clearing. Another truck was following with the medical orderlies. That must mean all the injured were out. He went inside.

The emergency room had overflowed into the lobby. It stank of smoke, burned flesh, shit and antiseptic. Under its lights, white, shocked eyes met his gaze, faces the colour of old paper, or blackened with soot. Flesh that had been seared to oozing brown pulp. Blood.

His pulse hammered, the lights seemed to brighten above him. He watched, fascinated, as steel sliced away burned cloth and flesh, as mouths opened to cry out. He watched human beings reduced to creatures of pain and reflex.

The door opened behind him. More of the injured were being brought in on stretchers. He hurried outside to the last truck and helped carry a stretcher into the hospital. The man on it was covered by a blanket almost to the eyes, but as they went through the doorway, he seemed to rouse and the blanket shifted. Under a film of instant bandage, the lower part of his face was a crimson and white ruin. The man's head strained back and choking sounds came from where his mouth had been. Grebbel realised the man was trying to cry out. He heard the scream in his head.

When they got inside, there was nowhere to put the man but the floor. A nurse with bloodstains on her bare arms lifted the blanket, examined the man quickly, then gave him an analgesic shot and hurried on to the next. Grebbel was left alone with the man he had helped carry. He looked down at him. The man was choking.

Grebbel turned to call a doctor from one of the other casualties, but suddenly his own hands knew what to do. There was a tray of instruments on a roller table in the middle of the room. He took a scalpel and sprayed it with antiseptic, then knelt by the injured man. He supported the man's head with one hand, and with the other he first sprayed the man's throat then slit the skin and muscle over the lower half of the trachea. When he could see the hoops of cartilage, he sliced between two of them. Pink foam appeared in the cut, and the man's breathing steadied a little. Grebbel sterilised a catheter and taped it into the incision as a breathing tube. When he had finished, the man was breathing steadily again.

Carefully, walking some internal tightrope, Grebbel took the scalpel back to the table and then picked his way back to the stretcher. He sank down beside it and stared at what he had done. Every muscle in his body seemed to be trembling.

Around him the chaos started to become quieter.

"You shouldn't be here."

Numbly Grebbel looked up. The worst of the casualties had been moved out. Carlo was staring down at him.

Grebbel indicated the tracheotomy he had performed. "He was choking. I was right, wasn't I?"

Carlo's expression softened. "It looks as though you were. There's nothing more for you to do now, though. Take a walk outside. We'll be able to give you a checkup for shock and concussion in ten minutes, but I don't think you'll have anything to worry about."

Grebbel nodded and stepped around the man on the stretcher and went to the door. The trucks had gone. When he looked back, the man was being wheeled towards the operating room. Grebbel locked his fingers together and failed to stop their trembling.

▲

"A bomb went off at the powerhouse," Chris said. He had just come in after lunch, while Elinda and Larsen were trying to assemble work plans for the following week.

Larsen sat up, his fists clenched in his lap. "Why ever did we go to the trouble of installing a datanet, when simpler methods are so much faster?" He failed to keep the strain out of his voice.

"The powerhouse?" Elinda asked. "The far side of the dam?"

"They were talking about it in the line-up," Chris said, almost apologetically. "Someone saw the trucks carrying them to the clinic. They were coming across the bridge. The word'll be everywhere soon"

"Some version will," Larsen muttered. "Myself, I'd prefer to know what really happened."

"Who was hurt?" Elinda asked quickly. "How many?"

"Couple of dozen, maybe more, from what they were saying," Chris said, giving her a questioning look. "Mostly construction workers, and one or two of the engineers. I didn't get any names."

"Discount fifty percent for observer error," Larsen interjected. "A bomb, you said. Was that a piece of hyperbole, or does this appear to be sabotage?"

Chris shrugged. "Someone heard the bang; and there was a cloud of smoke still there, a good ten minutes after. I saw it. And they're not supposed to be doing any more blasting this year."

"Do you think," Elinda said slowly, "there could be any connection with those leaflets?"

Larsen had turned to the computer. "You mean, they plant pieces of paper that have no effect, so two days later they switch to explosives? It seems a devious course to take for anyone with concrete goals in mind. Don't you think?"

"We don't know what their goals might be," she replied, "whether they're concrete at all, or even rational. The whole point of the leaflet was that there might be people who didn't care what they did. What about that interruption to newsfeed-night the other day? I think we can guess—"

"We do too much guessing." Larsen's fingers tripped over themselves on the keys. He inhaled sharply, paused, then carefully reentered the command. "What does your *vox populi* have to say about motives, Chris?"

Chris looked uncomfortable. "You hear all sorts of rumours. People believe the craziest things at times."

"In other words this could be serious. I hope we're not priming ourselves to turn into a lynch mob. If we develop a vigilante mentality here, we're doomed." The strain in his voice was obvious now. His head jerked as the screen flickered. "The voice of authority is speaking."

The other two looked over his shoulder as the announcement scrolled up the screen.

A public meeting was called for that evening, to discuss the recent events and their implications for the security of the settlement.

"That's very fast," Larsen muttered. "Here are the casualties. Serious, they're serious. No names."

He pushed himself upright and fumbled for his coat. "I need

some air," he said. "You might too. Lock up if you both leave the office."

Elinda stayed at her desk. Her hands were trembling. She hadn't really believed Grebbel could have got himself caught in the blast, had she? "Straight after dinner, they want this meeting," she said to Chris. "I hope they've actually got something to say." So he was that far under her skin already. And with Barbara left to rot in the mental ward.

"He was right," she said. "I need some air."

▲

She found Grebbel in the lobby of the clinic, moving a gas cylinder on a kind of wheelbarrow. He moved stiffly, as though pulled by wires, and his eyes were vacant. But when she stepped into his path, he saw her and stopped. She went and held him. His arms closed rigidly around her.

"What are you doing here?" she whispered into his chest. "I didn't know where you were." Her voice was threatening to break up.

He answered hesitantly. "We're clearing a storage room. Extra bed space. They're doubled up in the wards. . . . I found I couldn't leave here. I brought them over in the truck, and then I had to stay."

"You were at the dam when the explosion happened?"

"I was over there, just outside the generator room. The blast hit me."

"My god. You might be hurt. Did they look at you?"

"Yes, when the worst was over. They gave me a check-up. Told me to go and lie down." There was more animation in his voice. "Let me finish with these cylinders."

For the first time, she noticed a partly cleaned brown smear on the wall, scrapes and wheel marks on the doorframe and floor. She helped him move two more cylinders of oxygen, and then he found his coat and they stepped into the chill sunlight. The wind surged and began to suck away the heat they had brought with them from the building. His expression was turning distant again. She found herself thinking of Barbara's total withdrawal, and flinched.

He seemed to make an effort to rouse himself and began

speaking. "Something happened to me. I've only been here a matter of days, and things keep changing on me." His voice was beginning to rise, and he broke off and fell silent. They walked slowly, staying close together. She was wondering if she should prompt him with a question, when he said, "I cut a man's throat in there."

She stared at him, and carefully, dispassionately, he explained about the tracheotomy.

She looked away at the mountains then turned to him again. There was an expression on his face she could not interpret. "You think you've done it before?"

"I must have, mustn't I?" he said.

"What then? Maybe they teach that in first-aid courses, for people going into the jungle somewhere."

"Then maybe I got my arm savaged by a Bengal tiger."

"Do you know why you felt you couldn't leave the clinic?"

He frowned. "Watching all the pain . . . I felt I belonged there somehow."

"To help." She pictured him in a smoke-filled space, pulling the injured away from machines and sparking cables. "I wonder if you were in a lab accident before you came here."

"My arm, you mean? Broken glass?"

"It could be, couldn't it? Christ, it's all guesswork though. Do you think it was sabotage this morning?"

"I think it must have been," he said. "Nobody seemed to believe anything like that could happen by accident. I saw someone in a brown uniform shirt talking to some of the victims."

"Security. In the clinic." Suddenly, her mind raced. "It's too close to those leaflets, they'll be looking for a connection. They'll think Barbara was in on this."

"Because she can't defend herself?"

"The cop I went to for help—I didn't realise at the time, but he could have had orders to delay looking for her." She stopped and peered up at him. "I'm paranoid, aren't I? Of course I am. I don't care. Do something for me, please?"

"If I can."

"Get to Schneider's lab again, as soon as you can—let's walk back now. Make copies of all Barbara's computer files. Don't ask me what I expect to find; if I knew, I wouldn't need to ask. I want to know what evidence there is, if someone starts to frame her.

You may not be able to open the files without a password, but the system will let you make backups if no one's put double locks on."

She left Grebbel at the clinic and returned to the office. Towards the end of the day, Larsen returned. He still seemed shaken. He said he had been at the labs to review the design of the next batch of experiments, and had seen some of the casualties.

The distress in his manner disturbed her. "It's been a bad day," she said. "Let's quit; let's get something to eat and then go to this meeting."

Chris said he would finish his simulation, and maybe see them in the Hall. Larsen seemed about to refuse, then looked grateful and nodded. He walked to the cafeteria with Elinda and they ate slowly, saying little, until it was time to go to the meeting.

The doors were open, but despite the cold, people were gathering outside. A tall red-haired woman with a pair of toddlers told them, "The choir's finishing rehearsal. The show must go on, you know. They'll let you go in if you promise them to be quiet. Of course there's no way I can take these two in."

"Should we wait, too?" Larsen asked Elinda.

One of the children was chasing the other in circles round them. The victim screamed happily and then tripped and fell against Elinda's leg. She looked a little like the child that had fallen in the fishpond earlier. "Let's go in," Elinda said.

Inside, the stage was cleared and the choir stood in rows facing the conductor. A few seats were occupied. Voices rose and fell like the waves of the sea. Only the stage was lit, and great veils of shadow seemed to loom over the empty seats. Elinda felt she was in a dank underwater cavern, filled with the moans of the dead. She wished she had stayed outside.

"A modern piece of hymn-making," Larsen muttered to her when the conductor lowered her baton to talk to the performers. "I admit I would rather have stood in the wind."

"You should have said so. Shall we go back out?"

"It must be nearly over by now. We may as well stay warm. I believe this was the kind of music I lived with as a child. It has a lot of obscure associations for me now—both joyous and wretched. The combination can be almost unbearable, but I hope I can learn to come to terms with the bad and still value the good. It may be salutary to listen."

The conductor lifted her arms again. The voices rose, from

the throats of men in shirtsleeves, women in boiler suits—an elemental cry, an appalling, inhuman sound uttered from the mouths of people she passed every day in the street. The music bypassed her mind and worked within her muscles, her guts. She closed her eyes and waited for it to end.

Finally it did, and she realised she had been gnawing her fingers throughout.

Larsen shifted in his seat. "And now the more mundane problems of the world."

Within a few moments, the choir had been hurried away and chairs and a long table were being set up on the stage. She looked around, waiting for Grebbel to arrive. The Hall was filling up: two or three hundred people, she guessed. A hand microphone had been put on the table, and Dr. Henry and some of the other council members were talking quietly at the side of the stage. Henry looked at his watch, then shooed the group toward the table and went to the microphone.

"First of all," he began, "thank you all for coming. We have a serious matter to deal with tonight, and I'd appreciate it if, as soon as you can, you would pass on what happens here to your friends who haven't been able to make it or see this on the net.

"As you know by now, there was an explosion in the new generating room this afternoon. According to the latest information I have, about forty people were injured, seventeen seriously. Relatives and close friends are being informed individually, but none of the injuries are believed to be life-threatening." Beside Elinda, Larsen gave an audible sigh.

"To be blunt, we believe the explosion was deliberately set, an act of sabotage. I see this doesn't come as a shock to most of you, which is another reason why I called this meeting. We have had suspicions for some time that a group in our midst has been planning to disrupt our life here—though we did not suspect they would go this far. We are going to need the full cooperation of every member of the community if we are to prevent a repeat of today's tragedy. I'll outline what precautions we plan to take and what new bylaws we shall require. But first I'll hand the microphone over to Erik, our engineering manager, to explain what we believe happened."

The engineer stood and described how the effects of the blast and how some quick forensic science had established that two or three sticks of plastic explosive had been used in the main generator bay. He described the effects of the blast and the type of injuries it had caused. Then he paused and put a cardboard box on the table. He lifted out some blackened pieces of metal and a length of wire.

"These are some of the fragments our team found. Some of them were taken from the thigh of one of the injured, where they had created shrapnel wounds. They are part of a lithium battery and a timing device. Personally I cannot see how this explosion can be anything but a deliberate attempt to damage equipment that is almost irreplaceable here, and to kill some of our most valued workers." Without further comment he sat down.

Dr. Henry thanked him and introduced the Security chief.

She stood and surveyed the audience for a few moments before speaking. "Several of you in this room," she said with emphasis, "are close to people who were almost killed this afternoon, and who may be maimed for life." She paused and looked at them again. "And, almost certainly, someone listening to me now either planted that bomb or knows who did."

Larsen muttered, "Here she comes, the witch-hunter. She will destroy us all if she sows distrust like that."

"We don't believe a large group was responsible," the woman continued; "but in a society like ours, even a single deviant can threaten the safety of every one of us. As the result of some recent events here, we have some idea of who is involved, and we are keeping our suspects under observation while we assemble our evidence.

"Dr. Henry has indicated that we'll be tightening security. I can't reveal all the measures we will take, but I think it fair to tell you that our personnel will be among you more often now. Some of them will be apparent; some will not. We have enacted the emergency powers regulations, giving all accredited members of the Security forces the authority to stop, question, and if necessary search any person they feel may be a threat to the safety of the community.

"Needless to say, we have emphasised to our staff that these new powers are to be used with the utmost tact and restraint. Nevertheless, I have no doubt that they are utterly necessary, and therefore I ask you all to give us your understanding and cooperation while the crisis lasts."

Dr. Henry summed up and asked for questions.

Out of the corner of her eye, Elinda saw Grebbel slide into a seat at the end of their row. Someone was asking how long the crisis was expected to last, and how they would know when it was over. Henry started to make soothing noises that made little impression on her. When he finished speaking, she surprised herself by standing up.

"Sit down," Larsen whispered urgently. "Don't make a fuss here."

"Yes," Dr. Henry said. "The young lady on the left."

"You believe there's a connection between the bombing and some recent events here. Can you be more specific? Were you referring to the leaflets put out the other day? And does that mean there's some truth to what they said?"

Henry looked at her appraisingly. Finally he said, "I could hand this one to our Security chief, but I'm sure she'd merely tell you that we can't divulge information like that until we're sure the criminal or criminals have been put away. If you have a particular reason for asking those questions, perhaps you could contact me at the end of the meeting."

Larsen tugged at her sleeve. "Sit down. Let it go."

She shrugged and took her seat. The questions continued, but she paid no attention. After a couple of minutes she caught Grebbel's eye, and he pointed towards the door. Larsen muttered, "Yes that's a good idea. Go now. I'll tell you tomorrow if anything else happens here."

She joined Grebbel at the back of the Hall and they left together.

"It's started, then," she said. "Did you hear all of it? I can't help wondering if I didn't leave a whole universe behind to get away from things like that—emergency measures and arbitrary surveillance."

"Why did you ask Henry about the leaflets then?"

Ahead of them, bronze and white clouds broke like slow-motion surf around a black pinnacle. One of the moons made an ivory crescent above the head of the valley.

"I was upset," Elinda said. "I wanted to see what he'd say. Barbara had something to do with those leaflets, but I'm certain she'd never start bombing people. If they're trying to incriminate her, to use her as a scapegoat, I want to know. Did you get to her lab, by the way?"

"Yes, of course," said Grebbel. "I copied the files. They're on a blue stick in Barbara's drawer." He looked less withdrawn than when she had left him that afternoon.

"Thanks. I'll look in tomorrow and pick them up. You want to go in here?"

A swinging signboard illuminated by a colour-corrected mercury lamp bore the name *Red Lion*. "This the tavern?" he said. "Sure. I've yet to see the inside of the place. And I'd say we could both use a drink."

Inside, dark wooden panels divided it into alcoves facing on a common bar. The lighting was a mixture of small shaded bulbs, perhaps from flashlights, and colour-balanced LEDs. In a far alcove, a man was singing off-key, something about falling down a rabbit hole. Closer, the benches were occupied by men and women in construction gear.

Grebbel and Elinda found seats on a padded bench beside a window, near the end of the bar. A waiter in a black and white check shirt came, and Elinda ordered a whiskey sour. "I know too much about their beer, and their hard liquor isn't something I'd normally drink straight, though it's getting better. Isn't that right, Pedro?"

The waiter grinned. "We always tell the customers we're getting better. Haven't seen you in here for a while though. Maybe you'd be surprised at what we've got."

"Surprised, maybe," she said; "delighted—I doubt it. If you don't want what I'm having," she said to Grebbel, "I'd recommend the vodka or gin."

He shrugged. "I'll try what you're having. Make it a double."

A man in a group at their end of the bar began describing a shuttle lift-off to the other waiter. At a table nearby, a couple were talking about the chances of finding the saboteur.

Their drinks arrived. Elinda swallowed a mouthful. Grebbel tasted his, then drained it.

She frowned to herself and shook her head. "I'm not doing very well yet. I tried tracing where the leaflets had come from. I found where the paper they were printed on went to, but now I don't think that tells me much. I'm not giving up, but I'll have to think of something else to try."

He squeezed her hand. "Just don't try anything that'll get you into trouble. Don't think of anything like that."

They were silent, gazing at each other in the tinted light.

". . . you can't see the laser beam, but you can hear it, at least it seems that way, the whole sky roaring—and there's the thrust chamber glowing like the sun, climbing like a bird, and the hydrogen not turned on yet . . ."

Glasses clinked. A group entered and another left.

". . . but that's the point—how much longer will they pour money into here if someone's trying to blow their investment apart?"

Grebbel reached across the table and took her hand. Her fingers stroked his palm. They shared a smile. "Things can't be important all the time," she said. "We can go in a minute."

Outside, they stopped and held each other. He rubbed her shoulders, stroked the back of her neck, she ran her hands along his spine. In the trees on the valley slope, the wind rose and roared and was quiet again. Masses of moonlit cloud turned ponderously overhead. Beyond the clouds, the aurora writhed. She muttered into his shoulder, "You're still wound up tight, aren't you?"

He nodded, rubbing his cheek in her hair. "We both are. Come on."

Two streetlights faded behind them, and doubled moon-shadows accompanied them up the slope. The stream sounded faintly among the rush of air through refurling branches. A four-winged creature like a silver bat, with its crested rider, swooped low over their heads and was gone. Above the clouds a sheaf of rose light shook open into a great orchid.

And then Elinda was fumbling for her key again, awkward with one arm still around his waist, and the previous evening was recreating itself.

"Take off your coat."

"Yes."

They spoke in whispers and moved slowly, putting their coats on chairs, then clinging to each other again; but still stiffly, inert.

"Last time, you were going to offer me a drink."

"All right," she said, and did not move. "If you'll help me look for it. And you'll have to make do with a cup."

"Maybe we should have stayed in the tavern then."

"You'd have to sleep on one of those benches. You'd get a stiff back."

In the dark, they found their way to the kitchen, and she produced a bottle and two ceramic cups. "I never did show you the house, did I? This is the kitchen. And through here, as you see, we have the bedroom."

"That's nice."

They were going through the motions, flirting until tensions relaxed.

They sat on the bed and poured whisky for each other. Leaning together, they took turns to sip from a single cup, one holding it to the other's lips, while the other's unencumbered hands explored and caressed.

At some point, when the cup was put down to be refilled, it disappeared. Turning to look for it, they fell against each other, giggled and kissed and toppled sideways on the bed. And quite suddenly their need sharpened and focussed. The play became urgent.

Elinda felt her body being caught up in familiar aching rhythms. The hidden, night side of her knew this version of the dance. That knowledge laboured within her, climbing towards the light, bringing its dark and fearful joy.

And Grebbel, with her face filling his sight, his skin tingling with the sensation of holding her and being held, felt a moment's pause. *Wait*, said his mind, *touch her there and she'll beg*. But then being inside her overwhelmed everything else, and when the climax came, it annihilated all awareness.

⋏

He was adrift in a place between sleeping and waking. He could no longer tell where his body ended and hers began. Their breathing sounded together in his ears, the fathomless sound of the ocean waves. He was a wrinkled creature, washed free of grit, wounds bathed and soothed, drifting on the edge of the ocean until the tide should roll in again and carry him back to the quiet dark.

Sluggishly he rolled in the water. *On his back*, said the waves, *turn him on his back. Turn him on his back. Turn his belly to the light, so we can see where he's hurt.*

Sea—where he's hurt, there he's hurt, there he hurts. In the white, in the light. It's the light, in the eyes, it's the sounds, in the ears, that's what hurts. Come to sleep in the deep, in the dimness and the peace. Heal the hurt.

It's too late now—see the wound. The wound. The wound.

JANUS

. . . severe laceration about the umbilicus, damage to the peritoneum, large and small intestines, lesions to the liver and pancreas. We'll need plasma—thirty units—dialysis. . . .

The ocean had vanished. He lay in the dark, his limbs tangled with hers, and stared toward the ceiling. His hands had come together and locked their fingers and begun to squeeze. When he made the effort to exhale, the air rasped in his ears.

He whispered, hardly daring to formulate the certainty that had appeared in his mind. "I was—a doctor."

She turned in his arms and muttered without waking. He peered at the blur of her face, a few centimetres from his own. Her breath was warm on his shoulder, her breast soft against his upper arm. His eyes tried to recreate details that had been familiar during the day. He ached. She stirred again, and he realised his body was damp with sweat.

He let his head fall back on the pillow and closed his eyes.

A doctor.

SEVEN

Chris glanced up as Elinda went into the office. "Early again," he said. "This whole place is turning upside down. Maybe even the boss'll take a day off."

The wind moaned about the building. Dry leaves rattled on the window.

"Don't get your hopes up," she said. "I'm just passing through. I'll be back, but there's order in the universe yet." She had sat down without taking her coat off and was entering commands through her keyboard.

As she was about to call up the residence directory, she suddenly realised that if Security was ahead of her, any attempts to reach Strickland might be monitored. She decided to gamble. She called up the directory and asked for addresses for half a dozen surnames at random, throwing in "Swale" and "Stackpole" as well. "Swale" proved to be the name of a real person living in the lower blocks, but "Stackpole" drew a blank. The system then displayed a block of names in alphabetical order centred on "Stark," the closest it could get. "Strickland" was third from the bottom of the list, with an address in one of the original settlement buildings off the Square. She memorised the address rather than writing it down, completed her search of dummy names, adding Jon Grebbel's as an afterthought, printed out a couple of the results for show, then said good morning to Chris and set out into the wind.

▲

She found half the Square roped off. A battery of lights had been set up near the Tree and focussed on the buildings at the far side. Militia in white jackets and gas masks patrolled the barrier, with riot guns in their gauntleted hands. She stopped. The wind surged and the icy waters of the river seemed to roil about her. Then she braced herself and walked up to the nearest of the militia and asked what was happening.

The hidden eyes swung towards her. It was probably someone she passed on the street almost every day—and the mask must be there for that reason as much as for protection.

"Keep back, please." A man's voice, but distorted beyond recognition. The furled tree fronds rustled and stirred above them, reminding Elinda of pinioned, groping arms.

"But what's happening?"

From the far side of the Square, someone shouted. A whistle blew. Three of the militia ran to one of the buildings and hurled something through a window, then forced the door and ran inside. After a moment there was a muffled thud and more shouting. Smoke streamed out. Then there was quiet. Elinda's eyes began to smart.

"Who is it?" she asked. "Who have they caught?"

But the mask was turned to the house across the Square and made no response.

The door opened again. The three militia emerged, two in the lead with a tall man in a dark green sweater between them. He walked heavily, seemingly unaware of the cold, his shoulders slumped. In front of the building, he twice bent forward and was shaken by coughs. His face was red; it looked swollen, and it was several moments before Elinda could be sure the man was Robert Strickland.

Another of the militia in the Square went forward to meet the three. He exchanged words with them, then said something to their prisoner.

Strickland leapt forward, was caught by his two guards. Elinda could see his face thrust up at the officer even as his arms were twisted behind him to force his body forward. His mouth was a black gash uttering sounds that were made unintelligible by wind and his own rage.

The officer turned away and Strickland fell quiet, letting himself be bowed forward, and coughing. Then he twisted his head up and shouted, and this time she understood his words. "You know why! Because of her! Erika! You know!"

One of the guards made a sharp motion, and Strickland fell to his knees. The guards began to drag him away.

"There was no need to hit him like that." She started towards him.

Strickland sprang to life. One of the guards fell and the other staggered against the wall. Strickland was crouching between them with one of their machine pistols in his hands. Now she could see him easily. "I remember your type," he was shouting. "Just fit for beating up grandmothers."

The militiaman dragged at her arm. "Get down!" The muzzle of Strickland's gun was swinging back and forth. If he pressed the trigger, he would probably cut her in half. "Get down!"

She dropped and put her cheek to the icy ground. As she covered her head with her arms, someone screamed. There was a brief clatter of shots. Then more screams.

For a long time it seemed that nothing was happening. She raised her head. Strickland lay crumpled at the base of the wall. His chest and the side of his head were crimson. There was a short chain of bullet holes in the wall where he had been standing. As she watched, a woman wearing a Red Cross armband went and bent over him, then stood up and shook her head. The two guards went to pick up Strickland's body.

Elinda pushed herself to her feet. The militia were taking down the rope barrier and the battery of lights and vanishing into alleys and side streets. People flowed back onto the Square.

She worked her way towards the building they had stormed. Now the tear gas was stronger, rasping at her eyes and the back of her throat. She stopped and wiped her eyes, coughing.

"You shouldn't be here," said Carlo when she looked up. Through wide goggles he was staring at her with an intensity she could not interpret. Awkwardly he added, "The gas won't clear for another five or ten minutes."

"I'll be okay. I want to find out what happened."

"They got the one who planted the bomb. There were traces of blasting compound in his room, and some spare wire and batteries."

"So it's over, then. It's all solved."

Carlo hesitated. "It looks like it."

"Assuming," she suggested, "he really did do it, and alone? But why would anyone do a thing like that?"

"Who can say?" Carlo looked away from her and peered across the darkened Square. "He might have been crazy. He was so easy to trace, they say, he might have wanted to be caught. And the way he stood there at the end, waving that gun, just inviting them to shoot him . . . Who knows what drove him to it?"

Someone knows, she thought, remembering Strickland's words to the officer. "He mentioned a name just now. Erika. That was the missing woman, wasn't it, the one mentioned at the newsfeed the other night? Do you think she was part of it?"

He turned to look at her, but then only shrugged. "What we've found is one man with some sort of chip on his shoulder; the rest is just moonshine. Sorry, now, but you'll have to excuse me. I'm wanted."

She watched him go, wondering if she was being paranoid or if he did know more than he had told her. Then either the tear gas or delayed shock made her eyes burn, and she hurried away.

▲

"You're back, I see," said Larsen, as Elinda came in, without adding "finally." Then: "Is something wrong?" They were alone in the office.

"I saw a man shot ten minutes ago." She told him what had happened on the Square. "It was a friend of yours. Robert Strickland."

Larsen faced her expressionlessly, and she realised she had been hoping to jerk some kind of reaction out of him.

"That's terrible," he said. "And they think he planted that bomb?" His voice was measured, as though he was trying to sound more concerned than he was. But then she saw that the colour had faded from his lips. His face seemed to age twenty years. "Shot, you said? Is he alive?" Now she could hear something in his voice, and it sounded like fear.

"I don't think he can be, no."

Larsen nodded and sighed, seemed to relax. Then he grimaced and turned away from her. Almost inaudibly he whispered what sounded like, "Dear god, what next?" His hands fumbled with a paper on his desk, crumpled it, then clenched on each other. "Dear god."

"Did you know him well?" she asked, beginning to feel she had drawn more of a response than she wanted.

"What? No—not well at all. It—it's just such a shock . . . after the bombing."

"They say they found evidence in his rooms that he'd been building a bomb. And when they brought him out, he said—"

"I'm sorry," Larsen interrupted, "I haven't got time to listen now." He turned away and bent over his keyboard.

Half an hour later, Chris came in and told her the underground version of what had happened. It added little to what she already knew, and in the middle of Chris's account Larsen left the office to check on the work in the labs.

At the end of the afternoon, Larsen had not returned. Feeling curious but guilty, Elinda went to look for him. As she had suspected, he was not at the lab. Schneider had spent only five minutes with him, reviewing what she had told him the day before.

It was the end of the afternoon when Elinda found her way to Larsen's home. She had been there only once before and had trouble finding it again. There was a pale yellow glow in one of the downstairs windows, but when she went to the door and knocked there was no response. She knocked again, louder, but still without result, and finally went to peer in the window.

Two white candles in black holders were burning on a coffee table set by the far wall. Larsen was kneeling before them, his back to her, his shoulders hunched, his head lowered. She could see no religious icons, but he seemed to be praying. Faintly through the triple panes, she heard slow, solemn music. His hands were held near to his face, and his shoulders heaved once as though with a heavy sigh. She backed away guiltily, ready to leave him with his private burdens. But then thoughts that had been waiting at the back of her mind suddenly fitted together, and she hammered on the door until it was opened.

Larsen looked at her in surprise.

"I'm sorry to trouble you," she began, "but when you didn't come back this afternoon, I wondered if you were all right—"

"Yes, thank you. It's good of you to be concerned, but it was just a temporary—"

"—and then I thought of something you might not want to talk about in front of Chris."

"To do with this afternoon?"

"Yes."

"I see." He hesitated. "Very well. Come in, then and get warm."

When he switched on the electric light, the room was as stark as it had seemed from the outside. The candles in stubby brass holders still burned on the dark wood table. The walls were pale cream; the furniture, glossy black and dark brown; the floor, polished, amber-coloured wood. She had forgotten Larsen's taste for expensive austerity. He excused himself briefly and returned with two glasses and a green bottle. The label had been removed, but Elinda guessed it had said something like *ExtraSolar Burgundy*. He poured, and handed her a glass, then went and sat down. He moved stiffly, his head high and his back straight, as though going to his own execution. She sat facing him on a hard chair with a thin cushion. From a single loudspeaker behind her the sound of discordant string music started and began to saw at her nerves.

"I overheard you the other day," she began, "when Strickland went to see you in the office. He was still looking for his friend, Erika, then, wasn't he? Before he gave up hope and got angry. I didn't mean to spy on you, but you were both raising your voices, and I was just outside the door."

"Whatever you intended, evidently you did overhear us. I take it you haven't come just to let me hear your confession."

"No. I heard something he said—that you'd helped him, but refused to help her. And in the Square, near the end, before he died, he was talking as though he remembered his life back there."

"Perhaps," Larsen said, "he was one of the lucky majority, who came through the Knot unscathed. Have you considered that?"

"Was he? I could ask around. I could find out."

Larsen met her eyes, then moistened his lips and looked away.

"And when you were talking to him," she went on, "you said something about the hippocampus. That's part of the brain, isn't it? Something to do with memory, perhaps?"

"I won't ask where all this is leading, but I would like to know why you think it concerns you."

"Strickland said if you'd helped her, she wouldn't have gone and done something else, gone to someone else, maybe. Now she's missing. I was looking for a friend too, but we found her. And when we found her, something had been done to her mind.

And now it seems as though she had been looking for someone. So: I'm clutching at straws, but I know of two missing persons, female, both probably looking for someone here—"

"Not necessarily the same person," Larsen interjected.

"But looking for someone. One of them is found with her mind scrambled, and there's some evidence that the other wanted something done to her mind, her memories. I'm trying to find out what happened."

"Let me be sure I understand what you're suggesting here. You believe, I take it, that Strickland came to me, and I did what the experts at the clinic were unable to do, I restored his lost memories. Then, because I refused to do the same for his girlfriend, she ran off to someone who damaged her in some way so that she hasn't been seen since. As a result of either his personal loss, or the trauma of regaining his past, Strickland became unhinged. He detonated a bomb at the dam, and was shot down this afternoon. In other words, you believe I am ultimately responsible for several maimings at the dam work site and for Strickland's death today."

"No, I don't believe that. But I think you do. I saw your face when you got the news each time. That's why I was worried about you today."

Larsen stared at her with an expression she could not fathom. Then he lowered his head and stared down at his hands.

"I can't help you," he said, in a dull, weary voice. "I don't know what your friend might have found, or whom Robert Strickland's friend might have turned to. Please do not ask me for more details of what I did. It was a mistake; I had plans, and they were misguided. The reason I refused to help the poor woman was that I felt I risked being found out if I continued. I am not cut out for heroism." He raised his head to meet her eyes. "Now you know enough to put me in jeopardy, and I have no alternative but to trust you."

He paused, and she waited, feeling sure he was going to add something.

"When you said Strickland had been shot—" he began, and looked up at her—"when you told me he was dead, I was glad. My first feeling at that man's death was relief that he would not be able to give me away. That is what I have been trying to come to terms with since I left the office."

"It's not so terrible," she said, unable to suppress a flicker of sympathy. "It's only human to be afraid for one's self, isn't it?"

"But I had set myself up to be above such pettiness—I had committed hubris. And now I am glimpsing the price."

She had no answer for him.

She wondered why she had come, and prepared to leave; and then her mind started working.

"Just a minute," she said. "You said it was a mistake, just now, restoring that man's past. Was it a mistake because he was what the leaflets said, a criminal—a psychopath or something?"

"I can't talk about this."

"It must have been bad luck, to pick someone who was damaged." She paused, then went on slowly, thinking. "The leaflet didn't say how many like that had got through, but we haven't had an obvious string of crimes. So there couldn't have been that many, could there? And only about a third of them would need their minds restoring. . . . What am I missing here? You did something. Something you won't talk about. And then you gave up after one bad experience."

She stared at him.

"I'm still missing something. How many were there like that waiting to be restored? How many potential monsters? Do you know who they are?" She stopped short, appalled at what had come into her mind, then forced the words out: "Is—is Barbara one?"

Finally he answered, with a bitter smile: "If I said yes, would you ask me if I knew what she had done?" He moistened his lips. "Would you want to know that?"

"Shit." Her nerve failed. Despising herself, she backed off. "All right, tell me this then—what has Carlo been doing, that you could fix people he can't?"

More confidently, but apparently choosing his words with care, Larsen said: "To the best of my knowledge, your friend has been doing whatever he can to make a difficult situation tolerable for himself and those close to him."

"Now that's a reply that raises more questions than it answers."

"If you really want them answered, you'll have to go to someone else." Larsen stood up. "And now, yes, I really have said too much. I wish we could both pretend this meeting had never happened. That's impossible, I know, but it must stop here. I'll say no more."

He ushered her towards the door. "Please go now, and don't talk about this again."

▲

Grebbel did not appear in the cafeteria while Elinda was eating. She considered looking for him at the address she had found from the directory, but decided to postpone that until she had thought things over more. Instead, after dinner she dropped in on Louise and Paulina next door.

She wondered if they would try to probe the state of things between her and Barbara, or between her and Jon Grebbel, but they seemed content to stick to less personal topics. Inevitably, the events in the Square came up. Elinda was the only one who had seen what had happened. "Someone told me he was so easy to find, he might have wanted to be caught," she said. "And it's true, when he grabbed the gun he just stood there. He didn't even try to hide behind the guards. He just stood there and made them shoot him down."

"If it's upsetting you to talk about it," Paulina said, "let's change the subject. Did you see they've released some new satellite data?"

Elinda shook her head. She had been too preoccupied to look at the bulletins.

"You know how big the continental masses are here," Paulina said, "there's hardly anywhere to put the oceans. But they're *deep*. Anything could be going on down there. Well, apparently they've been picking up strange radar contacts from the middle of Dante's Bay—been happening for years, but no one had been able to record more than a vague flicker. Only now there's a clear five-second signal and an infra-red signature to match. The thing's effective temperature was about twenty-eight Celsius, just a bit warmer than the water there. And someone did a computer analysis of the wave patterns around the blip. To cut a long story short, they're talking about a twenty-five-metre tylosaur—a goddamned sea serpent!"

"Someone thought it would be a good idea to take a boat down there," Elinda said. "I wonder if he's changed his mind." She remembered images of black volcanic islands combing the currents, and whole sargassos of gold and crimson vegetation spread on the waves. Now there was something new and purposeful beneath the bright surface.

She sipped Louise's tea, brewed from herbs she grew in their boxes of compost under artificial sunlight. The conversation drifted. Elinda found herself wondering who these people really were, with their apparently inviolable memories of another life. She realised how much the day had been a strain on her.

At the back of her mind was Larsen's question—if she found out that Barbara had been a criminal, how would she handle the knowledge? What would it do to them? She had run from the question in Larsen's home; she wanted to run from it now. But she sensed it would pursue her into her dreams.

"Have you seen the latest bulletin from back there?" Louise was saying. "Langston's campaigning in New England. A pretty face, but the man's a total null. The only good thing in his platform is, he wants to remove sterilisation as a legal penalty. And he got that line from Sherry Tsang. Do you remember seeing either of them? I think they were on one of the broadcasts a couple of weeks ago. We remember them back from when they were running for local governorships—we always had a weakness for a good glitzy bedroom farce, and you can't beat a big election for that. It's one thing we miss out here. . . ."

Elinda's attention had wandered again. Something in what Louise was saying had snagged her attention, but she was unable to focus on it. Too much had happened today. She needed time to think it through. After a few more minutes, she pleaded tiredness and excused herself.

Outside, the wind shrieked and roared through the valley. Snowflakes stung her cheek.

Grebbel materialised from the darkness ahead of her. "Don't run," he said tensely. "It's me. I looked for you, but you weren't in, so I stayed. I was walking around here, waiting. . . ."

"My god, come in out of the wind."

In her house they reached for each other and clung together while the world moaned and shivered about them.

"A bad day," she whispered and wondered how she could have been reluctant to look for him earlier. "You heard what happened in the Square? I was there, I saw it. It was Strickland, the one who lost his girlfriend. I'd talked to him the other day, and then he was just something smashed down at the foot of a wall. And when I got back to work . . . no, never mind."

"What?"

"No, nothing."

"It must be something. To do with what happened at the Square?"

"I can't talk about it; it's not important anyway. What happened to you today? You're as tense as I am. Did you have a bad session at the clinic?"

"I had a session, and it'll be the last one."

"Why? What happened?"

"Nothing happened," he said. "That's the trouble. It's just the same as all the other times. Glimpses of another life, another world. But it's somebody else's life, it's not mine, and I don't know what my life is."

"But you're still going to give up? I'd been thinking it might be best just to let it go after all, but you're so torn up by this—"

"Torn up. Right." He gave a harsh chuckle. "My arm's been shredded, and I haven't a clue why. Was I a part-time lion-tamer? Or maybe the scars mean what they seem to mean. Maybe the thought of coming here was too much and I tried to open my veins at the last minute. I can't even tell if that's ludicrous or not. Or perhaps the leaflets were right, and there's a file on me in some institution, with a twenty-five-dollar name for what put me there. No I'm not giving up. But I'm not going back to that machine either. There's enough evidence in my own mind. Whatever they've been doing to me, it's not getting me any closer to finding out real answers. I opened a man's trachea the other day. I told you. I knew what I was doing, my hands knew." His gloved fingers slid to her neck, pressed coldly against the cartilage of her throat. "Just there. Quick and clean. I'd been trained to do it. I know that, I'm as sure of that as I am of anything." He shook his head, whispered: "If I'm really sure of anything, even of you . . . Christ, I don't know what I mean."

She resisted the temptation to rub her throat, got up to open the blind and look out.

Snow blew across the window, heavier now; the sky was a mass of churning cloud shot through with pale streaks of light. Her breath started to mist the glass.

"It's a cheat," he said suddenly. "A trap. It's—" His voice lowered. "There's something dark here, eating away, in here where my life should be. . . . Secrets." He stopped and turned to her, staring. "You cared too, didn't you? Now you're giving up. And you won't tell me what happened at work today. You too."

He swung her round to face him. "You know and you won't tell—"
Then he stopped. He pushed her away and turned his head to the
sky. His eyes were clenched shut but the pale light glimmered on
his cheeks. "Oh god," he whispered. He twisted his head from side
to side. "I was ready to hurt you. You're all I've got to hold onto,
and I was going to hurt you. I'm scared, Elinda. I don't know
what's happening. Come here. Please come here."

When she went to him his arms gripped her so that she could
hardly breathe.

After a while, he stepped away, stood beside her. He did
not speak but she could hear his ragged breathing. His fingers
quivered in hers. The wind shrieked and fell, shrieked again. She
cleared her throat. "I think," she said, "I'd better tell you what I
found out this afternoon."

The next morning, while she and Larsen inspected a new batch of
corn seedlings, Elinda told him she had betrayed his confidence.

"When you decide to do a thing, you waste no time, do you?"
he said. The dawn wind roared outside. Rain and hail rattled on
the window. "Is there something in you that insists on putting
yourself in the wrong? I suppose you have a reason for this?"

She started to tell him about Grebbel.

He nodded. "I know of the man. Menzies, his foreman, was my
associate. If you know so much, I may as well tell you that. He has
mentioned your Mr. Grebbel to me too."

"Will you help him, then? Will you do whatever it is you've
done before?"

"After what happened yesterday?"

"But that was because you wouldn't help her—Erika."

"Or because I did 'help' poor Strickland."

"In this case, you'd do more harm by refusing Jon. He's
suffering," she said. "I don't know what he'll do if he can't get
help."

"A suggestively vague threat," Larsen said. He peered at
a discoloured leaf, put the plant aside for examination later.
"Meaning, I take it, that what I decide will determine not only
this man's welfare, but perhaps yours and my own as well." He
bent and tightened a clamp on one of the nutrient hoses. "I

already told you I'm not the stuff heroes are made of." He did not look at her. "Give me time to think. If I can schedule something, Menzies will contact your friend."

▲

In Barbara's lab the door was open and Osmon, the technician, was coming out. "I have to go in for a minute," Elinda said. "There's some data I need for the Greenhouse here."

He hesitated, then smiled. "As you like. But I'll have to be locking up in five minutes."

She switched on Barbara's computer and entered the password. When she brought up the file directory, it was incomprehensible at first. Then she mentally eliminated files that were clearly part of Barbara's work. A few stood out. FAILSAFE, for one, and RABBIT.

She debated whether to try guessing Barbara's other passwords, but then checked the memory storage. Four of the files, including the two she had noticed, were empty.

She switched off. A clumsy, and probably hurried, piece of cover-up. But by whom? Security? She had to assume so, which meant she should stay away from this terminal, in case it was monitored.

She flipped through the desk drawer until she found the memory stick Grebbel had copied the files onto. Stupid not have devised a safer arrangement for getting the files to her. But if Security were still keeping a low profile, maybe whoever had sabotaged the online memory wouldn't have come into the lab and gone through the backups yet. She put the stick in her pocket and left before Osmon returned to lock up.

▲

Through chilly rain squalls she hurried up the hill to her home, went to the couch and from under the seat cushion she pulled the papers she had found in Barbara's room. She scanned them quickly, selected half a dozen sheets that looked promising and took them with her.

Then she made the long walk back through the rising wind past the Greenhouse. She opened the office and switched on her computer.

When she loaded them, the files Grebbel had copied seemed to be intact. She looked at the sheets with Barbara's writing and tried to decide which one might hold the password.

It took an hour. Several times the files erased themselves when she entered too many wrong guesses, and she had to reload them from the stick. But finally she unlocked them.

FAILSAFE contained the text of the leaflet, with instructions to broadcast it if Barbara failed to get in touch the following morning. It must date from the time Barbara had vanished. And it must have been sent over the net, to Jessamyn. She closed her eyes and took several long, deep breaths.

This certainly wasn't going to get Barbara off the hook. If Security had found this and they were going to try to hang the bombing on her as well, there seemed to be only one way out. She would have to follow Barbara's tracks and prove that Barbara had been right.

She opened the file named RABBIT. It evidently consisted of some dialogues held over the computer net. The original exchanges must have been in volatile storage, forcing Barbara to make notes afterwards. A few times and dates had been highlighted, and some of the entries had received comments in capital letters: OTHERS BEFORE ME? E.F.? Near the end was an entry that read: *Trap 01:00. Recorder. Weapon?*

Elinda winced. Setting traps and looking for hidden things? She shook her head Then finally she remembered what the nurse had said about Barbara's compulsion to keep moving and her hint about a cave.

EIGHT

"Just what I needed," said Grebbel. "I'm barely off the shuttle, hardly got to know her, and she drags me up the side of a mountain." They had stopped on a bend of the trail, where it gave a clear view into the valley. The settlement was spread out below them, as he hadn't seen it since his first night in the dirigible, but this time clear and detailed in the daylight. A truck edged back across the causeway to the near bank, like an ant on a pencil. As it turned, its windshield caught the light and for an instant became a tiny sun.

Elinda scowled. "Sourpuss. Misery. I even did without the ropes and the ice axe just to make it easier for you."

"Hah. I bet you wouldn't know one end of an ice axe from the other." He paused, frowning, "When we . . ."

"When we what? When we who? Jon? Have you remembered something?"

He paused, then shook his head. "No, just a funny feeling. It's gone now. So where's this cave you want to look in?"

"It's a place Barbara and I sometimes hiked to," she said. "Farther along the valley and up. I don't think we're going to get there before dark. I still think in terms of twenty-four-hour days half the time when I try to plan things."

And maybe, Grebbel thought, *you're not totally happy about bringing another lover to one of your former trysting spots.*

"Oh, look," she cried, and pointed. Out of the sun's red glare, riding down the wind, the pair of raptors came sweeping towards them. Steel blue wings cut the air like scimitars; the crimson heads and orange crests might have been arrowheads loosed from a titan's bow. The two creatures passed twenty metres below them, their round, amber eyes staring, the talons at the first wing joint clearly visible, and the needle teeth in their jaws.

"Scaly eagles," she whispered. "Such an ugly name. I've never seen them this close before." She leaned against Grebbel and he put his arm around her shoulders.

The two eagles dwindled down the length of the valley until they were almost out of sight. Then they banked and turned across it, two drifting flecks of light against the bluish foliage the trees. They soared over the river and back towards the head of the valley, where the elongated bubble of a dirigible was gliding into their territory. If they mobbed it, they were now too far away to be seen.

Elinda let her head rest on Grebbel's shoulder. "It's still the same, isn't it?" she said. "We keep teasing each other, playing games, because we don't know what's real behind the play. Even now, even here."

He rubbed her neck, his gloved fingers stiff and clumsy and comforting. "Let's leave the masks on," he said. "Right now, the play's the thing."

They followed the trail almost up to what passed for the treeline, where it widened into a clearing that overlooked the valley. Clouds of green creatures the size of houseflies buzzed in the shade, but did not approach them, but once Elinda was bitten by something that lurched away through the air and fell to the ground, twitching.

Slabs of grey stone were thinly covered by earth where spongy turquoise leaves grew among fallen boughs that looked like the limbs of fallen dragons or angels, and the trees formed a living shield between them and the rock face. Spray from a hidden waterfall glimmered in the shade there, and that dark wall swayed and shivered with the voice of the sea.

Grebbel prowled, examining the site.

"Does this suit Madame? Let's see if I have this right. Note the scenic view from the front bedroom, and the fashionably elegant decor in grey, brown, and leaf blue. The lighting is entirely natural, and it comes with its own built-in timing mechanism specially adapted to this planet. And, here, the back bedroom leads to a bathroom with shower and constant cold running water. Over there is the eastern bedroom. And in the western bedroom we have—someone half buried under a collapsed tent."

"That's okay, there's no real hurry. Finish your guided tour, sit down and have a good laugh before you come and help."

"We obviously learned this in different schools. The way I was taught, you look around for the best spot *before* you pitch the tent; it saves the effort of keeping it on the poles when you move it. But I suppose your way's more interesting. *That* goes in *there*."

"It's out of the wind here; the nearest glacier's five kilometres away; I know for a fact that the chances of being hit by avalanches, lava flows, meteorites and—giant squid are no more than twenty percent in this particular spot. And we can look across the valley without getting up. Or do you want to do a geological survey first?"

"That's a thought," he said. "But I don't think we've got time."

She stuck out her tongue, and he grinned and backed to the entrance. "Hand me the pegs, and I'll fix the guy ropes."

When it was done, they lay in the tent, looking across the valley. Far to the south a trail of smoke grew from a pale blue peak. Orange light flickered at its crest. They watched it and heard only the wind and a trickle of water. "Well," she asked finally, "how's the western bedroom now?"

"I admit I've seen worse. There's no snow on the ground, for one thing." He frowned. "It can be rough, camping in the mountains, in the snow. . . . What are you doing?"

"A survey—what does it feel as though I'm doing? A geological survey." She put her tongue out again.

"Come on," she said a little later. "Wise guy, tent erector. *That* goes in *there*."

"So it does," he whispered. "My god."

"You may be wondering," she said, frowning in concentration, breathing rapidly, "why else I asked you here today."

"No . . . actually, I . . . No."

"I was—hoping—to remind you. Of certain things. Now that you've decided to look for your past . . . by yourself. In case . . . in case you had any ideas of—giving up . . ."

"Who said—?" he began, and lost the thread of his thought. After a while he tried again. "Who said . . . I was giving up . . . anything? I didn't say that."

But now she was beyond replying. Her eyes had closed and her face was soft, though she gasped like a woman drowning. At each movement he made, she moaned and writhed as though her nerve endings had been stripped bare. He watched her with a remote intensity, in fresh astonishment at what a simple motion could trigger in her. Then she screamed. And her convulsions tore him from his detachment and flung him across an echoing, void.

She came back slowly, like a great chord booming and shimmering into silence. The sunlight dappled the tent roof, flirted with her eyelids when she let them close to feel herself closer to him.

They lay together until hunger roused them and they dressed to find the food in their packs and collect wood for a fire. There were piles of dry leaves for kindling. The fallen branches that they piled onto the fire burned aromatically with yellow flames and a thin blue smoke that eddied above the trees and was lost along the upper slopes of the mountain.

The next morning, they packed the tent and set out again. The path was muddier now as she led the way through the watery afternoon sunlight. They came round a stone outcrop, and stopped. A creature like a maroon, six-legged bear stood in the middle of the trail, half-heartedly nibbling at wiry scrub. It raised its eyeless head towards them, and patterns of light and shade rippled over the hair on its flank, then froze into place as though it was sensing them with its coat.

"What is it?" Grebbel whispered. "I'm not sure. I've heard of sightings, a few tracks. "

He took a step forward.

She grabbed at his arm. "Wait. What are you doing?" He was bending to pick up a long rib of frond, like a spear, and going forward again. Suddenly there was a thin shriek above them and a small black creature fluttered down. It landed near the bear and scuttled to it, pulled itself up by the long fur. In a moment the outline of the bear's head changed and two small black eyes stared forward.

The bear shook itself as though waking up, then swung its head from side to side and hissed at Grebbel. Its mouth was a black and cruel-looking beak.

Grebbel stopped and took a step to one side. The compound creature hissed again, then quietly trotted past them along the trail and vanished behind the outcropping they had just passed.

Elinda and Grebbel looked at each other wide-eyed, then suddenly burst out laughing. But the sound seemed so out of place, they fell quiet again. "And what were you planning to do with that pointed stick?" she asked.

He shrugged and dropped it. "I wasn't sure it would get out of our way. Probably wouldn't have, the way we found it. What do they say—two minds are better than one?"

"Even if they're in the same head?" she asked, and immediately wished she hadn't. "We're almost there. Around this bend."

Ahead of them a cliff gleamed like a brow ridge. Beyond a screen of vegetation the dim sun showed a dark opening. "Palace Cave," she said, and then was reluctant to say more.

They made their way into the entrance. There were marks in the earth that might have been bootprints, but she could not guess how recent they might be. "Flashlights now," she said, but Grebbel was already unpacking his.

The cave seemed to be empty. Their lights glimmered on grey limestone, the roof receding in narrowing crevices up into the cliff. "Barbara left something here?" Grebbel asked. "Any idea what we're looking for? I don't see any tracks."

She went forward cautiously, crouching under the low roof. "Anything at first." She realised she was whispering. The air was damp and musty and filled with the murmur of trickling water. "Careful. It goes down here; it's like a couple of steps." After ten paces, the ceiling was high enough for them to stand, and the cave opened to the right to form a small chamber hidden from the outside.

Uncomfortably, she recalled the last time she had been in this cave. Barbara had prowled restlessly, climbing ledges and testing out the echoes of her voice.

She glanced back Grebbel was standing stiffly just under the higher ceiling. His face was drawn, his eyes closed. The flashlight in his hand twitched, and sent a fan of light along the pleated wall.

"Jon, what's wrong?"

"The air in here . . . at the bottom step, I thought I smelled . . ." His voice shook. "No. Forget it." He cocked his head. "Listen to the water dripping, further in. These caves must go right into the mountain."

"You want to go that way? There's a place we had through here. . . . I'd like to look there myself."

"Okay. I'll call if I find anything."

Elinda had been unpacking their lunch, that last occasion, listening to her call back as she explored. When she went to fetch her, Barbara had vanished, her voice throbbing out of the empty air in the main cave. The sounds had seemed to come from everywhere, and Barbara had decided to play hide and seek. It was ten minutes before Elinda, following the calls of "warmer" or "colder," had found the way up to the hidden cleft in the wall.

This time it took longer and she found the layer of soil and rock fragments on the floor thicker than she had remembered, a pile of dead leaves that looked like an abandoned nest, a litter of what must be bones and broken eggshells, and two or three angular fist-sized lumps that must have broken from the ceiling.

If Barbara had been here she'd hidden her tracks pretty thoroughly.

Before she could do more than start sifting through the debris, Grebbel called and then reappeared, "I think there is something in there." he said somberly. "If I'm right we probably ought to find it together."

"Just a moment. It's so quiet, it used to be beautiful in here with just the torchlight." She reached up on tiptoe to where a stalactite grew above their heads, and touched it, finger to finger. She felt a bead of moisture transfer itself, and when she brought her hand down into the light, a bright transparent gem quivered on her fingertip.

His arms slid around her. The light clicked off and for the duration of a few more breaths they held each other in the dark, in the stone dream.

They switched on their lights and edged into the mountain. Grey walls enclosed them, with the steady trickle of water sounding somewhere out of sight. Was there a flicker of motion just at the edge of the lights, a quick rustling, almost too soft to hear? The beams flickered over columns and spears of stone, impending swords, the walls of tunnels and chimneys. To Elinda it suddenly felt like entering a stark and sombre dream.

Together they worked their way downward. Every minute or so, Grebbel pulled out a chisel and scraped a cross in the wall as a marker. Often they were only centimetres apart; their breathing and the scrape of their footsteps seemed the only sounds in the world, and a word spoken would resound between them from the cold rock walls.

Grebbel's breathing was becoming ragged, though he had shown no sign of exertion on the climb up. On a bulge of rock his boot slipped. He cursed and flung himself against the wall. A piece of rock the size of his fist fell and shattered with a sound like a hand grenade.

He said nothing. With their lights lowered she could barely see his face. After a while his breathing became quieter and they went on. Their hands brushed together and he linked his fingers in hers.

Finally they entered a cavern where the sound of water seemed to come from all sides. They switched off their lights. The limestone spines and columns were dimly illuminated. "Daylight," he whispered. "We're near another entrance."

"I think I can hear the river," she said.

"We're still high," he said. "But not all that far from the buildings."

"You're right," she whispered. "I can smell it now. Something rotting."

"The air must circulate freely through all these caves, or it would have been obvious earlier."

"It could just be an animal that crawled away to die. Or one that was hibernating and didn't make it."

"Of course it could," he said, switching on his light, "for all we know. Let's go on."

A few minutes later he flashed the light onto something in a crack in the ground. She looked. A piece of brown and green ceramic in the shape of an oak leaf—a large and clumsy earring.

I've been through this before, she thought. *Once was enough.*

Their search ended soon afterwards, in a gallery that narrowed to a chink between stone pedestals. A shape like a sack of potatoes lay in the dark. Elinda's flashlight beam touched it briefly and flicked away.

"The missing woman, I imagine," Grebbel muttered. "What was her name?"

"Erika Frank," Elinda said, staring. She shook her head, unable to look away. "Look. She was crawling. She was trying to get further into the mountain. There isn't even any water."

"Thirst isn't the most painful way to die in this situation. Hunger is worse. And the cold would hurry things along." He was bending over the remains. "I wonder if there's any clue to what sent her here."

"Don't touch her."

"What's wrong?" When he faced Elinda, Grebbel's eyes glistened deep in their sockets and his forehead was oily with sweat.

"You look like a predator, crouching over her like that," she whispered. "Let's get out. We'll have to leave her; we can't carry her without a stretcher or something. We'll have to come back, or I'll tell Security, and they'll fetch her. And I'll tell Barbara, I'll have to find a way to tell Barbara."

"Do you still want to look for whatever Barbara was planning to do here?"

"No. I don't think she got here. I think she wanted or was supposed to come here, but she fell near where I found her, and didn't get any farther."

⁂

In her bedroom the following evening, Elinda returned to the recorder that held all that was left to her of Barbara's last day of sanity. She scraped the battery contacts with her nail file, experimented with the device's little set of filters. But even after she recharged the battery and turned the volume up all the way, nothing came from the tiny speaker but hisses and dull rushing sounds, faint bursts of crackling and the banality of the last words Barbara uttered as herself.

"Testing, testing . . ."

And then only wind and echoes again.

⁂

After his last session with the memory machine, Grebbel had gone down to the river. Twice he had flung stones into the dark for minutes at a time until his arms felt like jelly. Once he caught himself screaming something. But as soon as he stopped, with his throat still aching, the words vanished from his mind and there was just the cold, the wind and the alien night.

Finally he had gone back to the lab, spent half an hour inoculating water samples onto culture plates, then sat at his computer and logged on to the main database. He searched for data on his past. Street names, restaurants, newspapers. Nothing brought a thrill of recognition. He gave up and walked back to the truck park. When a truck came free he worked the rest of the morning, trying to put all his energy into the job and ignore the confusion in his mind. But when he went for lunch, nothing had resolved itself.

Outside the cafeteria, he met Partridge swaying along in his black exoskeleton.

"How's tricks?"

Partridge pivoted to face him. "Fine. Just great. See, I'm turning somersaults, I'm so pleased."

"What's up, then?"

"Nothing's up, except bits of the generating station, maybe. These joints are wearing again. Grating. Hard on my nerves, that's all. I used to see a man about some—graphite lubricant, I think he called it. But now he can't get it for me. I'm down here, just where I always wanted to be, stirring the mud with my tin toes. People keep treating me as some sort of free bulletin board, when they don't think I'm the greatest guinea pig for new inventions. The sky's up, five hundred klicks up, and I'm not. There's a saboteur on the loose trying to kill us all. Everything's great."

Grebbel saw the tremor in the man's hand, the tight muscles in his neck and cheeks. *Withdrawal symptoms,* his mind said, and began to calculate.

"There's something you need?" Grebbel asked. "Something like 'graphite lubricant' to make life go more smoothly." He had the sense he'd done this before, finding a cure for people's ills.

"That won't fix anything. It won't get me out of here any more than your memory's gonna be brought back tomorrow." Partridge squinted around at the shadows and the long swathes of light from the cafeteria windows. "But it would help. Keep away some of the night sweats."

"Any preference?"

"All right! The man's only been here a couple of hours and he's got the whole pharmacy dropping into his hands. How about you find out what there is first, then what you can get a hold of, before you start trying to do business? Advice from a pro—more than you deserve . . . At any rate, that's what they tell me. I don't know anything, except what I hear. Clean freebase, that's good enough."

"Right," Grebbel said. "But who says I'm trying to do business?"

Partridge shrugged. "Sure. You're just making idle conversation, same as usual." He peered down the valley, at the aurora and moonlit snow streaming across the mountain peaks. "Real nice weather we're having, wouldn't you say?"

"If I were trying to do business, would it be worth my while? What could you have that I might want?"

"Me? All I've got is what's common knowledge. Like the fact that some folk here don't have all their memories; and what they get given back in return isn't always a good imitation—but sometimes it is. And some farmer types know more than they need just to keep the turnips growing. Or so people say. I don't necessarily believe a word of it. But then my thoughts don't flow as smooth as they did when they were properly lubricated."

"Okay," said Grebbel. "I can take a hint."

⋏

Elinda watched the recovery party come down from the valley wall with Erika Frank's body wrapped up on a stretcher. She attended the memorial service, where Dr. Henry talked about the dangers of exploring a world that was perhaps less well understood than it seemed. She listened to the gossip and debate that briefly flared afterwards but did not participate. The fragility of human relationships oppressed her. She could not understand how anything human could survive its own internal changes and conflicts, let alone the threats from a mostly hostile outside world. Remembering Robert Strickland's desperate need and what it had led to, she wanted to weep.

She visited Barbara twice, and came away depressed after finding only silence and blank unawareness. She remembered Barbara scrambling out on a spur of rock over a hundred-metre drop, to where an iridescent insect was shrilling its life out in the webs of a carnivorous plant. She had worked the trap apart and eased the dark living jewel into her hands, almost undamaged. She had lifted her cupped hands to hear it whirring against her palms. Then she had flung it into the air and spread her arms, and laughed at Elinda's concern as the wind fluttered her jacket like wings.

Now, looking down at her, Elinda felt a crippling sense of loss, as though something small and achingly precious were sinking away into darkness.

Grebbel had become quiet and withdrawn, seemingly unwilling to do more than the work he had agreed to. Whenever she found him in the lab he was busy running tests with Osmon, the paper-maker. But she saw that his computer was connected to the library database, as if he was still searching for his past. She visited him once in his room and they made love that night, with a cold urgency that left her feeling bruised and empty the next morning.

At work, Larsen deflected her questions about helping Grebbel. Now that the injured were being released from the overflow rooms in the clinic and there was more room to work, he spent several afternoons in the lab helping set up the germination experiments. Chris passed on the news that Freya, the head of the Factory, had changed lovers, and the chief of Security was said to be pregnant.

Elinda met Louise for lunch one day when the sun was up, and they were outside, watching a dirigible taking video pictures of the settlement when the contrail of an incoming shuttle split the sky like a knife-cut. "Just like home," Louise said, as the tiny spearhead of light vanished beyond the mountains and a sound like distant thunder filtered down to them. "Well, almost." The two raptors had reappeared and were mobbing the dirigible.

Then came the weekly dance at the tavern.

She had told Grebbel about it; they had arranged to meet. She had put on her best black jeans and some makeup. And he was late. She sat at one of the tables that had been pulled near the wall. Coloured lanterns hung from the ceiling, branches that looked something like evergreens had been pinned to the walls, and gave off a faint, slightly metallic aroma. At the far end, the band was setting up: a short, intense-looking man with pale vivid eyes was tuning a violin. He produced two or three screeching sounds and then something that sounded like two cats in heat or in agony. Behind him were a couple of guitars, a small drum set, an accordion no one had claimed yet. The tune-up went on with abrupt bursts of jagged rhythm interspersed with squawks and whines from the amplifiers; she was reminded of more creatures in distress or ecstasy.

The room was filling up around her. She scanned faces coming in, and Grebbel was not among them. In the crowd she thought she saw Carlo, and then she did see Chris with a short, dark girl in a white sweater. She even thought she spotted Dr. Henry. The band had assembled and seemed to have finished their preparations. The lights dimmed. A yellow spot lit the stage, and the first chords crashed out. After a minute, Elinda got up and worked her way to the bar.

When she came back with a whiskey sour, the dance floor was full. She sipped her drink and looked around for Grebbel again. At the end of one number, Chris and his girl caught sight of her, came and sat down. He introduced the girl as Marsha, and she smiled vaguely at Elinda, who tried to estimate how much of their pupil size was due to the subdued lighting.

"You hear the latest about the guy who did the generators?" Chris asked.

"I saw them get him," she reminded him for Marsha's benefit. "What else?"

"They think he did the power line last winter, too," Marsha said.

"And probably the leaflets," said Elinda, "and the last five computer crashes; I expect he spent his weekends blocking drains, pushing kids in the fishpond and corroding the water pipes."

If the others caught her sarcasm, they gave no sign of it.

"Guy was nuts," Chris said, "a real wig. Gotta be. Deserved all he got."

"I thought," said Elinda, "they would be looking for accomplices. He might not have done it by himself."

"Nah, they're easing off," Chris said expansively. "They got what they wanted, probably his accomplice too, they can't afford to keep half the labour pool playing watchdog."

"Chris, who tells you these things?" she said, trying to sound amused.

"Oh, just things you hear."

"When I was fixing the motherboard in Nixie's terminal," said Marsha, "Gerry—you know Gerry Sugamoto? Oh, well, he's the technical officer in Admin, and he told me there was a new message going on the Security computer net about the leaflets—

they're writing it off, too much bad publicity. I hear lots of things like that."

"Maybe I'm in the wrong career," Elinda said, and wondered if she could glean anything else without seeming too inquisitive. But then the band started again, and the other two got up to dance.

There was still no sign of Grebbel. The music drove at her like heavy surf. She picked up her glass and found it was empty. On her way to the bar, Jessamyn looked up from a corner table and watched her expressionlessly.

As she returned with her drink, a man moved to her table. "Do you mind if I join you for a moment or two?"

She turned, ready to object, and stopped. It was Dr. Henry.

"Just for a few moments," he repeated, and smiled.

"I was waiting for someone—but no, of course, please sit down."

"Thank you. I noticed you seemed restless. But I need to sit down for a while, and there aren't that many tables available. Should we introduce ourselves? I'm never sure if it's presumptuous of me to assume people know who I am when I'm out of my normal environment."

"Oh, I recognised you, I'm sure everyone does," she said, and told him her name.

"And you're much too polite to ask, but you're wondering whatever possessed me to come here like this. Actually, that reveals something about you. If you came here regularly, you'd know that I'm here quite often. Noblesse oblige. I'll tell you in strictest confidence, I'm not much more comfortable here than you are. This isn't my ideal kind of music, either."

"What makes you say that about me?"

"I was watching you," he said. "When the music starts, you look as though you're riding punches. It's doing something to you, but you're not sure you like it."

Defensively she said, "Is that what you come here for, to watch the other customers?"

"Well, some are more worth watching than others. But what sort of an official would I be if I didn't take some democratic interest in the pleasures of the majority? One can't listen to string quartets in the ivory tower all day, after all. And this is a strange society, given to all sorts of quirks and foibles. Individuals going off on strange tracks, following their own secret convictions, pursuing private needs and telling no one. It's as well to have a finger on the pulse so to speak.

"And if you stay around, you'll find the reason I'm here tonight." He lowered his voice a little and leaned towards her as the music continued. "As your friend isn't turning up, why don't you tell me what you do?"

"I help feed us all, when there aren't too many distractions in the way of sabotage threats."

"Well, I think you'll find that's all taken care of now."

"You think so?" She took a breath and plunged on. "Maybe he had help. Aren't you trying to find out?"

He laughed. "Please don't look at me as though I'm judge, jury and god almighty. If I didn't know better, I'd think you were trying to flatter me. I don't have any final authority on what sort of investigation is carried out. I'm just an experimental psychologist who got kicked upstairs into administration. Thank god, they still let me find time for some research work now and then."

"Is that what brings you here, then? Looking for experimental subjects?" She wondered if she could turn the talk back to the state of the investigation.

He laughed again and leaned back a little. "That makes me sound like one of those mad scientists in the horror films, prowling the night with evil eyes aglow. It's true in a way, but I've found my subject for tonight—you'll see. Actually, I've never really aspired as far as evil—just a little roguery now and then. I don't suppose I could interest you—"

"In some roguery? Not tonight, thanks. Only on the sixth Thursday, provided there's an *r* in the month."

"Well, how about a little experimental mnemonic therapy?"

"That sounds very much like the same thing. What makes you think I'm in need of what you offer?"

"My dear, I've been what I am long enough to know the signs. I admit I wasn't more than eighty percent sure until you asked just now, but that's close enough. And I would like volunteers: I'm still modifying some of my procedures, and a willing subject is invaluable." He waited until she nodded for him to go on. "Let me explain. That machine we use in the clinic is human in at least one respect—it has a great deal of unused potential. With the right software, and the right concepts behind that software, it's not clear where its ultimate limits will lie. Right now, I'm exploring its possibilities as a therapeutic tool—a way of realising and adjusting the contents of an inaccessible mind. I like to think of it as the equivalent of the light-pipe that lets a surgeon explore the blood vessel he's trying to unblock—the same light-pipe that then carries the laser beam that burns away the blockage. But at the moment, we're still running tests and calibrations. So your help would be most welcome, and you'd be helping the advance of medical science. No, really."

"Sorry, really. I've got too much going on right now to get involved in anything like that."

"Ah, a great pity. But I know when a lady has her mind made up. Though that doesn't mean I may not try again when the portents are more auspicious. In the meantime, though, please forgive my unchivalrous departure, but I must try and collect my innocent victim before midnight comes. *Lente, lente currite, noctis equi.*"

He stood and gave a brief ironic bow and was gone.

She turned to look for Grebbel once more, but the mass of faces near the entrance were all unfamiliar. As she turned away, she caught sight of Jessamyn again, watching her from the far side of the room. Jessamyn turned and spoke to the woman sitting beside her, then looked back at Elinda with a gaze that was openly curious.

Elinda looked at her empty glass and decided to get another drink.

When she returned to her seat, a couple of spotlights had been turned on the stage, and Dr. Henry was standing up there with a tall blonde woman. He drew polite laughter by saying he had been asked to justify his place here, and then started talking about the untapped potentials of the human mind and body.

She knew what Grebbel was doing. He was with Larsen, and he hadn't made the effort to tell her. She wondered if he would know her whenever he saw her next.

Henry was talking in quiet insistent tones to the blonde woman on the stage.

"When I snap my fingers, you'll remember only that you want to walk to the far end of the stage and come back. What you remember is what you are, and what you are is what you do. What I tell you to you remember is, for the next five minutes, what you'll be."

The woman's eyes closed, her face went slack. Only a moderately deep trance, he told the audience. The woman turned her back and began describing the people at the nearest tables. She accurately recalled hair colours, missing buttons, a cracked lens in a pair of spectacles.

"It might seem from this display," he said, "that the capacity of the human memory is bottomless. But if the information the young lady is recalling right now is to be available tomorrow, or next week, it has to be stored where it can be found. And here is the problem. When some of us came through the Knot, parts of that stored memory were lost. Not destroyed, necessarily, but mislaid. Imagine editing a play by taking out every speech by one character, every mention of him. You might make very little difference at all, but if it's a good play, with a job for every character, you'll change its meaning, you'll probably reduce it to gibberish. . . ."

Suddenly the performance sickened her. There were too many questions in her head. She picked up her coat.

▲

At the end of that afternoon's shift, Menzies had approached Grebbel. "Your girlfriend told you about us, I think—Niels and me—that we might help you."

Grebbel had nodded, tight-lipped.

"I think we might have something for you today, if you still want it."

"Of course I do!" Grebbel took a couple of breaths. "I'm very grateful."

"Give me a minute to finish checking this motor here, and we'll go on over."

Grebbel put his hands in his pockets and peered past Menzies' shoulder, then walked round the other side of the truck, watching the ice sheets turn purple-grey and a whorl of clouds build as evening crept towards them. The winds were still quiet; he wondered if that meant more fury when they did rise.

He came back to the front. "Anything I can do to help?"

"Try standing where I can't see you, or stop fidgeting."

"Sorry."

He thought of Elinda, and wondered what they would be to each other two hours from now—who or what he might be.

He pulled his hands out of his pockets and looked at them. The fingers quivered. In the dim light the scars were almost invisible. They held more of his past than the shell of memory he had been found here.

"You ready, or are you going to spend the evening moongazing?" Grebbel turned. "Yes," he said quietly. "I'm quite ready."

They walked away from the river. Grebbel could make out footprints in the gravel path, and wheel ruts, but he did not recognise the route they were taking. The sky was a deep violet, with two stars pricking through gaps in the cloud, and one moon shining clear. After a few minutes he heard the sound of a stream.

Menzies muttered, "We'll stop by the waterfall."

The fall was about a couple of metres high. The stream billowed over it in a dull roar, making a dim flapping whiteness like sheets on a clothesline. Just below the fall, the path turned inland along the bank and passed a hollow under vertical slabs of rock like a tent at the crest of the falls. Branches tossed in a first gust. Green lights flickered among the undergrowth. A man was standing there.

"Mr. Grebbel, is it?" the man said. "Make yourself comfortable. There's a dry ledge outside this cleft, and you can sit with your back to the rock. I don't think we're been formally introduced, but I believe you know who I am."

"You're Niels Larsen," Grebbel said into the fog of water sound. "This is a strange place for a therapy session."

"Treat it as an initiation. We have to decide how committed you are to recovering your former identity." The rush of the falls hid almost tone and inflection, leaving a bare outline of a voice.

"I don't understand how I'm supposed to convince you."

"We'll come to that in a moment. You realise that the restoration is not easy."

"I'm willing to do anything you want to pay for your efforts."

"I wasn't referring to our difficulties, Mr. Grebbel," Larsen said. "I meant the difficulties of the subject—yourself. For some hours or days the subject must expect to struggle with two identities. There is the personality he has lived as in order to accommodate the memories he acquired here, and the old personality built on the original memories. The subject must identify his true past and integrate his two personalities. The process is difficult, if not actively painful. There is no way to carry out a normal existence and pretend that nothing is wrong while one undergoes it. You would call attention to yourself—and to us—very quickly. The simplest solution is to carry out the treatment while the subject is incapacitated by some genuine injury or illness that can be used to mask his disorientation. In the past, we were opportunistic—we would wait for a suitable virus infection to strike, or an accident at the work site—until we decided to abandon our plans altogether. In the present case, a more direct approach seems necessary, since we must be cautious now. And conveniently, that also gives us a test of the subject's commitment."

"I see."

"I hope you do. We are working in your best interests—but we also must safeguard ourselves. We have trusted you enough to reveal our identities. Now we ask you to trust us in this."

"What am I supposed to do?" Grebbel asked. "Dive off this rock? We'd both find that a bit hard to explain, wouldn't we?"

The wind was rising, sounding like a river. Clouds rolled across the stars.

"You went for an evening walk," Larsen said. "It got dark among the trees earlier than you expected and you weren't sure of the path any more, so you started hurrying to get back before it got too dark to see. You failed to notice the ledge in time, and you slipped and fell."

"You think they'd buy that?"

"They will," Larsen said, "if they've no reason to be suspicious; and I wasn't intending to give them any cause to be."

"So, if anything goes wrong, it's my own fault."

Something screeched twice above them, sailing the wind.

Larsen shrugged. "I'm merely stating the conditions under which we can help you. I understand that you want to postpone the injury, if not the decision itself, as long as possible, but we haven't got all night."

Grebbel swallowed. "I don't think much of your sales pitch—"

"We are not selling soap, Mr. Grebbel. Lives are involved in this."

"—but if you want proof, I'll give you proof of sincerity."

He turned towards the rock and swung his hand. There was a wet thud and his arm filled with sick pain to the shoulder. He staggered, went down on one knee. Then he turned towards them with a rock in his other hand.

His arm came up in front of his face and struck like a snake. Struck again.

Before they could reach him, he had slipped to his knees. He could taste the blood in his mouth.

"Proof," he gasped. "Proof of commitment. You want more?"

Menzies grasped Grebbel's wrist and twisted the rock from his hand. He got an arm under Grebbel's shoulders and tried to lift him. Grebbel wrenched free. "I'll stand by myself. When I'm ready. Are you convinced? I can do more." He lurched upright. "Whatever it takes. You talked about trust. What does it take to buy your trust?"

"Enough. That's enough now," Larsen said harshly. "Let's get you some attention. You're going into shock."

"I'll walk. I'll walk by myself."

To the south, lightning arced over the mountains. Rain blew into the men's faces.

The other two stayed on either side of Grebbel, and at the edge of the trees, when the light from the Square reached him and he stumbled from grass to gravel and his eyes rolled up, they reached out and caught him as he fell.

NINE

Outside the tavern Elinda hesitated. In a black, churning sky, the moons glinted and vanished, ice-blue lightning arced. The wind sent spiked rags of tree membrane scuttling along the High Street. A few raindrops spattered on the road. She had no reason to go home yet, and there was still the chance that Grebbel would turn up. She walked off at random, aiming to come past the tavern again as often as necessary, until either he did appear or the wind got the better of her.

Then, *No*, she decided. *No.* He had just forgotten. This was a world of erratic memory after all. She would go and give him a polite reminder. Very polite. Icicle-in-liquid-nitrogen polite.

And he would . . . ? Laugh at her? Fall on his knees and apologise? Ask her what the hell she was doing there uninvited? Lower the pseudo-whisky bottle and peer at her in bewilderment?

Or if he was out? If his living room, his home, his bed was empty?

And some other bed was occupied. Or—

It's colder near the water, isn't it? She inhaled sharply at the memory of hiking the trail with Charley.

Then she found she was heading for the clinic, and the tightness in her chest confirmed that she had not gone that way by chance. *He's late*, she thought, *he's stood you up, and you're already seeing him wrapped in bandages or . . . How long have you known him, for Christ's sake?*

She would give him until tomorrow morning. Then if he didn't turn up, she would go to Security. But not before then. To go now would be to tempt fate.

As she was about to turn away, a side door opened and a man came out of the clinic. He kept to the shadows and walked quickly, huddled against the wind, but she thought she recognised him in the shimmer from the sky. She was curious enough to follow at a distance.

He seemed preoccupied, his hands clenched at his sides, his head lowered as he hurried past the darkened homes and the spidery or convoluted Earthborn evergreens that grew from boxes in front gardens. Even before he turned onto White Falls Crescent, she was sure it was Larsen. But what could he have been doing? Not even he would be checking on the lab experiments at this time of night. She had hardly seen another soul since she had started following him.

Behind her, the row of streetlights went out for the night. Among the scudding clouds both moons shone, and two shadows paced at her side.

Larsen had been doing something in the clinic, not checking on the experiments, and that had to mean—

She started back towards the clinic.

"Why so quickly?" said a man's voice.

She stumbled, but didn't look round.

"Such a hurry," he said. "This moonlight deserves more honour." His footsteps were suddenly close behind, almost at her side, louder than the wind. The street was dark and empty. She wondered if she should run.

"You don't honour the moons? I thought all women were Dianas nowadays. Free-spirited goddesses, plucking wild music from the strings of their hunting bows." Osmon the technician, the paper maker. He was at her shoulder, his shadows entangling her own. She did not look at him. "And yet, here, where the goddess has two lamps to her glory, you scurry away as though you were the one hunted."

"It's late," she blurted. The wind shoved at her. "I've got to get home."

"My dear young lady, do forgive me for not recognising you. You are the one who is interested in paper, who works at the Greenhouse and visits the clinic after hours. You must be nervous these days, after what happened to the dam. All that willful destruction . . . But haven't you taken the wrong path to be going home? Surely you have. Here, let me guide you." He moved closer. She waited to feel his fingers on her arm.

She remembered his forearms, his hands in the paper mill. They would grip like steel clamps. It was too late to run. Scream?

"It would be much better if you went home now," he said. "Believe me, much better." Without a change in inflection, he went on. "Here there is nearly always a moon to hunt by. Hadn't you noticed that? I did, long ago."

Scream—but those hands could be on her before she did more than draw breath. And if he did nothing and someone came, what could she say?

She had stopped walking, and he stood in her path. Leaves like scraps of paper blew between them.

"But you are the violinist," he said. "The musician who has lost her calling. Is it because she wants to lose it?" He moved to her side. She flinched away, and suddenly was walking up the hill. Ahead of her the woods were dark; and, an impossible distance away, was the dark row of housing where she lived.

A creature the size of a large dog, with pale golden bars glowing along its head, crossed the path and scurried out of sight.

Insane. Do something. Run, scream. Anything.

But he was at her side, still speaking quietly. "Does she still yearn to feel the bow in her hands? The huntress's bow if not the artist's. But finally, the two are the same, of course. Think of the shrieks of the creature impaled by the huntress's arrow, and think of the song of the strings. In unskilled hands they are not to be distinguished. And that is because they are both songs of pain. Only, the instrument of art is the crueller and more refined. It disguises the torment of the flesh by its form. You rack the creature's guts when you tune, do you not? And tighten the strings to the unbearable edge of breaking. If they could cry out then, would they not scream? But they have been stretched, racked until any movement is intolerable. So when it is plucked, the string, the brute inarticulate matter of the string—yelps. And when you stroke them, when you draw a harsh unrelenting bow—the huntress's instrument—across those racked and agonised cords, when you rack them beyond all bearing—they sing. And the song, like all true beauty, is built of pain."

He was silent for a dozen steps, as though timing his next speech. And she waited to hear him, hypnotised. "Eventually," he said, "the tortured string can sing no more, and breaks. But that is the inevitable price of beauty. I have always felt, myself, that a true spiritual experience is worth whatever price it exacts. Don't you agree?"

"What are you saying?" She felt herself trying to break the spell. "Do you believe any of that, or are you just trying to scare me?" As soon as she had spoken, she was appalled at her recklessness. You were supposed to humour maniacs, not antagonise them.

"Even if I wanted to," he continued smoothly, "how could I be frightening someone who is merely hurrying home to get a good night's rest? After all, we're just walking in the moonlight, discussing the origins of music. In fact, you are much safer now than before our fortunate meeting. The woods here, how dark—and who knows for sure what may hide in them? There must be caves and gullies there, where one could be hidden for days, out of sight, and out of earshot of all who pass by—where even the loudest and most desperate cries would be heard only by the one who had brought you there, and who might find in them the purest exaltation."

"Someone like you?" The words forced themselves out of her. In a moment she would believe where this was leading and be too terrified to utter a word. "Cut the bullshit. If you're going to try something, get on with it." *Insane. Insane.*

"I do like a woman with spirit," he said, looking her up and down. "But I'm really not sure what you can mean. I was offering to protect you from whatever dangers might be abroad tonight. Though, come to think of it, I have noticed that those who have never experienced acute suffering are the ones most inclined to precipitate its occurrence."

"You've noticed that have you? I wonder where." Why was she goading him? "For all you know, I don't need your protection. I might carry a nasty little gun with me on my late night walks."

"Of course you might. Though it would have to be a very small one, and even so, I doubt you could get it out in time to foil a sudden attack. But such weapons are frowned on, and I don't think you're the type to flout the local conventions. No, on the whole, I think you are unarmed. Whereas I . . . but let's not slice away the skin of decorum from the flesh of our discussion. I always find a little uncertainty sharpens the perceptions remarkably, and this is such splendid night, it would be a pity not to experience it fully."

And then he was silent, walking quietly at her elbow until they reached the dark corner of her road. If she had had a weapon, she would have drawn it then.

"Well," he remarked, "the time has come. All things must end, and our little adventure has reached its finale. A pity we cannot achieve a final cadence of true poignancy, but we must content ourselves with a mere *andante morendo*. I mean, of course, that now I must abandon you to the uncertainties of the night. But I've enjoyed our little discussion immensely: you have suggested several interesting possibilities to me, and I can only hope you have found it instructive as well, because if we meet again like this, I'm certain we'll be able to extend the scope of our investigation and explore some of these topics more substantially."

Her tongue was shrivelled in her mouth. Before she could speak, he had turned and was walking back down the slope. Immediately she began to run up the slope, and that was a mistake, because it released the fear she had been holding in check, and she could not tell if he had really gone, or was playing with her, stalking her again, closing in on her under cover of her footfalls. She allowed herself one look back over her shoulder, then forced herself back to a walk. A monster. A psychopath. Barbara's leaflet was right. She *should* have run, she should have screamed for help and run. But the voice had held her, the rhythm of the words-how could she have fled while he was still talking quietly of music and pain?

She concentrated on controlling her breathing. *In* four steps, *out* four steps. The wind roared about her. That exit line of his had been a threat: *If I catch you there again. . . .* The last curve in the road was coming up ahead. Cold spectral lightning bloomed among the pillared clouds. Another hundred metres. A hundred steps, twenty-five more breaths. A threat. How much did he know? Had he seen her following Larsen?

Was she going to have to be on her guard the whole time now? Was every hour going to be as harrowing as this until she got to the end of whatever tangle she was unearthing? It was too much. The fear would exhaust her.

She looked at Paulina and Louise's home, but all the windows were dark. Her own home was closer. She broke down and ran the rest of the way.

With lights on and the door locked behind her, she let herself collapse. She dragged herself to the bed and lay, still dressed, staring at the light. It churned up images for her: Larsen's candles, the paper-maker's elegant horror, and some that did not fit.

She felt that if she went and looked out of the window, the dark would be held back by a row of purple-white mercury lamps on chipped concrete poles scrawled with graffiti. There would be cars parked along the curb—rust buckets with twisted bumpers, cracked windshields, broken headlights, their paintwork smeared with dust that the kids' fingers had turned to blackboards, all colours bleached to anonymous greys by the streetlights.

She closed her eyes and shook her head, but the picture only became clearer. She got up and walked through the house, switching on lights, and it went with her.

There were flattened beer cans in the gutter, milk cartons, torn candy-wrappers, scraps of newspaper, blackened leaves. A gaunt mongrel rooted there, then lifted its head and scuttled away towards the bank of the dead canal beyond the row of lights. A patrol cruiser was entering the street, a dark bulk above the parked cars. Blades of red and blue light rotated from its cupola.

Her hands knew what to do. They found a black pencil and copies of Barbara's leaflet. They slashed a group of horizontal lines along the back of a sheet, poised to make other marks.

The patrol car was outside, was stopping, its lights beating against the window blind. Blue, then dark, then red. Footsteps on the steps outside, approaching. Stopping.

Dark.

Blue.

Dark.

Red—

The door thundered.

Her pencil ripped through the paper and snapped. Then she was in the kitchen, blocking her ears with the rush of water. The sink filled, and the ceiling light glared back at her from a thousand jagged facets. She moaned, unable to look away, then let her head go down. The cold burned her face, bit into her eyes and ears, until there was only a high singing sound from somewhere inside her. Air plopped from her mouth; water forced itself into her throat in hard lumps. She retched and straightened up, spilling water over the floor. The pictures had gone. She was sick and trembling all over, but the pictures had gone. And she no longer wanted to know what buried memories they had come from.

She pulled out a chair, sat. And began to force the world back into place.

▲

Pain scored Grebbel's arm. He floated in a grey space, where pictures and sounds circled at the edge of awareness. Sometimes they drifted closer, where he could examine them. One was a thought: *I can't feel my face.* Others were images: faces in white masks looming like clouds. Red and white dapple. A mouth straining open, showing the tongue and the stained molars, the cheeks white and beaded with sweat, rucked up in folds against the clenched eyes. There was no sound with that image, as though whatever should have accompanied it could be properly represented only by silence.

"Mr. Grebbel."

He recognised that the voice was from outside the greyness. He thought words in reply, but could not push them into the air.

Now there was a woman's face lit by moonlight. The air was freezing, and they clung together for warmth. Behind them was the long snow slope down to the fence and the trees. Orion reared above them.

"Jon Grebbel."

He thought words again, and this time there came a croak from the void where his face should be.

"You can hear me. Good. Listen to what I say, but don't try to move. In a few minutes we'll be ready to begin."

The voice continued, but he was out in the snow, holding her for warmth, then turning, trying to shield her from the wind.

"They've given you a heavy dose of analgesic. You may not be fully aware of what's happening to you, but the procedures should work well enough. Afterwards you'll be disoriented for perhaps several days. Try to remember not to say anything that will reveal what happened to you. As far as possible, don't speak except to answer questions. We will implant a hypnotic suggestion to that effect, but it's as well if the conscious mind has the same instruction. We'll be starting soon. Don't be alarmed if you feel yourself being moved."

She was laughing with him and the snow was whipping past

them unfelt. The world darkened around her. She glowed for him in the night, moonfire, moonsilver, and his reflection lived in her eyes.

"We're wheeling you into the treatment room now. We've got the place to ourselves. In a minute you'll feel the headset being put on. Then we'll uncover your eyes. After that, we'll have to put you under for an hour. You may feel the needle, but nothing else. When you come out of it, we'll be finished."

He held her until he could not tell where his body ended and hers began. Still he strained towards her. For a moment the wind screamed icy words in his ears. Then he broke through into the light that annihilated all thought, pain and fear.

⋏

Niels Larsen straightened from the oscilloscope screen and looked across at Osmon. "He's into phase epsilon. Cut off the drug now until I tell you."

"Whatever you wish."

As usual, if there was irony in Osmon's subservient manner, Larsen couldn't be sure of it. Mercifully, Osmon was an almost pathological follower, without initiative; it was all that tempered the other sides of his nature. But at least he seemed to be behaving himself now.

They looked at the man in the bed. He was wrenching at the straps, his eyes staring blindly from above his bandaged cheeks. "Yes," Larsen muttered, "it's working now."

⋏

Consciousness came and went for the man called Jon Grebbel. Sometimes, when the drugs released the storms within him, he seemed to be a creature of the tide flats. He squirmed and howled in the wind and the harsh sun, and then the dark waters would return and hide him in their depths.

Most of the time then, all was dark. Sometimes he would glimpse one of the deep's unearthly offerings, but it would be gone before he could understand it. There would follow an interval of absence, when he knew nothing, but the currents and the sea creatures worked on him, and at the next change of the tide, the creature that bore his name was left gasping on the sand in a new shape.

When he floated free of the drug, he knew his eyes were bandaged again, but he was aware of the changes in light and shade that marked the passage of time. He tried counting days, but could not tell how many mornings he had seen and how many of them he had dreamt. Sometimes there were voices, and when he tried to answer them, they vanished into the dream world; or dream voices would insist, and would become those of flesh people ministering to his body.

Even when the drug did not hold him, he lived among brilliant dreams. Some were so poignant and familiar that, when they returned to him, under the bandages he wept, and afterwards wondered what they could have been to have moved him so. Some were recent and forced themselves in front of him, and he regarded them with awe that he should have given and received such tenderness. But most of the dreams pulled him down into the dark sea where half-seen mouths snapped, and eyes glared. When he could, he tried to study them, and would think, *That was me?* And then: *Yes, that was me.* And later, with controlled anger: *No—that is me. I will be what I always was.*

▲

The following morning, on her way to visit Barbara in the clinic, Elinda was told that Jon Grebbel had been admitted with concussion and fractures after a fall.

"We've got him on electro-ossipagation," the technician told her, in what must have been meant to be reassuring tones, while she stared at him numbly. "The bones'll be knitting nicely in a few days, and they'll be better than new before he knows it."

"Is that why he's still unconscious?" she demanded, her throat dry.

"Well, no, actually." The technician looked uncomfortable. "There's something wrong in his head. It must be the concussion. I'm not meaning to alarm you now—we don't think there's anything organically wrong, nothing that won't fix itself with rest—but if we don't keep him deeply sedated, he squirms and thrashes about. Does his bone casts no good at all, you can imagine. Looks as though he's having nightmares. We're still working up the test results, but so far we can't find any sign of brain trauma; and sometimes he's been quite lucid. So we'll just be keeping him under observation for a bit longer."

"Can I see him, then?" Her voice sounded almost normal.

"Sure, you can see him. Just don't expect too much. We've uncovered his eyes for the moment, but he may not know you. Then again, he may—depends on how he is this morning."

She went in. Grebbel's arm was in a sling. A bandage hid half his face. His eyes were closed and he seemed to be sleeping peacefully. She touched his hand with her fingertips, then held it, tracing the bones and tendons under the smooth skin. After a few moments, she sat on the bed and looked at him. His eyelids flickered, but he seemed unaware of her presence. He had gone to Larsen, she was certain, and now he was—different.

If she spoke to him, would he recognise her?

At least they hadn't fastened his wrists, she thought; he didn't bite. She felt ready to scream.

Then he murmured something and his fingers closed about hers. She bent forward until her forehead was on his chest. Her shoulders shook, her throat swelled and ached. His fingers were in her hair, stroking the back of her head. But when she sat up finally, his expression seemed unchanged, as though he had dreamed her and did not believe the dream.

Compulsively she scrubbed at the tear stains fading into the sheet. She wanted to spend the rest of the day sitting and watching him sleep, pretending they were cocooned from the rest of the world. And then she knew she was hiding from her own fears, and that they would only grow the longer she ignored them. She bent and kissed him, and felt his lips twitch in response. Then she got up and left.

TEN

In the office, she called the Security office over the net, and asked for the officer who had been with her when she found Barbara. She reached Charley as she was going off shift and arranged to meet her for lunch.

"Concerned about your Mr. Grebbel?" Larsen asked from his desk in the office. "I assure you, he was fine the last time I saw him."

She turned to look at him. "Don't worry, I'm not turning you in. And what does 'fine' mean? I just left him, he's wrapped up like a goddamned Christmas present."

"I meant, he's doing as well as can be expected, given the choices he made," Larsen told her, erasing her last doubts about what Grebbel had done.

She was searching for a reply when Chris rushed in and started talking about the latest gossip to come through the Knot.

Larsen pointedly turned away from her and called up the page. Making an obvious effort to focus, he said, "These young people, this group—they are musicians?"

Chris nodded. "Andropov and the Marxes, they're giving a concert in support of more payload deliveries for us—there's even a chance they'll come through and play here for the celebrations, if the memory thing can be beaten in time. Here in the main Hall, live."

Larsen shook his head. "However did we become worthy of such an honour?" he asked with a painful effort at levity.

"Well, don't get too worried, nobody would *make* you come and watch."

"Not today. Let's hope we still have such freedom when your musicians finally arrive."

Larsen made a show of returning to his computer, turning away from both Chris and Elinda, and leaving her with a handful of unanswered questions.

▲

At lunchtime, Elinda met Charley at the tavern. Charley had bought a sandwich—"Your pseudo-cheese, plus my own sprouts from my own window box"—and Elinda bought a bowl of onion soup and some crackers. They sat at a corner table facing the doors and the Tree as it undulated gently outside in the wind.

"I didn't have time to make sandwiches this morning," Elinda said. "And last night, something happened." She described her encounter with Osmon, without mentioning Larsen or what had happened to Grebbel.

"For Christ's sake," Charley said. "You let him walk you up past the woods? What in hell were you thinking of?"

"I don't know. It just seemed impossible to . . ." She shook her head. "Anyway, the point is, what can I do about it?"

"You could stop going for walks by yourself at night till you get some common sense into you."

"That's just it. I think I may need to do more of that—and I don't want my freedom of movement restricted in any case."

"Of course you don't." Charley said, and frowned. "Well, you *could* lodge a complaint, your word against his. . . ."

"But—?"

"Exactly. There's been some strange rulings lately. I can't tell what will be followed up and what won't any more. Gordie, on the desk, he's a decent sort, but I get the feeling he doesn't have as much say in things as he wants us to believe. If you made a formal complaint, you might wind up charged with mischief yourself, for all I know."

"Shit. I haven't got time for that. What, then?"

"Learn some self-defence."

"I haven't got time for that, either." Elinda brushed cracker crumbs from her sleeve, then looked at Charley. "I need a weapon, don't I?"

Charley spread her fingers on the table and stared at them. "What do I say? I enforce laws restricting private weapons. It's my job. I don't know. If you went around with a large kitchen knife in your coat pocket, you could be charged. And I don't think a knife would be what you really need anyway. If we found an unregistered gun on you, we'd have to charge you, and you'd be in serious trouble. I can't see you getting permission for a firearms certificate either—at least, it would almost be quicker for you to learn tae kwon do. I'll tell you, we know there are unregistered weapons circulating here, including some small handguns; and someone who wanted one could probably get her hands on one if she tried, but that's all I can say."

Elinda considered. "Okay," she said finally. "I guess I'll have to live with that."

Λ

The fog began to clear from Grebbel's mind. He stared about him, tested his thoughts for the blurring of the drugs, and trusted himself to ask, "How long have I been here?"

The nurse turned to him with a faint smile. "You've asked me that every day for the last week," he said. "Sometimes twice a day. But now you look as though you'll remember. This is the end of your second week. There were some complications, but the worst's over now. You should be on your feet tomorrow, I'd say, and then we'll probably let you out for a few hours each day, for the next two or three days, to see how you cope."

His jaw still ached. He mumbled, "How long before I can use my arm again?" He tried to test his muscles in the sling and the cast. "I've been driving a truck," he added. "Can't do that with one arm."

"We've been giving you electrotherapy to encourage the bones to knit. For your head too. You had a nasty contusion there—hairline fracture as well. It's well on the way now, but we had to keep you doped—you kept tearing the electrodes off. The bones should be able to look after themselves about now. They'll be a bit delicate for another ten days or so, but then you'll hardly know anything happened to them."

"You said I'd be let out on parole for a few days. When do I get out for good?"

"Within a week, I'd imagine, provided you keep testing clear of brain damage."

"Right."

"I wouldn't worry about that. Your reflexes look good. Any problems you're aware of? You are an amnesiac, aren't you? I thought so. It might be harder for you to tell then—but you don't notice any changes in your memory? No gaps you can't explain, no scrambled connections?"

"No. My memory's as good as it ever was."

⋀

That evening, Larsen came to visit him. "I heard you'd come out of the transition phase. How do you feel?"

"Fine," said Grebbel. "Just fine. Can we talk freely?"

"We should be a little discreet. We're not under actual surveillance, but I wouldn't want our business shouted down the corridor. How is your memory?"

"Fine. Just fine."

"You can be less discreet than that."

"So far, I'm a satisfied customer just waiting to see how far things develop."

"Good. I have a number of questions for you, and I imagine you have some for me. I gather you're going to be out for a few hours a day in the near future. I'll arrange to meet, and we can talk then."

"Okay, Tomorrow, or the day after, then."

⋀

Fine, he thought, *as good as ever.*

Except that the chaos Larsen had released in him had not yet stilled.

Except that he was not sure how much was memory and how much dream.

Except that the person named Jon Grebbel on this world was little but a puppet, a painted mask for the real Grebbel beneath. And that deeper reality . . . He lost the thought among glimpses of remembered dreams.

She had been part of the dreams. He remembered her here in

this room. He remembered her tears. Were they only tears for the mask?

Mountains, he remembered, like those outside this room. And years of training. Dissections. Treatments for shock and trauma. The easing of pain. The highest calling, the amelioration of human suffering. That was a true mask—the blank green that covers the surgeon's face, while under it, the lips curl, and with each breath, the whisper: *I am! I am! I am!*

Only, here they had fitted another mask on him—had grown it into his flesh. And now, when it was prised loose, it tore open, and lacerated him. Slowly he was identifying which fragment of memory was mask and which was the face below. The veins and tendons of a forearm as the fist was clenched. The crease at the corner of a mouth. A ruined body being strapped into a chair. Excitement. Pity. When he had pieced together enough to be sure of which was which, he would decide what to do. To fit the two together, mask and flesh, and live as one. Or to make a choice— which to reject and which to wear in the world. The mask or the face.

⬥

Elinda spent ten minutes with Barbara, who stared at the wall and murmured once or twice, but gave no sign of recognising her. Elinda came out feeling empty and began preparing herself for whatever Jon Grebbel might have in store for her.

Carlo was waiting outside the door.

"It's too cold for spring," she said at random to cover her surprise. "I'll never get used to this place."

"Actually," he replied, "I don't think it is particularly cold. Maybe you're running a temperature?"

"Me? No. Why, do I look sick?"

"You look as though you're under some strain. I was hoping to meet you; there were some things I felt I should talk to you about."

"Yes?"

"You're concerned about your friend in there—about Barbara, I mean. You're concerned enough to be trying to do something about it."

"Is that a question, Carlo? If it is, the answer's yes, of course.

I don't understand how she got the way she is, and no one else seems interested in finding out what happened."

"I mean, if you're trying to do Security's job—"

"They don't seem too interested in doing it themselves."

"Have you asked yourself why you're so compelled?" Carlo went on. "Guilt can be devastatingly—"

"For Christ's sake, Carlo, keep your coffee-room analyses out of it. What are you trying to say?" *And* why, she suddenly thought, *why are you and Dr. Henry, with all the time and resources you have, unable to do what Larsen can manage to do in secret, part-time?* At that moment only her fear of exposing Larsen stopped her from uttering the question.

"If you're looking for someone," Carlo went on, "if there really is someone to find, you'd be putting yourself in danger. I don't know how much you've thought of that."

"As it happened, I took this out of the kitchen drawer a couple of days ago. Something happened that made it look like a good idea, and the rolling pin wouldn't fit in my pocket."

He looked at the paring knife she showed him and frowned at her. "Scratch someone with that, and you may cause more trouble than you avoid."

"I'd more or less worked that out for myself," she said. She considered, then pulled Barbara's recorder from her pocket. "I've started carrying this with me too. If something interesting looks like happening, I'll turn it on. So if anything does happen to me, you know what to look for." She met his gaze. "Do you have any better ideas?"

"You could let it go and stay out of trouble. I'd be a lot happier if you would."

She pursed her lips and lowered her head. "No I couldn't," she said quietly. "Sorry, Carlo, and thank you for the thought, but I couldn't." Then she drew a breath and looked him in the face again. "You know more than you're telling me, don't you?"

He sighed. "You're making this very difficult. I've seen . . . I want to—help you, but there's too much I can't say. I was talking to you about therapy a while ago. . . ."

"And I said I wasn't ready to stir all that up again. That's even more true now. I've got enough to worry about." *Including how far I can trust you or anyone else,* she suddenly thought. "What can't you tell me? Why not? Come on, Carlo. You've been claiming you're my friend. How can I believe you if you won't trust me?"

Carlo winced, then said slowly, "I still think you'd be more comfortable if you had come to terms with your past. But that wasn't the point I wanted to make now. The therapy machines—how they work is, they feed signals into the brain. If the signal matches a pattern that was there before—a latent memory, that pattern is reinforced and can be made conscious. But the input signal always comes from outside. And even if the signal doesn't match anything already present, with enough applied energy—"

"Stop bullshitting me. Get to the point. Why can't you restore my memories? Jon's? Are you really trying?"

He hesitated. "There are . . . limits on what we can do. There are safety precautions and other restrictions. I've been doing everything I can to help you."

"You have? Really? Why am I supposed to believe that? And you didn't answer my question did you? What do you mean by helping me? Why can't you talk about it?"

"It's . . . political. Not everyone agrees about this place, not here or back there. Not everyone knows . . ." Before Elinda could respond, he turned away, muttering, "I'll explain it later."

Dr. Henry had come in. "Good evening to you both," he said brightly. "Spring is definitely in the air these days, isn't it? Ah, it's the young lady with the unusual taste in music. You found your friend that evening, I trust, or I'd be regretting my tact in abandoning you so easily. Did I hear Carlo telling you about our new developments? Much more eloquently than I could, I imagine. We're still working on them, so we shouldn't be giving out news until we're sure of our results, but I think we can say it's looking promising. I've always maintained this machine had the potential to be a major therapeutic tool." He looked quickly at his watch, as though timing the length of a scene. "But I'm afraid you'll have to excuse us now. We have a case to discuss."

She watched them leave, stifled a couple of curses, then checked at the desk and went on to Grebbel's room. The bandages had been removed from his face, and the sling from his arm. His face was swollen but he seemed to be sleeping when she went in, and she waited, peering at his eyebrows, at the faded bruise on his cheek, the way his hair straggled across the lines on his brow. His lips were slightly parted, making him look both vulnerable and brutal. She listened to his breathing and watched his closed eyelids twitch and flutter. Finally she stepped forward and stroked his hair back from his eyes. He shook his head weakly, but did not wake. She sat on the bed, and after a moment lay down beside him, uncaring of the open door behind her. Her muscles felt waterlogged; she just wanted to lie there beside him and sleep.

Grebbel stirred and blinked at her. For a moment his face seemed riven by turmoil, and then it was a mask. It took him two attempts to find his voice. "Elinda. I wasn't expecting you." But his gaze never left her face, and just then that was more important than anything else.

A breath she hadn't realised she was holding quietly escaped through her lips.

"I think that's what I like most about you," she said. "The passionate greetings."

"I'm sorry. I was dreaming, I think. I haven't come back from it yet."

"You want to tell me?"

He closed his eyes and shook his head, turned his face from her. "It's—muddled. I don't understand it—couldn't explain it to you anyway."

She reached out and put her hand on his chest. "You've remembered, haven't you? Niels did something."

He nodded, his closed eyes turned to the ceiling.

"How much? How much have you got back?" He did not move. "You did go to Larsen, didn't you? You wouldn't tell me, and you ended up in here. You're here because of what he did, aren't you? Jon, talk to me. I've been scared enough these last couple of days. Talk to me."

He turned slowly to face her. First his good hand, then both hands reached up to grip her shoulders. When she heard his breath grate in his throat, she forced herself not to flinch. His fingers were like icicles, but she felt his gaze on her face like the glare of the sun. She told herself that it was the dim light that made his expression so unreadable.

"You—came here." His voice was barely recognisable. Slowly he nodded. "It's all back, or all that matters. I'm everything I was." His eyes stared. She could see a red vein in the white above the pupil. Then his face twisted. "And you came *here*." He released her and rolled onto his back. His breathing was rough with what might have been laughter.

She swallowed. "Then you've got what you wanted. Are you happier for it?"

He swung back towards her. "I feel as though I'm just waking up from a long dream. I'm learning to walk again, I'm feeling the wind on my face." He shook his head angrily. "I—I can't describe what I feel." He had lifted his clenched fists but seemed unaware that he held them quivering between himself and Elinda. "Happiness has nothing to do with it. The first fish struggling up the beach into the air and the sun—did it care about being happy?"

"Then you're not happy."

"Haven't you been listening?"

"I've been listening to you trying to convince yourself that you're better off than you were. How do you expect me to believe it if you don't?"

He shook his head, still staring at her. "I can't explain it any better. You wanted it too, you wanted to be whole again. Now it's happened to me. If you don't like it—"

"You can't explain it at all, because *you* don't like it." She had to struggle to keep herself from shouting, but when she lowered her voice, she could hear how close it was to breaking. "If it's so wonderful being whole again instead of a fish in the sea, why aren't you telling me what you remembered? Come on—you're whole again, you're what you were before, back there. What *was it?*" She did shout then, and his face seemed to close against her.

"I see," he said. "It's fear, isn't it? You're scared of what you might find in yourself if you looked—you can't bear to think that someone else might still need the truth."

"To wallow in it, you mean. To sink back, to turn into . . ." She broke off. "Yes, I'm scared. I'm terrified of what'll happen—that we won't know each other any more."

He gazed at her, and now his eyes narrowed, his cheeks were drawn up, in pain or concentration. "I've regained my past," he said slowly. "I—haven't thrown away what I am . . . was."

She exhaled raggedly, and listened to the wind buffeting the walls of the clinic.

"You're like me," he said. "You wanted yourself back, and now you're scared, but we're the same. By the stream that time, it started to come back. A snow slope, a road and a fence with lights. Remember? The wind cutting through our blankets, snow up to our knees. Blankets and rain gear, one groundsheet, that's all we had, and fifty klicks to the freeway junction. Then the sirens when they found we were gone. And the searchlights. Remember? Eight of us made that break. I knew just two of them. One of the strangers was a woman. We were together when the choppers came over and the others scattered. We knew nothing about each other; we didn't talk much, that night we had together with the choppers going over every twenty minutes, before they found us and brought us back. Remember, Elinda?"

"No I don't! I don't remember!"

"But you could. There needn't be any trouble. Then you'd know. You'd understand why I needed this, and it wouldn't have to be between us."

"I see." She sat back and looked at the ceiling. Her arms were clutched across her belly. She was starting to tremble. "So I'm worthy if I agree to have my mind tampered with too, but otherwise, I'm just a liability?"

"You're twisting things. You've let them drive you into your little cave, and now you daren't even stick your nose out to smell the air. You've become what they're trying to make you, and you like it."

When he had finished, he turned away and lay still. The silence stretched. She could find nothing to say that wouldn't make things worse. And she wasn't going to cry in front of him now. Except that if she didn't, she would hit him, bruises or not. She sat up. "I'd better go."

"You're overwrought," he said. "You haven't even tried to find out what I remembered."

"I don't want to know! If it was something you were proud of, you'd have told me."

She closed the door quietly behind her as she left.

▲

The afternoon sky arched over Grebbel from mountain wall to mountain wall. He shook his head and flexed his right arm.

"Take it easy, remember," said Carlo at the door of the clinic. "We can't do miracles."

"On the contrary—I feel reborn." He gave Carlo a broad grin and started toward the dam.

The sign showed 143 days to completion, an increase since the last time he had seen it. Beyond, trucks whirred with their loads of gravel. The river gleamed in the sun, flared white against the growing dam.

A truck turned into the parking bay and stopped. Menzies swung down and waved Grebbel to him. "Feeling better, are you?"

"Still a bit confused, but I'm a new man."

"That's good then." Menzies was eyeing him closely. "Niels would like a talk with you. Can you meet him at your place in half an hour?"

"He said he would," Grebbel said agreeably. "It's something I've been looking forward to."

He walked slowly to his building, watching the life around him and trying out a consciously worn mask of amiability.

Larsen arrived a few minutes early. Without preamble, he said as he sat down: "I have a number of questions, but perhaps you'd like some things explained first. I'll be whatever help I can."

"Yes, I've got questions," Grebbel replied easily. "One or two. We might start with who you are and how many people you've managed to restore. After that I'd be quite interested to hear what they—*they*—think they're doing and why they imagine they can get away with it. And what are you planning to do about it? Why don't you start on those questions? I'll probably find a couple more as we go along."

"Who I am, in the sense you mean, isn't important," Larsen said. "Consider me as what you see: a technician with certain scruples but a preference for a quiet life. What I was before I came here, I keep to myself." He flexed his shoulders stiffly. "How I started this is a longer story than we have time for. But, in brief, after I'd been here a few months, I found that my apparent self kept slipping away, giving me glimpses of what was underneath. And then I learned—never mind how—to strip away the mask completely."

"That's what I call it, too," Grebbel said. "A mask."

Larsen looked hard at him, then went on. "I became myself, but I had had the experience of living as the mask; and the two personalities made me whole—for the first time, I think. I felt such a liberation—I wanted to liberate others too. I thought we could gather enough of our kind to compel the authorities to see the error of their ways. At the time, I was helping set up the labs in the clinic, doing some software development. It wasn't hard to get access to their programs."

Larsen paused, and lowered his voice. "I moved too quickly,

too uncritically. And then I began to understand what I might be liberating. I realised how naive I had been. And yet, what they do, wiping out a human portrait—once, I might have said 'a human soul'—and replacing it with a charcoal sketch is monstrous. . . ."

"Okay," Grebbel interjected brusquely. "What about them? I got only the inside view of the business. What's their game? Whoever they are."

"At heart it's a typical bureaucratic compromise. Two social experiments, with controllable parameters—or nearly so. One in the growth of a new society, and one in the reconstruction of criminal psychologies. Add to it the possibility of cheap labour to help develop the new colony here, the remoteness of the social laboratory from the home world, should anything go wrong, and the use of isolation and minor hardship as forms of punishment to satisfy Calvinistic factions, and you have a politically saleable case for what you see around you."

Grebbel considered. "Fascinating," he said dryly. "And, remind me again, what were you thinking of doing about it?"

"I still have some plans, but they will have to wait for the right political climate. There's nothing to be gained by recklessness. At the moment, I see no way to do more than I am at present."

"As far as I can see, that means just sitting back and watching until somebody twists your arm."

"Let me explain two things to you, Mr. Grebbel. What I originally did was not done casually. I did it because I was convinced the net result would be to bring more good than evil into the world. But I made errors of judgement. I helped restore personalities that even I must concede should not have been brought back." Larsen's gaze was fixed, but it was not clear whether it was focussed on Grebbel or on something beyond the room they were in. "In your case . . . in your case, I have to have faith that I have done more good than evil. But I walk a knife-edge. I will not be a party to violence or disorder."

Grebbel started to speak, but Larsen cut him off. "Let me make my other point. It relates to what I have just said. The process of restoration is not in practice reversible. It seems that the tissues of the brain, the structures and connections that make up memory and personality, can sustain only so much manipulation by these rather primitive techniques. Twice, the authorities discovered someone who had been restored, and tried to reprocess them. I have seen the results. Of course, the apparatus and the level of expertise here are not all they might be, which must add to the difficulty. But the result, in terms of my portrait metaphor, is not another charcoal sketch, but rather a child's scrawl, partly erased. The organism still looks human, but a detached observer, I'm sure, would assign it to a zoo. I said I've seen this twice. I hope never to see it again. Nor does anyone else who understands what is happening here."

Grebbel had pushed himself to his feet. He paced stiffly then turned to Larsen. "I see," he said. "That's how you keep your merry men in line. I take the warning."

"I've been telling you why I do what I do, and under what terms. Now I have a few questions for you."

Grebbel tensed, then exhaled deeply and leaned back against the wall. "I suppose you've earned the right."

"Thank you. First, you have regained your past. What were you back there, and what made them decide to send you here?"

"I was trained in medicine. . . . No. If you have your pride and shame, allow me mine. What's your next question?"

"I could insist," Larsen said after a moment. "But we shall have to start trusting each other sometime. However: you know what you did, and you have lived another life for some weeks now. How do you feel when you look back?"

Grebbel gazed at him and did not speak. His jaw muscles tightened, his hands locked on each other. "They took away my past," he whispered. "They—tore it out by the roots. . . ."

"You see," said Larsen, "if you won't tell me what you did to be sent here, I must at least know what you plan to do with yourself now. Have you been making plans?"

"I thought you talked about trusting each other."

"Believe me, I try to and I want to. But you have to understand that you can't have complete freedom now—none of us can. We're too closely tied to each other. If one of us draws the attention of the authorities, we are all endangered—"

"Only if he's stupid enough to get caught and weak enough to talk; and this doesn't look like the sort of setup that goes in for heavy interrogations. Or is that something else you didn't tell me about?"

"They'd threaten you with re-treatment. And, as I said, that would probably leave you barely fit for a zoo. What would you do then, Mr. Grebbel?"

"I'd cut my throat," Grebbel whispered. He met Larsen's gaze and lowered his voice further. "I'd dig my fingers into my eyes and rip them from the sockets."

Larsen flinched and looked away.

Grebbel took a step toward him. More calmly he said, "I mean, Niels, I'm not one to betray a trust. Not to someone who's helped me as much as you. But I value my privacy. I have my own plans, for my own life, and they don't concern anyone but me, unless I invite them to share it."

Larsen stiffened himself visibly and said, "I must insist. I need to know now and in the future what actions you intend—"

"You need know nothing that doesn't concern you," Grebbel snapped. "And I'll be the judge of what that is."

In a ragged voice, Larsen persisted. "If necessary, with a few words in the right places, I could have you reclassified as a psychiatric case. You'd find your freedom to determine your own actions much more severely curtailed then, I assure you."

Grebbel smiled and approached him. "But, Niels, what do you think they'd find if they examined me? And I could put a few words in the right places too, couldn't I? No, don't get up." He placed his hand on Larsen's shoulder, and Larsen sank back into the seat. "I think you've more to lose than I have. You're not one to take risks. And you've just bankrupted your authority by making a threat you can't back up." He moved back a pace. "Niels, you've put the whip into my hand."

He rocked back and forth, clenching his fists and flexing his damaged arm. He watched Larsen with a faint smile as he did so.

"As a gesture of good faith," he said, "I think I will tell you what you wanted to know—why I was sent here. It may amuse you. First, though, let's think about masks and faces a little. Let's say we each have a mask, something we've learned to use to hide our secrets from the world. And what's behind the mask is unsure of anything but its own existence and its mortality. How am I to know I am real and safe, and myself, unless I can be sure I'm separate from you? How can I know that you—the real, vulnerable, quivering you—acknowledge me as real, if all I see of you is the mask you wear each day? Well, I *can* prove I am real and different from you, I can split your mask a little and see what's inside it. Have you guessed how?"

He snapped his fingers in Larsen's face, and the tendons in Larsen's neck jerked as he held himself from flinching away.

"It's simple," Grebbel said. "It's if you hurt and I don't."

He looked at Larsen, then went back to his chair and sat down. "I was a doctor," he said conversationally. "I told you that, didn't I? A healer of the sick, the infirm, a comfort to the dying. Where I worked last, the-patients had a name for me. They'd tell newcomers what to expect. I'd built up a reputation, you see—by hard work and initiative, the way one is always supposed to."

He paused and rubbed the bruise in his jaw reflectively. "It started small, of course. At the beginning—this was in my home town, still—I'd be on call at the station when they brought in a suspect. Often he'd struggle, try to use his knee or his feet— occasionally it would be a woman—but there were always four or five officers to one suspect, and they'd carry him if they had to. I'd see them go into the interview room, and then one of them would come out and turn up the rock station on the ghetto blaster outside the door, and go back in. Afterwards, they'd explain about the slippery stairs in these old municipal buildings, and ask me to do some tidying up and pay no attention to any delirious accusations I might hear.

"After a few weeks of this, when they decided I was reliable, they showed me where the real work was done. I had to learn to treat the effects of certain drugs, often given in conjunction with electric shock or other procedures. That treatment chair almost brought back memories the first time I saw it. The work was quite delicate—not just patching up breaks and contusions—it was often a case of keeping the patient conscious, or alive, long enough for the business to be concluded successfully.

"Then I moved to the big city and, with my references, I was able to do the same work there. And when I went abroad on an international aid program, I was welcomed into the government anti-terrorist team. I had got to be quite good at the work. I was able to make suggestions. I found I was often able to judge what approach would be most fruitful, or when a different one should be adopted. Then I began to devise improvements. They knew my worth by then, and encouraged me to experiment. I did. I learned to improvise, and when we went into the mountains after the guerillas, I acted as intelligence liaison officer and was in charge of all interrogations. About that time, I gathered I had acquired a reputation and a name. Of course, when the coup happened, it wasn't a good idea to be famous in that way. . . ."

He gave a twisted smile that froze on his face, and said no more. Silence filled the room.

"What are you going to do?" Larsen whispered.

"Go back to the clinic and sleep; they're expecting me," Grebbel said and gestured at him wearily. "You can get up now, you can leave. I'm sure we'll meet again before too long."

▲

Elinda sat and stared at the recorder. She sensed she was letting Barbara slip away from her. Her memories of their times together now seemed as remote and vulnerable as the whispers of her voice on the recording. The metal shell was cool and impersonal, she had to remind herself it been held in Barbara's hand. She pushed buttons, found the list of current files, their time stamps, their sizes, the memory-space and battery power remaining when the recording was made, memory locations, signal-to-noise quality. She understood from somewhere that the latter was related to the battery level.

She froze. "My god." She had recharged the battery; it had quickly got too low to drive the speaker, just work the display screen. "How blind stupid can I get?"

When Barbara had made her little sound test, there had been another two hours' worth of battery power available. But the battery had started dying when Elinda got it home. Nothing more recent was listed in memory. So something like ninety minutes' worth of recorded sound was gone, lost.

Erased.

It wouldn't stand up in court, but it confirmed what she had known in her bones for weeks: Barbara had met someone that night and whatever she had recorded then had been destroyed. And the one who had done it had then sent her out into the night to die.

ELEVEN

In the clinic, Grebbel smiled for the orderly who connected him to the test apparatus; he laughed at the jokes that came with the dinner tray, and finished every scrap on the plates.

But that night, he dreamed of Elinda. *You've remembered, haven't you?* she said again, and her face filled his sight as though he were looking into the sun.

Yes, I'll tell you, he said, *I'll tell you all of it.*

The words died soundless at his lips. Her gaze pierced him. He felt it would cut out his heart.

He ran from her. Fled along white echoing corridors, crossed shadow-filled excavations on planks that fell away as he leapt from them. Came to a closed door. It was a high wooden door, with a loose brass handle, and he knew that on the other side of it were steps leading down. He reached up to turn the handle.

You've remembered everything, haven't you?

It was dark, and somewhere an icy wind was blowing, and he was shivering, huddled around the warmth of his body, his torn arm. . . .

You've remembered, haven't you?

Keep back, he said, not turning to see her. *Don't make me—*

When he awoke, her face remained beside him as it had been in the dream, the face of a woman on the rack, contorting in response to his slightest movement. But when he reached out to touch her cheek, his fingers brushed a shadow on the pillow, and he fell into full awareness. And was alone.

▲

Elinda sat beside Barbara, and watched her sleep, while her thoughts eddied aimlessly; finally she left and went along the corridor to Grebbel's room. At the door she hesitated. It would be the first time she had visited him since their fight. She could turn away now, and never have to deal with what he had become.

She rapped on the door and pushed it open. He was in bed, with electrodes taped to his temples, connected to a recorder beside the wall. He looked up and saw her. His face tensed, then his eyes widened, he relaxed and smiled.

"Friends?" she said.

He beckoned her. "Yes. Friends. Yes, yes."

She went in.

▲

Two days later, Carlo was waiting for her, in the clinic lobby. "I'll walk part of the way with you," he said, fastening his coat.

"Well, okay," she said, preparing to continue their last exchange.

They went out into the evening, turned towards the Square.

"How are things?" he asked. "Are you still bent on playing detective?"

"I'm not playing. I may not be professional, but I'm not treating it as a game."

"Sorry. I was wondering if you'd changed your mind about it, or anything else."

"Like having more sessions with your new machine you mean? No thanks, Carlo, I've not changed my mind about that." *Because it's a fraud isn't it?* she almost added.

"Have you thought about why you don't want to go back there?"

"Perhaps I'm not ready to recover my memories," she said, cursing herself for the half-truth. "After this business about there being mental cases here, I've been getting flashes of something that feels like the past, and I don't like them. Whatever I was, maybe I should just settle for being who I am, here."

"What you mean," he said carefully, "is that you're afraid. And that's quite reasonable. If there are some old bones in your psychic closet, it's quite logical that you'd be nervous about disturbing them. But that probably means that's exactly where the problems are, and where we have to go to tackle them."

"I don't mean to be obtuse, Carlo, but I had the impression that my most pressing problems were here in this pleasant little community, and right now."

"Some of them are," he agreed. "Perhaps more than you realise—or you're ready to admit. Last time, you talked about something scaring you. That's why I got you this." He turned towards the shadow of the Tree. "Come over here where we can't be seen."

Under the leathery fronds, he pulled a cloth package from his coat and handed it to her. "I tried to find something that would be easy to use. I looked for something that would discourage an attacker without necessarily injuring him badly—but most of the devices like that are either restricted or they need training and practice. I had to settle for something under the table, and it's nastier than I'd like. It's what some of the cops use as unofficial backup weapons. Ankle holsters and so on."

It was a short-barrelled, ancient-looking black revolver. She could just see the blunt noses of the bullets in the cylinder.

"If you have to use it, hold in both hands, point it and pull the trigger firmly. I didn't get any spare rounds, but it's for one emergency only. Then you'll lose it."

"It's small," she said, thinking it looked like something you might find under a damp rock, "and ugly. Thank you, I think."

"I had to do it for you."

She looked at him questioningly.

"Something happened," he said, and moistened his lips. "Back there. Someone I was close to, I should have protected. I couldn't watch it happen again, to you."

She shoved the gun into her jacket pocket. "Christ," she muttered, "is everything we do driven by guilt?"

"Elinda—I went out on a limb to get that for you. Don't be seen with it; there's no way you could legitimately own it. And— please be careful. If you find you need to use that thing, you've got yourself further into something than you should have."

"You're not going to tell me any more than that, are you?"

"I've told you all I know for sure." Through a chink in the

cloud ceiling, one of the moons glimmered down. Carlo's face looked carved from chalk. With his potential arrest warrant freely handed to her, she couldn't bring herself to challenge him directly.

They walked on, the black metal weighing against her hip. "The last time we talked," she said to fill the silence, "you were going to tell me something about the therapy machine."

"Yes. The treatment itself," he began, sounding a bit more comfortable, "—it's more complicated than you probably think. Several decades ago, there was a well-known psychiatrist who tried to make his reputation by a technique he called psychic driving. It became infamous later—he'd been using hallucinogens and brainwashing techniques, at a time when clinical practice was still highly experimental and standards were lax. What this machine does is a kind of psychic driving." His tone made her sure he was leading to a conclusion she would not like.

"You mean it reprograms—brainwashes—people?"

He hesitated. "It can—it could, if things weren't properly controlled. The thing is, there's no absolute guarantee that what it restores is real. So, we do our best to minimise any distortion, we look for obvious patterns and self-consistency. . . ."

"But you're mostly working on faith?" Elinda said.

"Faith and experience, among other things. If I knew what you were asking for, I might be able to help you more."

"I'm not asking for anything yet, Carlo. Just let me think about it for a bit. I'm not sure what I want." What she did want, she realised, was Carlo to stop hanging up veils of secrecy; perhaps if he kept talking, something would slip out.

"I know you're not asking," he began quietly. "You haven't asked me for anything. You didn't ask me for protection, for the gun?" He turned to look into her eyes. "But you accepted it when I offered. If I offered this, would you accept it?" He hesitated. "If I offered more?" he said hoarsely. "I could, you know. I would"

She wondered whom he was seeing when he looked at her, whether there were two moons in the sky for him, or just one.

"Oh, Carlo, I'm sorry. I wasn't ready for this. I've got all the complications I can handle right now. Don't push it. Please."

"All right," he said, after a pause. "Forget I said anything, if you like. Let it go. Forget it."

"I'm sorry, Carlo, but it's the best thing right now."

"It was stupid of me to bring it up. I knew it was, I wasn't going to. But you started asking about the machine, and there are things I can't tell you. And I don't want to see you hurt."

"It's all right. I'm going to be careful. I'm glad you care, but let's call it a night now. Let's talk again later, from where we were before, okay?"

▲

At the start of the weekend Grebbel was released from sleeping in the clinic. In his rooms, he stared at the strange, familiar walls and thought about how much had changed. He clenched his fist and flexed his healing arm.

That evening Elinda knocked on his door.

They gazed at each other. Then he stepped towards her. Without speaking they held each other tightly, without moving more than to breathe. To both of them it felt as though he had come back from another world.

▲

The next day, Grebbel worked a full shift at the dam. The sun was down, and the evening storm roared. Spears and sheets of blue light leapt among the mountain peaks. Under the ghastly flickering, bleached faces recoiled from the reverberations of distant thunder. Rags of cloud blew low along the valley. Trees groaned and bent.

Grebbel worked through the morning, while waves piled up against the dam and lathered across the causeway; beneath the arc lights, spray flew like diamonds. His arm was stiff and at times sore, but most of its strength had returned.

At lunch, he looked for Elinda, but she did not appear. Instead, as he was leaving, he found Partridge, balancing against the gusts as he struggled with the cafeteria door. Grebbel helped him inside.

"Well, if it isn't the new boy at last," Partridge said, beating water off his coat. "Been in the wars, have we?"

"You're looking great yourself. How's it been going out here?"

"Just the way it always goes, mate. Three steps forward, three back and a couple of falls on the arse. You look as though you know something I don't—or you think you do, at any rate."

The cafeteria shook and hail rattled against the window.

"Maybe I do," said Grebbel. "But not as much as I need to know. Weren't we talking business for a while there? You tell me what the wind's blowing your way, and I look for some better . . . lubricant for you?"

Partridge turned to him, and for an instant the hunger behind his eyes was obvious. "The stuff I've been getting lately's been pretty thin, and that's the truth. Just about hear my eyeballs grinding in the sockets when I wake up in the morning. What do you want to hear rumours about?"

"For the time being, something fairly simple. The flights to and from the Flats must go on some sort of schedule, but I haven't been able to find out what it is. I'd like to know when they run. If you can find that out, maybe we can go on from there."

"Okay. I reckon we can do something along those lines."

▲

At the end of the afternoon, there was a gap in the storm. High overhead, pink strands of light tangled above the ponderous turning mouth of a great cloud funnel; and beyond the aurora floated the two moons and an icy scattering of stars.

When Grebbel did his voluntary shift in the clinic, he announced that he was going to learn to use the computer program for predicting the biological activities of new compounds from their molecular structures. "I want to be ready for when we start harvesting some of the biosphere around here." He then managed to work in twenty minutes of exploration of the database where the drug inventory was kept. He got to within a couple of passwords of the inventory itself, and then closed down the search for the day. Too much access time might become suspicious. But when he left the lab he was confident; he could feel his plans coming together.

After dinner, he waited until he met Larsen hurrying through the rising wind away from the Greenhouse, and accompanied him, mentioning the talk they had had in Grebbel's rooms. "I didn't say all I had to say then, and I think I was wrong to keep some things back."

They were almost at Larsen's home, and Larsen uncomfortably asked him in.

JANUS

Grebbel paced the living room. He noted its austerity and the cleanliness marred by candle grease on the floor and the soot marks on the ceiling. "A man with a conscience?" he wondered aloud as a window rattled. "Perhaps a badly troubled conscience? I can sympathise. We all have to wrestle with the different sides of our nature—but then what are 'we' that do the wrestling?"

"Do you want a philosophical debate? Or is this just your stalking horse for something else?"

"If you're asking whether I've come to a decision—yes I have. But all in good time." Grebbel stopped and turned to Larsen. "Do you value truth, Niels? I think you must, to have done what you did. And trust. Admirable, courageous qualities—qualities that can ride a man and make him do more than he would ever have believed himself able to do."

"Whatever you came here for—I wasn't the one who harmed you. All I did was help you. Your anger should go elsewhere."

"Time enough for that. For the moment this is just about you, and what you can do to help me again." Grebbel smiled. "Trust and truth, those are the keys. You see, you have some information that I need. You must have an impressive group of graduates, of alumni, here, and I'm afraid their potential is going to waste. I'd like to discuss some changes in the set-up, in the rules of the game if you like, with the whole membership. Except, you seem to be the only one who knows the membership list."

"There are good reasons for that," Larsen said thickly. "As you know quite well."

Wind made a thin shrieking sound through some part of the building structure.

"Of course there are. Of course. But surely, you must agree, there can be exceptions for exceptional circumstances. I think this particular rule has outlived its usefulness as an absolute and should be waived for once. And, you know, it's very undemocratic of you to keep this all to yourself. You don't think so?"

Larsen shook his head.

Grebbel went over to him and rested his arm on the man's shoulders. "Trust is a great quality, you're right. Something that is prized in all societies, and rightly so." His free hand tugged at Larsen's sleeve. "I'm asking you to give me that gift a little longer, now that I've told you about myself. Trust me. Tell me the truth. Won't you?"

Larsen shook his head and started to pull away.

"A pity," Grebbel said. "But I had to learn some basic manipulative skills back there, and develop a certain physical strength. And I was good at my work."

He tensed, gripped—twisted. Larsen gave a short cry and fell backwards.

▲

An hour later, Grebbel rose to leave. Larsen did not hear the door close. He remained crouched against the wall and shivered. Gradually he accepted that it was over and he was alone again. He had broken so easily. Two or three prods in the right places and his will had collapsed. Once he had given up the answer to the first question, it had become impossible to stop. Grebbel had needed little more than the threat of further pressure.

He levered himself upright against the wall, then lurched to the bathroom. He vomited into the lavatory bowl. At some point during the ordeal his bladder had released. He undressed painfully and washed. Then he looked in the mirror. There, at least, the shell of himself seemed to be intact. Except for the eyes. In them he could see his own destruction. Would he be able to look anyone in the face now without displaying what he had become?

His sanctuary had been violated. The nighttime agonies, the meditations before candles, had been reduced to nothing by the simple fact of applied pain. And it was not over. Nothing had changed, beyond the apparition of one more failure to be lived with, and one more compromise to make with the unforgiving conscience.

He fumbled and set the candles on the dark wooden table, lit them. He stared hopelessly at the bobbing flames. How much pain was a man supposed to bear?

▲

In his room that night, Grebbel emptied the folder he had found in his luggage onto the table. The fabrications on which this life had been built here were spread out in front of him. He shuffled them and placed them like a fortune-teller's cards. Then, one by one, he began to tear them up. Letters: Dear Son, Jonathon, Hey

Lover, Dear Mr. Grebbel. Photographs—smiles and arms round shoulders, shadows and trees and bricks and hands and sunlight on a lake—"Lie," he whispered, and tore them. "Lie. Lie."

It was all gone, everything they had tried to make him build on—gone the way of Santa Claus and his dreams of being a shuttle pilot. He sank into his chair. Now his hands shook, tired from tearing, ached to tear again. The quiet suburban neighbourhood they had tried to feed him, the modest technical school obscurity—lies. And here, the menial work, the sense of life lived on a hollow stage without support, without roots. They had been inside him, eating away like a shipworm at his innermost self, inside, inside with their lies, their manipulations. It was all fake, false as makeup plastered over a tumour. . . .

In his mind, two crimson-headed raptors circled over the mist-choked valley. He gave a short cry and pushed himself back from the table.

The gold-painted hatchback was real, and the holding cell where he had looked down the snow slope and known that he was facing a kind of death. And the room with the whitewashed walls that were always splashed with brown because the cleaners were too anxious to get onto the next corridor—they had heard the sounds made in that room. That was real, and the other rooms, the basement room—dark as a cave, with grimy windows you could see your face in if you went up on tiptoe, and the handle you had to use both hands to turn, gripping in front of your chest, and straining because your hands would hardly fit around and the effort made your chest hurt. But the handle had to turn, had to open—

"Lies," he whispered once more, mechanically. His hands clenched and opened and clenched again. The retching sound that might have been laughter broke from him again.

⋏

Osmon was the first on his list, a kindred spirit, a willing follower, with some animal intelligence to go with his actual muscle. A deputy, an enforcer, a fixer. Grebbel turned to look for foot soldiers.

⋏

Réjean Lafayette turned to Grebbel with a practiced-looking smile. He was a small man with bitten fingernails, white, even teeth and a thin grey moustache. There were deep lines between his eyes and curving from his nose around the corners of his mouth. His movements as he chopped vegetables in the kitchen were quick and nervously precise.

"You look happy in your work," Grebbel commented after they had introduced themselves. "It must be an interesting job you've got there."

Lafayette's eyebrows lowered fractionally, but his smile did not waver. "Mustn't complain, you know. You looking for a position here or something? I gotta tell you—they'll only assign if you go through channels. They got real strict about that lately."

"Is that right?" Grebbel frowned. "He didn't tell me that. Just said I should come over and look at the work—even gave me your name. You know the guy, don't you—Larsen at the Greenhouse."

"I've met him." Now Lafayette's expression was carefully bland. "Didn't know he was involved in work assignments, though."

"Actually, it wasn't anything official. He just thought you might be able to help me. Something about you owing him a favour."

"Said that, did he? I don't suppose he said what kind of favour?"

"It's not the sort of thing we'd talk about in public, is it? I suppose I owe him the same. That's really what I came to talk about."

"You need help making the pieces stay fitted together, is that it, eh? Sure, I can help you keep your feet on the ground if that's what you really want."

"I was thinking we might be able to help each other. If you're interested in more than chopping vegetables, maybe we can arrange to talk someplace where we won't be disturbing everyone."

⁂

So the first step was taken, Grebbel thought, and it could have been much less promising. Larsen had obviously been very ambitious and very busy when he started his reclamations. Grebbel decided he could begin by ignoring all those with irrelevant backgrounds—the irredeemable kleptomaniac, the two child abusers, the wife-poisoner—and most of the women.

He would still have the makings of a reasonable core of helpers if those he approached were as sympathetic as Lafayette seemed likely to be. He considered his next moves.

▲

He wasn't sure if there were female sumo wrestlers, but if there were, Karina Fujiwara looked as though she could have been one. He found her in the vehicle maintenance shop, up to her elbows in transformer fluid. She heard him out quietly, without shifting attention from her work. He couldn't read anything from her manner or her expression while he talked, but finally she nodded.

"You talk some more," she muttered. "I listen. Then we see."

▲

In one of the workshops behind Hut Seven, Kurt Winter was using finely powdered rouge to grind the blank for an astronomical telescope. "It's a bit more than a hobby with the boss," he told Grebbel, "and a bit less than top priority. No question, though, we could use a mirror this size, in a permanent mounting. We've got a site marked out for the dome, and we hope to start building this summer." He explained how he had helped modify the spare furnace and adjust the composition of the charge to cast good blank discs. He pretended to glance over his shoulder and winked. "I learned this back there. I think the boss guesses I've got more old circuits working than I used to have, but she says nothing, I say nothing, the work goes on."

"You like being a glorified window cleaner?"

"Hey, when I was a kid, this was my dream. To build a real telescope. Like Newton, you know, like Galileo. Only I grow up and find they do everything by robot, unless you got three doctorates in engineering and a computer degree. Anything else, it's just a toy. You wait for a power cut to take the streetlights away, and no cloud, and then you can see the power sats, if you're lucky, through the photo-smog. And even the secretaries down the road, they all close their blinds before they get ready for bed. . . . Here, what I make is real. Even with the orbiters, even through this deep an atmosphere, there's enough here for everyone. We'll be doing real measurements with this one, a year from now, if she silvers right. That's always the tricky part, getting the surface down good with what we've got to work with." He seemed to be relishing the challenge.

"So all you were back there is behind you now."

"Back there, I was someone who wanted to make telescopes. What else I was isn't important, it isn't real any more. It's gone. Done with."

"Say it often enough and maybe you'll believe it," Grebbel snapped, and immediately knew he had gone too far.

Winter peered intently at his mirror. "I'd imagine we'd both have more important things to be doing than talking about what's best left alone. I can tell you I have."

"Then I'll let you get on with it." Grebbel turned and walked out into the sunlight.

▲

After Kurt Winter, he found Hendriks, Shelling, Abercrombie, DeWitt. Enough for the time being. He resisted the urge to cast his net wider and increase the risk of being discovered. He felt vibrant, confident in his decisions, so that where they led was almost irrelevant. If he had believed in such things, he would have said he had found the path to his destiny.

He met Partridge and delivered a package.

"Manna from heaven," whispered the astronaut. "Ah, you've got a good heart in you, mate. The nights have been pretty rocky recently, I don't mind telling you. And what do you want from the wind's whispers for next time?"

"I'm curious about weapons," Grebbel said.

▲

Elinda watched the clouds blowing across the mountain peaks as she walked, snow and cloud mixed against the deep purple sky. She was haunted by unformed memories of liver-coloured skies and dark, greasy water. On days like this, when the memories seemed ready to congeal into reality, angular rhythms would sound in her head, like the outline of something from another room heard faintly in the night.

She knocked at Grebbel's door and went in.

There was excitement in his manner when he saw her. "Surprise, surprise," he said. "Fancy meeting you here."

"Where else?" she asked. "You haven't been around anywhere else I've looked."

He seemed uncomfortable for a moment. "I've been busy. Making plans. I've . . ." He shook his head and stared at her. "What's been happening to you? You're looking exhausted."

"I've been planning, too," she said. "Or trying to. Hard work, this planning, isn't it?" She stifled what felt like the start of a hysterical giggle. "I think I need some help. Because I've gone so far now, I can't give it up." She tried to unknot her fists. Her arms were trembling as though she had been up to her elbows in icy water. Now he was closer to her than he had been for days, and there was a restlessness in his eyes, an animal intensity that suggested to her a predator turned prey.

"It's in you too, isn't it?" she said. "It's fear—the fear you feel when you know you're going to walk through the graveyard at night, and you could back out, but you won't because you've committed yourself and something in you would break and die if you changed your mind."

He looked at her steadily and nodded. "Break and die. Yes." He had moved close to her. The corner of his mouth twitched, but his eyes still stared. He swallowed and seemed about to reach for her, and she felt herself quiver like a drum. Then he closed his eyes and twisted away.

He sat down at the desk by the window and pulled a box toward him. "I tore up all the props they gave me, all the mementos of my so-called past life." He gave a short, choking laugh. "I was wondering what I would replace them with, when you came in. . . . You're right: I've been avoiding you."

She sat down. Now she was cold all over. "Because of what you've remembered?"

He nodded, not looking at her.

"What is it," she said hoarsely, then cleared her throat. "What have you remembered?"

"Lots of things," he said, so softly she could barely hear him. "A white stuccoed house on a quiet street. The colour of the first car we owned. My father's aftershave when he kissed me goodnight. The smell of gin that sometimes went with it. The pictures in the anatomy texts I used to sneak away and read—

the nightmares they gave me. And the cat. Lots of things, from a normal childhood."

She swallowed, and uttered the words calmly: "What else?"

Slowly he turned to look at her. His eyes were steady, watching for her reaction. His lips thinned in what might have been meant for a smile. "I was a doctor."

TWELVE

She was compelled to listen.

He talked for a long time, in a quiet, controlled voice, describing what he had been and what he had done, giving details, all the time with his gaze fixed on her, hardly blinking. He was tense and still, making no gestures, hardly ever turning his head or looking away while he found the right words. The speech came out of him as if he were reading it from the air between them.

"So now you know," he said finally, and waited, still watching her.

The cold had sunk into her bones. She could feel nothing but the tension that petrified her, that would shatter her if she tried to move. Then she saw how the same rigidity held him; she saw his eyes looking out from it. "You'll never be happy now," she whispered. "Never again."

He flinched, as though a cold gust had struck his face. His gaze lost focus, then returned to her with full intensity. "That's all you have to say to the monster? You're not appalled."

"It's in the past, what you did," she said, clinging to the last illusion. "It's over."

"Is it?"

Of course it wasn't over: he was making plans. She said nothing.

"If you're not appalled," he whispered, "you should be terrified." There was intense concentration in his face now. She could almost see the opposing tensions threatening to pull him apart. "You should get out of here and run for your life."

If she moved, he might spring at her. If she got up, if she left, she would tear herself open. "Is that what you want?" she asked. "Do you want me to run away from you?"

He shoved the chair back and stood up. For a moment he loomed towards her. Then he had turned and was pressing his forehead against the window. "I enjoyed it, what I did—I still enjoy it. You realise that? And to women. You don't know what you're risking. You haven't seen—you can't know . . ." He swung round to face her with his fists held shaking in front of him. His face was white. It contorted, and was immediately expressionless again. Through bloodless lips he whispered, "Why are you doing this to me? Why did you come?"

"What am I doing to you? Say it. Say it, say it—because otherwise I've gone mad and tied myself to a monster that doesn't care for me or anything human."

"Care for? Is that what you want me to say?" For the first time, he was shouting. "Care? Like a six-year-old with a best friend— with a kitten? Did the arena bull *care* for the dart in its flesh? Does the whale *care* for the harpoon? If I could rip you out of me, I'd do it, and be myself again."

"But you can't," she said, and was briefly, shockingly comforted. "We can't."

"No," he said flatly, "I can't . . . So we're tied to each other. Is that what it's come to? Conjoined twins? If one is destroyed, the other goes too."

"And if we try to cut the bond, we bleed," she acknowledged. "But it doesn't have to be that way. We can help each other. We can be stronger than we were separately. Oh god—don't look like that. It must work. It has to. We've got to make it work."

"That—that leaflet was right. We're insane, both of us. Or if we're not, this will drive us mad."

"Jesus Christ. . . . Yes I know."

He had been gripping the back of the chair with both hands. Now he scraped the chair across the floor and moved towards her. "Why did you have to come here today? I was . . . I had it all coming into place. Everything was clear. It fitted: who I was, what I was going to do—and I'm still going to do it! I am! They'll see what I am, all of them. They'll hate me, they'll scare their children with my name, but they'll remember. . . . And you'll hate me. You hate me now, part of you does, and you hate yourself for being here. Hate and pain and fear—they're what make people act, they make us what we are, because you can drive out anything else with them. Anything at all. And they last. Have you seen a man who's been broken by pain, or who's just discovered the strengths of his own terrors? He's marked for life—deeper than if he'd lost an arm. And love—have you seen what happens between a man and a wife when pain is used to divide them? Or between a mother and child?"

"Stop it! You don't have to do this, you don't have to be this way. Give it up—"

"Don't I? Don't I really?" He fumbled with the fastening of his sleeve, then tore the button off and ripped the cloth back from his arm. He brandished his scars at her. "How do you think I got these?" Before she could speak, he snatched up a glass and swung it against the edge of the table. Shards flew and the remains glittered in his fist.

"Glass," he said, and thrust it towards her. "It's sharp, it cuts. It hurts." Then he brought the splinters to his arm and began to rake them along his scars. She saw his wrists quiver with strain, his free hand spasm and clench.

"There was a window," he said, between ragged breaths, "in the passageway from the garage, when they took me to the treatment centre back there. It looked into a storage area. An old window in a grey wooden frame. I disabled one of the guards and put my fist through it. Then I raked my arm. They had a tight schedule; I knew they wouldn't have time to get rid of the scars. I wanted something to remind me, when I got to this side. If necessary, if I'd had time, I'd have gouged an eye out. I'd do it now."

On his forearm the glass left ragged white furrows that turned red and dripped. He faced her until her gaze was wrenched back to his eyes. "Tell me now it's not necessary," he whispered. "Tell me I can give up anytime. Tell me I can stop being what I am."

"God damn you, you can try! Is hurting the only thing that matters to you, is that all you understand? You think because you do that to yourself, because you're in pain, it justifies anything? It doesn't. It's a show, it's to convince you more than me."

She had risen and moved close to him; but when she reached for the glass in his hand, his wounded arm jerked up and he seized her wrist. The shards with their red smears and globules threatened her face. "I am," he muttered. "Not some puppet they think they've made."

She forced her gaze back to his eyes. "I won't beg." Her tongue was shrivelled, her lips numb. "Either use that thing or give it to me."

"You wouldn't say that if you'd seen what happens. So many of them start out like that, saying they won't talk, they won't confess, they won't beg."

"Add me to your list then, or let me go. Your arm needs bandaging."

She moved her free hand, found his shirt sleeve, felt towards the wrist. She would not look away from his eyes. His skin was hot and damp. His hand quivered, but was immovable as the handle of a locked door. She dared not look down to see if her fingers were smeared with blood. She found the glass, sticky when her thumb brushed a sharp edge, then smooth and cold. She tugged, and it came into her hand. His fingers slipped from her other wrist.

She did look down. The glass was clutched in her fingers, a cruel, leaking gem. On her other arm were yellowish marks, as though she had been manacled, darkening as she watched. Carefully, she reached out and put the glass on the table. It rattled as it left her fingers. She pulled her arm back and turned to him. Her mouth spoke. "Let me see your wrist."

Her body made its way to the bathroom, found bandages, returned. It wrapped his arm like a parcel, with fingers as brittle as glass tongs. When it was finished, her hands tied the bandage, and, marionette-like, she walked back to the bathroom with the remainder.

When she returned, he had picked up the broken glass from the table and was testing its edges with his thumb.

She screamed and ran at him.

"Throw it away!"

Glass shattered on the floor. She struck out, shouting, trying to hurt, then to seize him, shake him—

And then they were clinging together, their shared solidity the only refuge in a world gone to chaos. There was no room in them for gentleness. Instead of warmth there was desperation, and passion in place of hope. Her body felt weak as if it had been beaten, so that she looked for bruises when she bared it. But there was only the pale vulnerability of a drowned swimmer in the light of the morgue.

He was faceless with the light behind him, tearing his shirt off—his head drawn out into a horned grotesque—and black as his shadow. Then he came to her, cold waves of light sliding across his skin, his face that of a man awaiting execution.

⏶

He went to her, and his shadow slid from her face to enshroud her body. His skin trembled, as though he had been charged with lightning, and to discharge that tension would flash him out of existence. And yet the tension would not be borne. He was compelled towards her; and though she was the one who gasped and arched when they touched, he felt the shock throughout his body.

Before, she had been motionless; now she seized him and writhed and choked against his cheek. He could no longer help her, only let her hold him, and hold to her himself, while something in his spine, in the back of his head, and finally close behind his eyes, tightened and pulled and stretched, and would not, would not break. His mouth strained wide. He had lost sight of her, and darkness covered his eyes. The only sounds were the sounds of suffering. And the tension bent him backward without promise of release.

She spasmed and moaned aloud, then fell silent, then moaned again. His eyes flickered open. Her face was crimson, crumpled like a newborn child's.

He bent towards her—and the tension broke. The shock of discharge surged through his limbs and erupted into his brain—a white incandescence of sensation beyond pain or joy, that obliterated all he had ever been.

⏶

Slowly he came back into himself, into suspension between the poles of his existence. His cruel hand smoothed and caressed. His clinical eyes watched, and were clouded. His awareness, his vision of future possibility was shrinking to encompass only this other human, this other sack of vulnerable struts and pulp. His practised fingers touched flesh, and they trembled.

She stirred, slowly and heavily rising from her private depths. Her eyes were closed, turned away from his face, their lashes wet.

Helpless, he held her against the hollowness in his chest.

Her jaw moved against his sternum several times before the words came. "I can't stay here. That's what it comes down to. We'll just keep torturing ourselves if we go on this way."

She slipped away from him and began to dress.

When she left, he watched her through the window until she was out of sight. The sun was sinking towards the mountain tops, and the inland passes were spilling cloud into the valley. Catching the sun as it came in along the river, a dirigible descended towards the landing field. He turned away and went to clean the blood and glass from the floor.

▲

The next weekend, Elinda let Carlo take her to a dance. In her closet she rediscovered a cream silk blouse and a maroon calf-length flared skirt. She tried to lose herself in the primitive energy of the music and her sheer physical exertion on the dance floor. Then she had one or two drinks too many. The bass was booming in her head. *Obstinate*, she thought, *obstinate bass, it never changes.*

Faces would swirl around her. After they had gone, she was able to identify them, wonder what they had said. Jessamyn with her friend, staring and frowning. Or had that been later, after she had bumped into Dr. Henry? Literally. Almost knocked them both down, him into the arms of the blonde beside him. She remembered apologising to him, and then talking for so long that Carlo got uncomfortable and left and came back with more drinks. Which perhaps was not the greatest idea in the world, because it was then that the faces started eddying past her and blurring, and she couldn't remember what she'd said to Henry or when he had left.

Some time later she was outside, with the divided moonlight freezing onto her face, and Carlo was becoming aggressively friendly. She tried holding him at arm's length, then pushed him away impatiently. When he tried again, she lost her temper and told him she'd find her own way home. There was an unpleasant scene that afterwards she could remember little of. In the middle of it, Carlo had shouted something like "You're not supposed to have met, you're not supposed to be interested any more."

Crazy drunken evening, she thought. Only when she was climbing the slope to her home and she remembered she was alone and unarmed did her mind start to clear. Then the pain in Carlo's face started to haunt her, and his last words.

"You're what I made." Had he really said that, or was it just part of the drunken chaos slopping about in her mind? "I tried to prevent all this, and you won't even let me show you the truth!" He had been staggering away from her, or she had been lurching out of his reach, and the streetlight had glistened on his face. He looked haunted.

Snapshots, she thought; *the mind playing games*. Already the memory, if was a memory, was sharpening, changing focus as she examined it. Had he been reaching for her hand then, or had she added that to the picture herself? She couldn't tell how drunk he had been, either. She could ask him what he had meant, but only if he had really said it, or believed he had said it.

Crazy, crazy evening. She felt lucky to have reached her front door without anything worse happening. The lights buffeted her when her hand slid onto the switch, and she moaned and turned them off again. She groped her way to the bed and dived gratefully into oblivion.

▲

Grebbel worked on the terminal in the lab, waiting until Osmon finished checking out the atomic-absorption spectrometer. He searched the database for the delivery schedules and payload capacities of both the shuttles and the dirigibles, and tried to estimate the amount of hardware in orbit. Finally Osmon disconnected his circuit probes and moved towards the door, and Grebbel called him over.

"I've been talking to some of the others," he began. "But I need someone I can trust. I think we have enough in common to be able to understand each other."

"Indeed," said Osmon. "Are you referring to private interests that go unfulfilled, or something larger?"

"Both. But mainly freedom. In the past, a hundred men, properly equipped, have been able to overthrow an empire. What do you think a dozen men—perhaps two dozen—properly organised, could do here?"

"Do you think there are two dozen of *us* ready to take such risks?"

"I think if a dozen of us got ourselves established, we could gather enough others to support a change in regime."

Osmon looked at him. "Getting established, though . . ."

"It will mean violence, of course."

"Not necessarily," Osmon said.

"What are you thinking of?"

"Something in the organisation of this settlement strikes a discord in my ears. That most unfortunate young woman who was found in the woods—she was not the first to be missing. And the way the matter was treated . . . There were accidents in the caves when the turbine rooms were first being opened up, and no effort was spared to find the missing. I believe that these investigations were stifled by someone in authority. If we knew who it was . . ."

"We might create an unwilling ally," Grebbel finished. "But is there time?"

"We set our own schedule, don't we?"

"Of course," said Grebbel, but his fists clenched and opened, then squeezed until the knuckles were white.

▲

Elinda slumped onto the hard chair beside Barbara's bed. Barbara lay on her side, facing away from her, apparently dozing, but her breathing was fast and light. Her hair, thick and long and dark brown, that Elinda had sometimes spent half an evening combing and braiding, hung tangled over her face, hiding her eyes. Elinda reached out, carefully, tentatively and smoothed it back. She wondered how long it had been since she had touched her former lover.

I've betrayed you, she did not say aloud. *I've left you in here and found . . . someone.*

She whispered: "I didn't mean to abandon you. I won't abandon you."

He's like us, he's lost his memories. But it's hurting him; it's hurting us both. I don't know what's going to happen.

"I'm trying to finish what you were doing. I'm trying but it's hard. Was it about our memories? We went—he and I—we went to the caves and we found Erika's body. Was that part of what you were looking for too, whatever sent her there? I don't understand what I'm doing, what it is I'm trying to find."

Barbara, why couldn't you have trusted me with any of this?

"Pal'ce," Barbara mumbled. "Do, do. Go, 'member."

Oh, why didn't you let me in then? Why can't you show me what's going on inside you?

⋀

Grebbel found Elinda in the Greenhouse, supervising the harvest of soya beans. "No shortage of volunteers," he commented, "even this late in the day. Does everyone work like this for the communal good?"

She looked at him. "There's a duty roster. Your name will come up soon enough. But, yes, several of them are volunteers. What are you looking for?"

"I'm always curious about things like group solidarity and the room for individual goals."

"This is only a social call, then." Just public enough to prevent another blowup. Very shrewd. "Except that I don't believe it. What do you want?"

He drew a breath. "I didn't want to leave things the way they were after last time. No, you're right, that's not the only reason I came, but it is one reason. Please believe me."

"All right," she said carefully. "Go on."

"I was wondering if you had made any more progress in finding out what had happened to Barbara. I still might be able to help." He paraphrased Osmon's comments, without saying who had made them.

"I'd already guessed somebody was pulling strings," she said. "But it's nice to know I'm not the only one who might be paranoid. No, I'm no further on, and I'm in no position to turn down help. Whatever the reason it's offered."

⋀

That evening she had invited Louise and Paulina in for dinner, and for the first part of the evening managed to engross herself with the business of slicing vegetables and cleaning the two-kilogram carp she had squandered her coupons on. She would have to live on fish stew for the rest of the week, but at least that would be better than the late-night snacks she too often resorted to.

Louise and Paulina still seemed warily solicitous, which made her wonder what sort of signals she was sending out. Over dinner, she realised she was babbling, while her two guests sat and watched her. Suddenly she ran out of energy, and there was an uneasy silence until Louise started talking about the latest political developments back on Earth. Elinda found it hard to generate any interest. Even when the conversation shifted to a new batch of satellite photos of the land to the south of the Flats, she felt remote from the discussion. Finally Paulina asked, "Have you been to see Barbara lately?" and Elinda felt the world close on her again with a snap.

"She isn't changing. I can hear her talking sometimes, but she's still not there with me, she's talking in her sleep, dreaming. . . . I should go and see her again."

Louise and Paulina exchanged looks, and Louise said, "Maybe you should worry about her less. You're putting yourself under a lot of strain. It's very good of you to be loyal, but if there's nothing you can do—"

"She's not dead. She's trapped in a dream. Maybe I can wake her. If not . . ." She fell silent, frowning.

"What, Elinda?"

"Maybe there's a way to get into the dream with her."

▲

A chain of creatures like great slow birds flew high across the twin moons. Each pair of wings glinted silver for an instant as it moved out of silhouette, then was lost against the sky.

Jon Grebbel's divided shadows strode ahead of him as he made his way to Hut Seven. Osmon was waiting when he arrived, and the others drifted in one by one: Lafayette, Shelling, Hendriks, even Karl Winter, having abandoned his telescope for the evening. They were all early, but Grebbel waited until the appointed time before starting to speak.

"Thank you all for being punctual," he began, "and for being patient until I was ready to start. I appreciate that sort of consideration. It shows good social adjustment, and I admire that. Patience, especially—and I know how patient you all are. It takes a particular strength of will, it takes real courage, to continue to live your lives, and know all the time you're living a fake." He paused briefly. They were watching him with guarded interest.

"You've all been shown the truth about this place and the truths about yourselves. You all know how you came to be here. And you've managed to put that knowledge aside, to go on living as though it doesn't exist. You've fitted yourselves to the clothes they hung on you. You're model citizens now, well adjusted, patient, punctual—and I admire you for all that. You, Joe," he said to Abercrombie, who had been leaning back on the crate he was sitting on and looking sceptical, "you've made a life for yourself here, haven't you? You've put all that past behind you; you don't get hankerings after things that are best forgotten. I think that's admirable."

He paused and looked at them all. When it seemed that the questions would start coming, he went on. "Let me confess something. I'm not like you. I'm not cut out to be a model citizen. I'm not a man with the sort of patience you have. If someone insults me, I expect an apology. If they steal from me, I expect the money to be returned with interest; I expect them to be punished so that neither they nor anyone else would be encouraged to steal from me again. If someone injures me, I expect recompense, and I expect them to be deterred from ever injuring me again. I expect them to suffer as much as I suffered. What should I do then, when someone injures me by stealing my own past, my own self, by prying into my brain, my mind, and wiping away the years of my life? If I were like you, if I were a patient man, perhaps I would be content, as you are, and do nothing. As you do."

There were stirrings now, shufflings; someone coughed and muttered.

"You had reputations, all of you. People knew your names. Some of them shivered when they spoke them. You had weight among them, you reminded them that life was not to be taken for granted. And now you'd show them how much patience a human being can possess—except that you can't show them anything, or you'd stop being the model citizens you're all so content to be.

"Or are you? Are you so content? After all, you're here. You came when I asked, and you could all guess what I wanted to talk about. And you all came here patiently and on time."

"We're stuck here at the arse-end of creation," Abercrombie called out, "with an armed militia breathing over our shoulders. What do you expect us to do? Storm the U.N. garrison from here?"

"I'm going to do something. You don't need to know what just yet. I fully expect to get what I ask without using force. But if I'm wrong, and they turn on us, and force becomes necessary—in self-defence—the militia won't be the only ones with weapons."

"You're asking us to risk our necks without even telling us what you've got in mind."

"I'm asking nothing yet. I'm giving every one of you the chance to be what you want to be, not what they tried to make you. If you want in, we take it from there. If you don't, the less you know the better."

Karl Winter stood up. "I think I understand you well enough. This is not my idea of the way to a better life. I'll leave now. As long as no one is hurt, I will say nothing."

"Thank you for you honesty," Grebbel said. When the door had closed, he paced for a moment, then turned to the others. "The rest of you will want time to think. Let me point out something, though. This colony is important to them. They've poured money and time and effort into it, more money than any of us can imagine. They're not going to give it up easily. And the fact that we're at the arse-end of creation here, as you put it, cuts both ways. No, we can't take over the Rio Council, but what sort of police action can they mount from back there—particularly if we don't force their hand until we're secure here? The militia aren't invincible. I know the type of men they are; they can be broken. And remember there are a lot of other colonists here. There's a name for people like that. They've been called adventurers or explorers, the builders of a new civilisation; they've been called misfits and escapees. But I've got a simpler name. I call them hostages."

He looked at them. "Now, if you're not interested in any more of this, you're free to leave. But if you're with me, we can start getting down to business. . . ."

▲

When the group had left, Grebbel closed his eyes and sighed, then saw that Osmon had remained and was watching him. "Yes?

You enjoyed the performance, did you? You'd like an encore?"

"I know one doesn't detract from a historic performance by adding frills to it," Osmon said softly. "I was just waiting to close up the hut."

"Oh," said Grebbel bitterly. "A devotee, a fan."

"I don't think I understand you. I was impressed. I would think you'd be well satisfied with the way things went."

"Understand me?" Grebbel muttered. "I don't understand myself any more. What the fuck are we doing here—?" He turned to Osmon, who had not moved. "Well, don't let me keep you from locking up."

"Of course. You've set things in motion now; there will be changes."

"Like the kids' slide, or the sled," he muttered, "when you feel the thing starting to move." *And you hear the ice under the runners and you know it's already too late—you won't be able to stop it, and the hill curves away, you can't see where the run ends, and the fear is part of the excitement, the fear of the dark under the trees at the bottom of the slope, at the foot of the stairs, the mewling sounds, the room—*

"For god's sake, stop staring at me and do your work." Grebbel turned and left.

◢

Partridge shifted uneasily under Grebbel's gaze. "There's a crate of assault weapons I know about, and five thousand rounds. More than this group of boy scouts could shoot off before their pensions run dry. You think you want some of that?"

"About a dozen weapons right now, with at least thirty rounds each. If we can get that much out without it being missed straight away, so much the better. But I'll want more later, maybe at short notice. I know where we can store things now, and I expect more recruits. When we're ready to go, we'll take every weapon and every round of ammunition we can get."

"Christ on a crutch. You're dreaming. You been sampling too much of the stuff you're getting me?"

"Let me worry about my dreams."

"You'll get caught, Sonny, if you don't keep it small and slow. Whatever you're planning, you'll blow it into the wind if you can't keep it quiet. And if you go down, I know where that'll leave me—"

"Don't worry. They may start to suspect something, but we won't get caught, because we'll move fast, before they're ready."

▲

The dreams were no longer waking him, though they still left him with memories of going down—of being compelled downwards—into a darkened space where something crawled and waited. The thing to do was to keep everything focussed on the main goal, keep so busy the mind had no time to wander. And there were more urgent problems than his secret night fears. . . .

He looked up from the map he had spread under the light. "We'll have to move on two fronts. That means synchronised operations, and without the chance for a rehearsal. The main thrust will be at the landing field, because we'll need a blimp. The secondary operation will be within the settlement. Tallis, I want you to be ready to lock up the communications network if necessary." He turned so that he could meet all their eyes. "Is everything clear so far?"

"Where: that is clear, yes." Werner Schuhman the former aerospace engineer. "But I do not understand the how or the why, and certainly not the when."

"You don't know when, because I haven't told you." He drew a short flutter of laughter. Encouraged that they were keyed up enough, and on his side enough, to respond to a comment like that, he went on. "Nothing is settled yet, and certainly not the timing. That depends on a lot of things, including the schedules for the blimps. I'll give you more details as plans become clearer. You'll get enough warning, don't worry. As to how—I'll answer this, since you've asked it—how is easy, up to a point. We take the landing field, and a dirigible, and we start detonating explosives here and there until they give us what we ask for. I have some more ideas about how we do that, but I'll save them for a surprise later. And as for why—if you don't know that, it's not something I can explain in a couple of words. I'll tell you what, though. Give me a hand clearing up at the end, and maybe I can show you something that'll help."

As the others began to leave in ones and twos, Grebbel said to

Schuhman, "We may have a use for that training of yours."

Schuhman waited, hands in pockets, shuffling from foot to foot.

"I've been wondering about some of the satellites," Grebbel said. "I think it would be a good idea to keep an eye on them."

"I'm not sure I understand. They do not change orbit. They are more reliable than any dirigible timetable."

"I'm not so sure about that. But we'd need a telescope. A good optical telescope."

"You mean Karl's—Karl Winter's. You'd have to talk to him about it."

"Come outside a minute, and I'll show you what I had in mind." They stepped out into the dark. Grebbel led way up through the trees until the lights were almost all hidden. "You're a friend of Karl's, aren't you? It's a pity he couldn't have come in with us."

"I've helped him grind his mirror sometimes."

"So you'd know if it would be available for something like this in a few days."

"The silvering went much more quickly than he was hoping. But he's very protective of it. I don't think he would let anyone else use it."

"You have talked to him about that, then."

"We talk sometimes, when we grind the mirror, yes."

"And you're not sure about what you've got yourself into here, are you?"

"A few doubts—that's only human, isn't it?"

"Oh, yes," said Grebbel. He had positioned himself so that Schuhman was silhouetted against the moonlit clouds. He tensed himself and flexed his fingers. "It's perfectly human. But very dangerous."

▲

Grebbel lurched against a tree and stumbled into a patch of moonlight. His hands were dark and sticky. They looked like talons grafted onto his wrists.

Water. He could hear a stream. A few seconds with running water and those hands would be his again. A few moments more and his heart would cease its hollow battering, his throat would ease, he would be able to breathe again. There was enough moonlight, but the world swam and blurred. The cold was making his eyes water, that was it, or sweat was running into them. It was important to explain these things, to keep a grip on reality, so there would be no doubt who he was and that he was still in command of his actions. Otherwise the mewling idiot that was trying to take control of his brain would come back, and they would have beaten him after all.

The ground slipped from under him and he almost rolled into the stream. For a moment he wanted just to lie there. But that was the weakling too. He had to do something. To wash his hands, remove the evidence. *The first,* he thought suddenly, *the first here.*

He plunged his hand into the water.

The cold bit his flesh. He watched dark stains unravel into the current until his fingers gleamed through the ripples like ice. Crouched on the bank here, he could only reach one hand into the water at a time. It would have been easier if the bank were lower here, or there were stepping stones in the water. . . .

The moonlight glittered into his mind from the scale-backed stream. Silver ropes and handfuls of coins tumbled and vanished and returned. Finally he pulled his hand out and stared at it. From each finger colourless liquid dripped. The flesh must be wrinkled and pulpy now, but the light wasn't strong enough to show that. His mouth whispered, ". . . a long snow-slope, with a fence at the bottom, and Orion rising above it." And a night breeze stirred the branches.

He shivered and plunged the other hand, thrashed it about in the water, then pulled it out, and rubbed the two together. Clothes, shoes—he would have to do a proper inspection. Osmon must have done his job by now. It was just a matter of keeping them off his trail until he was ready to strike. They would find the bodies in a few days, and then the search would narrow. He would have to be ready to act before they closed in on him.

◤

Elinda met Carlo outside the clinic. "Come in," he muttered. "We'll be less conspicuous inside than out." It was after hours and stars glinted among high clouds.

"I'm not worried about being seen," she said.

"You may be, later. In any case, I am."

"You said you wanted to talk," she said briskly as they went in. "That's fine, because I need help in reaching Barbara, and it looks like you're the only one who can provide it."

"You're very cold. You're not making it easy for me."

"I'm sorry, but I haven't got a lot of spare sympathy any more. If you don't want to talk, let me tell you what I've been thinking."

"I don't know what we can do for Barbara that we haven't already tried."

"Some time ago Dr. Henry was talking about your machine being like a surgical tool, a light-pipe. It took me a while to make the leap, but finally I got there: does it mean you could go into someone's mind, that you could look around in it, and find out what was wrong and help them, even if they couldn't talk to you?"

He frowned. "Things like that have been tried. But it's not easy, and no one's proved there've been any real benefits. There are problems in matching two brains, maybe two minds, separating what looks like real communication from illusions created in the connection, or even one's own submerged fantasies—the thing behaves more like a badly cracked mirror than like a window. I think I can guess why you're interested, but I'm not going to encourage you. There are some real risks for the users, too— one or two psychoses have almost certainly been triggered by experiments like that."

"I'll leave the clinical therapy to you; what I want is to find out what happened—that's all I can do for her for now. And you're saying this idea might work."

"You're talking about leaping off a cliff that might be two metres high or twenty kilometres." Carlo took a step away from her. "Supposing it does work, you manage to get into her mind, you do find something in there, and you both come back after the experience—how are you going to be able to trust it? We're fishing in very muddy waters here, polluted as likely as not, and some of the things down there can bite."

"If it's come from her mind, I can check it out afterwards."

"It may not be that simple," he said. "These machines—I've been trying to make you understand—they play with both your minds, you might stir up fantasies from your own subconscious— you might never make contact with her at all. Or, if you do make a link, god knows what sort of illusion the two of you could unknowingly produce."

"I understand that. It's a risk I'm prepared—"

"Let me finish this, please. Or I'll never be able to say it. These machines—one of their functions, not their main function, is to impress illusions on a suitably prepared mind. These illusions can be quite abstract; the machine and the operator look into the subject's mind and find images, sense-data that will make them real."

"You use the machine to create a fiction—an imaginary life."

"A legend, it might be called in some areas. But of course. there's a major difference. The fiction is written into the subject's mind, so it is no longer fiction as far as that subject is concerned: it becomes part of the mind. It can amount to a new personality."

She was staring at him. "You said—the other night you said you'd created me."

"My job here is to implement the instructions given me—to install past histories compatible with the required personality types I'm asked to shape. You were one of them. I was given a program to break you out of certain behaviour patterns. In some respects at least, I haven't done very well. But still . . ." He hesitated. "I don't know all of what you were before, but what you are now is in large measure a product of the machine and my own efforts."

"Jesus Christ." she whispered and closed her eyes. "I . . . I can't deal with that now." Then she looked him in the eyes. "You've no choice but to help me."

He stared at her.

"You're being stupid, Carlo. You've already given me an illegal gun, and now you've told me this place's secret. You'd better do exactly what I want."

"Christ, you're serious, aren't you?"

"Clever man."

"Oh god. . . . Well, we can try. But not yet. I need time to test out the programs and check over the machines. And we'll have to find an evening when things are quiet."

"I'm sure that's all within your capabilities. I have complete faith in you, Carlo. Just don't leave it more than a week."

⋏

Grebbel levered back the lid of the crate and flicked his flashlight beam over the contents. He nodded. "Ingram machine pistols.

They'll do for close-range work. Get them out of here and put the crate back at the bottom of the rack." He looked towards Shelling crouched with his black box inside the door of the darkened weapons store. "How much longer can you keep the alarms quiet?"

"Maybe ten minutes, before they change codes. But the guard'll be round before then."

"This'll have to be enough. Find the azoplas explosives and let's get this lot into the cave."

⋀

"You look as though you haven't been sleeping," Elinda said to him. "That's what you told me before, but now it's you." They were walking outside the cafeteria, the smoky daylight warm on them.

Grebbel gave a short laugh. "Who has time to sleep?"

"I saw the eagles again this morning," she said as they walked on. "I thought I might go up there, to the caves, again sometime soon."

"No," he said. "Don't do that."

"No? Have you found something else—? No: it's to do with what you're planning, isn't it—whatever's keeping you away at night? And we don't talk about that, do we?"

"I'm going to talk to Carlo," she said. "He started to tell me something about our memories, and I want to get the rest of it out of him. And there's more. I think I know how to reach Barbara."

"Don't tell me, Elinda. You're trying to force me to tell you what I'm doing, and I can't."

"You won't. If you're so ashamed of it, then don't do it."

"It's not a matter of shame, it's deeper than that. And anyway—" He broke off and shook his head.

"It's too late? You've sold yourself already?"

"Not sold. Maybe bought, reclaimed. Yes, reclaimed, at a price."

"I'm going to ask Carlo to help me, and if he can't or won't—"

"*Don't tell me.*"

⋀

Larsen and Menzies were walking beside the dam. The air was warm. His head lowered, Larsen pulled his hands out of his pockets and squeezed them together. "You're sure about it?" he asked. "You've seen him with the others?"

"I've seen enough to be sure they're holding meetings. Our Mr. Grebbel is planning something."

"It's good of you to say 'our,' but the responsibility is mine, I'm afraid. I should have checked on him myself, but I suppose I didn't want to believe he would go so far, or so quickly."

"Don't try to take everything on you again. It's ours. We have to decide what to do."

"Thank you," Larsen said. "You're right. The trouble with knowing both sides is that there are no illusions left. And the woman in my office, Michaels—she's been asking questions. She suspects something. I don't think Grebbel can have confided everything to her, but she has her own interests, and she'll be in danger if she follows them much further."

"She's still trying to find out what happened to that woman they found in the woods?"

"Yes, and she's part of this somehow, and Michaels may cause things to unravel from that end if she's not careful. I fear that whatever we try, someone is going to be hurt, and if it isn't us, it may be someone more innocent."

▲

Five days later, Carlo told Elinda the arrangements were complete, and she met him that evening in the clinic. "I shouldn't be letting you do this," he said. "If we had any formal regulations here I'd never get away with it. Back there, they'd have my licence before I could get out of the door."

"But this is here, and any willing help is useful, isn't it? So let's get started, shall we. . . . I don't mean to snap, I'm probably more uptight than you are, that's all. I'm grateful to you, if that makes things any easier."

They wheeled Barbara's bed into the instrument room. She was sleeping fitfully, loosely penned under an elastic sheet. Carlo set up an IV drip beside the bed.

"What's that?" Elinda asked. "I thought she was drugged to the eyeballs already. I want to reach through to her, remember?"

"I don't think her conscious mind is going to be much use to you," he said. "We've used this before. It seems to allow the unconscious some ease of expression. We'll give you a light dose too, to help the contact."

JANUS

Barbara muttered and blinked as the needle was taped to her arm. Watching, Elinda felt a stab of guilt at reducing Barbara to an experimental subject. She slid onto the bed next to her and closed her eyes while Carlo finished his preparations.

Then came the connection of the headsets. The rigid plastic hood went over her face, plugs fitted into her ears, closing out sight and sound. "Hold still," Carlo's voice said in her ears. "I'm going to inject a mild muscle relaxant." There was something cold and wet against the inside of her elbow, then a faint pricking. In the quiet dark she floated alone.

THIRTEEN

"I'm going to run some tests now," Carlo's voice said. "I'll ask you some questions and monitor your brainwave patterns when you answer. It'll help me adjust the impedances on some of the feedback circuitry. Later on, you can just think of the answers, but at first I want you to speak them out loud. Is your name George . . . ?"

For several minutes, she answered simple questions, some of them more than once, and then thought of sensations as Carlo asked her to. He muttered into the microphone occasionally as though he was having trouble adjusting his settings, but finally he was ready to make the link.

"I'm energising the transmission circuits now. You may feel a slight disorientation." She did: it was like being on an unlit stage and having the curtain go up to uncover a darkened auditorium. "I'm going to flash a light on and off in front of Barbara's face. Let me know when you see something."

For an unmeasured pause, nothing happened. She felt like a creature of the ocean depths groping for sunlight, or a swimmer in the toils of a muddy canal. Then came a pale, moth-like glow, through which she could still sense the surrounding darkness. It faded before she remembered to call out. "There! Just then, I saw it!"

It flickered again. Strengthened. "Yes. It's there, it's coming clear!"

The ghost grew flesh. It shrank and focussed, drew near.

Eyelids blinked across it. It was a small, blue-shaded angle lamp, and the wall of the instrument room was dimly visible beyond it.

"Good," Carlo said. "Let me lock that in. Now I'm going to lift her arm. . . ."

There was a lot more. Tactile sensations, then hearing. For smell, he waved a bottle of acetic acid under Barbara's nose; for taste, he touched her tongue with a swab dipped in saline solution. It was pedestrian and uncertain, Carlo admitted, but still the best way they knew to open up any contact.

"I've done all the fine-tuning I can," he said at last. There's not much more I can do to help. You'll have to try to find her though her senses. Try to feel what she's thinking, try to hear what she remembers."

The drug had left Elinda lightheaded. Now she found herself feeling without touch, groping without limbs into a soft, resonant darkness.

She smelled tobacco smoke—as clear as moonlight breaking through clouds, and then gone. A moment later came a glut of sensations as if she had opened the door to a brilliantly lit room full of shouts of laughter and screaming and the hot pungency of sweat and woodsmoke, and then the door had been slammed before she could identify any faces.

Even as she was trying to sort out her impressions, larger, vaguer patterns began to form. They seemed to be some distance from her, and she pushed through the dark unspace toward them. She heard voices. At first she could not understand them, could tell only that there was at least one man and one woman, and they were shouting. She found herself listening for another sound, another different voice, and was both disturbed and relieved at its absence. Then the voices became quieter. She began to recognise isolated words, but their sense slipped away before she could link them together.

She wanted to see, to understand what was happening. But as she tried to move closer, the voices faded and were lost. She felt as if another door had been closed in her face.

Barb, she thought into the emptiness. *Don't shut me out. It's me, it's Lindy.*

The darkness churned, and was still.

Barbara. Please let me in.

The world was shaken as by a great sob. Close by, or from

the edge of existence, came the keening of a cold thin wind. She sensed black limbs swaying under icy stars. The night was full of the sound, mindless, tormented and insistent. Suddenly there was a white room with recessed ceiling lights and padded walls. The door was cushioned, too, with quilting where the handle should have been, and pads over the hinges. It was opening.

The room had not seemed dark, but as the door swung wider, an unbearable white light blazed in from outside, and the walls seemed to become dark mist. In the midst of the light, the angel entered.

The angel was dark only in comparison to the light that accompanied her. Her hair was yellow, her skin white, but she was tall and terrible in that room. She had the face of a holy inquisitor, living in an ecstasy of transcendence while performing horrors. "Filth," said the angel. "You are a debased creature. You are an affront to decency, a wart on the face of existence. You deserve no better than to rot in here. But I have accepted the task of redeeming you, and I must do what I can." The angel began to undress.

When she was naked, she came forward. Her eyes were cold and calculating, her hands like pale talons. "You'll have to show me what to do," she said.

The room vanished. Somewhere, far away in the dark, was the high keening sound; then it too faded and was gone. She was alone.

"That wasn't me!" she cried aloud. "I've never seen you in a cell!"

But the angel's last sentence had been hers. She remembered saying the words, the first night in Barbara's old room. And behind the cruel exalted mask, the angel's face had been hers, too. And the manner—?

She wanted to cry.

I'm sorry. I didn't understand. I didn't know what you needed, what I was doing to you. Don't shut me out now, please let me help you. Let me in, show me. . . .

She looked for light, and found none. She felt around for a doorway, but there was nothing. More urgently, she groped for anything that broke the silent stifling void.

She seemed to fall. And suddenly, the darkness thickened about her. It blocked her nose, forced itself into her throat. She began to choke, made frantic sweeping motions with her arms. She did not know whether she was soaring into the depths or diving toward the surface, but she sensed that what had happened so far was mere preliminaries, that the real revelation was about to appear before her.

She struck bottom.

The darkness crushed her down. She choked and struggled and tried to scream, and something opened beneath her, and again she fell.

She became aware of rough warmth—old bedsheets and a crumpled pillow. Stale, unventilated rooms, a leaky kerosene stove, diesel fumes from the bridge to the docks, and a chemical stink from the canal. There were always trucks on the bridge. She could feel the vibrations in the air, but there was no sound. There was no sound—but she could feel the abrasion of air in her throat when she breathed, and the pounding of the blood in her head.

She reached out under the sheets, her eyes still closed, wanting the feel of hard flesh, even the gritty stubbled cheek, rather than emptiness now. But there was nothing. She was faced with the day again, alone. Hopelessly she opened her eyes. The light through the blinds was brownish—the perpetual sodium lights of the dock road filtered through the smog over the canal. Her clock radio with the missing LEDs showed either 2:23 or 3:23. Still the middle of the night.

But she had to get up. Something had pulled her from sleep and was still pulling at her. Her hands were trying to sketch motions in the air; her lungs, her mouth were hinting at revelations to be taken out and studied—just as soon as she could get to that machine in the other room, just as soon as she could deal with what was pulling at her. Just as soon as she could stop it and get enough peace to listen to what her mind was offering her. But the silence choked everything.

It was the silence that had dragged her from her sleep again. It blocked her ears, it stuffed her throat until she wanted to gag. Even her eyes burned from it and ached to close. The silence had been keeping her awake for too many nights, choking off her work for weeks. Now it was making her get up and tend to it when she could feel the work finally throbbing for attention within her.

Push back the sheet and the heavy blanket. Cold wooden floor underfoot. Walking without sound. Measured breathing: in, two three four, hold, two three four, out, two three four. The door handle is loose, doesn't rattle. Don't look across the living room to the machine with its keyboard and headphones, not yet. The silence comes first. Into the other room. Turn on the light.

There it is—on its back, face screwed into scarlet wrinkles, its toothless mouth strained wide and drooling—each heave of its tiny lungs forcing out the silence. Silence that begins to split the brain like a wedge.

Beyond the open window is the grim and oily surface of the canal.

▲

When Carlo finally lifted the helmet away, she was weeping uncontrollably.

"I pulled you out as fast as I could," he said. "You were gone so long—"

"Her baby. She drowned her little girl in the canal."

"You got that from the link?"

She nodded, choking. "Near the end. I couldn't bear it after that."

"I heard you. I'm sorry. . . ." He took her hand. She seemed not to notice, and after a moment he turned away and began fussing with the equipment, turning off switches, rolling up lengths of cable.

"Carlo, please get me out of here. I'm too weak to move." She had begun to shiver. "I shouldn't have done this."

He turned off two more switches and came back to her. "That needle will wear off in a few minutes. I'll help you into the one of the other rooms until then."

"Yes. Thank you." They reached the door, she leaning heavily on him. "Carlo, I'm sorry. I made you do this and it was all a waste. I didn't learn what I wanted to know, and I found out things I shouldn't have known. What's worse, I've told you about them, when I had no right to."

He helped her to a chair. "Don't worry about that now."

"I have to worry. If it isn't my responsibility, whose is it?"

"It may not be anyone's. I told you before we started, what you find with that technique may not be real."

"Oh god, that was real."

"It seemed real to you; there's probably a real emotionally

charged experience underlying whatever you found—but it doesn't mean that what you found really happened. I don't believe the link was working properly a lot of the time there. I was worried—something was happening but it didn't look like the sort of communication we've seen before. But then, we've never tried it in these circumstances. You might have picked some random aberration out of the electronics, and built it into whatever you saw."

"You mean it's all been a big game of electronic Rorschach?" she said. "Putting my own interpretation on random data. You think I wanted to believe that of her?"

"I didn't say that—"

"But it follows from what you did say. . . . And, god help me, it may be true, I think it's true. She showed me how I'd used her: I'd turned to her here—*been* turned to her here, Carlo—when I really needed something else, and she knew it. Everything I've done for her since has been done from guilt. She made me realise that, and I hit back at her, by believing that about her."

"When I hear a piece of self-analysis as facile as that, I always suspect it's there to hide something else. I think you're being too hard on yourself right now. I think the truth is somewhere else."

"No, I think it's true. I tried to get rid of that load of guilt by dumping it on her when she couldn't fight back. No wonder I feel sick."

"Well. We won't settle that now. Where do you go from here?"

"That's a good question, Carlo. I suppose I have to keep working on it the way I was before. I can't see anything else to do." She struggled to push herself to her feet. "I shouldn't have made you do this. Now I'd better go home before I do any more damage."

⋏

From the edge of the dam, Grebbel watched a dirigible drift to the landing pole. A cloud shadow slid from it, and the gasbag acquired an orange arc of highlight. He timed the stages of its approach as it butted into the headwind. When the airscrews were clearly idling and the gasbag was anchored, he turned his truck and headed back to the gravel pile. Menzies passed him on the way and rolled down his window as they crossed. "You've seen them often enough by now, haven't you? We're slipping behind as it is, without everyone stopping to gape at the traffic." There was more than impatience in his tone.

At the end of his shift, Grebbel met Osmon outside the clinic. "I think people are beginning to notice things," he said. "The foreman chewed me out for watching how the blimp came in, and I don't think he was just bothered about the production on his shift. I don't think he can do much without putting his own ass on the line, but the sooner we're ready to move the better."

"Yes," said Osmon. "The sooner the better. Security found Schuhman's body this afternoon. I think they're going to be asking questions, and I saw another party going into the caves. Not the section where the arms are hidden, but they looked ready to make a search."

Grebbel inhaled sharply and held a long breath. "She told them," he muttered. "They're forcing our hand." Then he nodded, and his shoulders relaxed. "Well, we're committed now. How far along are the preparations?"

"We've checked out the automatics as far as we can. We have the azoplas ready for installation."

"Right," Grebbel said and shivered. "The sooner the better, then. This weekend. To be safe, keep an eye on Larsen. Have Tallis help you. I'll try to watch Menzies myself."

⋀

After two days, Elinda went back to try and see Barbara. She found Carlo talking quietly with Dr. Henry in the entrance to the clinic. They stopped when she approached, and Henry turned to her with a smile.

"The young lady from the tavern. You've come to visit your old roommate, I suppose. She seems to be making some unexpected progress. We're all very happy about it, I don't need to say." He took a step towards the door. "In fact, I'm going to indulge one of my many vices in celebration. They won't let me practise it—or most of the others, it seems—inside here." He stepped to the door and pulled out a metal case, produced what Elinda recognised as a genuine-looking cigar and a lighter. "It's an abominable luxury that I really shouldn't indulge in," he said, but I find it soothes the nerves at times—helps difficult decisions resolve themselves. Be seeing you, I hope." He fastened his coat and put a flame to the cigar, puffed vigorously, then walked briskly away.

She turned to Carlo. "She's getting better? Can I see her?"

He frowned. "It's not quite that simple. There are encouraging signs, but so far, mainly clinical: we think her alpha rhythms and her sleeping patterns are coming closer to the normal range. Don't get your hopes up: you may not find a great deal of improvement. You can see her later—someone else is in there now, and she's sufficiently aware of other people to be tired by too much contact. I'll have to see how she looks when this visit's over."

"You're not telling me who's seeing her, but I think I can guess. . . . Did our experiment have anything to do with the change?"

"It's hard to say. If we look back at her records, we can find indications that things may have started changing a week or ten days back. And there have been other influences on her—it's not what you'd call a controlled experiment."

"When can I see her then?" she asked.

Jessamyn came out of the corridor when Barbara's room was. She stopped and spoke to Carlo. "She's tired now. I thought I'd better let her rest. But she knew me. She talked to me. She's going to make it." Her eyes were wet.

"Does she know what happened to her?" Elinda demanded.

Jessamyn turned to her. "I didn't ask her that," she said. "I thought there were more important things to worry about right now." To Carlo she said, "I'll make another appointment as soon as I can," and hurried away.

"Let me see her, Carlo, please," Elinda whispered. "I won't disturb her."

He looked at her, then shrugged. "I'll have to check on her first."

He came back a minute later. "I'll let you have a couple of minutes, but I'll have to stay and supervise."

"Okay. Thanks, Carlo."

They went in. Barbara was lying with her eyes closed, half turned towards the door. Elinda bent over her, tried to smooth Barbara's hair back from her face. Without opening her eyes, Barbara stirred, muttered, smiled. Elinda bent closer and whispered, "What, Barbara? I can't hear you."

Barbara muttered and opened her eyes.

When Elinda came out with Carlo two minutes later, she was trembling. Carlo reached for her hand. "I'm sorry. I'm very sorry."

"It's all right," she said stiffly. "It's not your fault. She just didn't know me, that's all. She thought I was Jessamyn again. It's not your fault." She freed her hand. "I'd better go and let you get on with your work. It's all right."

But it wasn't all right. As she walked back towards the Greenhouse, she still felt Barbara's rejection. What had she tried to say, at the beginning, before she had opened her eyes? *Car? Scar? Scarf?*

She remembered helping to carry her out of the bush. The red mud from Barbara's boots had rubbed onto her parka. It had looked like drying blood and had appalled her afterwards, so that she had spent an hour the next day cleaning it off. But when she had picked up the same mud from the cave in the mountain, it had hardly bothered her. And the day before Barbara had been found, when she might have gone looking, she had been oddly intrigued by the new arrival she had seen walking from the dirigible with Carlo and Dr. Henry.

Her mind swept her away from that, to memories of Barbara since then. The inert figure who had given no response to her until that strange meeting in the electronic unworld. She tried to remember how it had started. Darkness, then a patch of light, then falling into the cell— No. Something else, before that.

Tobacco smoke.

Cigar?

Barbara's words came back to her: "Do. What remember. Do. Do."

This time, without effort, she filled in the rest. *What you remember is what you are, and what you are is what you do. What I tell you to remember is what you'll be.* And then Dr. Henry, the hypnotist, had begun his performance in the bar. . . .

Dr. Henry. The last person to see Barbara before Elinda and Charley found her? Dr. Henry, the puppet-master?

She walked faster to try and control her trembling.

That evening she began to make enquiries. On the computer bulletin board, she found what might be clues: a reference to a rabbit hole, a comment on missing persons, female. But when she tried to follow them up, she found only whispers—something that Marcia had heard from Eric who had overheard Kwan-li talking to Jacqueline at work about what Jean-Luc had been told by someone who could always be trusted.

She went to Carlo and asked in general terms about corruption among the authorities. He insisted he didn't know anything for certain, but warned her to be careful. He hinted that there were things going on that some of the people back there didn't approve of, though others did.

There was such an edge of nervousness in his manner that she believed him enough to be sure she was on the right track.

Then she looked for Grebbel. It was the night of the Council meeting, and she was half convinced she was going to have to confront Henry herself.

Grebbel's room was empty. His heavy clothing and pack were gone. She started to wonder what that meant, then tore herself away and headed for the Council meeting.

She sat at the end of a row near the back, behind most of the usual sprinkling of spectators. She listened impatiently while the group on the platform debated schedules and labour assignments while deflecting most of the questions from the floor. Dr. Henry looked controlled and businesslike, keeping the discussions moving, making sure that voices were heard, opinions recorded.

At the end, as the meeting was breaking up, she approached the front. Henry was involved in a discussion with two other Council members, and she wondered how she was going to attract his attention. But he turned to her with a genuine-looking smile of recognition.

"The young lady I keep running into," he said. "We should introduce ourselves properly someday. You have some suggestions for running the Council meetings? Believe me, I've been looking for some way of streamlining these Procrustean exercises in time-dilation for years."

"No—actually I wanted to see you about something else—about memory problems."

"Ah. Something specifically concerning you?"

"Well—not me directly," she said, letting herself stammer a little. This game was obviously going to be played on more than one level, and something that looked like a transparent excuse might make her more credible as an ingénue with a crush. "A friend of mine—she told me about it. She gets these dreams, you see. She wakes up and she can't quite remember what she was dreaming about, but she's sure it was her past. And she's scared. She's convinced she did something horrible then, but she doesn't know what. It's driving her crazy. She doesn't know whether she wants to find out what's the truth behind it all—if that's possible, I mean—or just make them, the dreams go away. It's dreadful—you're scared to go to sleep, and when you wake up in the morning, you know you'll be thinking about the dreams all day, trying to remember them, and all the time just terrified of what you'll find. That's what she told me, I mean."

"It doesn't sound as though your friend's in an immediate crisis," he said. "Has she had any help from the clinic? They're the people for something like this."

"She did go for a while. But it didn't seem to be helping. If it was doing anything at all, it was making things worse. But then she heard somewhere that you could sometimes help people like that—you being the inventor of the machine. So she asked me, since I've talked to you before, to come and ask if you could do anything for her. She'd—we'd both be very grateful."

"It's welcome to see someone so anxious to help a friend. I don't know if I can do much myself, though. I get so little time to do clinical or experimental work these days, I'm afraid my meagre talents are getting quite rusty."

She had a sudden urge to say, *All right, we've both shown we know the script: can we just skip ahead to the end of the scene and get on with the next?* Instead, she shook her head—no, she was certain he was being too modest, everyone talked about how brilliant he had been—and he had no idea how important it was to her—her friend, she meant.

And so the scene played itself out. He reluctantly agreed that he might be the best one to help her; he realised that the rest of his evening was free and suggested they discuss the problem in more comfortable surroundings. They walked through the divided moonlight to his darkened home.

Inside the entrance hall, he reached around her shoulder, and dim yellow light filtered from hidden places in the walls and ceiling. She was in a long, narrow and curved room with the highest ceiling she could remember seeing in a private home. The two longer walls were covered with unfinished logs set vertically to give the impression of a dense forest. The air was filled with the scent of pine overlaying the tang of tobacco.

"One of the few indulgences my position permits," Dr. Henry said. "I always found those low-ceilinged little boxes so sterile and oppressive." Instead of recognisable furniture, there were large, semi-rigid cushions in broad stripes of pastel shades scattered across the floor. He pushed a couple into shape and beckoned her. "I think you'll find these more comfortable than you might expect. But then you don't remember the tiny little lunch boxes most of us had to live in back there; so you see, being without a past can have its advantages."

"It's my friend who has the problem," she said, wondering if he was trying to trap her. "I didn't say I had."

"Right. Of course. I was merely recalling our earlier conversations. I didn't mean to imply anything else. So what do you think of my little solitary indulgence?"

"It's very nice. Is that a real fireplace?"

"Yes. Two things I love particularly, and I had them built into this house—my own ideals of luxury: natural materials and illusion. The fireplace illustrates the first—I can burn hardwood logs or other things if I choose in that grate, and they will burn well, with little soot and smoke. As to the second"—he reached forward and picked up a flat remote-control unit—"part of the attraction of illusion is the way it can reveal unsuspected truths about ourselves. Let's see what we can find here."

With a faint whirring, a section of the log wall pivoted about a vertical axis and was replaced by a boxlike machine with an astonished-looking cluster of lenses at its centre. He pointed the control unit again. Light flickered from the lenses towards the lower part of the wall in front of her, and the wall glowed and seemed to recede into oceanic depths.

"From some points of view," he said, "we live by manipulating illusions." Beneath his voice, orchestral sound began to stir. "Words are masks we've learned to recognise in place of the things they label. We count them like coins, valuing them for the face they bear—just as the coin itself is a bronze or nickel mask for the true gold—which in turn is a mask for what we would use it to achieve. You see, what lies behind all the masks is something within the skull, within the mind, something that lies hidden among our dreams and fears. We may look back along our lives and think we glimpse the secret in memory, but memory can be the most precious and most deceiving coinage of all. Memories shift and merge or vanish when we try to examine them. They fade like a half-developed photograph if we ignore them, but distort under the glare of too close a scrutiny. Yet what would we do without them? Do you like this music?"

"I—don't know. I don't think I've heard it before." Until he spoke, she had been too intent on trying to follow his words to be aware of the sounds building in the background.

"Ah, I didn't ask if you recognised it. But your body seems to know it—your hands do. It's shifting between 5:4, an uncommon rhythm, and 2:4, and you're following it perfectly. I noticed the first time we met in the bar, you seemed to have hidden talents. Isn't it odd, the things people do without realising they're doing them—not to mention the motives they have and never recognise? Don't you find that?"

"I hadn't thought about it much, I'm afraid," she muttered. This was getting more complicated than she had expected. "My friend—"

"Oh, but you should think about it, both of you. Look for the little mental quirks you can't explain. That's the way to ensnare those elusive memories: go on with your business as though you hadn't noticed a forgotten thought was peeking out. Just keep it in the corner of you eye until you can tell it's come too far to get back-then turn and seize it." At the last phrase, as if to demonstrate, he reached out and took her by the wrist.

She flinched, but converted the reaction to a stifled giggle. His fingers were large and soft, but their grip was unpleasantly strong. "I must try that—I'll tell my friend too. That's your advice, is it?"

"That depends on what you and your friend really want. Won't you tell me her name, by the way? I like to know whom I am helping. Tell me more about yourself, too."

"You're going to help us, then"

"Of course I'll do my miserable best. But you still haven't fulfilled your part of the bargain. It's necessary, as well as desirable, that I know more about the people I'm dealing with. But I'll let you think about that while I look for some refreshments."

He rolled out of his cushion and went to a wooden cabinet in the corner from which he produced glasses and bottles. She tried to watch what he was mixing, but the kaleidoscopic shifts of the hologram before her kept drawing her gaze into it. Every time her attention wandered from him, the music tugged at her mind, simultaneously familiar and elusive.

"Here we are." A tall glass beaded with condensation was put into her hand. She sniffed at it, sipped. The drink soothed her, then burned deep. She sipped again, then took a swallow. A lightness began to spread through her.

"Now," he said, "why don't you tell me more about yourself and what you want."

She appalled herself by starting to cry.

"Ah," he murmured, and stroked her shoulders. "That's it now. Let it come out, let it flow. Tell me what you need."

She shook her head and hid her face in her hands, in fear of what might escape her lips if she tried to speak.

"Tell me," he repeated, holding her now. "I can't help if you won't tell me what's wrong. Why did you think you had to invent a friend as an excuse to come to me? Did you think I'd laugh at you or turn you away?"

"I don't know—I was scared."

"But not more afraid than you are now. And why did you pretend to be something you're not? You're too bright to think I'd believe that little charade. Did you imagine I'm one of those who are only attracted to intellectual midgets?"

Miserably she nodded, wondering how long any of her pretences would last.

"But now you know better, don't you? Now you can trust me." She nodded again, and he asked. "Then why are you still afraid?"

"I don't know," she cried. "The dreams—" And when she said it, she found it was in some sense true.

"Then we'd better look at them, hadn't we? Try to relax and keep watching the images." He took up the control box and moved to her side, where she could barely see him if she watched the images on the wall; but she sensed he was watching her face intently.

"What was in that drink?" she mumbled.

"A mild relaxant, to make you more in touch with your feelings. Nothing I wouldn't take myself. Now lean back and relax. I'm going to adjust the aural stimuli in a moment. . . ."

▲

It was a black midnight when she found her way home. The evening had been harrowing and fruitless. Henry had managed to turn her into a puppet with all its strings cut. She could no more have turned the scene to her advantage than she could have shouted down a mob. She wondered what he had got out of it; the serious pass she had been prepared for had never materialised. Maybe he just got off on playing therapist-confessor to young women in his own parlour. Or maybe he was letting her build up a debt he would collect later; she had agreed to return the following evening.

She took out the recorder she had carried with her, and tried replaying the talk with Henry. After a few sentences, it became unbearable. She stopped the playback and erased the whole record.

She slept for a while, but then woke, and knew she would lie awake until morning unless she managed to understand what had happened to her and decided what she was going to do about it.

He had found a route to her deepest fears. That much was clear—she had been terrified. But also, when she tried now to understand where the fear came from, she found no focus for it, only grief and pride in something she could not identify, and inexplicable guilt.

She recalled some of the illusory images he had conjured before her: waves like the sluggish ripples on stale brown water, and like the intertwining voices of the music that had accompanied it. . . . Why had she thought of that now? She was trying to distract herself when there were things she had to face. Like how she was going to be able to confront Dr. Henry if she did convict him in her own mind. Like what he had stirred up in her and how. Like what those amorphous images and sounds seemed to mean to her. Like guilt.

And part of the answer was obvious, and she had been skirting it for hours. Somehow, Henry had been knocking on that walled-up room when her past was hidden, and the dry bones were stirring.

Yes, she thought, that explained the terror. That explained the terror all right. She lay under the dark ceiling with her sweat soaking into the sheets and too exhausted to cry. Desperately, she tried to plan.

FOURTEEN

As he hurried to the clinic, Larsen was remembering. Not the
snow, the mountains and the narrow waters that were the
traditional emblems of his home, but the sights and sounds he
had grown up among—the squalid rows of lime-washed huts,
their roofs dripping icicles, mongrels fighting for scraps in the
frozen slush between them. Here around him was the mythical
country of his childhood, the vast depths of sky, the snow-peaked
grandeur, and bedecked with glowing creatures from a dream.

He almost paused to look around at the play of the aurora and
the living lights among the trees. But that would just have been
to torment himself with what might have been. The worm was
in the apple, the snake was in the garden, and had always been,
even before one of the children had named him, and he had gone
to public trial. So now he hurried, head lowered and hands in
pockets, driven more by the fear of failing his precarious ideals
than by a rational concern that he might be watched. At the
entrance, Sidney Tallis at the desk raised his eyes as Larsen went
past, but said nothing. He was committed; if Tallis was Grebbel's
now, Larsen had put his head in the trap.

In the corner of the analytical lab, he sat at the main terminal.
Schneider was at a meeting of the safety committee. Osmon was
off duty. If he came back, Larsen would say he had to do some
groundwork for a batch of memory restorations, test out some
new parameter values for the machine. He had rehearsed the
speech in his head until he was almost sure he could make it

sound convincing. Anyone else on staff who turned up could be given some doubletalk about his ongoing research project with Schneider into local mutations and zoonoses.

He brought up the main directory and keyed in the password for the medical databases. As long as no one looked at the screen and asked how he had got access to that dataset . . . He pulled out the file he had created with the list of names and identification codes, their backgrounds and prognoses. He could print out a copy here, while he was sure the information was intact. No—there was too much risk of being interrupted. He spent two or three nerve-wracking minutes copying the file to the open medical bulletin board, and from there to the Settlement datanet, and then hiding his tracks.

With the screen clear again, he went over his next steps. Print out the list and get a copy, or the file itself, into the hands of Security. The hard copy would be best; he wasn't sure he could feed a dataset into the Security files without leaving a trail. But first he had to know whom he could trust.

He switched off and stood up, wiping his palms on his thighs. From the doorway Tallis was eyeing him curiously.

"Anything wrong?" Tallis asked. "Find something you didn't expect?"

"No—no. Maybe I'm coming down with something. Virus, it could be. They must mutate here the way they did back on Earth, I suppose. . . . I was just trying out some new parameters for the machine."

"You expect to be using it again soon, then?"

"Yes, I don't see why not. Do you?"

"I'd be careful. Security's tighter these days—and you can't be sure of who your friends are."

"Yes," Larsen said. "It's bad when you cannot trust the ones you must work with. A society that's built on trust can get along without most laws; without trust, all the law books in the world won't save it."

"I'm sure you're right. People don't like to think they're being betrayed. They get nasty sometimes, very nasty." Tallis eyed him coolly. "It's not always safe at nights now. I'd be cautious about running unnecessary errands if I were you."

"I intend to be very careful," Larsen said tightly. "Just a few pieces of business to finish off, just one or two, that's all." The words dried up in his throat.

"Right. Be careful how you go, then."

"I shall. Very careful. Yes."

▲

Grebbel awoke in the dark. With the blinds drawn, he put on the lights and examined his previous night's work spread out on the table. There were two units in grey boxes, each small enough to fit in his hand. He checked for loose wires, then fitted the covers on the boxes. He picked up the box that had a round button on the top and walked across the room with it. He depressed the button twice quickly, then held it down with his thumb.

After ten seconds he lifted his thumb. From the unit on the table came a faint click, and a spark leapt between two contacts. Grebbel nodded and folded the two boxes separately in bubble-wrap and wrapped them with his lunch.

He left his room and walked out into the cold dark. Now he sensed that the net he had woven for himself was constricting. He thought of the sled leaping down the slope. The exhilaration came with the danger, when you were committed and could only hope to ride out what you had started. *Then* you were alive—then you knew what it was to be human. And at the end you could rip off the mask and feel the air icy clean on your face.

Would they take him as the head of Security? He thought he could make a good enough case, even without the azoplas and the hostages. But that was down at the bottom of the slope, and the ride had hardly begun.

Osmon met him beside the trucks.

"How quickly can you be ready to move?" Grebbel asked.

"You've decided, then?"

"Yes." The sled was just starting to slide. But every instant, the momentum grew. One more push, and there would be no going back, for any of them. "They'll stumble on something of ours soon enough. We can't sit back and wait for them. Some of the azoplas charges are made up, and I know the dirigible schedules. How soon?"

"As soon as we can contact everyone, but—"

"That's good enough. Today, then." He handed Osmon the wrapped unit with the spark contacts. "I'll give you the detonator circuit back. I tested it with the trigger this morning. You did a good job. I'm afraid I'm too likely to be watched, so get Joe to install it with the charge."

▲

Elinda woke haunted by the music Henry had played her; and when she walked to the Greenhouse the dark air quivered with sinister glissandos. Ominous chords, just above audibility grew like distant thunder. She had a sudden vision of a performance—the triple timpani, two players crouched over the skins, with the cellos sawing away, double basses giving out sporadic plucked notes like approaching gunfire, while the hoarse growl of the trombones began to rise towards fury, and, massed at the back, the horde of human voices was poised to erupt.

I'm going mad, she thought. That bastard did something to my head with his trick drink. For that piece he had played, whatever it was, had been electronically synthesised—no timpani, or trombones, certainly no massed choirs. But it wouldn't leave her head. The twin moonlight appeared to her as a *sforzando* diminished seventh on horns and trumpets, the pale snow fields were piccolo shrieks, the wooded and shimmering slopes were the burnished voices of cellos and violas slithering down from discord to discord.

"Lovely morning," said Chris when she reached the office. "Halfway to sunrise and there's hardly any frost on the window. Do you think winter's over for this year?"

"My god, I hope so."

"You see there's a new report of the sea serpent? They picked the wrong hemisphere for the biologists. Schneider'll be having fits if that thing's real and nobody's ready to play Ahab."

Somehow she was going to have to work while her head was swimming with last night's chaos. Chris being sunny and talkative didn't help. Nor did Larsen when he came in, late, silent and preoccupied. She wondered what he had learned to disturb him, but with Chris chirping away beside her, she had no way to ask.

Chris tried to ask him about the codings for a promised batch of chick embryos, but Larsen was staring hard at his own terminal and couldn't help. She shook off her inertia and helped

Chris find what he wanted. Then she returned to her own tasks—reports to prepare, production data to evaluate—with her head full of sick tension and hallucinatory music.

▲

At the dam, Osmon wandered over to a group of men taking a lunch break from the shift in the turbine rooms. He sat down with them on a mound overlooking the river. Another man joined them, wearing a striped rugby shirt over a high-necked sweater and carrying a sports bag. Under the arc lights, the men exchanged sandwiches while they talked and gestured at the caverns on the far bank. When they packed up their belongings, it was not obvious if everyone had recovered his own property. The man with in the rugby shirt went across for the afternoon shift in the turbine rooms. He carried his bulky sports bag with him.

▲

Elinda worked into the afternoon and then got up and put her coat on.

Grebbel was not at the dam site. Menzies, the foreman, gave her a sour look and said everything was getting disorganised; who knew which shift anyone was on nowadays?

She walked to Grebbel's building and found his door locked; there was no response when she hammered on it. She lowered her hands and forced herself to be calm. The clinic, then. He might be working there. He might still be prepared to help her.

When she got to the entrance, the lights in the administrative offices were going out. The man at the desk was struggling to carry a large parcel into the room behind, and she slipped in without disturbing him. There was no sign of Grebbel. She paused at the end of the corridor where Barbara's room was. She wondered what she could achieve by going in, and then wondered why she was looking for excuses not to. Approaching the door, she heard movement and turned the handle. The door was locked.

She knocked, then called out and tried the handle again.

"I've got the key," Dr. Henry said behind her.

He was breathing deeply. "What a pleasant surprise," he

said. "We can continue our recent discussions. In fact I'm quite anxious to do so." His fingers clamped onto her upper arm. "I think we need a good old-fashioned heart-to-heart."

She was still holding onto the door handle, but he pulled her away. "Don't make a fuss, please," he muttered. "I'd prefer to avoid messy scenes, but there are still Security staff on duty, and they'd help me if I summoned them."

In her pocket she slipped the *record* switch. "What were you going to do to her?"

"All in good time. This way, please."

"Where are we going? Is she all right? You can tell me that, can't you? How is she now?"

"A bit late in your concern, perhaps? Could it be a sign of a troubled conscience? She's well enough for the time being. In here please."

They were in the instrument room. *If he tries to lock the door*, I'll fight, she thought—*go for the eyes and the balls. I'll use Carlo's gun and splatter his brains on the wall.* But he guided her to an armchair beside the bench and sat facing her. He was between her and the door, but a visitor would see only the dedicated physician having an informal discussion with his patient.

"Well?" she said.

"Patience, my dear." He seemed in control of himself now, but tense. "We have the whole night ahead of us." Resting his chin on his fists, he regarded her thoughtfully. "I think we might start by hearing some more music."

⋀

Larsen had worked all day, without stopping for a meal. When the other two left, he locked the office door and returned to his terminal. He pulled out the sheets with the names and identifications of the possible conspirators, and worked his way into the files on the status of the workforce, to see if he could find any pattern of absences that might give a clue to what Grebbel planned and how many were involved.

⋀

On the path from the caves, Grebbel stared toward the landing field. The children with their kites were led out and the gate in the fence was locked. He had seen the procedure often enough to recognise it even from this distance. Beside him, Lafayette and Mahmoud fingered their new machine pistols. "All is usual?" Lafayette asked.

"Yes, so far. Now—we haven't had time to go over it as well as I'd like—you understand what you have to do? The whole thing depends on your disabling the alarms in the control tower—making sure no one sounds a warning until we're established."

"What is to understand?" muttered Mahmoud. "We make exercise of our skills, we are quiet. We save these"—he gestured with the gun—"for when it is hopeless. These are old rules for an old game."

"Then all you have to worry about," said Grebbel, "is getting in there without raising any suspicions. Come on, let's go. I've got to meet the others."

▲

Niels Larsen looked at the pattern emerging on the monitor screen and knew he was too late. The sheets of paper with the names were at his elbow, but the important ones named there were already acting. Several, in office jobs, had reported sick, others were currently untraceable; and there was no response when he tried to test the alarm circuits at the armoury. So he had to assume they had weapons. There was no way now that he could act in time to prevent anything without revealing himself—and he didn't even know where they would strike.

He scrabbled at the keys, searching the databases for clues. If he knew where they were, perhaps he would be able to fake an alarm, a fire, anything to get the authorities involved. But sending unprepared firefighters into the middle of an armed attack would be murder. . . .

Behind him, the locked door thumped, then splintered and sprang open.

"Working late here, too?" asked Sidney Tallis. "I've seen you do that a lot lately. I don't think it's good for your health."

Larsen tried to bluster, but the words died in his throat. Tallis came and stood over him. He produced a large, pointed knife and flipped the papers at Larsen's side with it. "You shouldn't have done that," Tallis said. He peered quickly through the window towards the landing field. "You're too late now, unless the sirens start in the next two minutes, and I don't think you'd got that far, had you? Had you?"

Larsen shook his head, clinging to any shameful hope that he might yet survive this.

"But you shouldn't have done that to us. If I didn't have to hurry, I'd take some time to convince you of that. As it is . . ."

"Tallis—it's me. I brought you back. *I* did. Don't use the knife. Don't—"

Oh Jesus Christ—if you exist, return and forgive me—

▲

Jon Grebbel was crouched in the dark beside the wire fence that bounded the landing field. He felt the safety catch on the Ingram machine pistol, and contemplated the level of commitment represented by one motion of a finger. Inside his coat was the trigger switch to the explosives, which might prove more important if they ran into difficulties. Osmon and the others were beside him, below the line of sight of the main windows, and half hidden by the undergrowth. The sky was a great cave of black and silver, and without the perimeter lights, the landing field was mystery of shadows. The moons were setting into a bank of clouds. Until the perimeter lights came on, they were safe from the control tower: anything on the ground in this direction would be lost against the dark of the valley wall. He glanced up at the nearest light mounted above the fence not fifteen metres from where he waited. If the power went on now, the field would seem incandescent. They would be spotted before they got ten metres. He wiped his hand on his thigh.

"What's happening in there?" one of the men whispered. "If they've killed the lights, why don't they signal?"

"Quiet," Grebbel rasped. "Keep listening."

There was wind, stirring branches on the step hill slopes. There was the rush of the river, the cry of a raptor—a brief flutter of wings. Something else. Grebbel tensed. The beat of airscrews.

"It's coming."

"Two minutes early."

"Shit."

"I've got its lights. Just below the skyline. Following the beam."

"Right. That's it," Grebbel said. "The field should have been lit by now, so I'm assuming the power's been taken care of, and we're going in. You all hear that? Into position when I move, then go when the fence is cut."

He crouched and ran to the fence. Beside him, Osmon bent and sheared the lower half of the wire, and they ran through. They thudded across the cleared field, the control tower bulked low ahead of them. Beside it, the beacon rotating on the landing pylon splashed red light across its slab walls and empty windows.

"Move it! If the building's dark, they won't land."

Their boots clattered on the concrete apron, and then the door was swinging open and they were in.

"Lights!" shouted Grebbel. "Lights first—then get in position."

Joe Abercrombie opened the circuit-breaker panel and started resetting the breakers. Lights flickered on in open doorways. In the entrance to the control room, Ahmed Mahmoud lay bleeding from the chest. A dead guard lay beside him clutching a long-bladed knife. Osmon crouched over Mahmoud and shook him by the shoulders, trying to ask what had happened. Grebbel pulled him away. "He's too far gone. Let him be. Get into position."

"We need to know what happened. If a warning got out—"

"There are no guards. That's enough. He did most of his job. Lafayette must be here too. He didn't get as far as the control panel, so we'll have to fake the talkdown ourselves."

"If they got out a warning—"

"Then we all say sorry and go home. Now let's get the comlink alive." He stepped into the control room. "Let's have the landing lights, but not all at once—and keep them erratic. Look as though we've got power problems."

"They're coming in on the receiver now," Hammond called. "We've got a voice link. They want to know what's wrong."

"Circuitry problems. Don't be too specific. It's coming under control. Fake transmission breakup if you have to, but see they get that they're cleared to land."

Grebbel, Osmon and four others found ground-crew jackets and put them on over their coats and weapons. Grebbel picked up a personal transceiver and checked that the control room team were reading him. Then he followed the other five outside to wait for the landing.

Stars glittered icily in a patch of clear sky. In the dark at the head of the valley the red and green riding lights of the dirigible were clear now. Grebbel watched them hungrily, and flinched away as the nearest bank of field lights blazed in his eyes. A moment later they were dark again, leaving the world a pulsating black void. "Give us a countdown," he called into the transceiver. "I can't see anything from here through the lights."

"Just over a klick yet. They sound a bit suspicious, but they're still coming."

"Deploy, everyone," Grebbel muttered to his group. "Check your weapons."

The aurora pulsed turquoise, silhouetting three skeins of cloud above the western range. The light dimmed to sea green, shifted to violet, and was lost against the sky.

"Two hundred metres."

The Ingram seemed alive in Grebbel's hand, growing light and then heavy, then light again. Around him, the others were shades, dim faces with flickers of eyes and teeth.

"They're over the pylon. Deploying the hook now."

"Okay," he rasped. "I've got them."

The dark, round cloud above them was swelling and starting to catch the light from the field. He could hear the motor whine beneath the throb of airscrews. Then the grapple on the pylon clacked home. The winch raced and began to pull. Now the airscrews were feathered, idling down to a steady flicker. He watched as the gondola beneath swayed and sank and halted, and found he had been holding his breath.

"They're opening up. Let's go."

The six ran forward and were waiting as the yellow light from the cabin spilled down the extending stairs to the concrete. The first of the crew appeared in the doorway. Grebbel nodded to the others to hold back and started up the steps.

The man in the doorway had not moved. "Hold it right there," he shouted. "I don't know you. What the hell's going on here?"

Grebbel kept climbing. "Security check," he snapped. "Blue triple-zeta. Flash just came over the satellite link. You should have picked it up. Explosives in the hold. The crew goes down for clearance while we check the cargo."

"Now you just hold it. Nobody said anything to me about this." The man turned towards the cabin. "Hey, Rolf, you got anything about a blue triple-zeta?" He turned back to Grebbel. "You got a flash from the satlink? Your whole comset was down—"

Grebbel took the last rungs in a stride and clubbed the man twice with the barrel of the Ingram, then kicked the body off the loading platform. The other five started up the steps behind him. From inside, someone called out, "What's going on down there?"

"Upstairs," Grebbel snapped, and burst into the entrance, then up clanging steps to the control room. A pistol cracked twice as he threw the door open. The second shot whipped past his head, and he fired a short burst. It knocked someone down and shocked the air with echoes. Grebbel saw that he'd let himself fire within thirty degrees of the gasbag. Two crewmen froze in their seat, their faces as blank as those of the dead.

Smoke was still eddying up into the air-conditioning vents when Osmon and the others pushed in after him.

Grebbel motioned Carl Davis to the controls. "Set things up and we'll get the others aboard."

The man he had shot moaned and tried sit up. Grebbel stared, then went and lifted his head by the hair. "Well, well," he rasped. "An unexpected bonus. Martin, old friend, old colleague. After all these years. How has life been treating you, eh?" He jabbed with the gun muzzle. "Eh?"

"Grebbel? Is that you?" The man gasped and shook his head. "It's over, all that. I'm not what I was."

"Now there's a funny thing," said Grebbel. "Neither am I."

Davis called from the pilot's seat, "I can't load the aerodynamics program. And our IFF signal's dead; we can't answer challenges."

Martin nodded weakly. "We had just enough warning. You'd better quit now, before you make things worse for yourselves."

"We'll fly this thing on our own if we have to."

"Where are you going to go? Not back to the Flats without the IFF unless you're bent on suicide."

"Then you'd better tell us how to switch it on again, hadn't you." He pushed with the gun muzzle, and twisted.

Martin groaned and tried to double up. The blood left his face and he gasped chokingly. Then he lifted his head. "It's over," he whispered. "Can't you understand? There's nowhere for you to go. Give it up now."

"Sorry, that's not what I want to know. Osmon, I'm going to be busy the next few minutes. Do you think you can persuade my old friend here to tell us what we need to know?"

"Oh yes, I think so."

"Do it yourself, Grebbel!" Martin cried. "Do your own dirty work. You always did before."

Turning away, Grebbel stopped, and seemed about to reply. Instead he lifted his transceiver and spoke quietly into it. "Let's refuel and get everyone aboard."

Osmon put down his pistol and went to crouch over the wounded man.

▲

Dying wasn't the worst, Larsen thought; it was the pain that destroyed. Pain stripped one bare of humanity, left one grunting and howling like an animal. But even worse than pain was the fear of it. It was fear that humiliated, destroyed one's own worth. It was fear that crippled the will and paralysed the flesh. That was why he was on the floor now, curled up like a foetus—unable to move or make a sound, hardly to breathe, for fear that he would wake the pain once more and it would blast him.

So it had all been failure, and now he could not even move to undo some of the harm. The computer link was there above him, on the desk. If he risked turning his head a couple of centimetres he would see it. But that would bring the first stirrings of the pain, and for what? To reach for the link, to pull himself up and set his fingers working on its keys, he would have to scale ridge after vertiginous ridge of agony.

That was how it was when you were led by conscience, but ruled by fear and pain. One passion unopposed would shape a life. But to fight fear one needed something as strong. Love? He had neither loved nor hated. In an earlier age, he might have found a god he could have served, and poured his fear and his need into that service until it turned to love. But his times valued knowledge over conviction, and he had acquired knowledge of what was right, without the inner certainty. Now even his knowledge was tainted. And all his pretences at love had been mere callous, squirming betrayals by the flesh.

Here was the final betrayal, as the flesh pinned him helpless even while the life oozed out of it. One betrayal following another. From the parish school and the children, to the university, to the trial, to this place, with half his mind cut away . . .

Deliberately he was working up something to fight the pain, something that began to feel like rage.

Rage then. If not love, then at the end of it all, hate. Something to fight the fear, something as strong as pain. His head turned, and the rent in his flesh seared, but his eyes had found the edge of the desk and the terminal, and they gave him a ledge to cling to. *Now. Now.*

His breath rasped, and once more the flesh betrayed, his muscles would not move.

Now. Damn you to hell. Now.

He was wrong. Nothing was stronger than pain.

The cry turned to a sob, and then to retching.

It was unbearable. It had to be borne.

It had to be—because now his elbows were on the desk, his fingers, shaken by spasms, were crawling across it and stabbing at keys.

Just five seconds. Three keys. One more breath. And it will all be over.

⋏

"Music is perhaps the highest of the arts, don't you agree?" said Dr. Henry. "At its best, it can evoke illusive and heightened states such as no other medium can approach. And yet it is so much more immediate than most of them."

Elinda said nothing. The room was full of a strange tangle of sounds whose fragmentary rhythms plucked at her nerves.

"This piece, for instance. I discovered it quite recently. It doesn't have the exalted scale of the great works, but I think it showed promise. I get the feeling the composer was not quite reconciled to the medium. The sound is all synthetic of course, but notice how closely it's made to resemble a small classical orchestra. Later, you'll hear synthetic approximations of voices, too. It's almost as though the composer would have preferred to write for chorus and orchestra, but knew no one would ever pay for such resources to perform an unknown work."

"Is this supposed to mean something to me? Or are you just filling in time?"

"I'm talking about potential, creative potential—or just simple, human normality and the prices it can exact. What you're hearing is the best—as far as I know—and probably the final work of a composer who might have gone on to become famous."

"Is this some kind of guessing game? Am I supposed to know what this mean?"

"Actually, we could make it a guessing game. For instance: why is this the composer's last work? No idea? How about a clue? Is she happier being unable to compose or not?"

She stared at him. "It's someone here, isn't it? One of your— Someone here, now."

"Would you like to try the next question? Yes, of course you would. The name. Think carefully while you listen."

She shook her head angrily. "Fuck you and your games. Get on with whatever you're doing."

"I am getting on with it, please believe me. Another clue, then. But not too big a clue, because now you have to think it out for yourself. She had a child, one child."

"God damn you, stop this."

"Can you think of a name now?"

"It's Barbara, isn't it? Barbara, after what you did to her. I don't know—how dare you—"

"That's an interesting response. Let's change direction for a while."

"Fuck you! I'm here because of Barbara—we'll talk about her! Was she onto you for the amnesia fakery or for what you did to Erika Frank? It doesn't matter does it? She was, what, trying to set a trap, trying to follow a lead, and you got her first? Was it here? You drugged her, hypnotised her, and when you'd finished whatever you did to her, you found her recorder and erased the evidence, you dressed her up again and sent her out into the mountains."

"Yes. Her and one or two others. A moment ago I was talking about prices. In my case, that means the price of maintaining normality, a functioning personality—means satisfying certain needs that periodically arise. When I am sane and in control, I am much as you see me now. I am calm and rational. I am also a good psychologist and a good administrator—in all modesty, I am of value to this society. But periodically, as I say, the need arises in me, and it rapidly becomes obsessive if unsatisfied. And then there is only one way to restore equilibrium. You understand what I mean."

"No, I don't understand! All right. Question and answer. Did some of the criminally insane come through the Knot?"

"I think you know they did."

"All right. Then how many? How many are there?"

"You're sure you want me to tell you?"

"*How many?*"

"About thirty percent, of course."

"What do you mean? The Knot—"

"The Knot does practically nothing to the human mind."

"Then what happens, the memory loss . . ."

". . . is done on the other side, before the criminal leaves. Theirs is the simpler task. They just delete memories, wipe away areas of the psyche, sketch an outline of the replacement. Here we develop and integrate the new personality.

"This place is an experiment. You're an experiment, I'm an experiment. Your friend the technician is particularly an experiment. We're rehabilitating the psychically damaged. Recovering good from evil. But, of course, there mustn't be any way to go back and find out that you really lived on a houseboat on a canal. Secrecy. And secrecy about secrecy, because if hints get out that something is being hidden, the whole starts to unravel. . . . So not everyone can know. Here or back there. And among those who know—here or there—not everyone approves."

He stood up and began loosening his shoulders, flexing his fingers. "Of course secrecy also serves some of my own interests."

She groped for something to keep him talking, to delay what was coming. "And Carlo?" she asked.

"A well-meaning simpleton. He knows just enough to keep his mouth shut."

"Oh god, he's covering for you, now."

He shook his head, frowning as though she had questioned his professional judgement. "I don't put my trust in simpletons."

Even as her fear rose, Elinda felt one of the knots in her stomach loosen.

Henry put the heels of his hands together in front of his chest, and pressed until his arms quivered; he seemed unaware of the effort he was making.

"Security's on our side naturally; she'd have to be. Here it's not too bad in fact. People mostly either go along or understand they shouldn't ask the wrong questions. Back there . . . well the wrong kind of publicity could be damaging to us."

"But you, you're just another of the monsters. You've said so. Is that why you're here?" she asked. "Out here rather than safe in some gold-plated research complex back home?"

Henry got to his feet and began pacing back and forth with a pensive, withdrawn expression on his face.

"There were rumours," he acknowledged. "A near-scandal, even, but no proof. I was offered a new appointment about as far away from my indiscretions as anyone could imagine. I do regret all this of course, but surely you see it is better to have a sane man in charge here than a ravening wolf—and the price, after all, is a life that would have contributed little to this or any other society."

"What—what did you do to her?"

"Oh, I think you can imagine. Though you might be glad to know that my needs do not require inflicting much overt damage. . . ."

"To her mind! What did you do to her mind? One of your hypnotist's games, was it, with your toys here to make it stick? So she walks into the woods and dies—with no overt damage. No one to accuse you, no corpse to dispose of, is that it? And the same with Erika Frank? My god, how many times have you done this? Sent someone crawling away to bury herself in the hillside like a dying animal? They must have known, the ones who sent you here, who set this place up. Were they still human back there, or had they plugged themselves so far in a datanet they didn't need bodies and didn't care about anyone who had a body? A field experiment—is that what we all are? Is that what I am to you, to them—a white rat to observe and play with and dispose of when you're tired of? Tie off her tubes and see if we can turn her on to women? See if we can switch her back, make her fall? What else? Did you care what you ruined? And Barbara? What about her music? A life that wouldn't have contributed, you said. What about the music you're playing now?"

He stopped pacing and gazed at her, his hands at his sides, fingers gripping and kneading the empty air.

"Oh, now, please think a little," he said. "Even without seeing her past profile, do you really believe your Barbara would have written that, or wanted to—or had a child? You know better."

"What? What are you saying?" She raised her hands to ward off something she could not yet see. "You're trying to tell me—" Her throat tightened, her cheeks were wet. "No. You're lying. You're lying to me to get yourself off the hook." She choked, forced the words out. "You want to destroy me too, to save yourself. You want me to believe that, that I—drowned, my, my . . ."

"Elinda, I haven't said any of that. . . ." He was watching her with interest. "But it was a fine piece of music."

"Damn you!" Now words were helpless against her despair. "Oh, damn you, god damn you to hell!"

"Yes, certainly. That goes without saying. But how do you judge me now?"

"Unfit to rot in the same ground as her!"

"Like you?"

"Yes! Like me!"

From the direction of the landing field, the wail of a siren rose into the night.

⅄

Grebbel came back and waved Osmon aside. He wrapped his fingers in Martin's hair and jerked his head back. "Come on. I can't hear you."

Martin retched. His face was bloodless, his lips like bruises. He mumbled and Grebbel shook him again. This time his words were audible. "Why couldn't you take what you had? It would have worked. No prison, no punishment? No suffering."

"No suffering?" Grebbel swung his scarred fist in front of the man's eyes. "You know what it meant to me. Look at this. Scars the length of my arm, so I'd remember. I'd have done more if I could. So don't think I'll turn back now. I want the IFF code."

Martin flinched, then shook his head.

"This is what you asked me for," Grebbel said. "Osmon, hold his arms."

"Pain does things to time, doesn't it, Martin?" he whispered. "How long is a scream, Martin? Longer than the time it takes on a clock, isn't it—much longer. But not as long as the time you helped them take from me. No, not a thousandth as long as that."

Behind him, one of the crew blurted, "There's no need for this. We can fly you out of here. The recognition system needs a new module—it won't work whatever you get out of him. But we could get you to the inner valley. We could drop you there and you'd have a chance."

Grebbel looked over his shoulder at the man. "You're next."

"Listen, it's your only chance, we can fly you out—"

"Can you?" Grebbel said bitterly.

"—to the highlands if you want. An hour's flight, hour and a half maximum. Or anywhere else you want. Just leave him here. He can't hurt you now."

"Except by being here. Except by living and pushing his treacherous face in front of me. They stole from me, and he helped them, they lied with my own voice. We'll lift when we're fuelled and loaded, not until."

"Tank's eighty percent now, full in about three minutes," Davis called. "The others are coming on board."

"We can run up the motors," the crewman persisted.

"Then do it! Osmon—watch him."

The cabin began to vibrate as the motors started. Boots thudded into the lower cabin. Then, from the corner of the landing field, the sirens began.

For the length of a breath, Grebbel froze, staring into the dark, a look of recognition on his face. Then he turned and snapped at the man at the controls. "Cut the lines. Let's go."

Martin rolled his head to one side and mumbled. Grebbel snarled and bent over him. "What? What now?"

"Don't—don't. It's over, for you—that's all. Was before you started. Seen it happen. You've been reprogrammed too long—split in two. You can't carry it off any more. No—stop! Just hear me. You're split in half, and there's no way out for you like this. And inside you know it—saw your face when the alarm went off. You're going to destroy yourself. Why else a suicide mission like this?"

The mooring grapple clanged and fell free. The beacon light swayed and sank beneath them. Under Grebbel's hands Martin cried out once more and became silent.

"I'm getting pulse signals on the downlink," Davis shouted. "One of the satellites is calling us."

"I can see it," someone said at the west port. "Above Glacier Peak. I'm going to lose it behind the gasbag in a minute."

"It's challenging!" one of the crew shouted. "I don't know the countersign!"

"You knew it twenty minutes ago," Grebbel snapped.

"Not to this. I've never seen it before. I tried the day password and the ship serial number, but it just keeps sending the same group."

"What's it looking for?" Grebbel barked at the crew. "Quick— or you'll fry first."

"The satellite IFF," said the crewman who had tried to intercede for Martin. "It's separate from the main module and the landing codes. We've only got seconds. There's no time to teach it to you. I'd have to send it myself."

Grebbel cursed, gesturing the man into the communications seat.

The crewman snatched up the headset and started keying in commands. He stopped abruptly. "They're not challenging, they're—"

There was a muted orange flash and a sound like thunder.

"Missed," someone yelled. "They missed us!"

Grebbel shouted them down. "Warning shot. Send that counter-challenge."

"They're not responding. They expect us to land."

"Let them expect. Send your signal."

The man's hands fumbled over the keys. Then the orange flash came again, and the thunder. But this time, the thunder continued and the lights went out. The cabin swayed, tipped— started to fall.

Grebbel drew his gun and clung to the door pillar as the floor tilted under his feet. The mountains spiralled upward across the ports.

⋀

As the sirens wailed, Henry and Elinda watched each other. Finally she muttered, "Well, aren't you going to find out what's happening?"

He moistened his lips, gave a thin smile. "That might be advisable." He went to the window and rolled up the blind with a snap. "You'd better put out the lights if you want to see anything out there."

She got up and slapped the switch and then went over to the window. The landing field was lighted—but only partially, she realised. A dirigible was moored at the pylon, a silver-black ellipsoid against the empty darkness of the valley. As she watched, it swayed. Henry inhaled sharply beside her. The dirigible started to rise.

"Your pager's been beeping for two minutes now," she told him. "Hadn't you better get back where you belong?"

"And leave you here alone, sweet child? Who knows what mischief you might get up to." He turned from the window and faced her. "Why, such innocents as you have been known to go about recording private conversations. How can I know you haven't done just that, using a machine you keep hidden on your person?" His fingers clamped onto her wrist. "I really have to be sure, you see."

She tried to pull away, suddenly realising that her coat, with Carlo's gun in it, was where she had left it on the chair. "You're crazy. If you don't answer the call—"

"There'll be an investigation, into a minor traffic irregularity while I was busy with a patient. Later—all later. But now, sweet child, angel of lightness and artistry, we have our own investigation to make."

"Is this what you did to Barbara? While you were playing with her head, with her mind? Jesus Christ!"

For an instant the window blazed orange. Then it was black again, and thunder rocked through the air.

Henry flinched, half-turned to the window. She clawed herself free and grabbed her coat. "Air-defence weapons this close to the Settlement!" he cried. "Who gave the order? It'll mean a full board of enquiry." He had got between her and the door while she was fumbling in the coat pocket.

"Child, the future is in ruins. All we have left now are whatever few hours we take for ourselves." And then he was on her.

She was driven bodily backwards. As her fingers clenched on cold metal, she slammed against the wall, head and shoulders. An explosion seared the night—from the window, the room, inside her skull, she could not have said. Shockwaves smashed the air from her lungs, twisted her fingers open and tore them empty.

She was drowning in a tide of sick roaring pain. Then air prised its way into her chest and someone screamed in fury. She made frenzied swimming motions, struck something that yielded, twisted away from the grip of claws. The screams must be going on, but she could not hear them, because the air was like treacle. It choked her ears, it was all she could do to heave it in and out of her throat.

The silence engulfed her, cold and palpable.

Overhead, if she dared to look up, would be the sodium lamps of the bridge.

The water reached up and seized her, shook her as a dog shakes a rat. She fought through it and strained to push it away, to break the grip of the hands that clung to her. They should have fallen away, hit with a splash, but the hands, the arms were larger than she could have believed, and appallingly strong, clinging to life. For a moment everything seemed wrong, she was casting away part of her self to drown, she had to stop and pull them both out of the water. But why were the hands so strong?

Then her sight started to clear. Some dark embodiment of the water clung to her, clawed and would not sink. She pushed at it, twisted and squeezed, tried to tear it and crush, where it spluttered and choked at the end of her arms and wheezed and slowly grew still. . . .

She found she was on her knees with her head in her arms, listening. There was her own breathing, hurried and painful, and another, rasping, a low gurgle. Dizzily she sat up. Her cheek felt as though the flesh had been smashed into the bone. Other pains were starting to penetrate the numbness of her body. She was shivering.

In the distance were sirens, men shouting, the roar of engines. She expected to see oil-scummed water and the concrete balustrade of the highway bridge. But there was just a room with toppled chairs and machines, and a man sprawled on his back. She found a light switch and turned it on and looked at him. Blood oozed from a wound in his side, above his waist. One of his hands was pressed to it. There were strands of blonde hair caught in the fingers. His face was scratched and his throat was marked with red bars that seemed to be darkening.

She looked at her hands. They were shaking violently. Two nails were torn back, her fingers were stiff and swollen. She rubbed them down her forearm as though scraping off water.

From outside came two sharp sounds, unmistakably shots, and more shouting. She sensed that at any moment she would understand what had happened to her here. Then she realised she was about to throw up. She lurched into a corridor, and found her way out into a night torn by wind and fires.

FIFTEEN

He crawled through pain. It burned and tore in his arms and chest and throbbed in his skull. He dragged it with him, clamped to the ruin of his ankle. Sometimes the pain obscured his thoughts so that he was unsure of anything but his own aching body and the need to crawl. To crawl downhill. That was central. That and his name. Grebbel. Jon Grebbel. His mouth shaped the syllables and croaked them even while it gasped for air.

Greenish lights drifted over him. Wings slid across one of the moons. He crawled. In front of his eyes a pale flower closed its petals, separated from its stem and shrank beneath a rock.

There was more light behind him, up on the slope. Something burning. And searchers: a strung-out line of them, with lights, calling to each other. But still behind him. That was important.

Crawl.

He bruised his knees on half-buried stones, and struggled through thorns that tore cloth and skin with equal indifference. After a time, he became aware of other light filtering through the undergrowth. The moons, rising. And with that, he began to understand where he was and why he was crawling.

Up the slope, that was the remains of the dirigible. When he had left it, it had been a black skeleton with flames pouring from it. He remembered the trees sweeping up outside the window, and then the shock. The gasbag must have ruptured and the fuel tanks exploded. He could not remember jumping clear—just the dark trees, and then the inferno above him as he lay crushed tothe ground. Some time afterwards he had become aware again.

He was scrambling away from the wreck as fast as his damaged leg would let him. He must have broken through the cordon of searchers converging on the fire. He had discarded the pistol. The pouch on his belt, where the spare magazines had been held, was empty, and his hands still remembered the hammering of the recoil.

Now he tried hauling himself upright and hobbling. He found a branch to use a staff. He made better progress with that, but limping on one leg over the broken ground taxed his balance and made him feel conspicuous. The first time he stumbled, the staff slipped from his hand and he fell back to his knees.

He crawled again.

In front of him now, patches of moonlight flitted among bark and stone and earth, like scraps of burning fabric. The roar of burning he heard was the wind moving through the trees, or the blood in his head. And the voice, the whispering voice that had been dogging him, tugging at his attention while he crawled, was drooling from his own mouth.

As he became aware of it, the voice stopped. The part of him that ached and burned stood back and waited to find out what the creature using his mouth had wanted to say. He had begun to shiver. The flesh was giving out, demanding rest. He would have to find somewhere to sleep.

His teeth rattled in his skull, and the voice started again. "Crawl. Down you go. Down the slope," the mouth slobbered. "Through the shadows. Feel with your hands, a step at a time. Down the stairs, through the dark . . ."

. . . through a darkness alive with hidden claws. Down, step. Down, step. One hand clutching the rail, the other out somewhere in front to grope, protect, ward off.

Down, step, down, and off the wooden stairs. The darkness silent again, after the noises that broke through sleep.

Rough cement underfoot.

Four steps now to the door.

Count—

One. Two. Three. Four.

There: hands reaching up to the handle, shoulder high. It slips between sweating palms. Turns. The door seems to fold inward, its groan lost under the hammering pulse. Despite the dark, pink spots flicker in front of the eyes.

Standing just inside the door, incapable of going on, unable to go back.

One hand is scraping its fingers over the whitewashed brick, clawing for the switch.

Is there a sound from the blackness in front? A moan, a single, unbearable syllable? In the furry dark, the mind creates a phantom communication.

The switch clicks. An explosion of white light—eyelids crimson until the terror forces them open. Light sears the white rough walls, and the things huddled in the far corner, one of which still moves. This thing looks up and reaches with its bloody claw, this thing that used to be—

Eyes prickling, mouth jerking uncontrollably.

"Dad—?"

The thing croaks and grins, slithers forward. Something grinds beneath it, and is pushed clear: a needle, with shards of glass.

And then the stairs lurching underfoot, the light pursuing, the shadows leaping ahead. Back into the little room and the frail door, the dark, the bed of nightmares. . . .

The light in his eyes now was the moons, rising together. The mouth had been muttering over and over. It fell silent and he stared into the dark in a dull astonishment that a vision from another age and another universe could leave his eyes still burning and his chest tight.

"Fake," he muttered. "Planted in my head. Layered defence. If I got through the first layer, there'd be this to explain where it came from—to make me feel—" He shook his head and hugged himself against the cold and rocked from side to side, shivering. "To make me believe I'm still a puppet. Just different strings. Fake. Fake."

He crawled.

Behind him, when he looked, the fire had sunk to a crimson glow. There were still occasional shouts from the searchers, but no more gunshots. Maybe they had realised he had slipped through and they were working their way back down the slope. He wondered how long it would take them to hunt him down.

He was shivering continually now. The aurora had turned the wood into a ruin of shadows and eroded columns, a boneyard. The sound of water reached his ears, and then he came to a clearing, with a boulder pushing through the loam like a huge buried skull. Heaped around it was a leathery, spiky mass of fallen leaves. He wouldn't find a better place to rest before shock and exposure crippled him.

A pale light silhouetted the peaks at the eastern end of the valley. The wind was beginning to comb through the branches—was a high shriek somewhere far above.

He hutched himself into the space between the boulder and the upper slope, where two trunks and their spreading roots hid him from higher up the valley. Reaching for armfuls of the dead leaves caused a thunderous crackling as though the forest were burning up around him. If the hunters were anywhere near, they would be onto him now, but he was too exhausted to care.

Inside the noisy prickling blanket, a feeling of warmth crept over him. He felt himself falling into the dark tunnel between worlds and selves. He had time to fear the dreams that waited there, and then the dark closed on him.

▲

She had fled from the sound of sirens, as it seemed she had done once before. Thorns clawed at her. Lights swam across her vision, snapped with tiny mouths. Vegetable fingers clutched at her limbs.

The world opened its mouth and roared at her. She was flung, pushed, battered, clawed. The air flashed and roared. Overhead, shapes like huge disembodied arms thrashed. Icy wind poured over her, filled her eyes, her nostrils, sucked the warmth from her body. Pale shapes scuttled away from her.

Something like a huge sail was whirled out of the sky. It screeched as it tangled among the upper branches. She saw a long, beaked head raised like a spire. Then it screamed again and was dragged out of sight.

She stumbled away, crawled, tried to hide from the wind, and was battered onwards.

Then an expanse of water lay glittering before her, the boundary of another existence. The limbs that had been twisting and roaring in the dark were suddenly quiet. The fractured light from the water engulfed her. She waded into the brilliant silence, a burden in her arms. She held the burden away from her. It clung to her for a moment, and she had to free it from her sleeve. She let it fall.

The silence shattered. Stingingly cold water crashed over her waist. The dark shape slipping away from her in the stream was only a log, and she wondered why she was screaming.

At some point she realised it was sunlight that glimmered through the flying clouds, and there was mist in the lower valley. She was staring into a mountain stream.

The water was clear and swift. It foamed over the yellowish pebbles and splintered the sunlight into her eyes. She did not know how long she had been sitting beside it, but her hands were purple and bright pink with the cold, and too numb to close. Her body shivered as though someone were shaking it.

She rubbed her hands together, then lifted them and stared at her bruised fingers. She tried to think.

She had seen the dirigible burn and had left the river bank, but been unable to get to the fire. A couple of kilometres from it, she had passed a stretcher party carrying two dark bundles toward a clearing to wait for a dirigible to pick them up. There were half a dozen militia with them, wearing gas masks and carrying pistols. They had warned her off the slopes. They told her that four of their own and three of the terrorists had been injured, as well as a couple from the crew of the dirigible. Three were critical but most of them were expected to live. She had pried out descriptions from them and convinced herself that Grebbel had not been among the casualties. Then the dawn winds had come.

Sometime later she had come across the stream. She had stooped to drink, and had been unable to move away.

She could hear the searchers now, working through the undergrowth again now that the winds were dying. So they hadn't caught him yet.

A dirigible was floating over the forests near the crash. It must have just arrived as soon as the winds quieted enough, and picked up the casualties. Stiffly she got to her feet.

Walking at random, she found her grasp on the present slipping again. She was on vacation with her parents the year before high school; she was walking with the rest of the nature class through the woods of Stanley Park; she was going over the second draft of her final year composition project, when Dr. Miller stopped the recording and pointed to the score on the screen. "Parallel fifths again." He shook his finger at her. "Three hundred years ago, we'd have failed you on the spot, young woman. But fortunately times have changed, and you at least have something to say. You should allow your instincts more freedom. Pretend you're writing for a real chorus." She was with Leon, on her twenty-fourth birthday, singing a snatch of melody, and conducting with a dog rose she had plucked, singing for joy of him and the life within her. She was walking with Barbara, skipping across the stepping stones at the stream, both knowing they were going to make love.

She came back to the present, and found she was climbing toward the area where she and Grebbel had camped. Would he be trying to get there? He had hinted he had material hidden in the caves there. She remembered their descent through the caves, the dimness around their light, the resonant dark. Then she tried to look back, to find a point where things had gone beyond rescue, looking for a moment where a phrase or a look might have changed everything.

The trail of crushed vegetation and disturbed dead leaves jerked her back to where she was. It had leapt out at her before she was aware of it. Now that she tried to trace it, it was elusive— as though she had merely connected a few random traces in her mind. But she followed her imaginings down the slope for ten metres, and just as she was becoming convinced she really had invented it all, there was an unmistakable gouge in the loam. A little further on there was a single footprint. She guessed he had been favouring one leg and crawled much of the time. He did look to be heading for the ledge where they had camped, the entrance to the caves. So she would be able to catch up with him. Provided the others didn't find him first.

But she lost the trail in a clearing. Shivering she wandered among the trees at the edge. Above her head a branch bore buds like bronze fingers. She reached up on tiptoe, and a drop of dew transferred itself to her fingertip, a tiny jewel of brilliance. The wind stirred, with the smell of smoke, and the new dirigible moved sluggishly along the valley. "They're going to catch you," she whispered. "Monster. There's no hope for you." She wanted to cry.

There was a sound behind her. A pile of dry leaves burst open and fell aside with a splintery crash. A figure crouched there, stretching a hand towards her.

"Water," croaked Jon Grebbel. "Get me some water for Christ's sake."

▲

She brought water from the stream in his empty ammunition pouch and he drank like a parched animal. She did not ask where the contents of the pouch had gone, but he must have seen the question in her. "I lost the gun," he said. "Threw it away when the shells ran out. They're looking for me now. For revenge, I suppose. Are you going to fetch them?"

"You know I can't. God damn you, I wish I could."

"All right then."

"But you could give yourself up."

"You think so? Now? You know what they'll do to me if they get their hands on me—after they've finished taking revenge for what we did to them last night."

"They'll put you on trial, you'll get a fair hearing."

"And then they won't even shoot me. They'll put me back under that machine. If they don't burn out my brain, I'll be less than an animal."

"No they won't. They're not allowed to do that."

"I'm a medical problem now. And don't forget that the head of the administration helped develop that machine and its uses. He wouldn't let me out of its clutches. He wouldn't waste another experimental subject."

"No—he isn't in charge. Not any more." She told him what had happened the evening before, what she had found out about Dr. Henry. "He could get away with what he did to those women only because so much had to be secret here."

"We could be together. It could still work." She reached for his hand. "We could have more times like the picnic."

He shook his head impatiently. "We can't go back. I'm not what I was when I arrived here. I'm what I was back there, and I don't have to pretend to be anything else. I'm not the person you met."

"I'm not what I was then, either. Don't you understand? Things have been coming back to me for days, but since last night, it's been a flood. I feel I'm living a dream and all that's real are my nightmares. We can't go back, either of us—we have to go on."

Another sound came through the air—a roar of engines. A large delta-winged aircraft appeared in the eastern mouth of the valley and followed the river. As they watched, it pulled up and seemed to hover, then put down landing gear and sank out of sight towards the landing field.

"Troop transport," said Grebbel. "And using real fuel. No expense spared. They've probably brought investigators, the top brass. Maybe the experiment's going to be reconsidered. Maybe its opponents have found some leverage."

He looked through the trees at the river and the dam, and then at the dirigible floating further up the valley. He lowered his head. "I remembered something last night. Perhaps their meddling stirred things up that I'd lost since childhood. A nightmare perhaps. Something in the cellar, our cellar. It had been human, someone close to me—and now it was rotting into something obscene. That must have stayed with me, even though I didn't know it, because when I was older and I found a stray cat in our garden, I took it down to the cellar. . . . I had to wash the blood off the wall before my parents came home. That was the first, long before the police station . . . if these are real memories." He shook his head and stared at her, his voice suddenly desperate. "But if they are real, does it mean I had no choice at all? Because, if that's the way it is, then it's all been meaningless, life's nothing but a sick joke."

"Don't think like that now," she said. She had sat down beside him and rested her hand on his shoulder while he spoke.

"What else is there?" he asked bitterly.

She hugged her arms to her body and swallowed. "I murdered my child," she said.

▲

Slowly the air brightened. As he listened to her and the pain in her voice, he watched the searchers working their way nearer. He eyed the dirigible, estimating the range, the allowance for wind and elevation. His hand clenched on an invisible gun butt and quivered.

Elinda finished speaking.

"They had no right to take that from you," he said.

"And they tied my tubes for it. And left me to believe that was what I'd chosen."

He put his hand to her chin and lifted her head. "I lost my gun, but I've still got one bargaining chip." He pulled out the grey trigger box. "We mined the dam. This is a trigger. If they start to play rough, I'll use it."

"Oh, Christ, no more."

"What should I do then? Hand it over and promise to be a good boy?"

"Yes! Yes. A fresh start. A promise of good faith. To show that you're different."

"Different? Am I?" He looked at her lowered head, at the red light on the ice fields, then back at her hair. "Yes, I'm different." He smiled to himself. "I'm the one they used to ask for—there wasn't a man or a woman I couldn't break. Who is this, sitting here waiting for them to come and finish their work? What am I doing here with you?" His voice rose. "It's what they put in me, spewing its thoughts from my mouth, pushing me out of my own mind."

The fluttering of the dirigible's airscrews came down the wind.

"It's too late for that. We have to do something." She stood up. "I'm going to wave. It'll look better if we attract their attention before they find us."

"I can't stop you, can I?"

The dirigible altered course towards them.

It hovered above the clearing. In the doorways, men wearing dark sniping goggles trained automatic weapons. An amplified voice blared. "Put your hands behind your heads and wait at the edge of the clearing. Don't move."

The dirigible sank until it was below the upper branches. A ladder dropped and three men scrambled down—two with assault rifles and an officer with a holstered pistol.

"We've spent all night and all morning looking for you," the officer said to Grebbel. "You've caused all the grief you're going to cause. Now it's our turn."

"I'm hearing every word you say," Elinda said loudly. "And I'm not leaving him until I'm sure he'll be safe."

"So you think. We have a say in that too." He gestured at Grebbel. "You—up the ladder."

Grebbel muttered and limped forward.

The officer grabbed his shoulder, tried to swing Grebbel round to face him. "What? What did you say?"

"I said, I've roasted better than you over a fire."

The officer's head jerked, and one of the guard swung his rifle butt into Grebbel's kidneys. "Murderers need to be taught about civil tongues. We just lost some good friends because of you."

Grebbel had fallen to his knees. Slowly he pushed himself

upright. He gasped into the office's face. "Amateur. Pathetic, piss-licking amateur."

The guard's rifle went back again, and Elinda grabbed for his arm. The other guard caught her by the throat and yanked her away. She stumbled and fell, and glimpsed the man tensing his leg for a kick. Grebbel's voice stopped them all.

"Listen to me. I can save us all a lot of trouble. Or I can make the sort of mess you'll spend the rest of your career explaining away." He was holding up the detonator box. He thumbed a button twice quickly, then held it down. "You can guess what this is. There's a few kilos of azoplas at the other end. If you want to find out exactly where, just keep pushing us around. Now we'll all get into your chariot and fly down to the field, and then we'll talk. Until then, this is staying right here in my hand, and nobody had better get any other ideas about it. I suppose from what I've seen of you so far, you'll need to be told that this button I'm pressing is a deadman switch and there's an independent timer at the other end. And you'd better give us some blankets. I wouldn't want to lose control of my fingers from hypothermia."

The officer glared at him and stiffened his shoulders, then gestured towards the ladder.

"Leave the door open," Grebbel said pleasantly when they were all aboard. "I'll sit by the fresh air. There isn't enough metal in these walls to block the detonation signal, but I wouldn't want anyone to miscalculate on that and take unnecessary risks."

"You're enjoying this," she hissed at him, pulling a blanket around her.

"Of course. That's what I've been telling you. . . . Can you stay out of those updrafts? We'd like a smooth ride down here. The bumps make my hands itch." Then he looked at her again, and grew quiet.

▲

Elinda watched the sunlight sparkle on the river below them. Behind her, she could still feel Grebbel's crouched presence. He would have to see there was no alternative for him; he would have to accept whatever the authorities offered. There might still be a life for them. Weed trails swayed in the current, a fish leapt. The future was as hidden from her as the ocean that lay beyond the mouth of this river. Shivering, she hugged herself and closed her eyes.

Faces drifted into her mind. Carlo, saying, *I made you what you are*. Henry, with his machines and his smooth rationalisations. Strickland's haunted look. Barbara. And Leon, Charley, Jessamyn, Dr. Miller . . . She saw them grouped around her, breaths drawn, waiting; and she sensed the river of sound that was dammed within them. They were waiting for her. And within her, there was only silence.

▲

The valley slid below Jon Grebbel like a tape rewinding onto its spool. All the control he had over his life now was held in his hand. The dam with its swirl of white water came into view. One twitch of a finger . . . And what would decide that? His own will or the cancer they had planted in him? His thoughts circled upon themselves like a snake eating its own tail. He had done—had built a life by doing—horrible things; and now he was offered redemption and love. But whatever he had been, the things they had done to him were worse, and the proof of that was that their taint still clouded his reason.

He had fled from a childhood nightmare into an existence founded on pain, and fear—had been driven by fear of the loss of self, so that love brought demands he could not endure; and he could make life bearable only by asserting his own separateness.

He had had pride, and power, had been in control of his life, had known what he was; and now they were beating him down like a mongrel dog, and twisting his mind to make him like it.

The two visions were clear and separate—and how was he to choose, when choosing relied on powers of judgement that had been defiled? The snake had impossibly gnawed its way up the spine and was devouring its own brain.

▲

"I'll tell you what I told them," Menzies said to Carlo. "As far as we know, it was just the one piece of sabotage, but most of the circuits in the workings blew. It'll be a while before things are back to normal."

The two stood uncomfortably together outside the Hall, where the new team from the Flats were in the middle of their preliminary interviews. The investigation was evidently just in its early stages.

"You really think they will get back to normal?" Carlo asked. "Dr. Henry's in intensive care. He was shot. By an illegal gun," he added straight-faced. "You didn't know? And apparently he was delirious when they found him, and some of his babblings are raising eyebrows. There was a recording too, apparently. He wasn't the man I thought I knew. There's going to be a big investigation, and the goals of this place are going to be questioned. You know what I'm talking about?"

"The memories, the deceptions. Yes, I know. I know more than you probably imagine. And Niels is dead. There's going to be questions asked about that too."

"Madame Security's in charge and apparently talking her head off. I can't see us having any anniversary celebrations—there's going to be a full enquiry."

"I'll be asking some questions myself—asking me, about things I thought I'd settled already. I relied on Niels a lot, you know, about what's right. And now I don't know. I'm going to have to look for my own answers."

▲

The dirigible was landing. The field was watched by troops in riot gear. Grebbel wondered if they'd been flown in from the Flats, or they were more militia who had appeared out of the woodwork. "Whose stable door do they think they're shutting now?"

"You wanted to talk," the officer said. "There are people in the control tower waiting for you. Let's go."

The world was becoming unreal. Among the crowd outside the armed cordon, he saw Carlo and Partridge, and they seemed to be creatures he had met in dreams. The astronaut was white-faced and shaking. In his black exoskeleton, he looked like a creature imprisoned in a cage that was growing from his flesh.

Inside the main building there were others, mostly in uniform; some Grebbel recognised, most he did not. Elinda was still with him. Carlo was whispering urgently to her. She said something, then handed him a small black instrument that he took away.

A few minutes later Carlo was called back to examine Grebbel's ankle. Carlo bandaged it and applied an emergency cast, then found an elbow crutch for him.

"They expect me to walk out in front of the firing squad myself, then?"

"Don't ask me," Carlo muttered. "I don't know what they're planning for you."

"How about your boss? Is Dr. Henry going on to another honoured research position? I'm sure he'd need a trusted assistant."

"He'll live, that's all I know. And keep your voice down. I'll have enough troubles when the storm breaks."

"Well, it's nice to think the old virtues of secrecy and self-interest haven't quite died out."

"Self-interest. Your friend Osmon died on the way down from the mountain. Are you interested in that?"

"There are worse fates," Grebbel said. "Or was he helped on his way?"

"Only by you, I'd imagine. It's not easy, but I'm going to have to decide—I'm going to tell them everything I know. You can plan your own actions accordingly."

"Commendable. Most commendable. Think you can stick to it?"

Carlo turned and walked away.

Others replaced him, with questions, demands, offers.

Grebbel's mouth talked. It made counter-offers, promises; answered or deflected questions; and he could not tell whether he or the cancer they had put in his mind was using it.

"... in the workings on the other side of the dam," he finished. "A time fuse and an antipersonnel fuse. I'm the only one left who could disarm it before the timer runs out. I'll disarm the deadman switch, now ... there. But I'll keep it with me, if you don't mind. If you want any other questions answered, you might prefer to wait until I've disarmed the timer; you've got twelve minutes before it detonates."

And then he was being taken to one of the trucks. She tried to follow, and one part of the chaos in his head rebelled. "Stay here," he shouted. To the guards: "Keep her away from me, or the deal's off, I'll let the thing blow." They looked suspicious, but they hustled her away.

▲

Elinda watched as Grebbel was escorted into the truck and driven across the dam. He must be going to disarm the explosive, but his manner looked anything but conciliatory. His arrogance was in full play, even as he limped to the truck. She tried not to think what he might be planning.

Carlo appeared at her side with a mug of fish stew and a sandwich. "You'd better eat," he said. "There's a long day ahead of both us. They're listening to the recording again now. I don't think you'll be in deep trouble, but there's going to be an investigation."

"Right. Thanks. And you? Where will all this leave you?"

"I don't know. They'll still need someone, I imagine, to do some of my jobs. . . . I didn't know what he was doing. Please believe me. Perhaps I didn't want to know, perhaps I should have checked up more, but I never imagined he could be hurting anyone. First I thought Barbara's conditioning might have slipped and thrown her into shock somehow. Then when she didn't respond to treatment, I started to wonder. I'd guessed some of the psychopaths might be reverting. I thought perhaps she'd run into one. But I never imagined, never for a moment, it could have been him."

"Right." The four men had gone into the workings on the far side of the river. The silence filled her head. She could not think or feel.

"I saw Barbara this morning before they brought you down off the mountain," Carlo said. "She's coming out of it, I think. She asked me what day it was."

"Ah," she heard herself say. "Jessamyn was good for her then,"

The river was bright in the sun, and the two raptors circled over it. The empty truck was still at the far end of the bridge.

Elinda turned slowly to face Carlo. "It's too much, right now," she whispered. "Did you ask her . . . do you think she'll see me?"

"I think she will, but of course . . ."

". . . things will be different."

▲

The truck with Grebbel and the three guards pulled up at the far side of the dam, where the turbine room was carved out of the cliff. "In there," Grebbel's voice told them.

"All right, but we're staying with you to keep an eye on you."

"It would be simpler for us all if you didn't."

What had made him say that? That drivelling voice they had implanted again?

Always the image in the glass was his face, and always the fist that shattered it was his own. "You made your last deal back there. Now get on with it."

He hobbled from the truck. The tunnel went into the rock for twenty metres before descending to the chamber where the new generators were still being installed. Some of the lights strung above had gone out, and the shadows forked from the men and wheeled crazily as they approached the steps.

The lights had all failed here, and they groped in the dim glow reflected from the horizontal shaft. Down. Step. Down. Floor underfoot. Eight steps now to the storeroom. Count—

"Get on with it, Grebbel. If you're going to open that door, do it. What the fuck are you laughing about?"

"I'm not—laughing. . . . The door's stiff. I can't get any purchase with one leg. You'll have to help me."

The officer cursed. As he stepped forward, Grebbel turned to the door. Then he pivoted. His hands blurred and struck. The officer cried out, then froze, gasping, pinned between Grebbel and the others, with Grebbel's fingers probing his pain centres.

"I wasn't laughing. Now I'm laughing. Can't you see me? Because it's all over, the last joke's been told—"

—And here it was, finally, the only thing he might hold onto as himself. The door in the dark at the foot of the stairs, the suffering body.

And the white light when he punched through the last illusion.

▲

There was surprisingly little sound, and only a flicker that might have been sunlight reflected from a wave. But when Elinda turned, the truck had vanished. A boiling white cloud obscured the excavations, and the end of the bridge sagged towards the water.

A white pennon of foam streamed from where the dam had been breached. Beyond it, a new cave in the valley wall loomed through the smoke.

She was already running. There were others beside her, ahead of her. Someone grabbed at her arm to pull her back, but let go when she clawed at his face.

She fought her way across the dam to where the bridge slumped into a muddy torrent. The roar beat at her. Its spray stung her eyes. And there was nothing to see. The cavern in the far wall was being scoured clean by the flood. The water carried nothing but mud and couple of logs. In the first furious release, the current had taken its secrets and its dead, and now bore them away to their dissolution in the shadowed reaches of the sea.

▲

"It's over," Carlo repeated. "They've heard the recording. They'll want a full statement from you tomorrow, or the next day. Get some sleep now." Elinda had spent forty hours being questioned and treated for shock and exposure, and then been sent away. Carlo had escorted her home. But now, at her door, the night winds were dying, and she did not want to go in and pace among those empty rooms. She knew she would not sleep.

Carlo's face was blurred by the dark; the sound of the wind in the trees obscured his voice. To the east, the clouds were streaming away and stars were coming out. "Things will change. They can't ship us all home, but they'll have to rethink what they expect of us. We'll have to remake our lives. . . . Elinda, are you listening? Go to bed. You must sleep."

She listened to the wind. She thought of clouds being torn apart on the teeth of the mountains and reforming over the valley. "I will," she muttered and put her hand on the door. "Later. Soon. Leave me alone now please." Her throat hurt. Her eyes were dry, but she could not remember when she had stopped crying. Silence seemed to fill her.

Sometime later she realised she was alone, and the sky was full of stars. The trees swayed about her and the stream hissed and sputtered.

She walked out onto the stepping stones. The water must be wearing them away every moment, changing their proportions minutely, so that after a season, a lifetime, a million years, their shapes would be quite different. Each layer worn away was a mask removed, but when you had peeled away the last mask, the whole of the stone was gone.

Perhaps all that was important was that the stones turned

in the current and presented different edges and faces to each other, and eroded each other in different ways. There was no core, just different planes and angles, like the phases of the moon.

After a while there were threads of silver among the stones. She knelt, and her fingers made slow caressing motions in the water, shaping the outline of a small body. Then she clutched her empty hands to her breasts and wept again.

When she looked, the moons were rising over the ice fields, gilding the distant serrations of the Angels' Hand. But Beta, the lower of the two, was almost invisible—dull red instead of ivory.

An eclipse, she told herself numbly. An eclipse on a new world. No human being had seen exactly this, though it had happened a million times and would return a million more.

And now she had only one moon shadow. She watched it darken the water beside her. Thinking about moon shadows, she made her way to the bank and turned towards her home. She thought of shadows stalking beside her like familiar ghosts, pale in early evening, but black voids at night. Shadows that slid ahead and forked into unknown darkness, or trailed her steps—at each dawn fading, stretching out and vanishing, to return, shrinking and deepening with the night. Shadows that lengthened and split apart, then reconverged and fused—that opened and closed like a pair of shears. Shadows inseparable from her, but inextricably bound to the shifting configurations of moon and sun, the cycles of sky and ocean.

In her mind she heard singing.

ACKNOWLEDGEMENTS

By a process I can no longer trace, this book grew out of Lester del Rey's story "Evensong." My original (dreadful) short story gradually developed into a novel-length manuscript, at which point a number of people contributed useful criticisms: initially, past and current members of the Lyngarde writing group, Jo Beverley, Hildegarde Henderson, Elizabeth Holden, Andrea Schlecht, Madona Skaff and the late Sansoucy Kathenor; followed by Candas Jane Dorsey, Karl Schroeder, Michael Skeet and Jean-Louis Trudel. Subsequent drafts were stimulated by valuable comments from David G. Hartwell and Virginia O'Dine, and aided by Candas Dorsey's indefatigable support.

Inevitably the writing was shaped by works I have read—to some degree, I suppose, by almost everything I have read—but the influences I am most aware of are William Golding, Fyodor Dostoevski, and Roger Zelazny.

Finally at ChiZine Publications, Brett Alexander Savory and Sandra Kasturi rescued the book from the wilderness, groomed its fur, polished its teeth, sharpened its claws and sent it out into the world with its head held high.

I cheerfully accept responsibility for any remaining defects, and offer apologies to anyone I have forgotten to mention. Thanks to you all.

ABOUT THE AUTHOR

John Park was born in Britain but moved to Canada in 1970 as a graduate student and has lived there ever since. He has done research in chemical physics and been part of a scientific consulting firm. Along the way, he developed a liking for Beethoven, became a graduate of the Clarion writers workshop, and began selling short stories (not necessarily in that order). His fiction and poetry have appeared in a number of Canadian, US and European publications. He lives in Ottawa, where he is a member of the Lyngarde writing group.

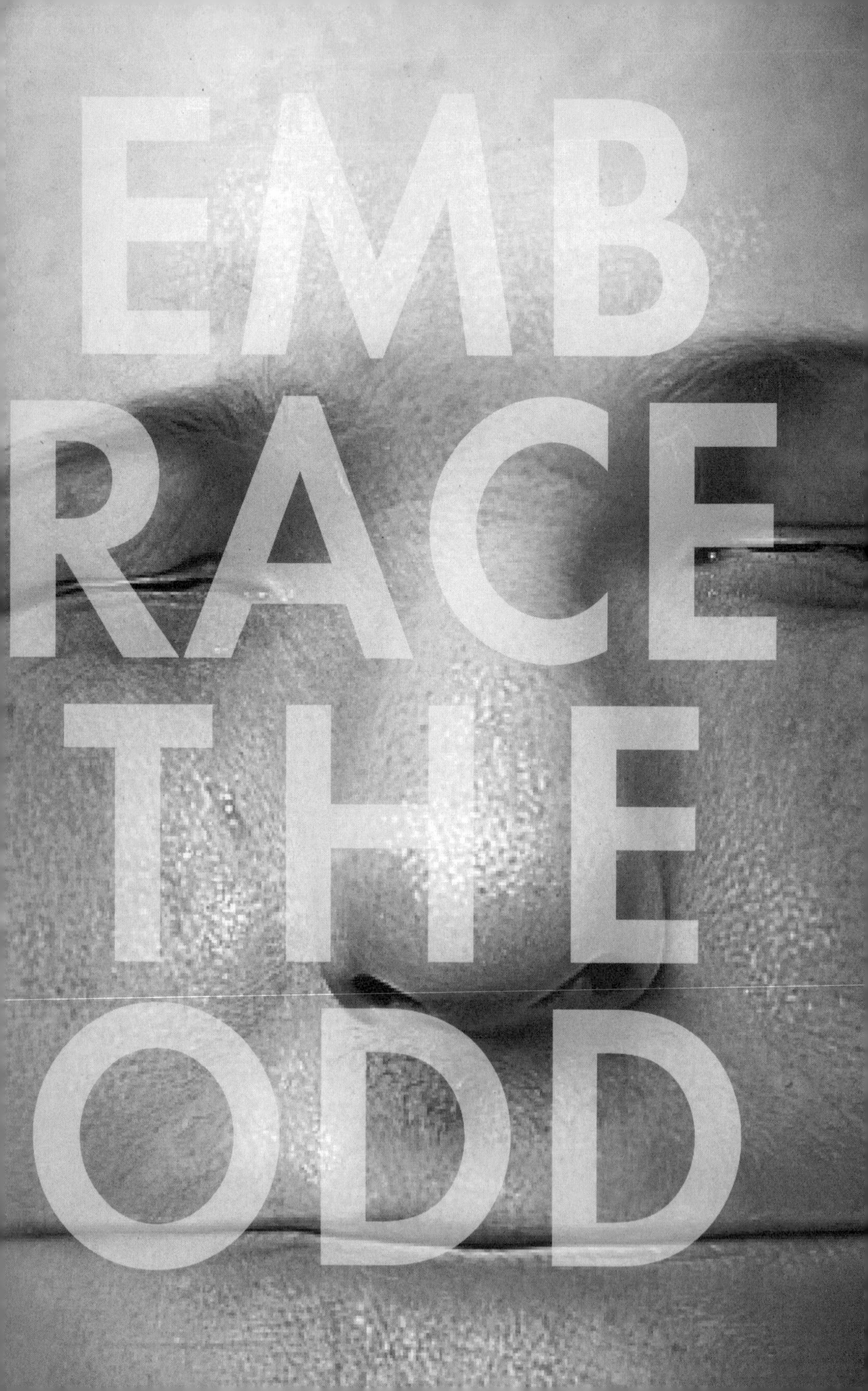
EMB
RACE
THE
ODD

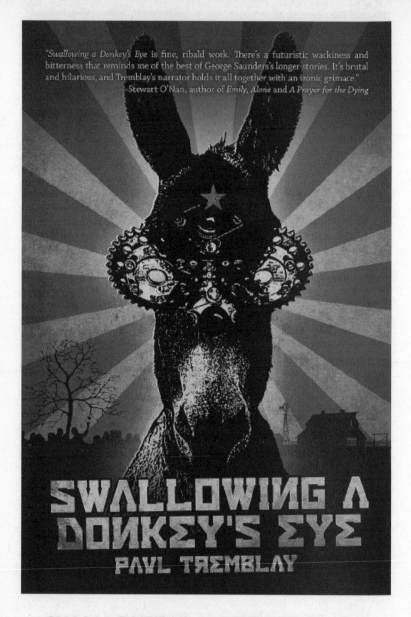

SWALLOWING A DONKEY'S EYE

PAUL TREMBLAY

AVAILABLE AUGUST 2012
FROM CHIZINE PUBLICATIONS

978-1-926851-69-3

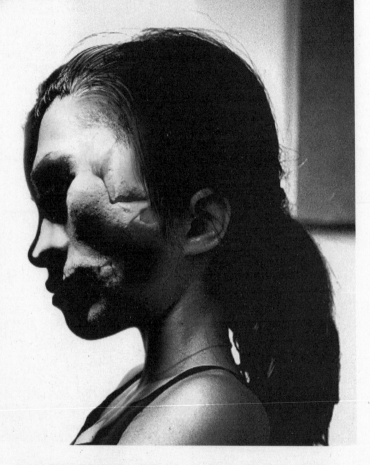

REMEMBER WHY YOU FEAR ME
THE BEST DARK FICTION OF ROBERT SHEARMAN

AVAILABLE OCTOBER 2012
FROM CHIZINE PUBLICATIONS

978-0-927469-21-7

THE BOOK OF THOMAS

ROBERT BOYCZUK

AVAILABLE NOVEMBER 2012
FROM CHIZINE PUBLICATIONS

978-0-927469-27-9

978-1-926851-54-9

JOHN MANTOOTH

**SHOEBOX
TRAIN WRECK**

978-1-926851-53-2

MIKE CAREY, LINDA
CAREY & LOUISE CAREY

THE STEEL SERAGLIO

978-1-926851-55-6

RIO YOUERS

WESTLAKE SOUL

978-1-926851-56-3

CAROLYN IVES GILMAN

ISON OF THE ISLES

978-1-926851-58-7

JAMES MARSHALL

**NINJA VERSUS
PIRATE FEATURING
ZOMBIES**

978-1-926851-57-0

GEMMA FILES

A TREE OF BONES
**VOLUME III OF THE
HEXSLINGER SERIES**

978-1-926851-59-4

DAVID NICKLE

**RASPUTIN'S
BASTARDS**

978-1-926851-35-8

TONE MILAZZO

**PICKING UP
THE GHOST**

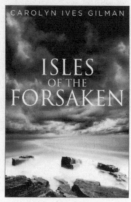

978-1-926851-43-3

CAROLYN IVES GILMAN

**ISLES OF
THE FORSAKEN**

978-1-926851-44-0

TIM PRATT

BRIARPATCH

978-1-926851-43-3

CAITLIN SWEET

THE PATTERN SCARS

978-1-926851-46-4

TERESA MILBRODT

BEARDED WOMEN

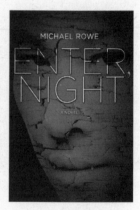

978-1-926851-45-7

MICHAEL ROWE

ENTER, NIGHT

"THE BEST WORK IN DARK FANTASY AND HORROR FICTION THESE DAYS IS BEING PUBLISHED BY SMALL PRESSES, HAUNTED LITERARY BOUTIQUES ESTABLISHED (MOSTLY) IN OUT-OF-THE-WAY PLACES, [INCLUDING] CHIZINE IN TORONTO. THEY'RE ALL DEVOTED TO THE WEIRD, TO THE STRANGE AND—MOST IMPORTANT—TO GOOD WRITING."

–DANA JENNINGS, *THE NEW YORK TIMES*

ALSO AVAILABLE FROM CHIZINE PUBLICATIONS

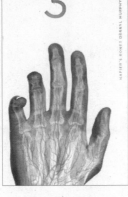

978-1-926851-10-5

TOM PICCIRILLI

EVERY SHALLOW CUT

978-1-926851-09-9

DERRYL MURPHY

NAPIER'S BONES

978-1-926851-11-2

DAVID NICKLE

EUTOPIA

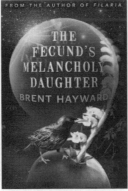

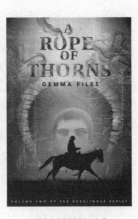

978-1-926851-12-9

CLAUDE LALUMIÈRE

**THE DOOR TO
LOST PAGES**

978-1-926851-13-6

BRENT HAYWARD

**THE FECUND'S
MELANCHOLY
DAUGHTER**

978-1-926851-14-3

GEMMA FILES

A ROPE OF THORNS

A BOOK OF TONGUES
GEMMA FILES
978-0-9812978-6-6

CHASING THE DRAGON
NICHOLAS KAUFMANN
978-0-9812978-4-2

CHIMERASCOPE
DOUGLAS SMITH
978-0-9812978-5-9

CITIES OF NIGHT
PHILIP NUTMAN
978-0-9812978-8-0

FILARIA
BRENT HAYWARD
978-0-9809410-1-2

THE HAIR WREATH AND OTHER STORIES
HALLI VILLEGAS
978-1-926851-02-0

HORROR STORY AND OTHER HORROR STORIES
ROBERT BOYCZUK
978-0-9809410-3-6

IN THE MEAN TIME
PAU TREMBLAY
978-1-926851-06-8-

KATJA FROM THE PUNK BAND
SIMON LOGAN
978-0-9812978-7-3

MAJOR KARNAGE
GORD ZAJAC
978-0-9813746-6-6

MONSTROUS AFFECTIONS
DAVID NICKLE
978-0-9812978-3-5

NEXUS: ASCENSION
ROBERT BOYCZUK
978-0-9813746-8-0

OBJECTS OF WORSHIP
CLAUDE LALUMIÈRE
978-0-9812978-2-8

PEOPLE LIVE STILL IN CASHTOWN CORNERS
TONY BURGESS
978-1-926851-04-4

SARAH COURT
CRAIG DAVIDSON
978-1-926851-00-6

THE TEL AVIV DOSSIER
LAVIE TIDHAR AND NIR YANIV
978-0-9809410-5-0

THE WORLD MORE FULL OF WEEPING
ROBERT J. WIERSEMA
978-0-9809410-9-8